A Cockpit in New Guinea

A Cockpit in New Guinea

C.M. McGee

About the Cover
The idea for the front cover is the author's own. However, the two airplanes depicted in combat come from a drawing by Mr. Iain Wyllie for the cover of "P-39 Airacobra Aces of World War 2" which was published by Osprey Publishing Limited in 2001. The technical art, especially the faded P-39 instrument panel in the background, is due to a huge assist from XLIBRIS graphics. The author extends a profound debt of thanks to both of these corporations.

This book was printed in the United States of America.

To order additional copies of this book, contact:
Xlibris Corporation
1-888-795-4274
www.Xlibris.com
Orders@Xlibris.com
83390

Cliff + JoAnn

Hope you enjoy

it

Prologue

New Guinea is the world's second largest island, over six hundred miles at its widest point, one thousand miles at its longest, 15,400 feet at its highest. At one time, the island was part of the Australian continent, but floodwaters severed the land bridge, creating what's now known as the Torres Strait. Inland, there's a formidable array of mountain ranges and valleys, an unlikely panorama of snowcapped peaks and nearly impenetrable tropical forests, fed each year by over four hundred inches of rainfall. These forests contain ever-growing numbers of endemic species, including over seventy different types of snakes, hundreds of known and unknown marsupials and crocodiles, and a veritable plethora of bugs, gnats, and crawlers.

New Guinea's first human inhabitants came from the Australian continent to the south and the East Indies to the north. The largest group, later called *Papuas* (Pah-poo-ahs), arrived some thirty thousand years ago. Over the centuries, the island's rugged geography splintered the inhabitants to such an extent that, even today, over seven hundred different tribes, languages and dialects exist.

The primitive, sometimes barbaric ways of the tribes remained unchanged when the island's east end was explored by Dom Jorge de Meneses of Portugal in 1526. He called the island "Ilhas dos Papuas," meaning "Island of the Fuzzy-Haired People." Nineteen years later, the Spaniard Ynigo Ortiz de Retes renamed the island "New Guinea" because the natives so closely resembled those he'd encountered on the west coast of Africa. To the explorers tasked to claim the island's natural ports, and to the missionaries sent there by the Spanish,

English, Dutch, Portuguese, and Germans, New Guinea was no doubt hazardous, forbidding duty.

But still the Europeans came, maneuvering against each other for control of the unique, mysterious island. In 1828, the Dutch took possession of the western half. In 1849, Capt. Owen Stanley of the British Royal Navy charted the southern coast and mapped from a distance the inland mountain range that bears his name. In 1885, the Germans annexed the northern coast, naming it Kaiser-Wilhelmsland. When Australia won independence in 1906, the English signed over their rights to the southern coast, which became the "Territory of Papua."

By World War I, Dutch, Portuguese, and Spanish claims were part of distant history, leaving the Australians and the Germans to fight for control of the island. The Australians invaded the German interests in 1914 and the two sides fought mostly to a standstill. After Germany's defeat in the Great War, a League of Nations mandate completed the task the Australian army couldn't, creating the "Australian Territory of New Guinea."

Then came the Second World War and the Japanese.

Fortunately, the Australians had allies helping them defend the island. The first was an extensive network of coast watchers, informants, and guides among the indigenous tribesmen, many who remained from the First World War. These networks proved crucial as the Japanese drove toward Port Moresby in the spring and summer of 1942.

Another ally was even more formidable than the first: the island itself. Despite their march through Formosa, the Japanese were no more prepared to deal with New Guinea's rugged terrain, extreme weather changes, strange diseases, and antihuman critters than anyone else.

And then early 1942 saw the arrival of a third ally, this one from the other side of the world: the U.S. Army Air Corps. Young, brash, optimistic-yet-barely-trained pilots were among 40,000 Americans assigned to the Southwest Asia Pacific Area. They left much behind them: futures in family businesses, gals, college, and the joblessness of the Great Depression; all swapped for the fears and dangers of war, and an enemy who was highly trained, more experienced, and better equipped.

Part 1

1

Staten Island, New York, spring, 1937

The skinny, five-foot-four sixteen-year-old walked through the main entrance of Curtis High School. He'd left home twenty-five minutes earlier, walked a block or so to Victory Boulevard and jumped on brand-new Bus No. 6, painted red at the bottom and white from the windows on up. He'd got off at the Richmond County Borough Hall, climbed a hill past the St. George Theater, and cut through to Hyatt Street. If the weather had been better, he'd have left his house on Melrose Street an hour or more early and walked the whole distance, just under four miles.

On the way to school he always saw lots of people, but he didn't speak to any of them unless they spoke to him first. It wasn't that he was impolite; he just kept to himself. It had always been that way.

Students were assigned to either the morning or afternoon session, but never both. The skinny kid was assigned to the afternoon session, which began with French class.

He hated French: couldn't read it, couldn't spell it, couldn't understand it, and couldn't care less about it. For some reason, though, his pronunciation was uncommonly good, whether he knew what he was saying or not. He was lucky that his older sister helped him learn an extra word or two. Maybe he'd scrape by with a passing grade and never have to pick up a French book again. Three more class periods would follow before the school day came to its merciful end.

Most students went to the cafeteria for lunch, paying fifteen cents for what might be their only balanced meal of the day. But the skinny kid never went to the cafeteria. He ate at home instead, but only if the old man wasn't around. This was the Great Depression; wasting food on lunch was frowned upon, even though he hadn't had breakfast. But today the old man hadn't come home during the noon hour, so the kid had made his standard fare: two eggs and a piece of bread.

Now he checked the clock above the office door. Good. He had ten minutes or so to drop by the library before class. He wished he had more. He loved the quiet of the library and the chance to look through the magazines. *National Geographic* took him a long way from Staten Island and New York City. *Time* put all kinds of interesting people on its cover, and *Popular Mechanics* was full of scientific ideas and new mechanical contraptions which hinted at an exciting new life. He wished it could be so, because he hated his life now.

The library was small and deserted, except for the librarian. Mrs. Blanchet looked the part: same dress every day, coke-bottle glasses, thin and frail, her gray hair pulled back in a tight bun. She was cranky, too, untrusting of all human life younger than herself, most likely anyone under eighty. And her laundry list of rules chased everyone away. You couldn't sit and read there. You couldn't do homework there. And God forbid if you were ever caught talking there. Nice library! Wasn't it ironic that the skinny kid loved going there so much?

Despite her vices, one could count on Mrs. Blanchet to have the library in good order. The day's *Staten Island Advance* and current periodicals were always neatly arrayed on a table in the far corner of the room. Followed by Mrs. Blanchet's wary stare, that's where the kid headed. It was too bad that the librarian took neither the time nor the effort to see the difference between students and troublemakers, for the skinny kid was truly interested in books and magazines. He would have welcomed the librarian's interest, or help, or guidance, but she gave him none of those things; just her stare.

The skinny kid walked to the corner table, and there it was: *Popular Mechanics*, Volume 67, No. 2, dated February 1937, with a small article, "The West Point of the Air," advertised on the cover. He picked it up, went right to page twenty-seven, and was soon lost in the article.

In the late 1920s, a young army pilot named William Randolph had been on a committee to name a new pilot training base. Unfortunately, Randolph was killed in February of '28, when his AT-4 crashed on takeoff. But in his honor, the War Department named the base after him. By the mid-1930s Randolph Field had earned the nickname "The West Point of the Air." There were three stages of pilot training: Primary Training at Randolph, Basic Training at Brooks Field, and Adv—

Something made the kid look up at the clock, which hung high on the wall behind the librarian's desk. 2:08 p.m. He was late for French. The bell for class had rung exactly on time; he never heard it.

"Oh no!" He hurried over to the librarian, still carrying the magazine open to the article.

"Mrs. Blanchet, may I get a library pass for French class? I got stuck in this magazine, and . . . uh . . . I'm sorry, but I need a pass."

She just looked sternly at him. "What's your name?"

"Donald McGanley, ma'am. Mrs. Blanchet, I need to hurry. I'm sorry, but I lost track of time."

"Mr. McGanley," she began.

Donald felt a pit in his stomach. Here it comes, a lecture while the clock runs. Mr. Bose would never let him into French class if he were more than ten minutes late. Class rule set from the first day. But Mrs. Blanchet babbled on.

". . . you can't expect me to stop what I'm doing when you don't pay attention to the time. And you can't expect a free pass to keep you out of trouble when the fault is yours. No, you can't have a pass. I'm tired of having pupils misuse the library and ask me to forgive their noise in this room or their failure to return books on time and their rudeness to their elders . . ."

Oh, brudda! "Excuse me, Mrs. Blanchet, but I have to get to class . . ."

It was useless. The old crow never stopped talking. Donald headed out the door with Mrs. Blanchet still jabbering about misfit kids and the fate of the country's future if left in their hands. At least her voice faded as he went.

Donald bounded up the stairs to the second floor of the three-story building and ran down the hall to Room 202. It was 2:12 p.m.; the door was locked. He debated knocking, dreading another lecture or an embarrassing berating in front of the whole class, or worst of all, having the door slammed in his face. Another kid might just forget the class, happy to be free to spend the remaining time of the fifty-minute period perfecting his excuse for being absent. He might even skip the rest of the day and wander around upper Staten Island until it was time to go home, parents none the wiser.

But Donald wasn't like that.

He rapped on the door. Mr. Bose looked annoyed when he answered. The man seemed twice as big as he normally was. He looked down at Donald, scanned the hallway, and announced, "Class is in session. Good afternoon."

"Mr. Bose, please, I was in the lib . . ."

As expected, the door closed in Donald's face. He turned around slowly and, back against the hallway wall, slid down to the floor. He was so mad at himself he felt like crying, but he was too old for that. Sitting there quietly, he began his own self-berating lecture. Why did he have to goof up and be late? Why did he stand there politely and take that lecture from Mrs. Blanchet instead of running to class?

He sat for a long while, knees bent with arms folded on top of them, head down. He had no idea how long he sat there, almost in tears but not quite. Perhaps he dozed off for a few minutes, but then a noise from down the hall startled him and his head shot up. He'd better get out of here before anyone saw him.

There was no way he'd tell his parents about this. His old man would kill him. He just had to hope he'd never find out. Donald got up and headed for the stairs and his third-floor algebra class. Damn it! This type of crap had gone on his whole life. He was sick of it and he wanted out. Some day he'd find a way, with nobody's help but his own.

2

Donald Thomas McGanley was the fourth of five children from the union of Edna and Johnny McGanley. The family had come to America several generations earlier, from County Meade and County Tipperary, near Dublin, Ireland. Most of the McGanleys settled in Brooklyn, moving later to Staten Island, though one or two branched out. A distant relative had been one of the Alamo defenders, though the complete story of the clan was never passed down.

Johnny was not wealthy, nor did he have the connections or savvy to take advantage of the Roaring Twenties. He wasn't able to save much as a young husband and father, but worked steadily, paycheck to paycheck, as the manager of Roulstons Market. He took great pride in this comparatively lofty position and was acutely conscious of his image. He worked six days a week, 7:00 a.m. to 7:00 p.m., arriving promptly each morning, shirts starched.

But as the Great Depression deepened in the early 1930s, Johnny was demoted to cashier, taking a double hit in salary and an even bigger hit in his pride. Still, Johnny worked long, hard hours, enough to keep the family fed but too many to be a dad to his five children. Instead, his kids often found him angry, sometimes physically abusive. Most days it was a bad idea to be around when Johnny came home, especially if dinner wasn't made or the chores weren't done.

Johnny married Edna, also of Irish descent, in 1913. There was an edginess about Edna, kind of a nervousness. She was vocal and opinionated one minute, scared and quiet the next. It was hard to tell which mood she was in. She rarely spoke of her upbringing with her children, so most of her family history, and all of her secrets, went untold and died with her. But she was a dutiful mother. She held her young kids when they were sick and ran the household like any other mom.

Until 1929. The stock market crash and the ensuing years were increasing difficult. Loss of status and dire financial straits were a huge strain on her. At the same time, her oldest kids were rapidly becoming less in need of her mothering. By the early 1930s, her own depression led to a nervous breakdown, leaving her virtually bedridden. Normal maternal chores of the household ended up being distributed down to the children. She would not improve until the latter years of the decade.

The firstborn, Elizabeth, was outgoing and fun-loving from the start, and became interested in singing and dancing at an early age. She finished high school and got a stage job in Manhattan, without Johnny's or Edna's knowledge or consent. They never tried to stop her, perhaps sensing that it would probably be a waste of time. The job often brought Elizabeth home very late, occasionally not at all. Edna would stay up waiting for her, even though her daughter begged her not to. Elizabeth, tough and independent, knew damned well what she wanted and wasn't about to let the slow, plodding, depressed life in the McGanley household get in her way.

The next three children were all boys, each two years apart. Victor, or Vic, was clever and strong-willed: not very tall but stocky and strong, a poor choice for someone to mess with. The boy was street-smart, always on the run and always into some kind of deal. In short, he ruled the neighborhood. It didn't take him long to figure out that school was not for him, and he dropped out rather than torture himself with unimportant matters like literature, math, and science. (Actually, the boy was *kicked* out of school as an "incorrigible.") For Vic, home was a place to be only if he didn't have business to attend to, and he came and went freely. There was money to be made, and Vic made it—lots of it. Later in life he would amass quite a fortune right there on Staten Island.

Roderick, or "Roddy," was next in line. Though not of Vic's stature, inside or outside of the home, he clung to his older brother like glue and matched Vic's abbreviated school career. A happy-go-lucky, mischievous fellow, Roddy tried to make his own name on the street. He'd fight anyone, anytime, about anything. As the middle of five children, one might expect him to be the forgotten one, but it didn't happen that way. At age seven he suffered a near-fatal bout of pneumonia. Edna stayed with him night and day, bonding in a way that would never be matched by any of her other children. Roddy reveled in it. His role as maternal favorite and sidekick to Vic kept a twinkle in his eye that would last his entire life.

Donald was next, followed by Ricky five years later. As the youngest, Ricky escaped the chores of the household. When Edna's condition worsened in the 1930s, he increasingly looked up to Donald as his full-time caregiver and babysitter. It would continue that way for several years. But as Ricky grew older he became more and more like his two eldest brothers. Like Vic and Roddy, he never finished school.

So the McGanley kids, spanning eleven years from top to bottom, self-indulgent, aggressive, and outgoing, were all pretty much alike—all except Donald. He was a loner, afraid of his father, the quiet one who seemed to accept life as it came, without complaint. These were unusual traits for a McGanley. His brothers recognized them very quickly and took great advantage of them.

With Edna bedridden much of the day, Johnny would typically assign weeklong chores to his kids. If the chores were not done by the time Johnny got home from Roulstons, punishment could consist of a whipping or a week inside the house, or both. Elizabeth and Vic were long gone, Roddy had no appetite for chores, and Ricky was too small. Donald would do his own chores, but could not keep up with the rest. When Johnny got home, most of the work would still be undone, and Donald would be the only one in sight. When the boy was seven, he spent almost his entire summer inside because of chores his brothers would not do.

Donald wondered why his father let things go on this way, but Johnny was too preoccupied with other problems. He wasn't making enough money, his wife was bedridden, and the daily news was almost hopeless.

One afternoon near the end of summer, Donald tried swapping chores with Roddy, hoping to get his brother to finally pitch in. But Roddy had more important things to do and was off with Vic when Johnny got home. Johnny noticed dust under the living room radiator and exploded.

"Donald!" The boy walked slowly toward his father. "Look at that!" The afternoon sun reflected off the dust. "Well?"

"Roddy and I agreed to switch, so I mopped . . . in the kitchen. He said he would dust." Donald turned to leave.

"Where are you going?"

"Out to play. I finished the mopping, Dad."

"You're not going anywhere. You stay inside for the week and finish the dusting."

Shocked, the boy stared at his father. Then frustration set in and tears swelled in his eyes. "But, Dad, I've done my chores and . . ."

Johnny didn't want to hear it. He balled his fists and moved toward Donald, who backed up, then turned and took off around the room, trying to get away. Johnny chased his son out of the living room, through the portal to the dining room, and finally trapped him in one of the corners. The boy struggled as Johnny lifted him up by the neck, holding him against the wall.

"Don't you talk back to me, boy! You'll stay inside if I say so!" Johnny raised his fist as Donald choked, then clamped his eyes shut, his face already beet red.

The boy started coughing, braced himself for the punch, and choked back at his father, "Go ahead!"

Johnny caught himself and relaxed his grip. His son sank to the floor, still coughing. Now free, Donald got up as fast as he could and fled the room toward the stairs, which he took at a dead run, ran to his room, and slammed the door. He leaned against it, and the tears came. He trudged slowly toward his bed and sat with his legs hanging over the edge, too short to reach the floor. He started rocking back and forth, and he cried . . . and cried . . . and cried. He couldn't get himself under control, though he choked and coughed in vain attempts to stop.

These past weeks, in fact, his whole existence, now unloaded on him all at once. "Why is this happening to me? What did I do?" he cried out loud, looking toward a small crucifix on the wall above his bed. He reached for it, lifted it off the hook, and gripped it tightly with both hands as he rocked and cried, rocked and cried, rocked and cried. "Why, God? Please tell me why is this happening to me? What did I do? Please . . . tell me!"

The bedroom door opened, and there was Johnny. The boy's crying continued, more quietly now, still choked with hiccups and sniffles as he tried again to get control of himself. His father simply looked at him and said nothing. Johnny walked over to the bed, looked down at him, expressionless, and snatched the crucifix from Donald's soaked hands. "You don't deserve this." Then he turned and left.

Donald knew then: he was all alone in this house. It wasn't that his brothers hated him. They didn't, and he didn't hate them. They razzed and wrestled and played their kid games, just like kids usually do. But when things turned ugly in the McGanley household, no one was there. No one at all. He was trapped, afraid, unloved, and alone, with no way to stop it.

3

And so the day at Curtis High School had been another frustrating day, just like that one years earlier. He went right up to his room when he got home, dumped his books at the foot of his bed, and flopped down. Now he lay there, staring up at the ceiling. There was no reason for Mrs. Blanchet to treat him that way. He'd always been polite to her. And he'd never been late to Mr. Bose's class, or any class, for that matter.

He was sick of being stopped in his tracks, sick of school, sick of home, and sick of being told what he couldn't do by his brothers, his father, and people who didn't know him from Adam. It had been the same way with the football coach, too. He'd shown up at tryouts, the first player out on the field on the first day, determined to make the team. But the coach had simply laughed at him, dismissed him because of his small size, and told him to go home "until he could wear long pants."

And the band: He'd joined it as a freshman to play the drums and picked up the skills pretty fast, or so he thought. He marched during halftime at football games and looked okay in his band uniform, but even that hadn't worked out. No one in the band ever talked to him. Jeez, they'd treated him like he was some sort of leper, and he had no idea why. He quit the band after a little over a year, and no one ever bothered to find out why or ask him to come back. Now he wondered why he was even alive, or if anyone would even miss him if he weren't. Life stunk.

He closed his eyes, must have dozed off for a while, opened his eyes gain, and looked up. The ceiling had gone nowhere and he'd accomplished absolutely nothing. He rolled over and looked at his algebra book. Inside was a never-ending list of homework problems. Why bother? He hadn't listened in class yet and hardly knew or cared about algebra or homework. He'd already flunked it once. And there was supposed to be a test the next day. God!

In all the silly self-pity, he'd forgotten about the *Popular Mechanics* magazine under his algebra book. Oh no, he still had it! No sense in taking it back to the library now. Mrs. Blanchet would say he stole it. He readjusted himself on his side, opened to the article "The West Point of the Air," found the place where he'd left off, and dug in.

> . . . *Advanced Training, the AT-6 is flown by pilots deemed to have fighter capabilities. Those pilots qualified for bomber or transport aviation fly the multi-engine AT-9 and AT-10. Cadets who do not show the skills needed to continue flight training can be assigned to the AT-11 for bombardier and navigator training. Flying cadets receive 65 hours of intensive training during each stage. Each cadet is assigned to a highly experienced instructor pilot who is an expert in aerial maneuvers and military tactics. As training progresses, so do the capabilities of the aircraft. By the time flying cadets reach the advanced stages, they are flying at speeds approaching 200 miles per hour. Strict performance standards ensure that each cadet completes training with the highest degree of aviation skill and personal confidence. Upon graduation, cadets are awarded their flying wings and offered a regular or reserve commission in the Army Air Corps.*

This was it! The way out! In his muggy room, seven o'clock at night, by himself, without his homework done, and with a renewed determination that came from somewhere down deep where no one else could reach, he decided, "I'm going to be a pilot."

✧ ✧ ✧

"What do you have there, Mr. McGanley?" Donald hadn't noticed his algebra teacher coming down the aisle. The students were supposed to be doing test problems, something like $3x - 5y - 7 = 5$ and "solve for Y." But having finished the *Popular Mechanics* article last night, Donald was now busy reading a book called *Your Wings* about pitch, roll and yaw, landing in crosswinds, tailspins, ailerons, rudders, and elevators. And then there were the pilot's instruments, tons of them it seemed: manifold pressure, the altimeter, the airspeed indicator, tachometer, vertical velocity indicator, and accelerometer, which indicated "G" forces. Assen Jordanoff's book *How to Fly* was tucked under his desk. That would be next. This was good stuff; the algebra wasn't.

"Uh . . . well . . . it's a book."

"I can see that. Why aren't you working?"

"I don't know anything about algebra."

"This is a test, you know, Mr. McGanley. Sometimes, I don't even know why you're here."

Me neither. "Well, I . . ."

"You'll never pass algebra unless you pass this test, let alone take it."

"Well, I . . ."

"Put down the book and get to work, Mr. McGanley."

Donald put down the book and stared at the test problems. He had no idea where to start. Too bad the teacher hadn't asked him how to do a slow roll. He felt helpless. What would Edna say if she saw his test score? And heaven forbid if she told Johnny.

But that's how algebra went, second attempt, for Donald McGanley. It was too late to save his grade now. Maybe it was a nice idea to be interested in airplanes, but he hadn't figured out that he needed to finish high school if he wanted to become a pilot. And there was no way to graduate from Curtis High School without passing algebra. When grades came at the end of the term, Donald received exactly what he expected: a failing grade in algebra, yet again.

Johnny never noticed, but Edna did. In spite of her weaknesses of the past, Edna saw in Donald a chance to succeed in education where her other sons never would. She scolded Donald for the failure and signed him up for algebra, third attempt, for the fall term. Donald was crestfallen, but this was one small push he needed.

4

Staten Island, summer, 1937

If you were a brand-new seventeen-year-old in the summer before your high school senior year, times might be quite good. The cutest cheerleader on the squad could be your girl, you'd have a starting position on the football team and there'd be dances and big events to attend, and graduation. This was surely to be the best year of your life.

But Donald had no such grand ideas. Graduation was an iffy prospect at best. He spent his afternoons working a paper route, making a nickel per month profit from each customer. On weekends, he bagged groceries at Roulstons for tips. Most of the money went toward the family food treasury.

Elizabeth was gone from home almost permanently now, spending a lot of time with some guy named Arnold, whom she said she planned to marry. Vic was only there for meals when he couldn't get them elsewhere, usually with Roddy in tow. Donald and young Ricky were the only kids home regularly. Johnny went about his business at Roulstons, virtually aloof from his kids.

When he wasn't delivering papers, Donald was thinking about airplanes. He'd read that *Popular Mechanics* article a hundred times but never got tired of it. When he picked up his papers for delivery, he scanned the newsstand for magazines with articles about airplanes or flying. He would be disappointed when he found none, but his little brother would keep asking him about planes and flying. Ricky didn't really care about it all that much, but he knew

Donald did. His desire for Donald's attention and approval kept the
questions coming. And Donald would not shun the kid the way his
elder brothers had shunned him.

"Are you going to be a pilot?"

"Yes."

"When?"

"After high school. I read about a place in Texas where they teach
military cadets how to fly. I'm going there." Donald hoped Ricky
missed the part about the military. He wasn't ready to tell anyone
about that just yet.

"Why do you want to be a pilot?"

Donald spoke more carefully, "Well, I'll be out on my own soon.
Being a pilot will be my career. You don't want to live at home the
rest of your life, do you?" Ricky didn't answer. "Tell you what. Let's
go down to the toy store on Victory Boulevard. I'll get you one of
those balsa-wood airplanes and you can build one for yourself.
How's that?"

"Great!"

Donald thought back to his younger days, when it was he who
built the balsa models. He'd fly them from his second-floor window
for hours. If he were lucky, he'd retrieve them before Vic or Roddy
got hold of them. His older brothers would toss the models around
until they crashed into something. Donald promised himself that
he'd never do that to his little brother.

"Will Mom and Dad let you?"

"Let me what?"

"Leave home to become a pilot?"

"Why wouldn't they?"

"It's dangerous."

"So is just about everything else if you don't know what you're
doing. If you want to be a pilot, you have to study aviation and practice
with an instructor. I have a couple of good books and magazines I
can show you."

"I wouldn't like it if you died in an airplane crash."

"Neither would I." Donald looked down at his little brother, who was staring down at the sidewalk. "Don't worry. I won't." Ricky looked up and smiled.

At Victory Toys, Donald went right to the balsa airplanes and picked out the cheapest one. Even that was a dime. Ricky didn't even notice; McGanley kids got very few gifts. He was just happy to be getting the toy. Who cared how or why or what it cost?

As they got to the cash register, Donald noticed a kid from school, Tim-something, sweeping the floor a few aisles down. They weren't friends, really. In fact, Tim was one of the hoods at school who got a big kick out of pushing smaller kids around. Donald avoided him. And now, with Ricky along, he just hoped that Tim wouldn't pay any attention to him.

But Tim had been watching Donald and Ricky since they entered the store and, apparently happy to see someone his own age, walked over toward the two McGanleys.

"Hi, Donny."

Donny? Donald was shocked that Tim almost knew his name, but he responded. "Tim, I didn't know you worked here."

The hood motioned for Donald to join him out of earshot of the cashier. "Didn't want any job, but the old lady found out that I swiped some jawbreakers from Mr. Beason's corner market, that little cheap joint down on Bay Street. Geez, everybody does it. That old geezer must be two hundred years old. Now I have to work here until I go to some army place."

"What place?"

"It's called Camp Dix, I think. Somewhere in Jersey. Shit! I offered to sweep out Beasons's store for a week, but he kicked me out and said, 'Never come back.' Then he finked to my mom. That night I got a whipping from my old man, and by the end of the next day, I got this job to do every afternoon. Shit! I still can't believe I got caught. My older brother did the same thing for years. He's in the pen now. Mom said she'll never let that happen to me. Now I have to join the CMTC." Tim started to walk away but Don stopped him.

"Tim, wait! What's CMTC?"

"Stands for Civilian Military Training Corps, or something like that. You have to go do like soldiers, sleep in a tent and get yelled at by stupid army men. Christ, I'd rather go to jail than do stupid shit like that."

"When do you go?"

"Next week, on the first, for thirty days. Thirty whole days! By the time I get back, Clara'll probably be messin' with someone else, and Beason'll probably be dead. Shit! There goes the whole fuckin' summer!"

Donald didn't give a damn about the hood's summer, but the CMTC was another matter. He asked, "How'd they sign you up?"

"My mom took me down to the Marine Hospital over in Vanderbilt. They sign you up right there with your parents' permission. Then some doctor gives you a physical. My mom spent a half hour telling this army guy what a dumb kid I am before she even signed the paper. You have to be seventeen. Shit, if Mom hadn't been there, I coulda told the soldier I was sixteen, that woulda been that, and I could spend my time showing Clara how to check me for a hernia."

Donald wasn't sure what a hernia was, but he knew who Clara was, so he could kind of figure out what Tim meant. He accommodated the stupid bully with a knowing laugh. But what he was really interested in was this CMTC. He wondered what Johnny and Edna would say if he told them he wanted to go. He decided that he'd just tell his mom. Tim said that only one parent had to be at the Marine Hospital with him, which meant he probably didn't need Johnny's permission.

Then Tim was talking to him again. "Hey, you're not gonna sign up for this, are you?"

Donald was conscious of Ricky standing next to him. Tim's swearing had made the youngest McGanley interested, and that was bad enough. As for the CMTC, Ricky didn't need to know anymore about it, or what his older brother might be thinking. "Nah. I just never heard of it. Sounds tough." And after a pause, he added, "Well, we gotta get going. We'll see you around."

They walked out of the store, free to go while Tim was still chained to his broom and his chores. Served him right; the guy had been a bully ever since Donald had known him. Donald and Ricky got a block or so away from Victory Toys before he spoke to his kid brother. "Stay away from that guy, Ricky. As long as he works there, stay away from that store. Okay?"

"How come?"

Don stopped and turned to his brother. He glared purposefully in Ricky's face. "Listen, Ricky. I said stay away from that guy—now, tomorrow, ten years from now. Understand?"

"But he was your friend."

"No, he wasn't. And he never will be. Look, you gotta understand that there's good people and bad people all over, even though you have to get along with all of them. You just have to learn to figure out who your friends really are. If some guy isn't your friend, then stay away from him. And it never does you any good to get mad or holler or get into some fight either. Plenty of other fellas do that. It gets them nowhere. Won't get you anywhere either. You got that?"

Ricky nodded and looked up admiringly at his older brother, clinging to his balsa-wood airplane. Donald was really neat. Ricky felt safe, with the best brother in the world.

Donald didn't notice any of that, with his mind on this CMTC. *Hmmm. You know, this could work!* It would be a lot better than being around the house all summer. More importantly, it was a step toward the army and getting out for good. And once he was in the army he could become a pilot. For the umpteenth time, his mind went back to the *Popular Mechanics* article about the "The West Point of the Air." *Pilot.* He wondered what it would feel like to really be one.

5

The Thomasson Act of 1936 created the Civilian Military Training Corps as a recruiting tool after the military drawdowns of the 1920s and the early 1930s. At selected posts around the country, the U.S. Army set up cost-free, all-volunteer summer camps for interested boys, all run by regular noncommissioned officers. It was a four-month program, one month during successive summers. The boys wore salvage army uniforms, marched, did close-order drill, and completed gunnery practice with a 1903 Springfield .30 caliber rifle. Advanced groups even did some basic artillery training. Uniforms caps had round metal discs with white felt background which distinguished each month of training: gold for basic, white for corporal, red for sergeant, and blue for reserve cadet officer, matching the intended four-year progression.

The CMTC had no military service commitment attached, but once trainees completed their fourth month of camp, they could be offered "reserve" status in the army if they'd done well enough. Some could even be called to active duty with a reserve commission as a second lieutenant, though such occasions were rare. Now, how could he sell this to Edna?

✧   ✧   ✧

Johnny, Edna, Donald, and Ricky sat silently at dinner: some vegetables, potatoes, and sliced bread. Edna glanced around, trying to think of something to say. Johnny never looked up from his plate. Ricky ate up his potato and was busy pushing peas around the plate.

Eventually, Johnny got up from the table and headed toward the living room. Seeing his chance, Donald spoke up.

"Mom, I heard about a free summer camp for boys. A guy I know from school told me about it today." He saw the quizzical look on Ricky's face and returned it with one of those *Stay out of this!* glares. Ricky had scattered the peas as best he could. He announced, "I'm done!" then got up and ran off.

"What camp?"

"It's kind of a play-army type of thing. It's at Camp Dix."

"Camp Dix?"

"Across the river, in Jersey, not too far from here. It's a month long."

Edna didn't speak at first. She looked toward the living room and then back to her son. "Have you spoken to your father? What about your job at Roulstons?"

"There's two or three delivery boys. Sometimes we just stand around all day anyway. I'd like to go." He sensed Edna's hesitation and kept talking. "I have to go down to the Marine Hospital for a physical, and they need you to be there to sign me up."

"When is this?"

"We can take the bus and go to the hospital tomorrow morning, and then I could be at Roulstons by noon. I don't go to the camp until August 1."

"I don't know."

"I really want to go, Mom."

"We'll have to ask your father."

"They only need one parent's permission. Dad's so busy with everything. I don't want to bother him."

"I don't want you to leave."

"Why, Mom?"

"I need you here. You're so good around the house."

"Mom, this is a chance for me to do something for myself. It doesn't cost anything. The army pays for all of it."

"Who's going to watch Ricky?"

"He's fine, Mom. You're here all day. He's got friends to play with down the street." Donald paused. "Mom, let me go."

"I'll go ask your father." Edna got up and went into the living room.

He heard low voices but couldn't make anything out. *Just great!* He'd hoped to leave his dad out of it. At least Johnny wasn't hollering. He was surprised when she returned. It hadn't been long at all.

"Your father says okay, but he doesn't have time to go to the hospital with you. I'll have to do that." She looked unhappy; he pretended not to notice.

✧ ✧ ✧

They arrived at the Marine Hospital just after 9:00 a.m. Donald was the only recruit there and saw the doctor almost immediately. After three or four questions about diseases, a cold stethoscope, a tongue depressor that made him gag, and a couple of knuckle taps on his back and stomach, he was done. Five minutes. Edna signed his release form, but said nothing all the way home. As he promised, Donald practically ran to Roulstons, but not before he passed off his paper route to Billy Bennett, whose mom was plenty happy to see her troublemaking son do something useful for a change.

On August 1, Donald got up early and met the 6:25 bus at the end of the street. The bus for Camp Dix wouldn't leave until nine o'clock, but he didn't want to take any chances. Still in her nightgown, Edna stopped him at the door.

"I don't want you to go."

"What? Mom, I'm all signed up."

"I know."

"I'll be back at the end of the month. It'll seem like no time at all. I've got to hurry to catch the bus." Edna could see that this was doing no good. She looked at Donald. She didn't move toward him to hug him; he didn't move toward her. Donald said, "I'll be fine. Good-bye, Mother."

"Well, don't disgrace me."

6

Camp Dix was the first real taste of freedom Donald had ever felt. He loved it. Around thirty boys showed up; Tim wasn't among them.

The boys were busy all day long, setting up their tents, digging their own latrines, hiking, building their own campfires, and cooking their own meals. As advertised, each was given the chance to fire the Springfield rifle during the third week of camp, the first time Donald had ever held a firearm.

The leader of the boys' camp, Sergeant Walter Malone, seemed displeased with the job. He hollered all the time but showed no favoritism toward anyone. And late at night he was the inevitable butt of the boys' crass jokes. Donald admired him, though. Even though Malone was plenty demanding, some might say harsh, he was aware of everything going on around him. He knew when to push hard and when to pull back. He knew who he was dealing with, not real recruits, but kids. It took a pretty intuitive person to understand how far he could go with them. Best of all, he always seemed to be telling kids what they *could* do, not what they *couldn't*, even while he was hollering at them. Donald found himself wondering what it would be like to serve under him in the real army. He'd follow someone like Sergeant Malone.

Two nights before camp ended, Donald was assigned the after-dinner-wood-gathering detail. Dinner had been later than usual after returning from a seven-mile hike with twenty-five-pound packs. The boys were whipped, and all had headed for the tents right after eating. Donald's job was to gather enough wood to keep the fire alive all night, even though no one would be tending it. The task was more about learning how much wood it would take to do the job, to gather enough—really, more than enough. As Donald dropped his second load and turned to gather more, Sergeant Malone stopped him.

"McGanley!"

"Yes, sir, Sergeant."

"Come on over here for a minute."

Donald stiffened and then walked slowly toward Malone, who was sitting on a log next to the fire. What was this about? What had he done wrong? "Yes, sir?"

Malone motioned beside him as he spoke. "Sit down here, son."

Donald was disarmed by the sudden compassion in Malone's voice; it was so different from the way he'd heard the sergeant address anyone over the last month.

"What did you think of the camp, McGanley?"

"Fine, sir."

Malone saw that as the boy answered, he looked down, never into his eye. "Yeah. Well, are you planning on joining the army?"

"Yes, sir."

Malone gave Donald a long, hard look. "Why?"

"Well, sir . . . I dunno."

Another long, hard look. Malone took a long slow breath and then continued, "You're a good hard worker, McGanley. You'll do well in the service."

Now Donald looked up, started to relax a bit.

"Are you in school?" asked Malone.

"Yes, sir, but I'm not doing very well."

"Why not?"

"Uh, I guess I'm not very good at school."

"Tell me, do you work as hard at school as you do here?" Donald paused at that, and Malone answered for him. "Why not?"

"I don't like it back home, sir. I can't do algebra any good. Nobody pays any attention to me."

"Who's 'nobody'?"

"Uh, well . . . I dunno."

"Well, what do *you* think? Can you do things good?"

"I dunno."

"Tell you what, McGanley. I've watched you plow through these last thirty days about as hard as anyone can. There hasn't been one task here that you haven't been able to do. And you've done most of them all by yourself. By choice, I imagine. Maybe you ought to choose to work that hard at everything you do, whether it's something you *want* to do or something you *have* to do. First key to success, son." Malone paused to let that sink in, but he wasn't finished. "Tell me, have you made any friends here, McGanley?"

"No, sir."

"Why not?"

"I don't know, sir. I guess I'm just a loner. People don't like me much, I guess."

Malone paused again and took another slow, deep breath. "Look, it's not hard to tell that you're an unhappy young fellow. You don't have to tell me why, but think about this. I'll bet you'll succeed a lot more if you don't spend your whole life trying to do things all alone. You'll hit bumps in the road, and at times you'll run into some lousy people, but that happens to everybody. Friends are good things to have. The army's pretty good at creating them all by itself. And you know, they're nice to have around when the shooting starts."

"I want to be a pilot."

"Okay." Malone could see what was happening here. The kid had a wall up, wouldn't tell anybody why he felt the way he did. But the sergeant thought the boy was worth finishing his point. "You gonna fly up there all alone?"

"Yes, sir. I'm going to fly in fighter airplanes."

"Don't you have guys up there flying planes next to you?"

"Uh . . . I guess so."

"So do I. Some day you'll need them, those guys flying up there with you, I mean. And they'll need you. If you go in the army, you'll make lots of friends . . . good friends. Don't waste your time listening to nobodies who get their fun by telling you what you can't do, or worrying about some idiot who does you dirt. And as for school, I didn't do algebra worth a damn, either, but I wanted to finish high school, so I got after it." Donald looked down and said nothing. He wished he'd kept his mouth shut. "McGanley, you hearin' me?"

"Yes, sir, Sergeant."

"Then look me in the eye." Donald did. "You really want to be a pilot, McGanley?"

"Yes, sir."

"Then remember this: there ain't no such thing as a squadron of one. So cut out the nonsense and go be a pilot." Malone got right up in Donald's face. "The only person in this world who can really stop you . . . is you."

7

Graduation ceremonies at Curtis High School took place twice a year, in January and June. The June 1938 ceremony would be much larger and more elaborate, with more graduates, speakers, a baccalaureate, a dance, and parties. As in all high schools, most of the seniors would revel in the glow as top dogs, looking forward to the spring pageantry that went along with proms, pomp, and circumstance.

But Donald didn't care about all that. In the fall of 1937, he took algebra for the third time, this one with Mrs. Richter, a pretty thirty-something who not only knew how to explain what variables were, but also had the patience to explain it a second or third time if you didn't get it. She was a darned good teacher at just the right time. Between Mrs. Richter's patience, Sergeant Malone's gruff-but-wise counsel, and Edna's determination to see her son complete high school, Donald had the push he needed and passed algebra with a "C." Just before the Christmas break he went to the principal's office and arranged to attend the graduation ceremony scheduled for January 12, 1938, in the Curtis High School gym.

He was the only McGanley there. His mother couldn't drive and never took the streetcar or buses by herself. His elder brothers had other things to do. Come to think of it, they probably did the smart thing by not showing up around Curtis High School. And so, Donald received his diploma along with twenty-two other students, only the second McGanley (after Elizabeth) to make it that far in education. With his diploma, he walked the four miles home, just like any other afternoon.

✧   ✧   ✧

Still too young at seventeen to join the army, Donald planned to spend the spring months working. Half his earnings would go to the family; the rest he'd keep for himself. Next summer he'd turn eighteen and go back to the CMTC camp at Fort Dix, but stay for three months. Maybe Sergeant Malone would still be there. If he worked hard enough, he could go all the way through the ranks and maybe get a reserve commission. From there he could join the flying cadets. A year or two from now he'd be in Texas, training to be an army pilot. His whole world would change in front of him, all for the better. The plan was perfect.

But the perfect plan got off to a rough start. Without connections, steady work of any substance was hard to find, and Donald didn't know anybody. Someone his age, high school diploma or not, was pretty much stuck with nickel and dime jobs unless they could dream up something better. A kid he knew from school named Alfie Posetti made himself a box, got some shoeshine paste and a brush, and set himself up in business. So Donald tried that. He went down to Baker's Barber Shop on Bay Street and asked if he could set up a shoeshine stand there. Baker agreed, in return for having his shop swept out twice a day. The deal was struck, but when Donald got home, Edna stopped the plan cold. "No! No son of mine is going to be a shoeshine boy!" Donald was left with the embarrassing task of going back to the shop and telling Mr. Baker that he couldn't work there.

Spring dragged on through March and April, with no regular job. Donald tried peddling magazines for street vendors and corner stores, but just like the newspaper job he'd had as a boy, most of the money was skimmed off by his boss. On Saturdays he pushed a three-wheeled cart delivering grocery orders from Roulstons, his only pay being whatever the customers would tip: perhaps a nickel, once in a great while a dime, most of the time nothing. In between these oddball jobs, Donald didn't do a damn thing. This wasn't working out, not even close.

Then finally, *finally*, he got a break. It was a rainy Saturday morning at Roulstons. One of the cashiers, a nice guy named Mr. Cox, was helping him load up an order for a Mrs. Hinson, a non-tipper who lived almost twenty blocks away. The order included a copy of the *Staten Island Advance* with a headline article about the WPA on it.

"Mr. Cox, what's WPA?"

"Works Progress Administration. Why do you want to know?"

"What is it?"

"It's part of Roosevelt's plan to get people back to work. Ever heard of the 'New Deal'?"

"I've heard of it, but I don't know much about it exactly."

"Well, people need jobs, so the government set up a whole slew of programs. So far it seems to be doing pretty well, I guess. The WPA is heavy construction: dams, roads, things like that. They've built a bunch already." (Indeed: After appropriations totaling eleven billion dollars, the WPA would construct 650,000 miles of roads, 124,000 bridges, 125,000 public buildings, 8,000 parks, and 800 airports and airstrips before it shut down.)

Cox said, "Lord knows I could use the money, over $40 a month. But I couldn't work there."

"Why not?"

"Fell out of a tree when I was little and broke my back. I have bad legs, too."

"Do you think they'd take me?"

"I don't know. Why don't you go find out?"

"How?"

"There's an office on Fulton Street in Manhattan, Fulton Employment, I think. Not bad I'm told. They placed one of my neighbors in the WPA about a year ago. He's been gone most of the time ever since. I'm sure his family doesn't like that too much, but they still have their house and an automobile." Cox put the last couple of items in the three-wheeled cart. "There, better get running off, son. Mrs. Hinson gets a bit snippy if we don't get her order there quick enough."

She was snippy all right. She complained to Donald about the rainy weather, her wet groceries, the tardiness of the delivery, and maybe a few other stupid things. But Donald heard very little of it, didn't even care that she didn't tip him. He was thinking about the WPA and Fulton Employment. If he could get a regular job, he could probably make some good money. And if it took him away from home, that was even better. He'd thought a hundred times about just taking off, but where would he go? Now he had the answer, and the WPA would be his ticket. This sounded better by the second.

On the first Monday morning in May 1938, Donald rose early, didn't bother to eat, and left home before anyone else was up. He took the bus to the Staten Island Ferry, which passed the Statue of Liberty and dropped him off at Battery Park. The Fulton Street address was still eight blocks away, but he decided to walk instead of taking the subway. He could save a nickel that way. And he was nervous; the walk would help.

✧   ✧   ✧

Fulton Employment was a poorly-lit, inner-building office with no windows. It was not exactly an upbeat kind of place. In fact, it was downright dreary. A single, cheap-looking picture hung on the wall opposite the entry door. Chairs lined two of the walls, but not nearly enough to seat everyone. A lone agent sat in a small office with a single desk, door open, occasionally talking to applicants but also talking on the phone with prospective employers. Donald filled out an application, placed it in a basket on a table with all the other applications, and took a seat.

The place was crammed full of men, even at eight o'clock in the morning. Some of them looked like they were eighty years old. Donald was obviously the youngest of the bunch. The waiting went on, hour after hour. Some got up and left; some looked at their applications and walked out before they ever got started. Since the agent's door was open, all could hear the interviews and phone calls, the same bland line of baloney each time. It was almost as though the agent was reading from a card or something. "Yes, sir, I have a nice young man here, good looking, and seems to be from a good family. We've checked him out thoroughly. He'll work awfully hard for you, sir. We at Fulton Employment take our placement job very seriously. Can I send him over, sir?" Most of the time, the answer was no.

"McGanley!" The employment agent stood in his doorway, Donald's application in hand. Donald got up and followed the man into the unfriendly, uninviting office. For all he knew, he could be in a police station interrogation room. A single chair sat opposite the desk, but the agent didn't offer it. With his back to Donald, he asked, "What type of work are you looking for?"

"Construction, sir. I'd like to join the WPA."

The agent turned around. "How old are you?"

"Seventeen. But I'll be eighteen in July. I have some identification, sir."

The agent shook his head. "WPA jobs are available only for able-bodied men, boy. Look at you. What are you, five feet and hundred pounds? The WPA is for heavy construction projects. They'd laugh me out of my job if I sent you over there. Besides, you have to be eighteen. Sorry, kid, but no."

Donald stared at the agent. Damn! He was sick and tired of being told "no!" The school football coach told him no, his mother and father told him no, teachers and librarians told him no, and his newspaper bosses either told him no or ripped him off. And now this creep was telling him no. Not one of these people lifted a finger to help him. Not one! He was sick of it! He balled his fists and started to shake, fighting back angry tears.

But he didn't take his eyes off the agent, who was slowly starting to figure out that this kid was a little shook-up. This wasn't the typical kid who came into the office, got turned down, shrugged, and left. The agent had read enough faces to know when he saw a genuine, driven, honest one. He decided to take a chance.

"Sit down, young man." The agent gave Donald a minute to compose himself while he got up, walked around his desk, and closed the door. "Mr. McGanley, ever had a full-time job before?"

"No, sir."

"And you just graduated from Curtis High School?"

"Yes, sir."

"Where's that?"

"Staten Island, sir."

"I'll tell you what. Suppose I get you a permanent job. Good work, good company, fair pay. I know of a few good openings for apprentice workers, but I don't want to waste my time and reputation filling them with loafers. What I want from you is at least one year's commitment to work hard and steady. Eleven dollars a week, close to what you'd get working a WPA job. What about it?"

Donald didn't know what to think. As he slowly calmed down, his mind raced to the plan for CMTC training this summer and raced back to the eleven dollars a week. That was good money. He needed it; his mother needed it. He could save more than ever before, and a regular job would get him out of the house.

"Sounds good, sir. What's the job, sir?"

"Lithographer with Field & Beattie. They're an advertising and sales agency for medical supplies. Good company. The owner is a friend of the family, my father's friend, to be exact. Well?" Donald hesitated. "What's the matter, son?"

Donald was wrestling with himself. Should he tell the agent about his plans for the summer and then his plans to become a pilot? He looked down and then back up. The agent could see the kid was pained; he just didn't know why. He asked again, "Son, what is it?"

"Well, sir, I was going to join the army."

The agent looked at his application. "Too young. You have to be eighteen. Look, I offered you this job because you seem to be a sincere, trustworthy young fella. This is good work, so I have to place the employee carefully. Now, I'm going to fill this job. It's yours if you want it, but I don't have all day. Make up your mind, Mr. McGanley."

For a change, someone was giving him a break. There were lots of people outside who obviously needed work more desperately, but the job was offered to *him*. That meant something. He took a deep breath. "I'll take it, sir. Thank you."

The phone call took less than five minutes. Gone were the scripted lines and plastic voice Donald had heard all morning. The agent now sounded honest, intent, and enthusiastic about the new prospective employee. For once, Donald felt good about the events around him. He actually smiled to himself and to the agent. And then the agent extended his hand. "Congratulations, Mr. McGanley. You start Wednesday at Field & Beattie right here in Manhattan. You live on Staten Island, right?"

"Yes, sir."

"The company will pay you a dollar a week for travel expenses."

Not bad at all. Donald felt good about this. He'd made the right decision, and he was truly grateful for the job. "Sir, what's your name?"

"Mr. Hampton." The agent looked up at the new employee of Field & Beattie. "Jack."

"Thank you, Mr. Hampton." Donald extended his hand. Hampton shook it.

"Good luck, Mr. McGanley."

8

Field & Beattie was a good company, just as Jack Hampton had said. The pay was good as well, and the job wasn't hard at all. He had to learn how to set up and work the printer and then deliver the products to customers, and that was it. Fellow employees were upbeat and friendly, and he liked the energy of the city, though he didn't engage with the people much. He was still small and obviously quite unsure of himself, so no one appeared to give him a second thought, especially women.

But Donald did the job well. He didn't show up late, didn't need supervision on the job, and didn't waste resources. In these penny-pinching times, he was a good worker to have, and Old Man Beattie noticed that. Donald earned a ten-dollar bonus for Christmas.

And life at home was better. Donald arrived from work only slightly before Johnny did and now found meals cooked and ready when he got there. Edna had reclaimed her role in the household, perhaps by necessity. Amazing how much a little money could improve life.

✧   ✧   ✧

By early 1939, it was obvious to Donald that his time at home, and perhaps at Field & Beattie, was coming to a close. He had already given up CMTC the summer before and still had his heart set on becoming a flying cadet. Field & Beattie had been a good place to work, but printing lithographs and delivering medical supplies would never get him into the air. The agent at Fulton Employment had asked him for a year's commitment, and he'd given that. Now it was time to figure out how to get into the flying cadet program. In early June, events sped up that process. Old Man Beattie himself called the eighteen-year-old into his office just before closing time on the fifth.

"McGanley, you've done a good job here."

"Thank you, sir."

"How old are you, Mr. McGanley?"

"Eighteen, sir. I'll be nineteen next month."

"Good. McGanley, how would you like to work in sales?"

"Sales, sir? What's that?"

"We're looking for an energetic young man to sell our medical products to hospitals and doctors. You'd be traveling all over New York and sometimes throughout other states in the northeast. Travel expenses will be paid by the company, including motels, if you're on the road overnight. Would you be interested in that?"

"Well, sir, I was hoping to join the flying cadet program some day and become a pilot."

"In the army?"

"Yes, sir."

"I see. Well, that's an honorable career. The military doesn't pay very much, though. As a sales representative with us, you'll make $19 a week to start, and there are opportunities for more, depending on what contracts you can bring in. But I need to tell you now that I'm looking for a solid, long-term employee for this job. Do you understand what I mean?"

It was a good offer, more than a 50 percent raise—tempting, but not as tempting as his desire to fly. Still he needed time to think it over. "Yes, sir. May I have some time to think about it?"

"Absolutely. But time is money, Mr. McGanley, and we need to fill the job. Let me know by Friday."

"Yes, sir." Beattie was all business, right to the point, and fair. Donald was grateful, but he knew he'd turn down the sales job. He suspected the old man probably knew it, too.

A few weeks earlier, Field & Beattie had closed early. Donald wasn't in such a hurry to go home, so he stopped off at the military recruiter's office on Whitehall Street. He found out that applicants for the flying cadets had to be twenty years old with some college, but if he applied from active duty, he could get the college requirement waived. The recruiter convinced him that the only way he could get into the flying cadet program was to join the army first.

Donald didn't wait for Friday. The next day he went directly to Mr. Beattie and told him he'd decided to join the army. To his credit, the old man made no attempt to stop him, and Donald agreed to work the rest of the month while Beattie found and trained a replacement. On the last day of June, Donald finished work, went to the front office, and collected his last paycheck.

In a way he was sorry for running out on a man who'd been so good to him, but he couldn't let himself wait any longer. He wanted to fly. As he walked out of Field & Beattie and headed for the recruiter's office, Donald realized that he'd finally be leaving home. There was nothing there for him anymore. He knew his mother wouldn't like it. She'd probably cry and try to get him to change his mind. Johnny? He had no idea what his father might say, or if he'd even care. They were practically strangers now; they'd hardly spoken in months.

All his experience roaming around Manhattan served Donald well. He went straight to Whitehall Street without missing a step. Thoughts of leaving home were behind him now. He was ready to enlist, excited about the future. He wondered where the army might send him. At the recruiter's desk he looked over his papers, reached for a pen, and stopped. The recruiter noticed the hesitation; he'd probably seen it a thousand times before. He pointed down at Donald's papers.

"You sign right there, Mr. McGanley, and I can swear you in as a private in the U.S. Army."

"Well, first I want to get something straight."

"Ask away."

"I can still apply to the flying cadets, right?"

"Yes, you can."

"And when I'm accepted they send me right to pilot training?"

"Yes."

"What if my enlistment time isn't up?"

"You'll be immediately transferred out of the infantry into the Army Air Corps Flying Cadets. Most likely you'll be assigned to training in Texas."

"And they'll waive the need for college?"

"Yes, they can do that."

"Well, I just want to make it clear that I'm not here to join the infantry. I want to be a pilot."

"Okay, then. Do a good job and I'm sure that when the time comes, your commanding officer will be happy to write a letter of recommendation for you. That's what normally happens when young men take your route to the Air Corps. I think this will work out very well for you."

9

Private Donald McGanley arrived home that evening, the same as he had for the past fifteen months, but almost two hours later than usual. It was past eight. Johnny and Edna were at the dinner table, just about through eating, it appeared. Ricky was gone, but his plate was still there, the vegetables pushed around to the edges to make it look like he'd eaten most of them. The meal on his own plate had long since gotten cold. There was no way to do this gently, so Donald just dropped the shocker on them.

"Mom and Dad, I'm in the army." If Edna's jaw hadn't been connected, it would have hit the floor. Even Johnny looked up, eyes raised, but he said nothing. "I have to leave tomorrow for Fort Jay, on Governors Island."

"When did you do this?" she asked.

"Today. Just now. I went to the recruiting office on Whitehall Street in Manhattan. They swore me in."

"What? But why?"

"It's okay, Mom. I'll be fine." Johnny got up and left without a word. They both watched him leave, and then Edna turned back to her son. He could see the tears coming.

"But why didn't you tell me? You . . . you can't do this now. We haven't talked about this."

"Mother, I'm eighteen years old. I'll be nineteen in two weeks. I can't just live at home forever." He paused. "Elizabeth left. Now she's married, and Vic and Roddy are gone, too. You didn't stop them, so why stop me?"

"You need to be here. This is your home. What about your little brother?"

"Mom, I'm sworn in. I have to go tomorrow. This is what I want to do, and you can't change your mind once you're sworn in."

"But where will you live?"

"They have barracks. All my meals are at a chow hall. I'll make $21 a month. Look, Mom, I'll be fine." Her look said it all. It wasn't worth saying anything more about it. He said, "I gotta go pack," then turned and walked away.

Not a word passed between parents and son the rest of the evening. It felt strange when he went to bed that evening. The house was dead quiet, as though he was the only one there. He laid on his back and let his eyes wander around his room. The small crucifix still hung by itself on the wall, the same one he'd clung to years before, right before Johnny had grabbed it away from him. He couldn't remember what he'd done after that or when he'd stopped crying. He looked at it now, unable to remember how or when it had been replaced.

Johnny had hardly reacted when he told them about the army. Just a look, but Donald couldn't tell what his old man felt, if he felt anything. His son was leaving home, possibly for a very, very long time, maybe even forever, but Johnny said nothing. It hurt. No doubt, it was time to go.

The next morning, Donald got up before anyone, as he'd done before, dressed quickly, and left.

10

Fort Jay is located on Governors Island in New York Harbor, less than one mile south of Manhattan and about a quarter mile west of Brooklyn. Originally named *Noten Eylant*, Dutch for "Island of Nuts," the island had no military purpose until 1776, when George Washington ordered earthen works built there, placing cannon that would later cover his successful retreat to Manhattan. *Noten Eylant* became Governors Island after the revolution, the new name reflecting its use as a retreat for royal governors during the war. In 1783, two military posts were established on the island by the U.S. War Department: Fort Jay in the south and Fort Clinton in the north.

Fort Jay was named for John Jay, a signatory of the Declaration of Independence, President Washington's secretary of state, and the nation's first Chief Justice of the Supreme Court. When Washington left office, Fort Jay was renamed Fort Columbus (after the famous explorer), retaining that name until 1904, when it again became Fort Jay through the efforts of Elijah Root, a succeeding secretary of state. Confederate prisoners were quartered there during the Civil War, and when Donald showed up, three ten-inch and one fifteen-inch Rodman cannon from that period still guarded the main gates. The fort was now home to the First Army Headquarters and Donald's new unit, the 16th Infantry Division.

There were four new privates assigned to Fort Jay on July 1, 1939. Three reported to the recruiter's office on Whitehall Street at 0800 hours. One never showed up. From Whitehall Street, they were bussed down to Battery Park and ferried to Governors Island.

They arrived at the "G" Company orderly room at 0915 hours, met there by Corporal Wendell Bellamy IV.

The recruits marched through the quartermaster's stations for uniform issue and over to the chow hall. After a breakfast of eggs and some weird, soupy beef sauce on a slice of toast, the new recruits marched to the armory, where they were issued Garand M-1 carbines, and then to their barracks. The carbines were placed in holders next to their bunks. Empty footlockers at the end of their bunks contained all their belongings and were to left open at all times when the recruits were on post.

By 1030 hours that first day, the recruits were on the drill field, located in a quadrangle courtyard surrounded by barracks. There they would practice left face, right face, about face, forward march, half step, half right, half left, mark time, quick time, and double time—again and again, day after day, until they got it right. Within a week, Corporal Bellamy added drill with rifles: port arms, present arms, order arms, parade rest, left shoulder, and right shoulder. It was all they did for two solid weeks. Once Corporal Bellamy pronounced them ready, the three new recruits joined First Platoon, "G" Company.

Enlistment in the U.S. Army ran for one year. For most of the soldiers Donald ran into, it was one year too long. Many had been sent by their parents, or were forced to join up because they couldn't find a job. In some cases they'd chosen to serve their country over serving time.

Donald liked the order in the army, the way expectations for conduct, dress, performance, even eating, sleeping, and housekeeping, were all laid out in the manuals, *for everybody*. Days started at 0530 with morning runs and calisthenics, and once a week there'd be an obstacle course run. Each Thursday, "G" Company ran the assault course with full packs and combat gear. Marching, close-order drill, shining boots, or cleaning rifles were always good time fillers. And twice a month, "G" Company headed to Camp Dix in New Jersey to fire forty rounds from their M-1s. In addition, each soldier was given a turn on the .50 caliber machine gun. Taps sounded at 2200 hours, but Donald rarely heard it: he was usually sound asleep by then.

Troops who followed orders and read the manuals did fine; those who did not were rewarded with extra details, or push-ups, or some form of unpleasant personal attention. One recruit Donald noticed, Paulie Nelson from the Bronx, tried hard enough but didn't pick things up very fast. Donald felt for him. He was small, even smaller than Donald was, couldn't tell his right from his left, and was hopelessly clumsy.

Paulie looked petrified half the time, an easy target for Platoon Sergeant Alfred J. Harris. Company First Sergeant Alan Masterson noticed him, too. They hollered at Paulie a lot. Masterson was old-school tough, not shy at all about getting on a soldier who marched out of step or dropped his rifle or fell out on a run. The platoon sergeants probably liked it when he picked on a recruit: it meant that Masterson wasn't watching *them*.

✧　✧　✧

It was an unseasonably hot day in early September; First Platoon was finishing an assault course run with full packs and rifles with bayonets. Donald was almost the last man to start, but he soon caught up with Paulie, who was so tired he just jabbed at a bayonet target, missing it completely. His rifle went flying as he sprawled to the ground. Harris and Masterson, watching nearby, were on him immediately.

"Nelson, get up!" Paulie staggered to his feet and started to slog on toward the next obstacle. "Nelson!" Harris was right in his face, looking almost straight down at him.

"Yes, sir, Sergeant!"

"Forget something?"

"Uh . . ." Paulie's shoulders slumped while he tried to figure out what Harris wanted him to say.

"Your rifle, dammit!"

Nobody saw him, but Donald broke off the course, ran over to Paulie and picked up the rifle. Before either of the two sergeants could react, he shoved it into Paulie's chest. "Here, Paulie, let's go!" He pulled on Paulie's arms.

"McGanley!" Now Harris and Masterson were after *him*. "What are you doing?"

Donald hollered over his should as he dragged Paulie away from the two sergeants. "Assault course, sir!"

"McGanley, get your ass back here!"

Donald ignored them. "Come on, Paulie, don't quit now! Let's go, let's go! Paulie, move it!"

The two privates finished the course together, then Paulie collapsed to the ground, prone. Donald gave him a minute and then sat down next to him. "Okay, Paulie, c'mon, sit up." They were both breathing hard. They weren't supposed to be on the ground, but Donald didn't want him to sit there alone. He waited for a few seconds. "You tired?"

Paulie laughed for the first time in weeks. He was still trying to catch his breath, but he was doing better now. "Yeah!" They both reached up under their steel pots and wiped sweat from their faces. "I didn't think I was gonna make it until you came along. Sarge was going to bite my head off. You really saved me."

"You'd have saved me, right? That's what they say we're supposed to do. C'mon, we'd better get up before they come after us again." Donald was up quickly and then reached down and pulled Paulie to his feet. A hundred yards away, Harris and Masterson were both smiling.

11

January 1940

Orders came down for five companies of the 16th Infantry Division to prepare for two months of maneuvers at Fort Benning, Georgia. New York City did not have the open spaces, and it was a better idea to conduct training relatively free from the ice and snow of the New York winter. Donald was glad that "G" Company would be among the deploying troops: it was a chance to get away from the normal routine. Most of the men would have rather stayed at Fort Jay where they could see their gals or take in the picture show, or better than that, frequent their favorite watering holes. Georgia was a planet's distance away.

Deploying units moved out on the twenty-fifth. They crossed the Buttermilk Channel by ferry and boarded the troop transport *Hunter Liggett*, bound for Charleston Harbor. To Donald it was a great, exciting day. For others, the overcast skies matched their gloomy moods as they left the security of home, most of them for the first time. Paulie Nelson was literally petrified as he marched up the gangway. Donald got in line behind him.

"Well, Paulie, we're off to see the world!" No answer. "Hey! Paulie! How're you doin'? You all right?" Still no answer. Donald could see that Paulie wasn't warming up to this very well. Just like the assault course; he'd have to look after him.

He followed Paulie on board, sat with him in the chow hall, and fortunately, bunked in the same quarters. Cabins were crammed full, with bunks stacked three high on three walls, the other open space just big enough to accommodate their gear and the door. Somebody had called them "sardine cans," like submarines, and now Donald could see why. Anyone who was claustrophobic would have a real problem on this or any ship.

The second day at sea, Donald leaned over the rails of the *Hunter Liggett,* staring at the ship's wake and the waves of the Atlantic. The skies were overcast and the sea was a bit choppy, row after row of swells topped by whitecaps. It was chilly, about forty degrees, and windy. Protected by his heavy jacket and a watch cap, he was happy to be here, headed somewhere he'd never been. He spun a slow 360-degree turn and saw nothing but ocean in each direction, fascinated at the view. He wondered how far he was looking as he fixed on the point where the sea met the horizon. He had no idea. If he hadn't wanted to fly so badly, he was sure he could be happy in the Navy.

But several soldiers were not enjoying the voyage as much as he. Some of them, in fact, a lot of them, were leaning over the rails or stuck in the head somewhere, actively seasick. He watched the ritual, pretty much the same after each meal, and half wondered why he wasn't sick, too. Then he caught sight of Paulie Nelson walking toward him. Paulie looked a little pallid faced, but not as bad as the troops leaning over the rails. He took up a spot next to Donald.

"How come you never get sick, Don?"

"I don't know. But you seem to be doing okay."

"That's because I didn't eat. Some crew guy told me to drink a lot of water and not to eat if I wanted to keep from getting sick."

"Good way to get real skinny."

"So's throwing up all the time."

Donald nodded and looked back over the water. He'd rather be left alone right now, just himself and the sea for a while, but Paulie hung around.

"Thanks for helping me."

"Don't mention it."

"No. You've been helping me ever since I got here. I really want to thank you, Don."

"It's okay, Paulie."

Paulie changed the subject. "Do you know where we're going?"

"Not really. Some place in Georgia. Can't remember the name of it, though. I know I've never heard of it before."

"Ever been on a ship like this?"

"No."

"Are you scared?"

"Of what?"

"Well, if this thing sinks, I'll be in trouble. I can't swim."

"It won't." Donald was surprised at the look of fear on Paulie's face.

"I've never been out on the ocean before. My mom thought the army would be good for me. She always said I was kind of slow and that it would be good for me to get out into the world. Heck, I think she just wanted one less mouth to feed. But I never thought I'd be out doing something like this."

"Well, we won't be on board very much longer, maybe a day or two." The two of them stared over the rails at the ocean, one happy private and one scared one. They were a study in contrasts: two young men somehow headed in the same direction but for very different reasons, and most likely on two very different journeys. Donald was glad for the few minutes of quiet, but finally Paulie spoke up again.

"Don, do you think I'm slow?"

Donald turned to look at him "What?"

"Slow. You know, kind of dumb. My mother thinks I'm slow. Teachers at school told me I was slow."

"I think you're fine, Paulie." This might be the first time anyone had asked for *his* approval. Paulie was even shorter than he was, was always the first private hollered at, and seemed to spend an awful lot of time cleaning latrines. Donald was glad he'd decided to look out for Paulie, especially on this trip. He hadn't been in this position since Ricky was little, and even if he preferred to be alone right now, it was kind of nice to have someone look up to him.

"Why did you join the army, Don?"

"To become a flying cadet."

"You want to fly?"

"Sure do."

"Why? I'd be scared to death."

Donald had no desire to get into the real reason he wanted to leave home. "Oh, I don't know. When I was little, I used to watch airplanes fly overhead. And if I could save enough money, I'd go buy balsa-wood models and fly 'em out my bedroom window."

"I never had a model airplane."

"They usually got busted up pretty quick. But I saw an article in *Popular Mechanics* magazine one day. It was about pilot training. I knew for sure I wanted to fly after that."

"How's this army stuff supposed to make you a pilot?"

"I can apply soon, right from the army." Donald turned back toward the railing. "Besides, I like the army life a whole lot better than the civilian world."

"Do you think there'll be a war? With us in it, I mean?"

He turned to Paulie again. "A war?" The question took him by surprise. "I don't know. Do you?"

"It's already going. I heard some guys talking about it. Germany took over Poland. It went so well for them, Hitler'll probably attack somebody else. Then we're going to be in the middle of it. I don't think I'd last a minute in a battle with the Germans, and we'll be the first ones to go because we're already in the army!" Paulie was talking a mile a minute. His eyes were half bugged out. He looked more scared now than he had a few moments before when he said he couldn't swim.

Donald hadn't thought much about all this, nor paid much attention to what was happening in Europe. Paulie might be right. The French and English had already declared war. If the United States ended up in a fight with the Germans, he might find himself in a foxhole or trench somewhere. That could screw up the whole works for getting into the flying cadets. He made an effort to keep his concern under wraps. "Ah, I don't think so. But I'll tell you one thing: if I have to fight the Germans, I'm going to do it in an airplane."

12

The 16th Infantry Division put in at Charleston on schedule, then proceeded west by convoy to Augusta, down through Macon, then on to Fort Benning, Georgia, just outside of Columbus. The 369-mile trip at 35 mph would wipe out the entire day. Donald was assigned a three-quarter-ton to drive, with God-knows-what in the back. He volunteered Paulie to ride with him. For food they had "C" rations, cardboard boxes with little green cans of ham and eggs, peaches, and something that was supposed to be chocolate cake. For a snack there was a weird-looking, freeze-dried "cereal bar" with a warning label to drink water with it; not too bad if you liked to eat cement. The convoy made two latrine stops on the way: one in Augusta and one in Macon.

Within thirty minutes, Paulie dozed off. They were supposed to stay awake, but Donald let him sleep. On his first trip to the Deep South, he was happy for the quiet and fascinated by the open terrain, the small towns, and the Negroes who stopped to watch them pass by. As they drove, he tried to remember the history of the slaves and the Civil War from his high school classes. He'd hardly spoken to a Negro in his life. Would they even talk to him? His curiosity only grew as they drove on. He was eager to experience new things. Joining the army was the best thing he'd ever done.

Paulie had mentioned the distant war in Europe. Donald admitted to himself that he hadn't really thought much about it. But if they went over there . . . wow! He'd never dreamed of going so far. He thought about flying, what it might be like to sit in a huge machine with nothing below or above you but air. He tried to imagine flying in combat. What would it be like to be shot at, or shot? He'd have to be a good pilot, the best in the Army Air Corps. No one was going to stop him from that, and . . .

"Don?" Paulie woke up and jerked Donald out of his thoughts. "Where are we?"

"Just past some little town, Sparta, I think. A little over halfway to Columbus. You ought to look around, Paulie; kind of interesting down here."

"Looks to me like we're out in the middle of nowhere."

"Well, we're a little over an hour out of Macon, and that's supposed to be our last stop. Not too much longer after that to Fort Benning."

"Is that where we're going?"

"Yeah, I asked Sarge when we got off the ship. It's a big army base, tons bigger than Fort Jay, he said."

"I wish I was home."

"I don't."

"Why not?"

"'Cause I'll never get to fly doing dishes at home."

"I couldn't fly. I can't even drive a car."

Donald thought, *Boy, this guy is really in trouble*. Maybe he ought to tell the Sarge about Paulie, but Harris was pretty busy with the troops on the road, and he probably already knew enough about Paulie anyway. Still, Paulie sounded like a little kid sometimes. Donald decided he'd just try to build up the guy when he could and help him finish off his enlistment. Maybe after the army, he could find something that worked for him.

"Well, you don't know if you don't try. Why not get your license as soon as you get home? They'll probably give us some three-day passes when we get back to Jay. You can borrow your parents' car. I passed the test, so I know you can." *Better not tell him it took me three tries to do it*, he thought.

"Maybe." Paulie turned toward the door and shut his eyes again.

They arrived at Benning just after 1900 hours. Long day: they'd been up at 0400 to debark the ship, then started and ended the drive in the dark. Someone thought ahead, though: barracks were ready for the dog-tired troops, who had just enough energy left to park their trucks, form up, march to the barracks, hop in their bunks and fall asleep.

✧   ✧   ✧

Fort Benning was a sprawling training complex. As Paulie had suggested, the Germans had indeed made an impression on the War Department. The place was buzzing with paratroop trainees who hustled through a three-week course of conditioning and countless mock jumps, where the harnesses jerked their backs and scraped their crotches raw. After five live jumps from eight hundred feet, they earned their jump wings.

Besides parachute training, Fort Benning's acreage played host to a long line of deployed units on maneuvers, like the 16th Infantry. They moved each day and bivouacked each night. On some days, there was a simulated assault, sometimes two. Occasionally, carefully planned maneuvers employed live fire. The work was tedious, relentless, and sometimes downright dangerous, but there was an urgency among the officers and the first sergeant that hadn't been there at Fort Jay.

Donald just did his job and spent much of his time helping Paulie keep up. The kid had been right when they'd talked at the rails on board the *Hunter Liggett*. He *was* kind of slow. But Donald was determined to help him through it, all the way through to the end of his enlistment and back to his mother. Paulie had no business in the army.

On the ninth day of the exercise, G Company completed an eleven-mile march through heavily forested, sometimes rocky terrain, ending with an assault charge against an old abandoned barn. So far, the training had gone well, with few incidents. Two men from their platoon had slipped on a hillside during the march, tumbling almost a hundred feet down the slope. But there were only small cuts and bruises, and some good training for the medics.

Now, with the day finally over, Sergeant Harris found a suitable place to bivouac. Having gone without a regular meal all day, the men dug into their rations and then formed into teams of two for the night. Donald and Paulie built a lean-to on the perimeter of a small clearing and settled in for some well-deserved sack time. Donald was almost asleep when Paulie spoke.

"Donald, are you awake?"

"No." He was dog tired. "What is it?"

"Do you think we're going to war?"

"I don't know, Paulie. Haven't we been through this?"

"I guess. But I'm scared. I don't want to be in the army."

Donald was a little irritated. "It's a little late for that now, Paulie, don't you think? Let's try and get some sleep."

"The only reason I'm here is because my mom made me go." Donald laughed to himself, but part of it filtered out, loud enough for Paulie to hear. "What's so funny about that?" Paulie asked.

"Nothing." No use trying to get Paulie to shut up now. He'd just have to suffer through this. Besides, now he really *was* awake. "My mother was exactly the opposite. Wanted me to stay home all my life."

"I'd give anything for that."

"No, you wouldn't." Donald hoped Paulie wouldn't ask about that, and he didn't. The boy was too scared for himself to think about anything Donald said.

"I can't seem to do anything right here. I know that you're trying to help me, but I don't want you to be getting into trouble because I can't do things the way Sarge wants me to. Donald, I just need to get out of here."

"Paulie, listen to me. Maneuvers will be over soon. What else can they have us do? We've force-marched, charged 'enemy' positions, built camps, then done it all over again—all of it, for almost two weeks. It's just routine training, like all armies do. I think you're worrying too much, and we need to get some sleep."

"No, there's more to it. All I want to do is go home. The army is no good for me."

"Paulie, look. We probably have to do this for a few more days. Then we'll head home. My enlistment is up in June. Yours is up in April, right?"

"Yeah."

"Okay. Then you'll get out before I will. We'll be fine, Paulie. Just stay up with me, and we'll be fine, okay?"

"Uh . . . I don't know. Something's going to happen. I know it. I shouldn't be here."

"Paulie, you'll be home before you know it. Look, they told us to pack up the live ammo today, right? That probably means no more live fire, which means we're probably heading home in the next couple of days. Sarge says we have to do fifteen more miles tomorrow. I don't know about you, but I'm beat. Now get some sleep."

Golly, this fellow's a mess! Donald wondered what Paulie's life must have been like before the army. It couldn't have been worse than his, but Paulie had practically been thrown out of the house by his own mother and told to join the army because he couldn't do anything else. What kind of a home could that have been? His mother probably did it more for herself than for her son. But that's as far as Donald's thinking went that night. Now, he was dead tired. He'd just watch after Paulie until they got back to Fort Jay.

13

Gunfire shattered the still darkness, jarring Donald out of a sound sleep. He grabbed his M-1 and scrambled from his lean-to, trying to remember where he was and what he was doing. Sergeant Harris grabbed his arm. "McGanley! They're attacking the encampment! Get two men and lay down fire in the direction of those shots!" He pointed to the muzzle flashes through the forest of pine trees. "And get out of this clearing. Now move it!"

Donald looked immediately for Paulie and yelled for him, but there was too much confusion and noise. He could barely hear himself, but at least his head was clearing now and he knew where he was. He stopped Al Jansen and Keith Harrington, the first two men he saw running from their shelters. "Sarge says we gotta return fire! Follow me!"

Harrington stopped short. "Shit! I don't have my rifle! Lemme go get it. Where're you gonna be?"

Donald motioned toward the flashes. "Right over there! We'll use the trees for cover. Hurry up! Just follow the muzzle flashes! And be careful, I can't see a damn thing out here!" Donald was right about that. It was pitch black, no moon. Whoever picked this time to attack their position knew what they were doing. McGanley and Jansen opened up. Now he knew why the live ammo had been packed up and replaced with blanks. They aimed into the woods, firing as rapidly as they knew how. Harrington rejoined them within a minute.

"Keith, you seen Paulie?" Donald yelled as he fired.

"Nelson? No. Sarge's grabbing everybody and pushing them this way, so he's around here somewhere. I don't think anyone's

66

attacking from the other side of camp. Too steep! Hey, this is really exciting, ya know?" Donald wondered how Harrington could keep firing and yakking at the same time, but he did. "Sarge is really sore, though. Someone might have been sleeping on sentry duty. I'd hate to be him right now!"

"Paulie!" Donald cupped his hands and yelled back in the general direction of their lean-to. No answer. Donald kept laying down fire and kept looking back for Paulie. There was no sign of him. *Where the hell was he?*

✧   ✧   ✧

Paulie heard the shots, too. He awoke, startled. "Don?" But his friend was gone, men were shouting, and he had no idea what to do. He got up and ran out across the clearing, half-asleep and unarmed, and saw the muzzle flashes in the trees to his left. He ran to his right, into the trees, but almost immediately, his foot gave way under loose earth at the top of a steep grade.

Paulie tumbled head over heels, rolled, and tumbled again. He picked up speed and smacked against rocks and trees as he went. He couldn't see a thing and couldn't stop himself. He screamed from a sharp pain in his left arm. Broken. He reached out with it anyway, trying to grab something, anything. His head struck the base of a tree. He felt nothing after that and kept tumbling and flailing, unchecked and unconscious. Totally helpless, Private Paulie Nelson died instantly when his head thudded and cracked open against a huge boulder. His body finally came to rest at the base of the hill. Two hundred feet above, First Platoon fought to hold their camp.

✧   ✧   ✧

The exercise maneuver ended less than ten minutes after it began. First Platoon responded quickly under Sergeant Harris, though Harrington had been right. A sentry had fallen asleep and been taken prisoner to keep him from warning the rest of the platoon. An officer showed up to make it damned clear to the frightened private that in a real attack, he and all of his comrades could have been massacred. But the defense of the camp was rated a success.

Harris ordered a roll call; one man was missing: Nelson. "Well, where the hell is he?" No one had seen him. Donald felt sick. Flashlights on, First Platoon spent the rest of the night combing the area for Paulie, without success. What could have happened to him? Did he run away? God, what a stupid thing to do! He'd told Paulie that they were almost ready to go back to Fort Jay, that his enlistment was almost up, and that they'd stick together and things would be fine. Why didn't he listen? *Jeez, where was he?*

The search went on for almost six hours before a private and two buddies from Third Platoon slid carefully down to the base of a large hill and found a body. It was Paulie, battered and bloody, almost impaled on the edge of a large rock. That afternoon, Donald sat on the ground, head in his hands, looking down. And cried.

✧   ✧   ✧

The inquiry into the death of Private Paulie Nelson lasted six days, ending in an official finding that the death was accidental. While the army studied the accident, maneuvers continued for the 16th Infantry. The following day they boarded a troop train bound for Arkansas, where maneuvers continued for ten more days before they finally headed home to New York.

Donald paid little attention to any of it. Paulie had been his friend, counted on him. And he'd failed. Maybe all those guys were right: his father, his coaches, his teachers, and his brothers. Maybe those guys were right! Maybe he wasn't meant to be here. His mind shot back to his bedroom years before, on his bed, holding that crucifix. No one would help him, not even God. He hadn't dared to think it then, but he sure thought it now: *Maybe ... I ... just ... shouldn't ... be ... here.* What would anyone say if he weren't? He couldn't forget Paulie, what he'd promised, and failed, to do for him. How could he live with it the rest of his life? He had no idea what to do, about being a flying cadet, about anything. He just had no idea.

14

May 31, 1940

Thirty days remained in Donald's enlistment. As the squad finished an afternoon run and calisthenics, First Sergeant Masterson intercepted him on his way to the barracks.

"McGanley!"

"Yes, Sergeant."

"Follow me." Masterson was a huge man, over six feet and two hundred pounds, and overbearing. All by himself, he was plenty of motivation for soldiers to do their jobs and stay out of trouble. What could this be about? Donald hadn't done anything wrong, at least he didn't think he had. Things had been pretty dull since they returned from their deployment, two and a half months ago.

Masterson led Donald to his office in the company headquarters, went around the desk to his chair, and sat down. This was intimidating. Donald was a sweaty mess from the exercise, sweating more as he racked his brain trying to figure out what he'd done. Mercifully, his answer came quickly as Masterson looked up and read Donald's face. "Relax, Private, no one's going to eat you. Sit down." He rested huge forearms on the desk and held up a paper in both hands. "It says here that your enlistment is up on June 30. That right?"

"Yes, Sergeant."

"So tell me, how do you like the army?"

"Okay, I guess."

"You've done a good job here, McGanley."

Donald felt sick. No, he hadn't. Paulie had died. He lowered his head and spoke softly, "Sir, Private Nelson wouldn't think so."

"That wasn't your fault, son."

"I was looking after him."

"And it was good that you did. That's the way it should be in my outfit." Donald didn't answer; he just looked down, and tried like a son of a bitch to fight back tears. To his credit, Masterson sensed what the kid was thinking. "McGanley, look at me." Donald looked up. "It wasn't your fault."

Donald choked out the reply, "He shouldn't have died."

"No, he shouldn't have, and I'm as sorry as you are. Private Nelson was one of my men." He paused. "McGanley, there was an official investigation and an official board of inquiry. It was done right. The board said it was a training accident. We have to accept that. You stay in the army long enough and things like this are gonna happen. In combat, people are gonna get shot and some of them are gonna die. The enemy doesn't care whether the guy they shoot is a stranger or your best friend. They just shoot! This isn't much different. It just didn't happen in combat. What we have to do is stick together."

"Yes, sir."

"Son, it wasn't your fault. Understand?"

"Yes, sir."

Masterson hadn't expected the meeting to go this way. His job was to reenlist Donald for another year. He sat quietly for almost a minute, hoping the time would take the edge off the kid's mood. "I recommended you for reenlistment, McGanley. I like the way you get to it. I think you're good for the army, just as the army is good for you. You'll make a good sergeant some day."

"I don't think I'm cut out for the infantry."

"Why not? It looks like you are to me. The Captain thinks you are. Both of us recommended you for reenlistment."

He knew this would come up. Donald spent plenty of sleepless nights thinking about it. This army gung-ho, teamwork thing was no good for him. He was better off alone. He'd had to learn that again, the hard way. In an airplane he would live or die by himself. All he wanted from Masterson, or Harris, or the captain was to get out of his way.

"I was going to join the flying cadets and become a pilot, sir."

"You have to go to college for that. No, this is where you belong, don't you think?"

Now Donald's attention was off the accident. What was this guy trying to do? "But I heard they can waive college if you're in the active service. All I need is to be twenty years old, and my birthday is July 15. Can I go to the flying cadets if I reenlist in the infantry?"

"Well, maybe, I guess, but you'd have to apply, and you'd have to wait until we get back from Florida."

"Florida? What's in Florida?"

Masterson didn't like the way this was going, nor did he like the way Private McGanley was speaking to him. His mood became less hospitable. "Maneuvers, at the end of the summer. You'll have to wait until the middle of next year before you apply for anything, and that's only with the captain's approval."

Donald's jaw dropped. He thought about what his recruiter had told him last year about applying and getting letters of recommendation. Now he'd just told Masterson that he wanted to be a pilot and gotten only reasons why he couldn't. Damn it! It seemed like everyone was trying to stop him.

No more. He was going to become a flying cadet, not in five months, not next year, but now! He'd worked his can off and done his details. Now it was his turn! He was sick and tired of being told no. Damn it! *Damn it!* Well, this was it. He took a couple of deep breaths. "Sarge, I'm going to get out."

"McGanley, France fell to the Germans last month. We're going to be in this thing pretty soon. It's not a good time to leave."

"Sarge, if we're going to war, I want to go in an airplane. I've told everybody I know that all I want to do is fly. All I get is one reason or another why I can't. Even my mother tried to stop me. Why? It seems like people care about their reasons for things and don't give a hoot in hell about mine!"

"Calm down, McGanley."

"But I can't, Sarge. If I don't speak up for myself, no one will. No one's ever told me anything but no! Well, I'm tired of it. I don't want to wait anymore. I want to apply now!"

Masterson took a long look at the kid. "Tell you what. If you reenlist for one year, I can check with the captain and see if he'll put papers through when the time comes."

Damn it, this is baloney! Donald looked down, then around, trying to buy himself some time to settle down. Then he looked straight at his first sergeant, again. "Sir, I want to get out. Can I get a letter of recommendation from you and the captain so I can apply to the flying cadets?"

Masterson almost laughed out loud at the McGanley's gall. He had to hand it to him: the kid had some guts, and he'd been a good troop since the first day. Maybe the captain wouldn't like his failure to reenlist the boy, but he'd have to live with it. Masterson's approach softened. "Okay, son, I'll ask. I can't speak for the captain, but you'll get one from me before you leave."

On June 30, 1940, Donald's U.S. Army enlistment expired. Before he left Fort Jay, Masterson handed him two letters of recommendation with his discharge papers, one from himself and one from the captain. Donald saluted, then Masterson extended his hand.

"Good luck, son."

Donald caught the Buttermilk Ferry to Brooklyn, then another to Staten Island, and went home.

15

July 1, 1940

For the second time, Donald walked through the doors of the recruiter's office on Whitehall Street in downtown Manhattan. This time it was not to enlist. The office had applications to test for the flying cadet program, together with a list of required attachments. Two recruiters tried to get Donald to reenlist, insisting that his application would be better received from someone on active duty. He'd heard that line before and it got him nowhere. And the recruiters made the mistake of giving Donald a pamphlet from the War Office: *Flying Cadets of the Army Air Corps: Aviation as a Career.*

The pamphlet laid out all the requirements: pass a physical examination, be single, male, at least twenty years old but not yet twenty-seven, and two years minimum of college credit. But there was an exception to the college requirement: applicants without it could still get in if they passed an educational exam. Donald looked at the date on the pamphlet: 1937. That meant that the bastards had the same pamphlet last year! If he'd known about the exam he could have spent the last twelve months getting ready for it, instead of listening to all the "apply from active duty" bunk. But all these guys cared about was their lousy recruiting quotas. He'd wasted a whole year! With the recruiter still in mid-sentence, he took the pamphlet and the application and walked out.

Fortunately, Donald kept the two recommendation letters from his first enlistment. The next day he went to Field & Beattie and asked to see the owner. Old Man Beattie remembered the young fellow, though it had been over a year since he left.

"Mr. McGanley, I thought you'd be a general by now."

Donald smiled. He remembered why he'd liked working for him. "No, sir, Private First Class. My enlistment ended three days ago."

"Well, I don't have an opening for you. Sorry."

"Well, sir, I'm not here to get a job. I'm applying to be a flying cadet."

"Why didn't you do that last year?"

"I couldn't, sir. You have to be twenty. But my birthday's on the fifteenth, and I'll be twenty then."

"Ah, yes, I remember now. Well, what can I do for you?"

Donald had two papers in his left hand, one in his right. "I need three letters of recommendation. I have one each from my former commanding officer and first sergeant at the Sixteenth Infantry, and I need one more."

"Well, I'm not in the service. I was too old for the Great War. I enlisted for the war with Spain but it ended before I had to report. So I'm just a civilian."

"I have the pamphlet right here that gives all the requirements, sir." He handed it to Beattie. "On page five it says all you have to be is a person of recognized standing in the community, and you can write a letter for me."

Beattie laughed heartily; Donald turned red. The old man appreciated the young man's raw enthusiasm; Donald missed the meaning completely. "Well, I hope I qualify," said Beattie, "I'll be glad to, son." He pulled out five blank sheets of paper from his center drawer and started writing, remembering to put carbons in between. "Says here in your pamphlet that the military wants everything in triplicate, so I'll just do that right here—one for me, one for you, and three for Uncle Sam." It took barely five minutes for Beattie to handwrite eight sentences. The letter, although short, spoke very, very well.

Donald took a minute to read it. "Sir, this is more than I expected."

"You earned it. Now, is there anything else? What's that paper in your other hand?"

"It's an affadavid, sir, to verify that I'm twenty years old. I don't know where my birth certificate is. My folks at home don't want me to join up. I was kind of afraid to ask them for it."

"Affada*vit.*" He smiled. "You have a driver's license?"

"Yes, sir."

"Let me see it." Donald pulled the card out of his wallet and handed it over. Beattie took a quick look and handed it back. "If it will help, I'll endorse that affidavit right here." He got two more pieces of paper from the drawer, slipped in a carbon, and wrote. He handed the papers to Donald. "There. If you find your birth certificate, you should probably use that instead. But if you need to use the license, this should suffice. Drop by the secretary's desk on the way out and have her put a raised seal on it. How's that?"

"Thank you, sir."

Old Man Beattie stood up and extended his hand. "Come see me when you get your pilot wings, McGanley. I want to see them." Donald's grip was as firm as he could make it. If the handshake hurt the old man, he never let on. Beattie just smiled at the young fellow and then asked for his hand back.

Donald practically ran out the door and down the three steps to the street level, then headed for the post office. Why couldn't more people be like Old Man Beattie? Why couldn't his own father help him? He wondered if Johnny even knew he'd gotten out of the army. Did he even care? It had taken a man he hadn't seen in almost thirteen months to get that last letter of recommendation. At the post office, he bought a large envelope, spent six cents for the oversized package, and mailed off the three letters, the affidavit, and the application (in triplicate) to the Adjutant General in Washington DC.

16

For the next three weeks, life at 31 Melrose went on as though Donald had never left. He went back to bagging and delivering groceries at Roulstons Market, just as before. He and Johnny virtually ignored each other, even though they worked only a few feet apart. Johnny looked up at him from his dinner plate once in a while, but that was it. Donald considered telling him about the flying cadets, but couldn't figure out how to get started. He'd been home a week when he finally told Edna about the application.

"But why did you do that? You just got home from the army?" She was almost in tears again.

"Mother, I've always wanted to fly. This is my dream. I hoped you'd be happy for me."

"I worried every day you were gone. Do you know that? It's dangerous. You don't need to be in the army; you need to be here."

"It's done, Mother. I'm sorry, but I have to make my own way. I should get something in the mail any time now."

Edna left the room in tears.

The days seemed to drag on forever. He hardly talked to his parents, except to ask Edna if any mail had come for him. After two weeks of nothing, the long, sad look on his mother's face told him the answer was finally yes. Edna handed him a letter from the War Department, Examining Board for Air Corps Flying Cadets, Mitchel Field, Long Island. *Finally!* Donald tore it open.

Your records indicate that you do not possess the necessary college credit to exempt you from the written educational examination. The next examination will be held on the

second Tuesday and Wednesday of August and the one
following will be held at this station on the second Tuesday
and Wednesday of November 1940. Applicants must
complete a physical and mental examination before the
educational examination. You will be advised when your
physical examination is scheduled.

There was some other garbage in the letter about changing addresses and bearing expenses, but Donald barely saw it. He was as excited as he'd ever been. He did some quick math: today was Thursday the 25th. Jeepers! He had only nineteen days before the test! Without a word to Edna, he took two stairs at a time up to his room, went right to the top drawer of the dresser he shared with Ricky, and pulled out the small 1937 Flying Cadets pamphlet. Page Seven said that:

Candidates for appointment as flying cadet must have the
following physical, nervous, and mental requirements:
Perfect uniocular and binocular vision; unimpaired
ocular muscle balance; an unimpaired optical organism,
anatomically and mechanically; good respiratory
ventilation and vital capacity; good hearing; a stable and
balanced equilibrium; a stalwart cardiovascular system, a
robust, supple, well-formed, well-adjusted, and coordinated
physique (minimum height, 64 inches); an integrated and
stable nervous system with that temperamental constitution
which makes for aptitude for flying.

Half of that medical crap made no sense to him, but no matter. He was healthy enough. After that came a description of the educational exam: American history, English grammar and composition, general history, geography, arithmetic, higher algebra (uh-oh!), plane and solid geometry, plane and spherical trigonometry, and elementary physics. Under each heading was a more detailed description of topics, then a list of textbooks used for exam questions. None of the books rang a bell, but the public library was only a couple miles away. He could probably find them there. There were also a few of his books left over from high school, and some in Elizabeth's old room.

The idea of a physical exam didn't bother Donald too much, but the educational exam was another matter. There was so much to learn, and fast; nothing else to do but get at it. From then on, in the evenings and on weekends, Donald was in the books like he'd never been before. After all the algebra struggles, Edna was amazed by this sudden diligence toward academics, but Donald's motivations were different now. This was about flying; he *had* to pass that test, and the days were speeding by.

The second Tuesday and Wednesday in August came and went with no letter from the War Department. It was just as well; Donald was nowhere near ready to test. On August 16, a second letter arrived from the Flying Cadets Examining Board. He was "requested" to appear at Mitchel Field not later than 0830 hours, September 23, 1940, for his physical examination. It would be followed by the mental exam, whatever that was. The army would provide "lodging" at the barracks for anyone needing to travel the day before, but no other expenses. Donald smiled at that one. After a full year in the army, he knew darned well what the barracks would be like. Still, it was better to stay at Mitchel the night before and get the recommended sleep, rather than get up at some ridiculous hour and show up half dead for a physical exam. Best of all, the letter meant that he wouldn't have the educational exam until November. There was time to get ready.

Donald pored over his books. Fortunately, Elizabeth was around more often during the summer because her new husband was away on business, and she'd stopped dancing while they tried to start a family. The answer to a math question that Donald asked her one day turned into full-time tutoring. She pushed her little brother, especially in math, as if she knew that he was the family's one chance for success in this world. She seemed to know just when to scold and when to praise. There was a lot of both that summer, but as the days wore on, little brother and big sister actually got to know each other. Occasionally, talk of geometric proofs or cosines of angles gave way to deeper topics between them.

"You're pretty intent on making this flying thing work, aren't you?" Elizabeth asked.

"Yeah."

"You're doing well."

"Thanks. I owe you a lot. You should be a teacher."

Elizabeth smiled. "You know, Mother doesn't want you to go away, Donald."

"I was gone for a whole year."

"I know. This is different."

Donald looked at his sister for a long moment. "You went."

"Yes, I did. She didn't want that, either."

"So why did you go?"

"Because I wanted to dance. I knew I'd love the stage, ever since I saw my first show. You weren't even born yet."

"So what did you say to Mom and Dad? Did you ask them if you could leave?"

"Well, no. I didn't really leave. I just went into Manhattan and auditioned on my own and got hired. I was so excited. But remember, I still lived here, at least for a while, until I met Arnie, you know."

"What am I supposed to do sitting around here? I can't just turn off my life because Mom doesn't want me to go. I want to fly just as bad as you wanted to dance."

"I know."

"Well, then, what do you think I should do? Stay here just to make Mom happy?"

"No, I think you should follow your dream, Donald." She said it gently, lovingly, almost motherly. It made him feel good. He couldn't remember if he'd ever felt that way in this house.

"So why don't you tell me how to figure out what a cosecant is." He smiled; so did she, and they got back to the books.

Over the following weeks, Donald spent less and less time at Roulstons and more and more in his room studying. Even Johnny began to notice; he even asked his son once why he wasn't at the grocery as regularly as before. Donald answered him, but Johnny seemed to dismiss it, as if he wasn't interested in the first place. Heck, the only reason Donald went to Roulstons at all was to get tip money, most of which he saved to cover the costs of two trips to Mitchel Field.

✦ ✦ ✦

Aside from being embarrassed by having to walk around shirtless in front of one particularly pretty nurse, the physical exam seemed pretty easy. The mental exam was too, even though Donald couldn't help noticing some sergeant feverishly scribbling notes as he answered questions about his family, his life, his jobs, and his friends. It was downright weird, but he put up with it. Before he left Mitchel Field in the late afternoon of September 23, he was told that he'd passed both exams, and to report back to Mitchel for the educational exam at 1000 hours on November 12.

✦ ✦ ✦

November 12, 1940

Johnny had already left for work when Donald said good-bye to his mother, mentioning that he'd be back late the next day. He took a ferry from Staten Island to Long Island, hopped on the Long Island Railway to the Hempstead Station. A bus dropped him a couple of blocks away from Mitchel Field. As he expected, lodging consisted of the barracks, the same he'd stayed in back in September. Still, it was good enough. The next morning he got up early and grabbed breakfast at a diner: eggs, bacon, toast, and coffee, the best he'd had in a long time. The bill and tip came to thirty-five cents, which wiped out his funds. He laid it all on the counter, at the same time wondering how he was supposed to get home with no money. Well, he couldn't worry about that, now. He had the test to take, and this test was his entire future. He *had* to pass.

Testing started promptly at 1000 hours. Donald sat in a converted office with six other young men and worked steadily over the next seven hours to complete sections covering the seven subjects. He was eternally thankful that Elizabeth had spent so much time with him. Here and there he came upon test questions they'd hit right on the button. It was a good feeling. The test moderator, a sergeant who seemed to take a dim view of babysitting two days away, dismissed the group a little after 1700 hours. Donald walked out, side by side with another candidate, who asked him,

"Well, think you got 70?"

"Pretty sure. How'd you do?"

"Terrible. And my parents'll kill me if I don't pass. My old man told me so."

Donald shook his head. "You're lucky."

"Lucky? What do you mean by 'lucky'? I didn't know any of that trignometer stuff, or the physics."

"You're lucky that your old man cares enough to kill you if you don't pass."

"I don't get it."

"Never mind."

"What'll yours do?"

"Nothin'."

"But what'll he say?"

"Nothin'."

Donald walked away as the kid stared after him. But now he started thinking about the test he'd just finished: how hard he'd studied, how much Elizabeth had helped him, and how good it felt when he knew an answer almost before he'd finished reading the question. He *must* have passed. The army sergeant giving the test told them they'd get the results in the mail in about three weeks.

Now there wasn't much left to do except go home. With no money, Donald hitched a ride to the docks, grabbed a lift on a fishing boat to Staten Island, and walked the four miles to 31 Melrose. He took in the streets as he passed, the same ones he traveled on the way to Curtis High School, the ones that took him to Roulstons, the ones where he picked up and delivered newspapers and magazines, only to be ripped off by a couple of chiselers. He went by the store where Vic took him to buy balsa-wood airplanes and three-for-a-penny gumdrops, the same store he took Ricky to several years later. He smiled at himself through all the memories, glad that they were finally in his past. He was ready to leave.

17

Donald stood by the mailbox and ripped open the envelope with the U.S. Army shield on it. The letter came directly from the Examining Board for Air Corps Flying Cadets. His eyes were wide with anticipation. He read. Then his mouth dropped open. Then it slammed shut. He clenched his teeth so tight that his face started to ache.

> We regret to inform you that your Educational Examination score of sixty-nine does not qualify you for the flying cadet program. If you wish to reapply you may do so in one year. Please see your recruiter if you have any questions.

He was crushed. A heaviness crept over him and his mind just stopped working. He felt . . . nothing, nothing . . . for several minutes. When his senses slowly returned, disappointment, anger, and frustration—all of them combined—welled up inside him. He'd put everything he had into this test and his dream of being a pilot, and now he'd missed the grade by one point. *One damned . . . fucking point!* He felt an urge to kill himself. He turned away from the street, walked slowly into the house, and flopped in a heap on the living room sofa. His mind went totally blank. Edna saw him at the mailbox and knew right away, walking tentatively in from the kitchen.

"What's the matter, Donald?" He was leaning forward, almost falling off the sofa. He slowly lifted his head and looked up at her. Edna sucked in her breath, startled at the look of total, sweeping hurt on his face. "Is it from the army?"

"Yes."

"What does it say?" Donald unfolded the letter and read it to her slowly, loudness and frustration increasing as he went. When he finished he just kept staring at the letter. There was no more response from either of them. Edna stood still looking at her son. No one knew what to say. Finally, Edna walked over and sat on the sofa next to him.

"I don't want you to be in the army." He didn't respond. She continued, "I want you to be at home. You can work with your father. You know you're always welcome here."

Now he was angry. "And what do you think I want, Mother? Am I allowed to do what I want?"

"I just want you here where it's safe."

"From what? All my brothers and sisters are gone! Even Ricky's not here, Mom. So why am I supposed to stay?"

"The army is dangerous."

"Dangerous? Is the army any more dangerous than what my brothers are doing right now? Do you even *know* where they are and what they're doing? Nobody stopped them when they strolled right out that door or dropped out of school. Nobody told them to go down to the market and deliver groceries for tips. So why am I supposed to take what I want to do and just throw it out the window?"

"Flying those airplanes could get you hurt or killed. I'm . . . I'm *glad* you won't be doing that. You need to be home."

"You're *glad*, Mother? You're *glad* that I *failed*?"

"I don't want you to fail. Donald, I need you here with me."

"Mother, everything I've done for the past three years—Camp Dix for that summer training, finishing high school, getting a regular job, joining the army—all those things I did because I want to fly. I needed to do those things so I . . . could . . . fly, Mother, not stay here for the rest of my life. I've already put one year into the army, remember? You and Dad did just fine without me. I was out to sea, on trains, in convoys, shooting guns with real bullets. And I'm *still* alive. I can't stay here and I won't stay here. I'm going to become a pilot, Mother, one way or another."

"Your father wants you to be home, too." Edna knew she was losing the argument.

"Dad? The last time Dad said something worthwhile to me was years ago, Mother. I'm going back to the recruiter in Manhattan, *right now*, and I'm going to figure out how I can get into the flying cadets. If he says I have to wait, I'll go right over to that employment office on Fulton Street and get a job until I can reapply."

"Donald, please don't. I need you. We need you." It was a waste of breath, and Edna knew it.

18

"You could reenlist right now, Mr. McGanley."

Donald wasn't about to play the recruiter's game. "No, thanks. I've already done one enlistment. All I want now is to get into the flying cadet program. Do I have to wait a full year or is there a way that I can reapply now?"

"You have to wait six months. But you may have a better chance of getting accepted if you're on active duty."

He'd heard that one before and didn't believe it anymore now than he did last time. "Will the recruiting office give me a letter of recommendation?"

The recruiter hadn't expected that one. "Well, uh, I'd have to speak with the supervisor about that. Normally, we can only give that kind of preference in very special cases."

"Like what?"

"Well, I don't know, but I'll take it up with the supervisor. I still think enlisting now would be a good move for you."

Donald had had about enough of this guy. A year ago, he might have bought this bullshit, but not now. He stood up. "Sergeant, I think I understand. I'll see myself out."

✧   ✧   ✧

Jack Hampton still worked at Fulton Employment, the same rundown old building and the same old desk. But apparently word had filtered back that Donald had been an able and dependable employee at Field & Beattie, even though that placing had been over a year ago. Success stories like that boosted Fulton Employment's reputation, quite valuable at a time when jobs were so scarce. When Donald came through the door, it was a half hour before quitting time after a long, unproductive day, but Hampton recognized him right away and greeted him enthusiastically.

"McGanley, come on in!" Donald followed Hampton into the same office where he'd been interviewed some eighteen months before. "Heard you joined the army."

"Yes, sir. Mr. Beattie was going to promote me to salesman, but I told him I wanted to become a flying cadet in the Air Corps. He was very fair with me. I left on good terms. At least I think I did."

"You did. Old Man Beattie himself called me after you left. Told me if I had any more around like you to let him know. Unfortunately, he's not hiring right now."

"Well, I wouldn't want to go back now, because I think I'd end up leaving just like I did last time. After I left the army I tested for the flying cadet program, but I didn't make it. Now I have to wait six months before I can reapply. I just need something to hold me over until I can get accepted."

"Why not go back into the army and apply from there?"

"I could do that, but the recruiting sergeant was feeding me a bunch of baloney. I felt like he just wanted me to fill up his quota. Then he'd stick me someplace I could never get out of. I just didn't trust him."

"Well, I've got an opening at Bissel, but it doesn't pay much."

"What do they do?"

"Carpet sweepers. They need a repairman. You go to the owner's home and fix the sweeper there. And you could probably pick up some extra tip money that way."

"I don't know the first thing about fixing a carpet sweeper."

"They'll teach you."

"Okay, well, I guess I've got to do something. When do I start?"

"Tomorrow. They're over on Staten Island. You live there, if my memory serves me right."

"Yes, sir, and tomorrow's fine."

"Here's the address. I'll let them know you'll be there at nine o'clock tomorrow morning."

Hampton was right about the pay. At eight dollars a week, the Bissel job wasn't as good as Field & Beattie. And his fellow employees, all two of them, were nowhere near as pleasant as Old Man Beattie's employees had been. Still, it was a job. Donald traveled door to door to do repairs in the home. Because transportation costs were not paid by Bissel, he walked from one job to another. Many of the customers would arrange to pay the bill by mail instead of giving cash to a repairman, which was okay, except that too many of them never paid the bill at all. As for tips, that was a pipe dream. After a six weeks of low pay, explaining to customers why walking from one job to another took so long, and returning to sour apple attitudes at the shop, Donald knew that this job was going nowhere.

Life at home was the same. Ricky had quit school after the first three days of the fall semester and was off to who-knows-where. Johnny was as detached as he'd always been, still unhappy about his demotion at Roulstons even though it had been ages since it happened. All he seemed to care about was trying to figure out how to make ends meet.

For her part, Edna was happier, thinking she'd won the battle about Donald joining the service again. But she was wrong. Her son lived there because he didn't have the money to live anywhere else, and he was rethinking his decision not to rejoin the army. Maybe it *was* the best thing to do, in spite of that knuckleheaded recruiter. Edna didn't know it, but the moment she dreaded was coming soon.

A week before Christmas, the owner of Bissel told Donald and his co-repairman that he couldn't afford to keep both of them on the payroll. Donald saw his chance. Before the owner's echo died, he volunteered to leave.

19

January 10, 1941

P rivate First Class Donald T. McGanley had been back in the
army for twenty-two days, after making it damned clear to that
clown in the recruiter's office that he would accept enlistment *only*
in the Army Air Corps, not the infantry, and *only* at a job where he
could work around airplanes, and *only* if he could reapply for the
flying cadets as soon as he became eligible.

Mitchel Field was the home for P-40 Depot Maintenance. Donald
worked the early shift in the 4th Materiel Squadron, fabricating,
repairing, and inspecting the bulletproof fuel tanks. The "Warhawk"
was a beauty. Donald wasn't on the job for a day before he told his
boss that he planned to apply to the flying cadets as soon as he could
and become a P-40 pilot. In the meantime, he learned his job quickly
and earned a reputation as a hard, reliable worker.

First Sergeant Daniel Combs had sent for him, though Donald
had no idea why. He hadn't been in long enough to do anything
wrong, and nobody'd said anything to him. He poked his head in
Combs' door, saw the sergeant was alone. At least that was a good
sign, maybe.

"Ah, McGanley! I've got some good news for you. Sit down."
Combs sifted through a stack of papers on his desk and pulled out
a brown envelope. "The recruiter's office in Manhattan just sent
over this letter. It's from the Examining Board for Air Corps Flying
Cadets. Says here you passed your educational exam for entry into
the program."

"But I got a letter six weeks ago saying I didn't pass."

"Well, seems they graded it wrong. You got five extra points for the enlisted time you had in 1939 and 1940. Once they got that right, your score came up to 74. I believe 70 is passing, right? Congratulations, Private. Looks like you'll be going to flying school."

Donald's heart began pounding and his eyes bugged out. He was literally stunned into silence. My God! This is it! "W . . . when do I leave for Texas, sir?"

"You don't, at least not right away. We can't let you go now."

"What?"

"We've got a measles epidemic here. Most of the guys are quarantined. We have no idea how long it will last. I need to move you to KP for a while. Can't have any of those sick guys playing with the chow, can we?"

Combs was making light of it all, but Donald wasn't amused. He couldn't believe it. "KP? But, Sergeant, you mean I can't go to the flying cadets because of KP?"

"Not just yet. We sent a message to personnel requesting a delay due to manning requirements." Combs read the shock in Donald's face. "It's an extra three dollars a month in KP, McGanley. Look, I know you're disappointed, but the captain won't let you go now. In fact, he wants to send you to the Air Mechanics School as soon as we start getting our people back."

Donald kept staring at Combs, his mouth agape in astonishment. *Air Mechanics School? What the hell is this?*

Combs' eyes returned to the papers in front of him. "The captain is very impressed with your work here, McGanley. So am I. Keep going like this and there may be a promotion coming soon." When Donald didn't answer, Combs looked up again. "McGanley . . ."

"You just said I was going to flying school, Sarge!"

"We'll see."

"What? Sarge, I passed this test six weeks ago! I wouldn't even have enlisted at all if they'd graded the damn thing right the first time. And now I'm denied my chance to fly for KP? And what the hell is mechanics school all about? Doesn't the captain know I want to fly?"

Combs' manner became stern. "He knows. Look, no one said you were being denied anything. We don't have any orders to send you to flying school, McGanley. All we have is this letter saying you passed your educational exam. If we get orders, we'll follow them. In the meantime, I need someone who isn't sick to shore up KP, and you're it. That's all I have, Private. You're dismissed." The look on his face meant that Combs didn't want to hear any more.

Donald turned to leave, but Combs stopped him.

"And Private!"

"Yes, Sergeant."

"Watch your damn language."

Donald couldn't believe this crap! They'd actually gone out of their way to request a delay. For all he knew, Combs and the captain already had his orders and were holding on to them until the right answer came back. Neither had shown any interest in Donald's desire to fly, and neither seemed to care that he should never have been in their command in the first place. They had a body and were determined to keep it.

Each day, seventy-one days in a row, Donald made a pest of himself, going by the orderly room at the end of his shift to see if orders had come for him. More than once, Combs threw him out of the place. He got in to see the captain once, but got the same run-around about Air Mechanics School and unit manning and KP. As the captain dismissed him, he also made it clear that he didn't want to see McGanley about it again.

Donald had no idea what to do. He still had almost a full year before he could get out again. There was nobody he could go see about it. He thought about writing a letter somewhere, but if Combs or the captain found out, there'd be hell to pay. And he sure couldn't go AWOL.

But Donald had a guardian angel, for once: it was the Flying Cadet Program. They had a qualified candidate and classes to fill. They didn't care about KP or Combs or the 4th Materiel Squadron's problems. On a bright, clear afternoon in early April, Donald swung by the orderly room, as usual. His bosses were nowhere to be seen. The clerk saw him come in and rose from his typewriter.

"Hey, McGanley, look what came in!" He handed Donald a single sheet of paper.

"Orders?"

"Yup."

"When did you get them?"

"About an hour ago. Take 'em. Sarge is in a meeting somewhere; I'll give him a copy when he gets back."

They were short and sweet, with four names on the list. He was to report to the Primary Flying School in Albany, Georgia, on May 1, 1941, as a member of Class 41I. He read the orders over and over. It was all he could do not to holler out loud. The clerk knew exactly how he felt, having been there every day Donald came by.

"Hey, McGanley!"

"Yeah."

The clerk was grinning ear-to-ear. "Good luck."

20

April 29, 1941

Donald would leave today. He was up early, unable to sleep after about 2:00 a.m. He spent most of yesterday packing up and cleaning his mother's 1936 Chevrolet, a gray two-door that and ran like a top. Vic had bought it several months earlier from the Chevrolet Garage on Bay Street for $422. But the car had seen little use around the McGanley home. Edna didn't have a driver's license, and Johnny never drove it, perhaps too embarrassed that his son could afford something he couldn't.

Edna had insisted that Donald take the car to Georgia. Strange! She'd tried so many times to stop Donald from leaving; now she was giving him the means to do it. He promised to bring the car back after pilot training, when he could afford to buy his own.

In the meantime, he'd found the three other recruits on his orders, all local college boys: Andy Cockrell, whose family lived in Queens, Al Rogino from Mattituck, and Gary Delks, who lived on 37th Street in Brooklyn. They agreed to split the cost of gas for a ride to Georgia.

✧   ✧   ✧

By 10:00 a.m., they were finally south of New York's metropolitan area on U.S. Highway 1, which they'd follow most of the way. No one said much for a while, except to direct turns here or there, whether they really knew the way or not. Once the traffic thinned out, the casual banter picked up.

"Good to be on our way," said Andy. "You should have seen my mother this morning. Cried like a baby. She's been tryin' to stop me from going. Hell, she'd been tryin' to stop me from doing anything since Dad died."

"Mine cried, too," said Al. "Made a big deal out of me leavin'. Last night they had the whole family lined up in the living room like some sort of reception. My mother got the grandparents and my uncles and aunts from Long Island and a bunch of cousins here from Saratoga; I got some cousins I didn't even know I had. One was really built; she started treating me like a real guest of honor. But I had to be careful: Ma woulda killed me if she caught us with her hand down my pants like that! My kind of action!"

"What was her name?" Andy asked.

Al laughed. "I don't even know! We had family out of the woodwork wandering around for the last two days. I didn't know half their names! Tell you one thing, though. I'm glad we left early. After all the boozing they were all sacked out this morning, so they didn't all pile out on the porch and embarrass the shit out of me when I left. But before I went to bed last night, they passed the hat like I was gettin' married or somethin'. Boys, as long as we don't detour all the way to California, we're going to make it to Albany with money to spare!"

Now Andy laughed. "I knew it was a good idea to bring a wop along. All I got is about twenty bucks. Mom doesn't have much so I gave her my travel money. I've been wondering how to ask you guys to spot me some dough until our next payday."

Gary Delks said nothing, mainly because his eyes looked bloodshot. He'd been half-asleep when he walked to the car and was fully out seconds after he got in. They learned enough to know that Gary's girl was against this whole thing, but she sure loved Gary and had let him know it, all night long.

Donald said nothing as the stories went on and on. Having been in the infantry and on deployment, he'd heard them before, especially the ones about exploits with girls. Just hot air. If half the stories had been true, the U.S. population would be twice what it was. Still, these guys seemed okay. He'd picked them up at Mitchel Field, they'd been on time, and it was a good thing they were around to chip in for gas. He'd introduced himself as "Don" McGanley. No more little "Donald."

His own departure was hardly worth mentioning. He said good-bye to Edna in the kitchen and then simply walked out the door and drove away. Ricky was around somewhere but did not say good-bye. His elder brothers were gone; probably didn't even know he was leaving. Johnny had left for Roulstons just like any other day. It hurt, all of it.

Except for Elizabeth. She'd been home the night before; they'd sat on the front porch and talked.

"I'm happy for you, Donald."

"If this doesn't work out, I'm not coming back."

"You know you always have a home here. You can always come back."

"That's not what I meant."

Elizabeth looked at her younger brother. "Don't talk like that. You've worked too hard. Be glad that you're finally going to get to fly, and stop with that . . . crap. You hear me?"

She'd embarrassed him. He'd embarrassed himself. He owed his sister a lot more than that. "You know, you're the only one in this family who ever tried to help me. I'll never forget you for that." He paused, started to say more, but stopped himself. Better change the subject. "You know what I really don't understand? It's that Mother didn't try to stop me this time."

"What could she do? You passed your test, you were already in the army, and you have the official orders. She feels the same, though, Donald. She doesn't want you to leave. She's afraid for you."

"How do you know?"

"She told me. We talked for a long time a few nights ago. She knows she has to learn to let all of us go. I just tried to get her to see the things you've accomplished instead of the loss she feels."

"You know, I can't believe she gave me the car to take."

"Well, she doesn't drive it. And that's a first step for her in letting you go, you know. Kind of a blessing, don't you think? She's learning. Give her time."

"I wish Dad would care, even a little."

"There's a tough one. He cares, though. He's determined to put food on the table, frustrated that he can't do more. He just doesn't know how to show other people the things he feels."

"He's angry."

"Frustrated," Elizabeth corrected. "Wouldn't you be if you were him?"

Donald gave his big sister a long look. There was no sense in reliving some of those earlier experiences with Johnny now, or telling Elizabeth things that would perhaps shock and surely sadden her. "You're going to be a great mom some day." They embraced.

✧   ✧   ✧

A sudden laugh snapped Don back to the road to Georgia. He realized that this was a happy day! He wished he'd kept that article from *Popular Mechanics* that he'd first read three years ago. He'd known from that moment on that this was what he really wanted to do.

And now here he was, on his way for good. He'd left a hundred dollars on his bed for his mother. The remaining travel pay, plus extra for "privately owned conveyance," was more money than he'd ever had in his pocket at once—fifty-five dollars. He could save most of it by driving straight through, even if he indulged in hamburgers and shakes all the way to Georgia. Yep, for the first time in his life he was *really* on his own. Staten Island was no longer home to him. Home was where he was going. He didn't give a hoot about how these other three guys felt about *leaving*; all he knew was that he was damn glad about *going.* He thought to himself. *Pilot!*

No better word in the English language.

Part 2

21

April 30, 1941

They'd driven straight through to Georgia, stopping only at places like the Nickel-Dime Burger for a quick meal, or at filling stations just to gas up, twenty-nine cents a gallon at most places. The roads were all paved; they'd made good time. Now he turned left off U.S. Highway 82 onto Route 19, slowing as he drove by a row of neatly parked airplanes.

They were at the Albany Municipal Airport. *Wow, look at 'em!* He felt like yelling at the top of his lungs, but didn't dare. These guys would think he was some kind of nut. Don pulled over and took his first good look at the future. His stomach was doing flip-flops; it was hard to imagine he was really here. He suggested, "Let's take a look."

Twenty-two PT-17s (PT meaning "Primary Trainer") faced inward toward a vast open field. There was nothing, dirt or paved, that even resembled a runway. In the middle of the field was a strange-looking wooden structure, like some kind of cross. No one had any idea what it was. A small building, more like a hut, stood alone in one corner of the field with a sign reading "Dispatch" attached to the roof, just above a window and ledge. It looked like one of those hamburger stands they'd stopped at along the trip. On the other side of the road was a small group of buildings: two two-story barracks and a chow hall, and one more building with a large sign that said "Darr Aero Tech."

In the late spring of 1941, Darr Aero Tech was one of a handful of civilian flying schools under contract to train military pilots.

But it wouldn't be just a handful for long. An intensifying war in Europe and a growing threat from Japan had the War Department's attention. Dozens of municipal airports virtually closed down civilian flying as schools like Darr moved in. Within the next few years, well over a hundred such schools would be scattered across the United States.

The Darr instructors were seasoned pilots. Some flew in the fledgling airline business, some had been with the mail service, some were veterans of the air races, and some even veterans of the Great War. They were good people: well-paid, to be sure, but also patient and skilled, well qualified to teach the PT-17 to the varied mixture of college kids and army grunts on their first stop toward becoming military pilots.

The PT-17, built by Stearman Corporation but designed by Boeing, was an open cockpit biplane with a metal fuselage and wooden, fabric-covered wings. The fuselage was painted blue and the wings yellow (unlike the navy version, which was all yellow). Under each wing was the Army Air Corps' white star on a circular blue field with a red dot in the center. (The Air Corps would drop the red dot in less than a year.) The tail looked a bit like the American flag, with horizontal red-and-white stripes painted on the rudder and one long blue band just forward of the stripes. The "Stearman," as it was more commonly known, was truly a sharp-looking airplane. It was also a solid one: forgiving, reliable, and easy to maintain. The military would order over ten thousand of them.

Don kept staring, wondering which one would be his. What would it be like to look down at the ground from above? How hard was it to learn to fly? Would he cut it? At Mitchel Field, he'd asked for a ride in a two-seat BT-something-or-other (it was a BT-13), but the answer had been no. Well, it was "no" no more. And another thing: he knew he wasn't going back to New York, whether he cut it here or not.

"Okay, Don, we'll go look," said Andy. "But just for a minute. If we get spotted by some big shot, he's liable to make us go sign in, and we don't have to be here until tomorrow afternoon. I don't know about you guys, but I have better things to do than run errands or clean up barracks. After this long, arduous journey into the Deep South, I think we're due for a motel and some beers, right, Al?" Rogino looked back like he wished he'd kept his mouth shut about the dough. "Ah, Albany, Georgia—I'll bet the place'll be hopping tonight! Don, you got two minutes!" Andy laughed heartily while Al looked annoyed, Don got out and marveled at the airplanes, and Gary stared glumly out the front of the car.

✧   ✧   ✧

They drove the four miles southwest to Albany and checked into two rooms of the Albert Motel, not a bad looking place on the main drag, almost exactly in the center of town. Don joined his three co-travelers for twenty-five-cent beers at a saloon a couple of blocks down from the motel, and followed that with fried chicken, potatoes, and collards at a diner next door. His first true Southern supper sat heavy in his stomach, giving him a perfect chance to beg off Al and Andy's desire to go back to the saloon and enjoy their last night of freedom. Gary Delks and Don headed back for the Albert.

Gary hadn't said much all day, but Don noticed that he looked increasingly miserable. Delks finally spoke up after they got to their room. "I don't think this is going to work out," he said.

"Why not?"

"Clara." When Don looked at him quizzically and Delks added, "My gal."

"Oh."

"We wanted to get married, but her parents wouldn't let us until I had a good job. Her old man fought in the last war and wanted me to join up. I knew damned well he was just trying to get rid of me. I signed up for the flying cadets before I knew that you couldn't be married. Her old man tricked me. Now I'm stuck."

"Don't you want to fly?"

"Oh, I don't care. Not really. I just couldn't find any decent work in Brooklyn, but I had two years of college time and figured officer pay would be better than a private's."

"You're right about that." Don thought about trying to talk things up with Delks, but dismissed the idea. He'd tried that with Paulie Nelson and look what happened. No sense in making that mistake again. Delks didn't seem interested anyway. It was just after eight, but Delks was already undressed. Without a word, he climbed into his single bed, turned his back, and went to sleep.

As for Don, he was too excited to sleep, even though he was dead tired from driving most of the way to Georgia. He tried to concentrate on reading the *Life* magazine Al Rogino had brought along from New York, but he realized after a short time that he wasn't interested. He couldn't wait until the next day. If it had been up to him, he'd have signed in and saved the motel money. So what if he had to run errands for some big shot. He was ready for pilot training—more than ready.

They were about to begin a three-phase program: Primary Training in the PT-17 followed by Basic Training in the BT-13, 14, or 15. Cadets that qualified for fighters would go on to Advanced Training in the AT-6. Each phase took place at a separate location, and each was twelve weeks long. The flying cadets at Albany were assigned to the War Department's Southeast Air Corps Training Center, which included most states in the Deep South, plus Florida. Don's class was only the second to start at Albany. Everything was brand new. If all went well, he would graduate as a pilot and second lieutenant on December 12, 1941.

22

Day One, May 1, 1941

Somebody blew a whistle and reveille sounded from the courtyard between the two barracks. When they signed in the day before, the new cadets had been told that their first duty would be a 0600 formation. Don McGanley had been awake all night. If anyone had been more anxious or excited about the first day of pilot training, he'd have been hard to spot. For Don, 0600 hours came at a crawl. Now, already dressed in his newly issued coveralls, he was off his bunk before the bugler barely got started. He would be the first man down the second-floor stairs and out to ranks. Two bleary-eyed guys, who'd taken full advantage of their last night of "freedom," shook their groggy heads as McGanley ran past their bunks.

"That guy's making the rest of us look bad. You'd think we'd joined the marines or something."

"Yeah? Well, think all you want. We'd better get out there."

The other guys must have thought the same thing. As soon as one started running, they all started running, throwing on coveralls and boots and stampeding out the doors. By 0612, everyone was out of the barracks, not bad for civilians but too slow for the Army Air Corps. Many of the guys in Class 41I looked a bit shell-shocked, as if it hadn't dawned on them what they'd signed up for. An army sergeant with a whistle around his neck stood impatiently as the sleepy cadets assembled. So this was the jackass who'd woken them up! Several steps away from the sergeant stood a first lieutenant, the only officer the cadets had seen so far.

The sergeant blew on his whistle. "All right, let's fall in! Form up in rows of twelve men."

One of the groggy heads muttered to his groggy-headed buddy, "You gotta be kiddin' me. Didn't we come here to fly? Now we're playing army."

"If the man on your left is shorter than you, then switch places." The flying cadets started shuffling about. "Let's move it, gentlemen, unless no one wants to eat breakfast." And after a minute or so, he added, "Now, look to your right and make sure you're lined up straight down the row." More shuffling. "Okay, gentlemen, every morning at reveille you begin right here. Same spot every day. Now, Lieutenant Jenkins has a few words for you. After that, we'll start with a little close order drill. When I'm satisfied that you all can march like a military unit, we'll proceed to the mess hall."

Lieutenant Jenkins didn't look much older than the flying cadets, but he was a big fellow and the military commander at Darr Aero Tech. He stepped forward.

"Welcome to Darr Aero Tech, gentlemen. I congratulate you on your selection as a flying cadet in the Army Air Corps. This is Class 41I. I am your commanding officer here, and this is my adjutant, Sergeant Hawkins. Before you start your training, I'd like to set a few things straight. First, although this is not a U.S. Army installation, let's not forget that this is still the army. You are no longer enlisted recruits, regular army, or civilians. You're flying cadets. When you finish advanced training, you will be commissioned officers. Starting now I expect you to look like officers, speak like officers, and act like officers. And I expect that your barracks will look like officers live there."

Don shuddered. He'd gotten up and run out the door so fast that it never occurred to him to make up his bunk. The fact that no one else did didn't matter to him. He felt like a dummy for having forgotten something so basic. The lieutenant went on.

"The training you start today is twelve weeks long. Each day, half of you will be at morning ground school while the other half is flying. In the afternoon, you will switch. Your daily duty will end around 1700 or whenever your instructor sees fit to release you. Even though the instructors here at Darr are civilians, they are your superiors and you will treat them accordingly. Report daily with a salute and address them as you would any military superior. Finally, in case anyone's curious, there's no need to ask about passes to town. Until further notice, there will be none. Your spare time belongs to the Army Air Corps, and you'll be too busy to waste it at bars and dance halls. I will decide when you've earned time for leisure pursuits.

Now . . ." he paused for emphasis, "look around at the man on either side of you, gentlemen. One of you three will not complete Primary Training. Another will not complete Basic Training. Your class is due to graduate on or about 12 December. Since the odds are not in your favor, I'm sure I will see your best effort. Gentlemen, good luck."

Don took note of the cadets around him. There was no way he was going to be one of the washouts. No way!

23

"Dan Metzer." The Darr Instructor smiled and extended his hand. He looked to be about thirty-five, maybe forty, obviously seasoned. He shook hands with the four cadets assigned to him: Don McGanley, John McIntosh, Pete Melford, and Al Morris. The cadets didn't know what to think. They shook hands like they were extending them toward a snake, still shell-shocked after marching to breakfast, to equipment issue, and over to the "flight line." Metzer had seen all this before.

"Everyone got their flying cap and goggles?" He was laughing under his breath at the obviously spooked cadets. The four of them nodded, intermittently. They looked like some out-of-sync barbershop quartet. "Good. Okay, then, who wants to go first?"

Don jumped. "I will."

"Okay, you are . . ."

Don saluted stiffly. "McGanley, sir! Cadet Donald McGanley, sir!"

"Relax, McGanley. Who's Mr. Melford?"

"I am, sir." A tall, red-headed fellow with an especially strong southern accent took an oversized step forward.

"Where're you from, Melford?"

"Meridian, Mississippi, sir."

"Okay. You can step back a little, Mr. Melford, unless you intend to attack me or something."

"No, sir!"

"Good." Metzer looked at the four cadets. "Fellas, let's get something straight. I'm not in the military, so you guys can lighten up. I'm here to teach you to fly the Stearman. Study your manual and listen up in ground school, and be ready to go every day. If you can do that, we'll get along fine. We'll each fly about fifteen minutes today, just to get started. Most days we'll fly for about an hour. McGanley and Melford, you come with me. McIntosh and Morris, you two just hang loose around here. And don't bug the sergeant in the Dispatch Hut, today or any day. I'll be back to pick you up in about an hour. Anybody have any questions?" They had dozens but had no idea where to start. "Okay, let's go."

Metzer turned to the two flying cadets as they walked toward the row of airplanes. "Ever flown before?"

McGanley and Melford answered together. "No, sir."

Don motioned to the wooden, six-foot-long, cross-shaped object in the center of the field, the one he'd seen when he'd first driven in. "Sir, what's that?"

"It's a Wind T, kind of like a weathervane on a barn. We always want to take off into the wind. So each time we fly, we'll look and see which way the T points. If you take off with the wind behind you, the takeoff roll will be longer, and you might not have enough room to get airborne. If the wind is from the left or right, it makes control of the airplane much harder. Always take off with the wind in your face. Shorter roll, better performance. Okay?"

"Yes, sir."

"Good. Now, either of you know anything about the Stearman?"

"No, sir."

"Great airplane: tough little 9-piston engine, 220 horsepower. It'll get us as high as 11000 feet and as fast as 120 miles per hour. We could go five hundred miles in this little buggy if we wanted to." Metzer pointed ahead to the plane with the white "26" stenciled just aft of the engine. "We'll take that one. McGanley, climb into the back seat and check the parachute. The harness clasps in the front. Don't forget to put the seat belt on."

"Yes, sir." Don was nervous. He was going to fly! His mind was racing a million miles an hour as he tried to calm himself down and climb into the airplane at the same time. But this was what he'd lived for, ever since he'd read that article in *Popular*

Mechanics. He couldn't believe he was here. This was the greatest day of his life!

Students sat in the back seat of the PT-17 with instructors in the front. Only the most basic instruments were available: an altimeter, a turn needle and ball, a tachometer, and a manifold pressure gauge. The gas tank was directly above the forward cockpit, attached to the upper wing, with a bad habit of leaking. Thanks to the windstream, any leakage usually ended up on the cadets. A glass gauge allowed the pilot to monitor the fuel remaining. There was no communication outside the airplane, but student and instructor talked—better yet—*yelled* to each other through a *gosport,* nothing more than a connecting pipe between the two cockpits.

Metzer directed Melford to the left side of the forward fuselage, where a starter crank was permanently fixed to the airplane. "Okay, Melford, I'm going to climb in and work the fuel primer. When I tell you, start turning this crank clockwise." Metzer then touched a half-dollar-sized ring next to the crank. "See this? It's the engager. Once I get the fuel lines primed, I'll yell 'contact,' nice and loud. Stop cranking and pull on this ring. That allows the gas into the engine, and she'll start right up. Any questions?"

"Uh, well, sir . . ."

"Look, don't worry about it. You'll be fine. I'll talk you through it. See the prop?" Melford turned and looked. "Try not to step back into it. The engine will catch in a few seconds. Ready?" Melford nodded a half-baked nod.

Metzer climbed in, strapped in, and yelled into the gosport. "McGanley, can you hear me? Just yell into the gosport!"

"Yes, sir!"

"Okay, we're going to crank it up, now." Metzer nodded back toward Melford as he pushed and pulled the fuel primer and set the fuel and air mixture full forward. "Okay, Melford, start cranking clockwise!" The engine started to whine almost immediately. Metzer yelled out the side, "Contact! Okay, Melford, pull on the ring!" The prop turned and the engine caught. Metzer waved Melford away, let the engine run for a few seconds, and then added throttle until the Stearman started rolling. Now clear of the parked airplanes, he checked the Wind T and turned into the wind with the open field in front of him.

"Okay, McGanley, we're going to take off now. Are you ready?"

"Yes, sir!"

"I'll push the throttle full forward. Listen for the air going through the wires. You'll hear a whooshing sound. Then the tail will come up, and I'll start pulling the stick back. In a few seconds, it'll just ease into the air. Ready?"

"Yeah . . . sir!"

"Okay, here we go!"

They rolled down the grass field, bouncing around like a ping-pong ball. Don, who had both hands on the rails of the cockpit to try and steady himself, forgot completely about the Wind T and didn't even notice the stick moving back or when or where they lifted off. All of a sudden, they were in the air. He gazed left and right at the wings, forward at his instructor, and up at the sky. He was flying.

They climbed to two thousand feet. He heard the rush of air, saw the view below, and felt the strange sensations as they rolled, turned, went up, and went down. This was truly what he wanted to do. He thought about how hard it had been for him to get here, and what a mistake it would have been if he'd taken up Old Man Beattie's offer to sell medical supplies the rest of his life.

"Okay, McGanley, come on the controls!"

Don was startled out of his daydreaming. "Who? Me?"

Metzer laughed. "Yeah! Get on the controls and follow me through! We're going to do a few turns! Once you get the feel of it, you can just fly it by yourself for a while!" Within a few seconds, Metzer yelled, "You got it!"

24

Don stood beside Dispatch as Melford walked toward him. Metzer then left with John McIntosh and Al Morris. The two "veteran" pilots sat down.

"What'd you think?" asked Melford.

"Nothing like it. Nothing. Can't wait to go up tomorrow."

"Well, I don't know about you, but I almost got sick. Didn't you feel sick?"

"No."

"Well, I'll get used to it, I suppose." He looked out across the field. "Where you from, Don? It's Don, isn't it?"

"Yeah. New York City. Staten Island."

"I knew you was a Yank right off."

"And you're a Johnny Reb. I knew that right off." Don smiled and they shook hands.

"Call me Pete. So, how do you like the conquered South?"

"Not bad. I was here before, in the army. I went in right after high school."

"Really? When?"

"Thirty-nine. Spring after that we were at Fort Benning on maneuvers."

"How old are you? No offense, but you look like you're about sixteen."

"Twenty-one. Well, almost twenty-one."

"Coulda fooled me. I thought you had to go to college to join the flying cadets."

"Not if you could pass their educational exam."

"Never took one. Nobody said anything to me about an exam."

"That was because of your college. You're lucky. It was an all-day exam. I barely passed."

"But you did and here you are. By the way, meet any belles on your march through Georgia?"

"Belles?" Don laughed. "No."

"So nothing interesting happened down here, eh?" Pete was grinning, his mind on one thing. But Don's was suddenly on another: Paulie. Pete saw his face tighten, the smile gone. He changed the subject. "Well, I think you'll like the South. We're pretty easy-goin' folks down here. I'm from Mississippi. Meridian. We're the friendly rebs."

Don didn't answer, so Pete continued, "I heard about the flying cadets while I was at school. I wasn't doing all that well in my classes, so I signed up. But I suppose I'm still a civilian at heart. This military life is pretty new to me."

"What did your parents think?"

"About what?"

"About you going in? I mean, didn't they try to stop you?"

"No. Well, they were kind of surprised, but I guess they were okay with it."

"Do you like it, the army, I mean?" Don liked the guy, even though they were opposites. Don was military first and civilian second, and only civilian when he'd been too young to join up. This guy Pete Melford was all civilian.

"Not sure yet. It's different, I'll tell ya that. I'm not too good at this marching around, but I'll get the hang of it; this flying thing, too. How'd you get down here, train?"

"Drove down. My mother gave me her Chevrolet, and I came with three other guys. One of them left already."

"Really? On our second day here?"

"Yeah. A guy named Gary Delks. He was nice enough, but you could tell he was second-guessing himself all the way down here from New York. Left a gal back home. After we signed in, he headed straight for the lieutenant's office while the rest of us went to get our coveralls. I guess it's just as good for him, since we were told we won't have much time for girls anyway."

"Don't bet on it." Pete grinned a sly one. "In the meantime, it's good to know you, Don McGanley from New York. If we stick together and play our cards right, I think we'll do okay."

"Sounds good."

25

The tighter they made the rules at Darr, the more Don liked it. He liked the order, the predictability of the day, and the high expectations. Each day began in ranks, just as it had the first day. Ten or fifteen minutes of calisthenics or marching drill followed, then they were off to the chow hall, where the food was plentiful and first rate. As a private, there had always been enough food, but nothing like this. Tables were arranged in long rows, with large plates of eggs and warm Parker House rolls, served family style by Negro waiters. Don became friendly with Esco Washington, his waiter, and usually left with a couple of extra rolls in his pocket.

The cadets' schedule alternated each week, just as Jenkins had said it would. Don preferred flying first; so did Pete. They felt fresher in the mornings and the air was smoother. Pete got sick every time they flew in the afternoon. The heat of the day usually brought thermals with it, causing updrafts as unstable cumulous clouds built up.

Classes lasted four hours, covering theory of flight, lift, the meaning and use of ailerons, rudders, and elevators, and navigation by dead reckoning using time, distance, and heading (corrected by wind). Instructors talked about navigation using radio beacons, but that was a tough one since there were no such instruments in the Stearman. On the third day of class, the instructor talked about "G" forces, the positive kind that drained blood from your head, and the negative kind which made the blood rush into the pilot's eyes. So far, flights had been nothing more than straight and level and a few turns, so the day after the class on "Gs," Don asked Metzer to show him what the instructor meant.

"Okay, hold on, McGanley!" Metzer banked sharply to the left and pulled the Stearman into a tight turn, then released the stick, rolled back to the right, and did it again. Both times Don was pinned into his seat, his vision clouded and narrowed. "Positive Gs! Did your eyes get dark?"

"Yeah!"

"Loss of blood from your head! It's called black-out. Okay, now tighten your guts and we'll do it again. Ready?"

"Ready!"

Metzer repeated the turns, but this time Don's vision stayed clear. "See the difference?"

"Yeah!"

"If you want to pull, just tighten up your gut and you'll be fine! Got it?"

"Yes, sir!"

"Okay, now we'll try negative Gs! You can't do much about it. Tighten your harness and hang on! Ready?"

"Yes, sir!"

Metzer was right. He rolled inverted and pushed on the stick. Without the lap belt, Don would've been tossed clear out of the airplane. His eyes hurt, but he clenched his teeth and said nothing. All he could see was a red glaze. After they'd flown half of an outside loop, Metzer got the Stearman straight and level again. Don yelled, "I'll never do that again!"

"Oh, yes, you will, if you find yourself in a dogfight some time! Just remember, if it's bad for you, then it's bad for the other guy, worse if he doesn't know it's coming! Learn how to deal with Gs and you'll be way ahead of the ball game!"

After that, most flights seemed pretty benign. They followed a daily ritual: the salute, the two-man procedure to start the engine, and the takeoff from the unmarked field, always into the wind. Once airborne, an increasing string of maneuvers followed: level flight accelerations while holding altitude, "S" turns back and forth across U.S. 19, "Pylon 8s," a maneuver to keep a wingtip on the road while turning back and forth, and the "slow roll," a blending of forward and aft stick pressures with rudder and aileron to keep the plane level as it slowly rolled 360 degrees. The slow roll was by far the toughest maneuver. Rushing through it just made it a repeat maneuver; too slow and the pilot made his task unnecessarily difficult. If the cadets were going to fail a maneuver, that was the one.

After the slow roll came forced landing practice. Metzer would suddenly cut the engine, leaving Don to find a field and prepare to land power-off. Less than hundred feet before touching down, Metzer would take back the controls, gun the power, and climb away. Then he'd do it again. In fact, he'd do it several times during a flight, always without warning. Finally, flights ended with landings and takeoffs—lots of them, ad nauseum. Over a one-hour training flight, Metzer kept his students busy. He was a damned good instructor.

Sure enough, the day usually ended around 1700 hours. The cadets would gather again for a few calisthenics, though that nonsense stopped after a few weeks. Then off to the chow hall for dinner. But the cadets weren't done just yet.

Because there were two classes in training at once, the "upper" class was traditionally responsible for teaching the new cadets about the military, which they did each evening and at least one day of each weekend of May 1941. Barracks inspections were followed by some in-ranks razzing by the senior class. Class 41I could only stand at attention, bark out answers to stupid questions, and take whatever verbal abuse suited their tormentors. One upperclassman hollered at Pete Melford about "expectorating" in ranks, but no one had the gall to ask what that meant. The creep probably made it up. Hazing routines went on, until of course, it was their turn to dish it out when Class 41J finally showed up the first week in June.

In the meantime, Pete and Don became good friends. Pete was an affable sort, more relaxed, and smart enough to let their friendship grow at its own pace. They became respectful of each other's personal space and supportive of each other's growing flying abilities. And Pete noticed something else about Don: He had an almost fever-like drive to be perfect every time up. He was merciless on himself for any lousy maneuver or landing. He'd lament anything and everything for hours. Occasionally, Pete would stop him.

"We're only students, you know? Give yourself a little time. Nobody expects you to get your wings the first day. I'll bet even Rickenbacker needed a few shots to get stuff right."

"Yeah, but you don't . . ."

"Has Metzer said anything to you?"

"No."

"Well, then, wake up, Yank. If Metzer doesn't like what you're doing, he'll tell you. Then you can worry to your heart's content."

Good advice, but never taken. Nevertheless, Don liked the guy. Pete was just the kind of friend he needed, whether Don knew it or not.

✧   ✧   ✧

After eleven days of flying, Metzer took the controls, landed early, stopped abruptly in the middle of the field, and jumped out. That was odd. Don unstrapped and started to stand up, but Metzer stopped him.

Don asked, "What's wrong?"

"Nothing. You just passed your first progress check. Congratulations, McGanley. Now get back in there and take her up. Run through your maneuvers and do two landings and takeoffs. I'll see you back at Dispatch in about twenty minutes."

"But, are you sure that . . ."

"McGanley, shut up and get going. We're holding everybody up." Metzer started trotting away and then called back over his shoulder, "And don't forget to strap in!"

It was pretty clever the way Metzer handled check rides. Cadets had heard over and over about the dreaded "pink slip." A failure on a progress check could cancel a solo, prevent moving on to Basic Training, or lead to a washout from the flying school. The check came any time the instructor saw fit, for good reasons or bad. There were no graded results afterward—just a handshake or a pink slip. Nothing was more nerve racking than a progress check. Metzer had instructed long enough to know all that. His students never knew they were taking a check until it was over.

Alone in the air, Don executed the best maneuvers he'd flown yet, including two perfect landings. He'd been so excited he'd forgotten about the Wind T and took off crosswind, but he actually forgave himself for that, even though Metzer read him the riot act when he got back. And there was one other thing he remembered to practice: high "G" turns, positive and negative, lots of them.

Don had been first in the class to solo. Lieutenant Jenkins mentioned him by name the next morning and further announced that they'd all been redesignated "aviation cadets" instead of "flying cadets." It was a small thing perhaps, but these things added up. He was on his way!

26

Day 26 of Primary Training

No one could mistake the sirens. They blared away from the emergency vehicles: a jeep, a fire truck, and an ambulance. The vehicles shot across the open field with the Wind T, beyond the greenbelt of pines to another field, to another beyond, and finally to the wreckage of the PT-17. The pilot was nowhere to be seen. Back at the Dispatch Hut, the cadets had gathered, dead silent. Faces were ashen and guts were tight. No one had gone through this before. Don looked around at the guys who were realizing that the dead man might have been any one of them.

It seemed like they waited forever for some real news, but it was barely half an hour. No one was dead. Aviation Cadet Danny Dukes from Huntsville, Alabama, the last to solo in Class 41I, had climbed into his PT-17 for his big chance. Danny wasn't your typical aviation cadet. His instructor cut the solo profile short for him, just two quick takeoffs and landings, and crossed his fingers.

But being a bit of a prankster at heart, Dukes decided to take his PT-17 for a little trip before the landing procedures. During his little jaunt over Highway 19 to the fields beyond, he decided to do one of those slow rolls so carefully taught in the first few weeks of the flying course. As the PT-17 rolled past ninety degrees to inverted, the class clown found out that he'd forgotten to strap himself in . . . and simply fell out. The slipstream whipped him back toward the tail, where he plowed into the elevator and broke his collarbone. He fell earthward, but still had enough sense to pull the rip cord in the center of his parachute. Dukes watched helplessly as his PT-17 passed him on the way down and crashed in a barren field. For his trouble, Danny Dukes became the only physical casualty of Class 41I Primary Training. He washed back to the next class, damned lucky he didn't wash out altogether.

As the true story of Dukes' PT-17 "kill" worked its way through the ranks, mixed reactions dominated the chatter everywhere. There was great relief, but wonderment at the incredible stupidity, and shock that he wasn't pinked right out of training. The guy was lucky he hadn't killed himself. Don knew he'd never make such a dumb mistake.

Lieutenant Jenkins had been right about that first-day announcement: Many of those seventy starters in Class 41I would not get the promotion to Basic Training, twenty-seven to be exact. Gary Delks had led the parade without even showing up that first morning. As the attrition grew, Jenkins got hold of a couple of ping-pong tables to keep the ex-aviation cadets busy as they awaited orders to other duty. The surviving cadets kept their distance for a couple of reasons: one, they were busy already, and two, they tended to look down their noses at the guys who "couldn't cut it." The washouts' new activity was called the "7-Ps" by the cadets still in training: "piss-poor-pilots-ping-pong-playing-party." As the washouts got wind of that, the decision to steer clear of them seemed wise indeed.

Now that the whole class had flown solo, all the training maneuvers had been introduced. Most of the remaining one-hour flights were solo, practicing the same events again and again. Metzer left on a two-week vacation once his four cadets passed that first progress check, leaving Don to fly ten straight solos. He practiced intensely, talking himself through maneuvers and debriefing himself after flights.

Pete interrupted him one day, "You having fun up there?"

"I can do better."

"That's not what I asked, Yank. I asked if you're having fun up there."

"Sure."

"Okay, just checking. You know, it's been great with Metzer gone, all these solos. I'll bet we have more solo flights between us four than the rest of the class combined."

"Yeah, well, we still have to pass our next progress check, and you can bet we'll get one when Metzer gets back."

"You worry too much."

"Maybe." In truth, Don had more on his mind than just progress checks. At the end of Primary Training, cadets would get a single course grade, either a "C" or a "D." A "D" meant passing, but the "C" was reserved for those few walk-on-water overachievers, the top one or two in the class who supposedly outshone the rest. Don wanted that C—*needed* that C.

Pete laughed. His New York buddy amazed him. He'd never met anyone so intense. "Don't you think Metzer would've told us if we were having trouble?"

"I suppose."

"Okay, then why not enjoy the fun while the cat's away? You'll have plenty of time to sweat it out later. And even after that, I'll bet you end up with one of those top grades."

"Don't you want a C?"

"I want to graduate and quit throwing up in the air. It's been better lately, but I still get queasy a lot. I don't think Metzer even knows I've been back there getting sick over the side half the time. Morris got sick right down the gosport once; smelled so bad Metzer pinked him. So all I wanna do now is do my sick thing over the side and get to Basic. They can give me any grade they want." Pete paused and then grinned. "In the meantime, if you want to worry about something, worry about girls. I don't know about you, but I could use some real inspiration."

Don couldn't believe this guy: sick stories one minute, girls the next, always grinning about something. In a way, he envied Pete.

✧ ✧ ✧

Sure enough, all four of Metzer's cadets got another progress check when he returned. Walking back to the Dispatch Hut, Metzer gave a rare smile to Don.

"Well, McGanley, looks like you've really learned to fly this buggy."

That was pure music. "Thank you, sir."

"I'll set up a navigation flight for Monday, kind of a break from the routine. We'll plan out a triangular route and figure out the times and headings. Gotta be disciplined about it or you can get lost in a hurry. Normally, we fly these flights together, but I'll let you go solo if you want. Think you're up to it?"

"Sure."

"Good. You're the first do the navigation flight. It'll be a little longer than normal. We'll plan it right after you get here from breakfast.

"Sounds good, sir."

The hard work had paid off. Maybe he'd get that C.

27

Lieutenant Jenkins finally loosened the off-duty rules for 41I, issuing unlimited weekend passes with the approval of individual instructors. Morale improved overnight.

But Don didn't want the distraction. He was happy in the barracks, having swiped a navigation manual from the academic building. He was on his bunk, leafing through it, when Pete walked in.

"Don, we're humans again! Lieutenant just approved passes for the weekend."

There was a whoop among the half-dozen guys lounging in the barracks. "'Bout time! Anybody for Columbus? We'll take off Friday night and make the rounds." Two of the three guys responded and began plotting how to round up a car.

"Well, Don, what do you say? You need to get out and relax."

"Nah, maybe next time. You know, some day we're going to have to know this navigational stuff. I'd just as soon get a head start."

"Look, we don't have to go all the way to Columbus. I found out about this place called Radium Springs. Local hot spot. Nice swimming area and lots of girls to swim with. C'mon, I'll even get you a date."

"Don't want one."

"Why not? Don't you like girls?"

"Sure. I just like graduating better. I don't want to get anywhere near a pink slip."

"Why? Has Metzer said you're having trouble?"

"No, not yet. Pete, let me just look this over."

"Oh, knock it off, for God's sake. You're the first out of bed, the first in the air, and you were the first to solo. For all I know, you're the first guy to pee in the morning. Can't you see you've got yourself all wound up over a pink slip that isn't gonna happen? You act like Metzer's the Grim Reaper with a handful of pinks in his pocket, all with your name on them. Look, you don't need to study that. You need to study some biology, feminine biology, up close. C'mon, let's go out to the Springs and worry about something important."

"Next time." Don had heard about Radium Springs. For more than one aviation cadet, weekend swims gave way to those pragmatic types of romances where everyone knew there was little time to waste with incidentals. Besides, he was barely over five feet five now; who'd want to take up with him?

"Okay, then. But I'm gonna keep askin' until you get smart. One of these days you're going to meet someone real nice, and you won't know what the hell to do. I'm tellin' ya, Yank, this takes practice. I, for one, am not going to skip this training."

Don laughed. "Have a good time."

So while cadets swam in the Springs and enjoyed the good life with the local pretties, Don spent weekends in the manuals.

Except once, when Pete's badgering finally made him give in. He went to Radium Springs with Becky Moore, a nice local girl who looked just fine in a bathing suit. They took smiling snapshots, ate a picnic lunch, and swam the afternoon away. But Becky wasn't his type, nor was he hers. They had the one outing together, and that was that. At least Pete didn't bother him about it anymore.

✧　✧　✧

The hard work seemed to be paying off. With one week of training left, Don knew he'd done well. He wanted that C, not the same old grade everybody else was going to get. And stuck in the back of his mind was that dreaded pink slip. After all this effort, wouldn't it be a hell of a thing to screw it all up now?

He didn't. Metzer said almost nothing on their training flights. Don's maneuvers were as close to perfect as he could imagine. And he passed his last progress check, just as Pete had told him he would. All he had left was a couple of solo flights to meet the required flying time and he'd be off to Basic Training.

The morning of his last flight looked like the start of a perfect day. A weather front came through the day before, bringing thunderstorms and heavy rain, but leaving clear skies and relatively cool, dry, still air behind it. Better yet, official orders to Basic Training at Augusta, Georgia were posted; McGanley and Melford were both listed.

Now they walked together toward Dispatch for a tail assignment. After this last solo ride in the Stearman, Don would go find his instructor and ask about his grade. He couldn't remember being in a better mood.

"Great day to fly," Don said.

"Yessiree, last one. You know, you're supposed to do something memorable on your last sortie. Whatcha got in mind?"

"Nothin'."

"Aw, come on. One of the guys flew inverted over the Wind T yesterday, and nobody said anything. I don't think they care as long as we bring the plane back in one piece. You gonna be the only guy who plays it straight?"

"Yep."

"Well, okay then. Can I ride with you to Augusta?"

"Sure." They got their tail number, waved, and headed off to the parked PT-17s with a cadet from 41J to help them crank up.

✧   ✧   ✧

Don set up for a Pylon 8 over Highway 19 below. He let his mind stray for a second, thinking about how far he'd come. He felt comfortable in the Stearman, but knew he was ready to go faster and higher. He was in the right place: in the military, training to be a fighter pilot. The Pylon 8 was perfect. He was a good pilot; Lord knows he worked hard enough at it.

Time for a slow roll. He checked his altitude at 1500 feet, set his power at 2,300 rpm, smiled to himself, and started rolling to the right, feeding in the left rudder as he went through forty-five degrees of bank. Passing ninety degrees, he added forward stick pressure and then felt himself get light in the seat, still rolling. So far, so good.

But he was getting too light. He practically fell against the forward cockpit, looked down, and saw that he wasn't strapped in! His eyes almost bugged out, right through his goggles. "Shit!" He snapped-rolled back to the left and pulled, cramming himself back into the seat, and hooked up his lap belt. He was shaking like a leaf. All he could make himself do now was fly straight and level, staring forward. "Jesus Christ. *Je . . . sus Christ!*" Don's last flight at Primary Training consisted of one takeoff, one Pylon 8, one quarter of a slow roll, forty-five minutes of straight and level flight, one landing, and one big lesson: "I'll never, ever . . . trust myself again."

Primary Training was over, but there was no satisfaction in that now. He never asked Metzer about his grade. He found out later, though. It was a D.

28

July 1941

Basic Training would begin at Bush Field one day before Don McGanley's twenty-first birthday. Bush Field was on the border of Georgia and South Carolina, six miles from Augusta, right along Tobacco Road. The 256-mile drive from Albany was easy compared to the two-and-a-half day overnight affair from New York. Given the whole weekend to get there, Don and Pete took their time, including a slow cruise through Augusta, more than four times Albany's size. They grabbed a quick dinner, but this time Don made it clear that he intended to head right to Bush and sign in. Pete just smiled through it. It was Saturday; he'd have much rather stopped by a dance hall, but he let it go. There'd be time for the girls later, and it wasn't his car.

Bush was another civil airport, just like Albany Municipal, except that it had a paved runway and was home to twenty-seven Vultee BT-15 "Valiants." (For some reason, the nickname Valiant never stuck: most guys just called it the "Vultee.") Only in production since 1939, it was even newer than the PT-17 had been. The Vultee was a closed-cockpit monoplane with fixed landing gear. But it *looked* like a fighter, at least to Don it did, and it was faster than the Stearman, with higher altitude capability and more range.

Best of all, cadets now sat in front, with a host of new tasks. Now *they* had to operate a dual-switch starter pedal about five inches long, located just to the right of the rudder pedal. Pushing with the heel started the energizer. They'd call out "Clear!" and rock the pedal forward with the toe of their boot. The prop would turn and the engine would catch, most of the time within five seconds. Forgetting to call out "Clear!" before starting the engine was a common mistake early in training, and a big one: worth a pink slip if the instructor felt like it. Another big change involved operating flaps for takeoff and landing using a manual crank and cable system. And finally, cadets had to learn to use the radio and the jargon that came with it.

Don's instructor was Bob Rearden, a nice enough guy and almost exactly like Metzer had been: all business. Don preferred it that way. Just like Primary Training, cadets on the flight line waited patiently by Dispatch for their one-hour training flight, except this time they had a bench to sit on, an upgrade from Albany. Someone got hold of a flight manual for the BT-15, so they sometimes passed that around as they waited.

The Vultee was nowhere near as forgiving as the Stearman had been. For one thing, the airplane was restricted from high "G" force maneuvers. About a year back, someone's tail had fallen off during a loop. Now cadets were constantly cautioned about Gs. Another danger was the approach-to-stall maneuver, a necessary skill so pilots could recognize how their airplane would act when it was too slow and about to go out of control. Cadets pulled the throttle back and slowed until the airplane began to shake, and the Vultee shook plenty. (In fact, it shook so violently some instructors called it the "Vibrator.") If the pilot did nothing, it would spin. The trick was to recognize the shaking and recover by adding power or relaxing the stick, or both. Approach-to-stall was only flown with an instructor aboard.

So instead of fast, hard maneuvers, Basic Training was more about instrument flying. Don was determined to master the art. Pete hated it. They sat in the chow hall after a long day, one happy guy and one miserable one.

"Had a good flight today," said Don. "Rearden let me cage the attitude gyro for a while and fly needle and ball. Back in the Stearman again. Good review."

"Don't you get tired talking about flying all the time?"

"Nope."

"In three weeks you haven't talked about anything else. I'm starting to worry about you." Pete leaned toward him. "I mean, we'd oughta be figuring out who the next lucky gal is going to be. C'mon Don, I thought you and Becky got along pretty well."

"We did. Nice gal."

"So?"

"So what?"

Pete frowned. "You're a tough one, Yank. You had Becky, I had Wanda, and Kaylee. But I guess I liked Lauren the best. Too bad we had to get through Primary."

Don was shaking his head. "Pete, I've got a progress check coming up. So do you."

"Yeah, I know. I'm not doing too well right now. My stall practice isn't very good, and I still get sick under the bag." The "bag" was a cover over the canopy that simulated flying in the clouds. "My instructor says I'd better start getting it. Geez, I don't want to get pinked out of here after I've come this far."

"You won't." *If you give the girl thing a rest and pay attention once in a while.*

"Doesn't your head get spun around under the bag?"

"A little sometimes. But I thought you were over getting sick."

"So did I, but the bag does it to me every time."

"I just try to fly as smooth as I can. Rearden is all over me if I don't. He said he almost killed himself in the weather one day, so he's real big about being smooth. And he said not to move your head around—just scan with your eyes. And spend more time in the link trainer." The link was nothing more than a box with a cockpit mock-up. The instruments moved while the box sat still. The guys hated it. "It's helped me a lot. I've gone over there on weekends to practice."

Pete looked across the table at Don. The more the guy talked about flying, the bigger his eyes got. How could anyone get excited about instrument practice? "I guess you're right. Tell you what, if I follow your advice and get through this progress check, can we go to Milledgeville and celebrate?"

"What's in Milledgeville?"

"College town."

Now it was Don's turn to stare across the table. "Figures."

✧ ✧ ✧

Basic Training proceeded uneventfully. Because of all the instrument practice, instructors were on board most of the time. If you were lucky, you flew in the mornings. Hot August afternoons brought that bumpy, unstable air that Pete hated so much, making the bag an especially unpleasant experience. On rare solo flights, Don felt an overwhelming desire to play with the cumulous buildups, but the G restrictions stopped that.

Eventually, Pete managed to conquer his airsickness, at least a little. He fell behind after a two-week bout with poison ivy, and the heavy flying to catch up seemed to help him out.

All the bag work, the link trainer, and some good tips from Rearden paid off for McGanley. With four weeks left in training, Rearden pulled Don aside after a flight.

"Think you're ready for a progress check, McGanley? Your instrument flying's coming along fine."

"Sure."

"Okay, how about going up with Dave Hogan?"

"Okay with me."

That surprised Rearden. Hogan was a notorious screamer. Worse than that, the list of pink slip recipients from his progress checks was as long as your arm. Cadets dreaded flying with him. Over dinner, Pete Melford tried to warn him.

"Look, Don, the guy's a creep. My instructor asked me the same thing today, and I asked him to fix me up with another check pilot.

He said okay. Why put yourself in a plane with a guy like that if you don't have to?"

"All I have to do is fly the maneuvers the way I'm supposed to, and everything'll take care of itself."

"With the guy hollering at you? You know, Yank, sometimes I don't get you. You spend all of your time sweatin' out pink slips, and now you're willing to walk merrily off the plank with the meanest SOB in the place pushing you along."

"If I do what I'm supposed to, there's nothing to holler at."

"You're kiddin' me, right?"

"I'm not going to get a pink slip, so there's nothing to worry about."

And during the progress check, there wasn't. Hogan told Don (in the back with the hood on) to give him a standard rate turn, forty degrees to the left. Don flew it. Then a standard rate turn to the right with a five-hundred-feet-per-minute climb. He flew that, too. They ran through the whole gamut of instrument maneuvers the same way. Finally, there were two unusual positions: one a nose-high with bank and the second a nose-low. Hogan told Don to close his eyes, then flew the Vultee out of position. Then he commanded "recover." Most of the time, cadets sneaked a peek at the instruments as the instructor flew because unusual positions were a common pink slip item. Better safe than sorry.

But not Don McGanley. He actually closed his eyes when Hogan told him to.

"You did what?" Pete asked later.

"You're supposed to close your eyes."

"Well, congratulations, McGanley, you're the first aviation cadet in history who didn't peek on his progress check. How many times did Hogan holler at you?"

"None."

"You're kiddin'."

"Nope. None."

"Well, either you're real good or Hogan got religion or something."

"Wanna know which one?" Don smiled. He needed this after that idiotic stunt on his last primary flight. He could have crashed that airplane, washed out right there. Now he'd passed this instrument progress check, and he'd done it the hard way. Felt good, *damned* good.

Pete let Don enjoy the moment for a second. "Tell you what. Let's celebrate. You still owe me a swing through Milledgeville. Why don't we head over there this weekend and see what we can find?"

The smile stopped. "Nah, you go, Pete."

A long pause. "You know, one of these days you're going to crawl out from under your blanket and figure out that there's a lot going on in the world. It's time for a break, Yank. Besides, I can't go without you. You've got the car, remember?"

"I'll let you borrow it if you promise not to smash it up."

"What are you afraid of? Girls or something?"

"You already asked me that."

"I asked if you *liked* them, not if you were *afraid* of them. I'll bet that's it. You are, aren't you?"

"Who? Me?"

"Yeah, you! You know, I haven't been bitten once. C'mon, we'll find a couple of nice ones, I'll make sure they don't bite, and we'll just go to the picture show or something. Or better yet, you can tell them all about your ride with Hogan. They'll think you're the greatest thing around. Won't be able to keep their hands off you!"

"Not my cup of tea, at least not now."

"Really?" Pete leaned forward, toward Don. "Then what is?"

"Flying."

"Well, there's no flying on the weekend. Got a better answer?"

"Nope. You'll just have to borrow the car and enjoy yourself." Don was getting more and more uncomfortable. He really didn't want to get into this with Pete or anyone else.

"Look, Don, the flying will be here when you come back. It's good to get out, you know? You gotta meet people. When's the last time you went out on a date, for crying out loud?"

"I've been out. Radium Springs, remember? And I went into Augusta with Jack Casey and Paul Morgan when you had that poison ivy a couple of weeks ago."

"I didn't know that! Well, Yank, you just moved up my list. What'd you guys do?"

"They went to meet some people, so I drove them." Actually, Casey and Morgan had met two local "ladies" working out of a "house" that provided various "services." Don sat in the car for half an hour while the two cadets dropped twenty apiece to produce the silly smiles they wore afterward. That was the first and last time he'd let himself get roped into a situation like that.

"You mean you just sat in the car while Casey and Morgan . . . ? Who'd *you* meet?"

"Nobody. I just drove. Look, Pete, let's not get into this. If you want to borrow the car, you're welcome to it. I appreciate what you're trying to do, but I've got other things to take care of, okay?"

Pete shook his head. Don was a good friend. He wanted to help the guy, but couldn't figure out how. "Okay, just answer me this, then I'll drop it."

"What?"

"When will you be good enough?"

"Good enough for what?"

"For anything?"

29

The rest of Basic Training shifted to approach-to-stalls and landing practice. Day after day, a short period away from the field was followed by a return to "Bush Control" and more landings than the cadets could count. Landings came easy to Don, except on days when the crosswind picked up. But then, they were tough for everybody. It didn't take much crosswind to cancel flying entirely.

Don took his last progress check, again with Dave Hogan and again without incident. Now finished with the formal part of training, all he was required to do for the last nine days at Augusta was fly solo once a day and practice. He settled into a relaxed routine: flying early, eating lunch, maybe hitting the link trainer for a half hour in the afternoon, taking a quick snooze before dinner, or "supper," as the Southerners called it. One afternoon with only a few days left, he woke up with a start at two cadets hovering over him, Jordan and Davis.

"Geez, you guys startled me."

"Just wanted to let you know, McGanley. You're next," said Jordan.

"Next for what?"

"Ah, everybody screws up around here, but since you haven't, we just wanted to put you on notice. We just got told that if they don't pink-slip us out of here, we'll be going to Barksdale."

Don was still just waking up. What the hell was this all about? "What happened?"

"I really smashed on a landing this morning. Damaged the gear. Boy, the instructor was really miffed at me."

"Ground-looped," added Davis. "Spun a real nice 360 degree after I landed. Went off the runway. We're just here to let you know. Hell of a day to fuck up! Now we're done for."

What was this? Don knew both of these guys, though not as close friends. "What do you mean?"

"Barksdale, if we're lucky. We just got our assignments."

"When? Where?"

"Over at the captain's office. I guess the instructors and the captain met at lunch or somethin'. Decided on assignments for everybody. One mistake and you're off to bomber command, or worse."

Don tried to think of anything he might have screwed up and couldn't remember a thing. He thought back to the slow roll at primary and shuddered to himself. Then he realized that Davis was still talking.

". . . and even people assigned to Craig Field are being told that their assignment is only pending. You have to keep your hands clean if you want to go to fighters."

Don wondered why these guys were telling him this. Maybe he was the only guy in the barracks right now and they needed to unload on somebody. Or maybe they heard his name being tossed around. He asked Jordan and Davis, "Were they posted somewhere? The assignments, I mean."

"Yeah, right outside the office, on the captain's bulletin board."

"Did you see mine?"

"Yeah," said Jordan. "It's Craig. But there're lots of bomber and transport assignments. Just wanted to give you fair warning. They're just looking for the chance to stick it to you." He was obviously bitter.

Don tried to think of something to say, but nothing came. He didn't know these guys at all, really, and they'd never shown much interest in him. He knew one thing, though. He wouldn't make those mistakes because he'd keep his eye on the ball, especially now, just having passed his last check. He'd noticed lots of attitude changes as the Class 41I survivors progressed through pilot training. Guys went from being scared and intimidated kids to increasingly confident, even cocky, with egos growing faster than their flying abilities. They talked long and loud at dances downtown, where they competed for female conquests by bragging about their four whole months of flying experience. Jordan and Davis had been among those guys.

But with so much to lose, Don had never played that game. He'd kept to himself: studied, practiced, and stayed away from distractions like beer and girls. And he knew he'd been right. Jordan and Davis had blown it; he wouldn't. Three days later, he drove with Pete to Craig Army Air Field, Selma Alabama, where Advanced Training would begin on Monday, September 29, 1941.

30

U nlike the civilian fields at Albany and Augusta, Craig was a real
army airfield. There were officers everywhere, many of them
AT-6 instructors and some barely out of training themselves. There
were civilian instructors as well, generally more experienced than
their military counterparts. Don never met his assigned instructor.
He was a civilian guy who'd managed to get himself messed up in
a motorcycle accident the summer before. Don ended up being the
Class 41I pass-around; he rarely flew with the same instructor twice
in a row.

But that wasn't a problem. He loved the look of the airplane.
The North American AT-6 "Texan" started from a hand drawing in
December 1934. It was a perfect, fighter-type trainer with retractable
landing gear and an air-cooled, 550 horsepower radial engine that
could reach 212 miles per hour and 21,000 feet. It also had a .30
caliber gun mounted on the right side of the engine cowling that
fired synchronously through the two-blade prop.

Everyone wanted this airplane. The Royal Air Force called it the
"Harvard," while the Australians called it "Wirraway." Other names
included the "I-Bird," "Mosquito," and "Yale." The U.S. Navy just used
the designation "T-6." The name Texan came about in December
1940, when North American opened a second, larger plant in Dallas
because the original plant in Inglewood, California couldn't meet
the army's production needs. At the height of its operation, Dallas
put out "batches" of one thousand. Over seventeen thousand AT-6s
were built, including rebuilds of earlier models.

Training was action-packed. After the hopelessly boring
instrument flying, there were high G aerobatics, Clark rolls

(360-degree aileron rolls going straight up), and something brand new: formation. With as many as five in a flight, the smoothness Rearden had insisted on during Basic Training really paid off. Guys who hadn't learned the skill could be downright scary in formation.

The pace was fast even when cadets weren't flying. A fully clothed dunk in the base swimming pool followed their first solo. One day was spent on the flight line learning how to change a sump valve (used to drain water from the gas tanks before flight). Cadets also learned to change tires, fuel up tanks, and add oil. Another Saturday they went to the base skeet range, firing shotguns at clay pigeons to learn how to lead targets. It was a prelude to the "rat race," an exercise flown in twos. The leader flew high G aerobatics while the wingman tried to keep his nose ahead of the leader as he closed to firing range.

Even takeoffs and landings came with a new twist. The AT-6's retractable landing gear required a brand-new habit pattern. More than one cadet forgot about that. Pink slips delayed plenty of first solo flights, and the quickest way to wash out of advanced training altogether was to wreck an airplane by landing gear-up.

AT-6 training went by in a hurry. The final week was reserved for air-to-ground gunnery practice out of Eglin Field on the Florida panhandle. It was by far the most exciting flying the cadets had done yet. They took off in flights of three for strafe practice in the Gulf of Mexico. The targets were small rafts with white fitted panels that looked like sheets hanging on Mom's clothesline. Cadets flew a box pattern starting at five hundred feet, rolling into a five-degree dive at the raft. They aimed through a *reticle*, a white Christmas-tree-shaped projection on a plate of glass mounted directly in front of the pilot. At 150 feet above the water, they opened up, firing only short bursts to keep from overheating the gun barrel. Each cadet had a hundred rounds of ammo with a specific paint color to allow spotters to score hits. Most cadets rolled aggressively toward the targets, took careful, calculated aim . . . and missed. However, the trips to Eglin by Class 41I were considered a total success: they all got a chance to strafe and nobody hit the water.

Don's last check pilot was Gary Gates, an easygoing civilian from Kansas and by far the most preferred check pilot among the aviation cadets. No one could remember Gates ever pink-slipping someone, but Don took no chances. He had three flights in three days to bone up on his "rat race" skills and landings after returning from Eglin, and used them wisely. Being a "taildragger," (only a small wheel kept the tail off the ground) the AT-6 had a reputation for causing problems in crosswinds, which kicked up a bit the day before the checkride. But Friday, December 5, 1941, was a perfect day to take the final progress check: crisp, clear, and no wind. McGanley and Melford were paired.

✧   ✧   ✧

Gates said nothing all flight long. As Don and the check pilot headed back to Operations, Gates turned and extended his hand. "Congratulations, McGanley, I'd say you're ready to go. I'll be happy to have a beer with you after graduation. See you then."

That was it? He'd imagined that something would be done to put the exclamation point on this achievement. Maybe a meeting with the commander, or a little speech by Gates about his future, or something. There was none of that. They shook hands, and Gates turned to leave, smiling at himself because of the dumbfounded expression on McGanley's face. He stopped and turned back to Don. The kid had performed well. Perhaps he deserved a little bit more from his check pilot. "By the way, I saw your assignment. Know what it is?"

"No, sir."

"P-40s, Morrison Field. You did well here, McGanley, better than most. Good luck to you."

"Morrison Field?"

"Palm Beach. Florida. Sunshine, beaches, swimsuits. Been there myself. You'll love it." They shook hands again and Gates turned away.

"Uh, sir . . . thanks!" Don gushed it out; his eyes teared. He choked off the emotion, glad that Gates had his back to him. The instructor simply waved as he headed back to Operations, and his next student.

Don almost choked again as he walked back to his barracks. This just couldn't feel any better, but the moment went so fast. One second he was an aviation cadet, a student. Next, he was a pilot. He wished there was a way to hold time still so he could live this a little longer.

He stopped, somewhere on the base, who knows where. Then other thoughts came to him, of his earlier years, thoughts of Johnny. He couldn't remember if his father had ever hugged him; all he could see was Johnny's fist. He remembered how awful he felt when he first received the results of the Flying Cadets Educational Exam. He thought of how he'd failed Paulie. And he remembered Combs, his sergeant at Mitchel, who put KP ahead of his pilot training. KP, of all things!

All those years he'd wanted to get away from home so badly, *needed* to get away, permanently. And the day he did, no one bothered to say good-bye to him. And now, no one was here. He started walking again, somehow feeling disappointed on the greatest day of his life.

He got back to the barracks and sat on his bunk, shoulders slumped and head down. Slowly his mind drifted to Elizabeth, and then to that CMTC sergeant; Malone, it was. And to Old Man Beattie. He lifted his head, sat up, and thought to himself: Don't these people who'd helped you along deserve more attention than the ones who didn't? He said out loud, "McGanley, what the hell is the matter with you? You should be thanking them now. Damn it, you should have thought of them first."

✧   ✧   ✧

"Hey, Don, I passed!" It was Pete, running through the door. "Took me two tries to get a decent landing, but I did it. Davenport looked at me like I was a walking pink slip; then he told me there'd be no more flights. I figured I'd be flying right up to graduation but he just told me that was all. Can you believe that? Oh God, I can't believe I made it!" Pete stopped short for a second. Don didn't look so hot. "Uh, you passed, too, didn't you?"

"Yeah, Gates did the same thing to me. These guys must get a big kick out of watching us sweat."

"Fantastic! Hey, I heard someone say that Barton's has our uniforms in." Barton's was the local tailor who was under contract for the new officer uniforms. "Let's go down there and get 'em! I'm going to put that rank on my shoulder and those wings on my chest and parade around like a peacock. We can go to the Exchange and pick everything up."

"We can't do that, Pete, at least not until after graduation. We're still cadets until the twelfth, you know."

"McGanley, for Christ's sake, would you relax for a change? We just finished pilot training! I'll go get the bars and wings. You can drive us down to pick up the uniforms, and we'll dress them all up. How's that?"

"We can't wear them around here, Pete. The other guys are still in training. I don't think it's a good idea."

"Well, then I got a better idea. Why don't you come home with me for a week? Meridian's only four or five hours away. We'll put 'em on and wear 'em home. C'mon, buddy, Mom's the best cook in the South. I'll even introduce you to my sister."

"Your sister?"

"You walk through that door in your spanking new uniform and she'll be yours forever!"

"Here we go again."

"Yeah, she's gorgeous . . . and twelve years old!" Don's expression must have been a doozy; Pete got a big laugh out of it.

"Very funny, Melford."

"Yeah, yeah, okay. C'mon, fella, loosen up! Let's pack up tonight and get out of here first thing tomorrow. It'll do us both good to get away from this place. Has anybody given you any details to do?"

"No."

"Okay, then. I, for one, am going to get out of here before somebody grabs me. And don't worry; we'll be back for graduation and act like we've never laid eyes on the gold bars or wings. Meantime, we can show off. Two hotshot pilots in their Chevrolet! We'll be the toast of Meridian, Mississippi!"

Even Don confessed to himself that it was a good idea. He was more than ready to wear his wings and lieutenant's bars. Plus, he'd never seen Mississippi, unless you counted the troop train almost two years earlier. And he had to admit that he hadn't been out much over the last nine months. "Okay. Better hurry downtown, though. I think Barton's closes at five."

"Oh, by the way, thanks for driving." Pete flashed his grin. Don nodded. Pete's enthusiasm was infectious, even on him. He felt a lot better.

✧　✧　✧

The lieutenants-to-be looked damned sharp in their uniforms. Since several cadets still had a sortie or two left to fly, they waited until the barracks was empty, and then dressed in their new duds. Don stood before the mirror in the latrine, staring at the prop and wing insignia on each lapel, the large silver wings above his left breast pocket, and the "butter" bars on his shoulders. He was awed by the sight, somewhat shell-shocked that it was he in that uniform. Not bad at all.

31

It took just over four hours to reach Pete's home, even though it was early on Saturday and there was almost no one on the road. Highway 80 was pretty rutted up in spots, so the going was slow. But no one was in a hurry. They had a full week with no obligations to anyone or anything. Don paid more attention than ever before at the world around him. The two "lieutenants" passed mile after mile of tall pines and scattered shacks of poor families, black and white. The 117 miles between Craig Field and the Melford home took them by Browns, Uniontown, Prairieville, Demopolis, Bellamy, and Cuba in Alabama, and then Kewanee in Mississippi. Some were towns in name only: to Don they looked as though a family or two took up a plot, built their place, and named it. Only Demopolis had a gas station, and he saw maybe three or four stores along the highway. It seemed a far cry from the sights along U.S. 1 on the way south from New York, or maybe it was just that he wasn't on some sort of mission now and had the time and sense to notice things around him. He was relaxed, he realized, for the first time since he could remember.

The Melford home was on the east side of Meridian, right along Route 80. Don parked in the driveway. They both got out, and Don stood aside while Pete announced their arrival with a honk on the horn. Twelve-year-old Leslie charged out of the house and literally jumped on her elder brother. The little girl was as cute as they came: she'd be a beauty one day. Gladys Melford hugged her son as expected, and then unexpectedly turned and hugged Don as if he had been one of her own. Mr. Melford greeted his son and the stranger with a solid handshake but didn't say much. He muttered something about chores and headed around the back of the house. Obviously, a man of few words, but at least he'd come out to meet them. Don figured Mr. Melford was probably a good ten years younger than he looked. And just as Pete promised, Leslie was smitten after her first look at the New Yorker in uniform. She gushed and giggled at him. It made him a bit embarrassed; intentionally, he figured.

Don liked the Melfords immediately. Even though he had just arrived, he was comfortable here. It occurred to him that he'd rarely felt that way in his own home. The Melfords showed an interest in him that he hadn't been prepared for. They talked in the living room for the next several hours, Gladys seemingly consumed with questions about the Big Apple. And after a while, Don realized that there was plenty to tell, with so many places to go and all the money in Manhattan, in spite of the Depression. The more he talked, the more he realized how fascinating it must be to these Southern folks who would probably never get the chance to see New York for themselves. Don was generous with his answers and grateful for their interest. Pete was right. This had been a good idea.

Pete had been right about something else, too. Gladys Melford was a fabulous cook. The ham, corn-on-the-cob, collards, hot rolls, and apple pie were all superb. In spite of Leslie's scrutinizing attention, Don truly enjoyed every minute of supper; not just the food, but the company as well. He guessed (accurately) that the Melfords took every meal together, said grace, and were genuinely interested in each other. They chatted on about daily events and each other's personal interests, and they laughed easily. This was obviously not a money-rich family, judging from the small house, the run-down front porch, and the beat-up '32 Ford out front. But they were rich in other ways that were a lot more important. Their home was as neat as a pin and a happy place to be. Don envied them.

Evening came quickly. The two officers were in Pete's old room for the night, Don on the single bed and Pete on the floor on a stack of blankets, which served as a makeshift mattress. Don had protested, but Pete assured him it was the best arrangement.

"Don't worry. I haven't fit in that bed since the seventh grade. I'd much rather be down here where I can stretch out. And I don't have to climb over you if I have to use the outhouse. Besides, Mom'd whip me good if she knew you slept on the floor."

"Ah, you finally got to the real reason."

Pete laughed. "Yeah, she really runs the show around here."

"I'll bet you had good years growing up here—good home, good family."

"It was pretty quiet until Leslie came along! But what about New York? I can't imagine what growing up in a city like that would be like."

"Lousy."

"You're kidding. How come?"

Don tried to think of a way to backtrack. He didn't really want to talk about his life growing up, but he couldn't think of a way to change the subject. "Oh, I don't know. It wasn't that bad, just different. My brothers and sister had other things to do. We didn't see that much of each other."

"I can't imagine that. What about your folks?"

"Oh, I guess Dad was gone a lot. His wages got cut way back when the Depression hit, so he had to work longer and harder. I don't think he said two words to me the last year I was home. Mom was sick all the time."

"Pop always worked hard around here, too." Pete paused. "Had a good football coach, though. He kinda took me under his wing, like a second pa. Since I'm so tall he made me an end on offense and defense."

"My football coach told me go on home until I could wear long pants."

Pete started to laugh. "No kiddin'?"

There was no answer. Just darkness. Pete tried to think of something to say, only came up with "pretty lousy." Again it was quiet, but it gave Pete a minute to wonder about his Yankee buddy: Why he didn't want to go out, why he was unsure about girls, why he had to be the first to fly and the first in ranks, and why he also volunteered to be the company bugler at Primary Training. And add to all that, Don was small, maybe five foot five or six inches at the most. The guy was as unsure of himself as anyone Pete had ever known. More than that, he just wasn't too happy in general. There was probably a lot more inside McGanley that needed to come out. Maybe it would someday. Pete decided not to push him, tried to lighten up the conversation instead.

"Well, Monday we'll head into Meridian and see what the ladies have to offer."

"Can't wait."

Pete laughed. "You're consistent, McGanley, I'll give you that. But this time you have no flying excuses. I know a couple of dance halls we can check out."

"Okay."

"Really? I'm shocked! I'll tell ya, I'm really going to enjoy seeing you wrapped in some lovely's arms, even if it breaks Leslie's little heart."

"Aw, knock it off."

"Yeah, okay. Well, I'm glad you came home with me. Good for both of us, I think."

"Good, we're finally in agreement, Pete. You've got a nice family. I really enjoy them."

"Then we'll enjoy some more tomorrow. Not much else to do on Sunday, except some chores. You don't expect to eat for free, do you?"

"Not at all."

"Good. Sleep well, Yank."

Don wasn't all that tired, or so he thought. He looked out the window but couldn't see stars. Clouds had been gathering all day long; probably in for rain tomorrow. Now the lack of moon and stars made it pitch dark. He was glad for that and for the quiet. He had no idea how long he stayed awake, but, thankfully, thoughts of those missed family years soon gave way to sleep.

32

Sunday morning. Heavy rains in already soggy conditions brought standing water close to the north side of the house. Normally the Melfords would have headed for church, but the flood danger changed the routine. Pete and Don spent four hours digging a drainage ditch away from the foundation, a project Mr. Melford had meant to do earlier in the year but hadn't gotten around to just yet. They were drenched and dog-tired when they finished, but they got the job done right. It was two o'clock in the afternoon by the time they dried off and cleaned up. And they were starved, too.

Right on cue, the South's greatest cook served up a feast: hot flapjacks, bacon and eggs, baked apples, and hot coffee. And Leslie, though she'd eaten hours earlier, took up a place right next to Don, rested her chin in her hand, and watched.

"You going to watch me eat?" Don asked.

"Yeah." She giggled. She was going to break somebody's heart someday.

"You waiting for me to drop something down my chin?"

"Yeah." She giggled a little harder.

Don smiled at the girl and turned to his hostess. "You know, Mrs. Melford, I can't remember a better meal."

"Well, you boys worked up a real sweat digging that ditch, and you skipped breakfast."

"Sweat?" said Pete. "It's raining, Mom."

"Well, you worked awful hard. Thank you so much, Don, for helping Pete."

"Glad to."

Between oversized bites, Pete said, "Well, that's good to hear, Yank, because we need to enclose the chicken coop and build a fence along the back boundary. All this rain'll make it easy to dig deep enough to set the posts. Mom said we've been losing chickens to foxes, and the deer are eating up the vegetables. Between you and me and Dad, we should finish everything before we have to get back to Craig."

"Fine." Don was perfectly willing to pitch in. Back home he'd done chores, had to sweat out whether he'd done them well enough or not, and ended up doing more than his fair share. He couldn't remember ever doing a project around the house with his brothers or his dad. It reminded him again how much he'd missed while growing up. He was envious of Pete. And one other thing: He was glad Pete hadn't pressed the idea of going into Meridian to get a hamburger or down a couple of beers or look for gals to dance with. Maybe all the chatter about that had been a bunch of bunk. No, he was perfectly content to be here, being useful at the Melford place, with literally nothing to worry about.

Don and Pete were just about to start a second plateful of food when Mr. Melford walked in, wiping himself down with a towel. He was drenched, too, having gone outside to put some finishing touches on the drainage ditch.

Melford had been gone all morning before that, trying to earn some extra money by tinkering with neighbors' home and auto repairs. He'd been employed at a paper mill in Meridian when the Depression hit, but lost that job in 1935. Fortunately, this house had always been his, passed down by previous generations. It wasn't a lot, but it was enough. These days Melford split his time between tending his animals and crops and trying to earn those few extra dollars. At least for now, they were doing okay.

"Oh, honey, you're soaked!" Gladys headed for her husband and helped him dry off. Melford looked a little annoyed at the babying but didn't protest; he'd given up on that a long time ago. He started to sit down at the table when the phone rang. Annoyed again, he went to answer it: Phone calls, incoming or outgoing, cost a nickel. This had better be important.

It was. "Alice says turn on the radio," he said. "The Japanese have attacked us." Without a word, he walked over to the radio, which sat on the dining room server, and switched it on. Normally, there'd be church music on, but not that day.

. . . . *have bombed Hawaii. Ships have been sunk at Pearl Harbor and the army base at Ford Island has been destroyed. I repeat from United Press: The Japanese have attacked Hawaii. Stay tuned to this station for further bulletins . . .*

Mr. Melford glanced at his wife, said nothing. Gladys gasped. It was 3:50 p.m., December 7, 1941. Pete looked across the table at Don. Plates were stuffed full of food, but all of a sudden, appetites were gone. The room was dead silent. Then Don said, "We'd better get back."

Part 3

33

Palm Beach was warm and muggy in winter, hardly what a New Yorker like Don was used to. Still, life was good. This was his first assignment as a brand new pilot. He was an officer. At $225 per month, counting pay, travel allowance, and rations, he was awash in more money than he'd ever known. He had status and purpose now. It felt good. Don and Pete found two more guys to split the gas cost and drove straight through to South Florida, arriving midday on December 12.

They drove through Morrison Field's "main gate" ready to fly, anxious to get a look at a long row of P-40s. The Warhawk was huge compared to trainers; Don remembered it well from Mitchel Field. The first lot of 199 had been delivered to the Army Air Corps in May 1940. Equipped with the V-1710-33 1150hp Allison engine, it could make fifteen thousand feet in five minutes and top out at just over 350 mph. Two guns on the nose and two on the wings gave it as much firepower as any fighter before it. If you couldn't get excited about flying a Warhawk, then you were in the wrong business.

When Don finally found Operations to sign in, there was no one there. Come to think of it, he hadn't seen anyone since he passed through the main gate. He stood out between the building and the airstrip with hardly a plane in sight, except for a couple of trainers.

A sergeant finally came up behind him, saluting. "Excuse me, sir, are you one of the new pilots?"

Salute returned. "Yes, I am. Lieutenant McGanley."

"Sir, Major Wurtsmith wants to see you."

"Me?"

"Yes, sir."

"Who's Major Wurtsmith?"

"Our CO (Commanding Officer), sir. He's over there in the headquarters building, Room 10. Told me to grab the first officer I saw and have him report. Since you guys were due to arrive this week, I just figured you were one of the new pilots."

"Okay. And, uh, Sergeant, what's going on here? For an active P-40 group, I can't believe how dead this place looks."

"I just got here yesterday, sir. Major Wurtsmith told me fifteen minutes ago to round somebody up. That's all I know. You're the first officer I've seen."

Major Paul B. Wurtsmith led the newly formed 49th Pursuit Group, a P-40 outfit with no P-40s. On paper, this assignment had looked like the big time to Don, but it was hardly that. The airstrip had one PT-17 and one BT-14 parked side-by-side, the two trainers Don had seen. And this was a fighter base?

Morrison Field looked more like some sort of railway depot. Trucks, jeeps, automobiles, and crates of war "matériel" of all kinds were stacked up like they were headed somewhere else. On the other side of the airstrip, there were a few hangars and several civilian planes parked rather haphazardly. Wurtsmith's office was practically empty, with only a desk and chair, nothing hanging on the walls befitting a major's career, and no orderly out front.

Wurtsmith was not terribly imposing physically: five feet nine, brown hair but thinning pretty fast on top, and a neatly trimmed mustache. Still, he was the highest-ranking officer Don had seen up close since he joined the service. His uniform was neatly pressed, his hair was perfectly combed, and his demeanor was practically godlike. As far as Don was concerned, he may as well have been God himself. Don saluted.

"Lieutenant McGanley, sir."

"Did you come straight here from Craig, McGanley?"

"Yes, sir."

"How many came with you?"

"Well, sir, three came with me in my car. We drove straight through. The rest of the guys are on their way, I guess."

Wurtsmith extended a single sheet of orders with a list of names as he looked up at the obviously uncomfortable second lieutenant. "McGanley, you're in charge of Operations. As soon as everyone gets here, I want the pilots in the air. Get as much flying as possible. You have one BT-14 and one PT-17 to use as you see fit. Sergeant Crandall will keep them gassed up for you. All you have to do is keep them flying."

"Uh, sir . . ."

"More orders should be coming in any time for all of you."

"Orders for what, sir? We're assigned to P-40 school here, sir."

"Not anymore. All you have to do is get as much flying as you can and see to it that everyone else does the same. You can start Monday morning. Any questions?"

"Sir, am I supposed to be in charge of all these people? I don't even know who's here."

"Lieutenant, there's going to be a lot of equipment arriving here the rest of the month. It needs to be inventoried and prepared for further shipment. I'm going to have my hands full with that, plus keeping the civilians away from our supplies. All I'm telling you to do is pass the word and make sure you *officers* get some flying time. I don't have time to hold your hand. Just do it."

"Yes, sir." Don saluted and left. The major was all business: no personable junk and no nonsense. Don liked him right away. The hard part would be getting these guys to fly when he scheduled them. After all, they were all the same rank.

Over the next day or two, the full complement of the 49th Pursuit Group arrived at Morrison from advanced training bases scattered from Texas to Florida. They were assigned a barracks and told where the mess hall was, and that was it. Don posted a notice on the barracks door announcing a formation for all officers on Monday, December 15 at 0900, but didn't sign it. It was the only way he could think of to get them all together and pass on the major's orders. Only he and Pete Melford knew what was up. As far as the rest of the officers knew, they'd be met, welcomed, and maybe even inspected by the CO. *Good! Let them think just that; at least they'll show up*, Don thought. Don and Pete headed for the chow hall, which was pretty sparse: only a few picnic-type tables and a small kitchen, one cook, one server, and no waiters.

"Smart idea with the notice, Don. I'm just glad I'm not you."

"Yeah? Suppose I tell these guys that you're my deputy, and they can refer all their gripes to you?"

"Cheap yank sucker punch."

"If anyone asks what's going on, just tell them you saw the notice, okay? That's all I'm going to do. Then I'll just pass the major's word on in five minutes or less. If they want to go AWOL over it, that's up to them."

A big fellow joined them as they walked, and the conspiracy talk stopped. "Where the hell you get chow around here?" the big fellow asked.

Don answered, "We're headed to the mess hall right now, but don't get your hopes up too high. There isn't much here."

"Place looks pretty damned bare to me."

"You just get here?"

"Couple minutes ago. Bud Rollins, Knoxville, Tennessee." He extended his hand. "Where're you guys in from?"

"Craig Field. Selma, Alabama."

"I was at Mariana, up on the Georgia-Florida border. You know, I looked around, and there ain't a P-40 anywhere, just a couple of flytraps out next to the runway. They don't even look like they'll taxi around your hat, let alone fly." The big guy laughed at his own joke.

"Pete Melford, Bud. That's Don McGanley." Pete extended his hand and looked at Don to see if he should say more. Don saved him the trouble and spoke up.

"There aren't any P-40s. I heard we were going to be shipped out again, but I don't know when. We'll just have to wait and see."

"Figures. In case the big brass don't know, there's a war on. You'd think they'd be gettin' after it a little faster than this. But I guess we'll find out tomorrow morning when the boss lets us in on all the secrets. Either of you guys meet him?" At least Rollins had been there long enough to see the notice about the formation of officers.

Don said, "Yeah, I did, but only for a few minutes. He's pretty busy."

"Doing what? There's nothing here."

"Well, he was pretty busy with paperwork when I saw him."

They sat at one of the tables and ate hamburgers and fries for lunch. The big guy talked about everything and anything, and kept on talking. Pete and Don heard all about aviation cadet training, as though they'd never been there themselves. But Bud got their attention when he told them about a flyby by four AT-6s at his graduation ceremony.

"The number four pilot, he was one of our second lieutenant instructors. Cocky guy. Tried to do a low-altitude slow roll at fifty feet. I guess he was gonna show us all how to really fly. But he didn't make it. He was inverted when he hit the ground."

No one said a thing, except Rollins.

"You know, those lieutenant instructors weren't so good. Most of 'em barely had twenty hours in the airplane themselves, and they were teaching us! If you were lucky, you got a contract instructor, civilian guy. They were a lot better, could really handle the airplane. All we could do with this dumb lieutenant was wave him good-bye."

Again, there was no reaction. Graduation at Selma had been quite different. Don and Pete and the twenty-seven remaining members of Class 41I met in a classroom at 1300 hours on December 8. Those who completed flying were told to depart immediately for their new assignments. Those who hadn't would fly final progress checks the next day, ready or not. If they passed, they'd be released to leave. No fly-by to make fun of; no ceremony, no parties.

Don had never seen a plane crash with the pilot still strapped in. Hearing the sirens at Albany had been bad enough. He was disgusted at this guy's callousness, but he kept it to himself. The Tennessean looked like the kind of guy you wouldn't want to tangle with. He was plain huge: over six feet tall and equally big in the chest and down his body. And he had a big head, literally and figuratively. The guy was loud and overbearing, perhaps because he thought he could be. Don didn't like him, neither did Pete. Lousy first impression!

34

The officers of the 49th Pursuit Group lined up outside of their barracks and awaited the commander. Once Don was sure everyone was there, he stepped forward and turned to face them.

"Major Wurtsmith is our CO. He wants us to fly as much as we can before we're shipped out. All we have is the PT-17 and the BT-14 parked over there. I'll put up a piece of paper, and you can sign up to fly. We'll do thirty-minute sorties in the local area, then we'll take thirty minutes to top off the gas and check the plane, and then off again. Go where you like, just be back in thirty minutes. We'll fly seven days a week, as long as the daylight lasts or as long as the airplanes will take it."

"Just one second." A tall lieutenant stepped forward. "Who's idea is all this?"

"Well, Major Wurtsmith just told me to keep the planes and pilots in the air. This is about the best way I can think of to get everybody up." Don figured this would happen, that they wouldn't like being told what to do by another second lieutenant. Well, too bad. Wurtsmith wanted them to fly, and that was all there was to it.

The tall lieutenant went on, "I don't know who you think you are, bub, but..."

"I think you've been given an order... *bub*! That means get your ass in the air and fly. Now what's so hard to understand about that?" It was Bud Rollins. He turned to Don, beamed a broad smile, and practically shouted, "Sign me up, Don!"

And that broke up the formation, quickly. Twenty minutes later, both airplanes were in the air, with several officers hanging around to take their turn. Don broke away from the sign-up roster and walked up to Rollins. "Thanks, uh, Bud was it?"

"Rollins! Knoxville, Tennessee. Home of the Volunteers!"

Don shook his hand. "I really appreciate what you did. Thanks."

"No problem. Guy's a jackass. Every army has one. Shut him up from the start and we'll never hear from him again."

"I guess not." Don smiled at Bud. Good second impression.

✧   ✧   ✧

With only two airplanes, flying time started to stretch pretty thin, about one flight every three or four days. In the meantime, Wurtsmith sent more operational orders to Don. Now that the country was at war, he wanted base defenses built. Those who weren't flying spent the next two weeks, including Christmas, filling sandbags and digging slit trenches around the base perimeter.

The slit trenches zigzagged every ten feet or so, like an accordion. In the event of an aerial attack, the slit design would prevent any fighter or bomber from simply strafing an entire straight-line length of trench, killing all the defenders in it. The same system of trenches was being engineered at all coastal bases on the eastern and western seaboards. Perhaps it was reasonable on the West Coast, but who in hell was going to attack them here in Florida, Germans? Not likely. Lots of guys griped, as soldiers do, but the trenches got dug. It was hell of a way to spend the holidays.

✧   ✧   ✧

January 2, 1942

It was barely after sunrise. Don was climbing *down* from the PT-17, his sixth sortie since arriving at Morrison. Not a large number, but more than anyone else had flown. It was a matter of desire. Guys who really wanted to fly lined up and got the sorties. Those who didn't, perhaps disappointed that the aircraft were beat-up trainers instead of the much-anticipated P-40, got less. He noticed Sergeant Crandall running across the tarmac. "Hey, Lieutenant! Major Wurtsmith wants to see you."

"Okay, Sarge. Go ahead and gas her up. I might just go up again if no one else shows up."

"You got it, Lieutenant."

Wurtsmith was behind his desk, as usual. He'd been burning the midnight oil and looked it. He handed Don a handful of papers.

"McGanley, these are orders to San Francisco for thirty-two officers. One passenger train and one freight train from Southern Pacific will be here this afternoon to transport the group. They'll line up one behind the other on the railroad spur on the other side of the field. Board at 1600, departure at 1700. You will command the freight train. Select an officer to accompany you as quartermaster and report here at 1500 to pick up the group records."

"Uh, sir, I don't know anything about freight trains . . ."

"You don't have to. There'll be a conductor and engineer aboard from Southern Pacific Railroad. All you have to do is watch over the freight and make sure it doesn't fall off into a ditch between here and San Francisco."

Don stood silent for a moment.

"Any questions, Lieutenant?"

"What about the route, sir? I mean, where are we going?"

"Fair question." He pulled out a map. "The rail line goes through Tampa, Tallahassee, and Mobile on the way to New Orleans. In New Orleans, we'll stop a little longer than normal to switch engines. From there we join the Southern Pacific Line "Sunset Route" through San Antonio, El Paso, Tucson, Yuma, and Los Angeles. There are two Southern Pacific routes northbound out of L.A. One follows the coast toward San Francisco, the other goes through Fresno before heading directly west to San Francisco. We'll take the Fresno route."

"Why?"

"The answer's above my pay grade, but if I were speculating, I'd say it's to keep us away from the coast in case the Japanese strike there. But keep that to yourself. No need to spread around more wild rumors than we have already. McGanley, I'm telling you all this only because I'm putting you in command of the freight train. The rest of the officers and troops know the method of travel and the destination only. Let's keep it that way. Any other questions, Lieutenant?"

"We're going to San Francisco, sir?"

"That's right. Once you get there, go to a place called the Cow Palace. Deliver the records there, and your job is done."

"The Cow Palace?"

"It's a large indoor arena where the city has circuses, prize fights, big events like that. The army leased it as a staging area for deploying troops. Just ask for directions when you get to San Francisco. I'll see you there. Anything else?"

"Well, yes, sir . . . uh . . . I've got this car. It's kind of the family car. I drove it from Staten Island to Georgia for Primary, then finally here. My brother bought it for my mother. I was going to try and get it back to her. What should I do with it?"

"Sell it."

"My mother's car, sir?"

Wurtsmith looked down and smiled. He slowed down a little, put down his papers, and leaned back in his chair.

"Look, McGanley."

"Yes, sir."

"We're off to San Francisco by train. From there we're heading west into a shooting war with the Japs that I don't think will end any time soon. Quite frankly, I don't think you'll need your car for a while, and there's no time to deliver it anywhere. If I were you, I'd take it downtown to a couple of dealers and see what you can get for it. Don't tell them you're leaving today. Once you've sold it, the least the dealer can do is give you a ride back to the base."

Don checked his watch: 0845 hours. He'd better get moving.

"You've done a good job here, McGanley. You have more sorties than anyone since you guys got here. You do what you're told without the griping. I picked you for the freight train because I need someone just like that to make sure this job gets done."

"Yes, sir."

"I'll see you this afternoon."

Don saluted and turned to leave.

"And McGanley!"

"Yes, sir." He turned back and saw Wurtsmith smiling at him.

"Let me know what you get for the car."

"Yes, sir!" Don saluted again. Just out the door he saw Pete heading toward the mess hall. "Hey, Pete! We're all leaving this afternoon!"

"What?"

"Yeah, we've gotta spread the word. We start boarding a passenger train at the spur at 1600. You and I have to pick up group records at the major's office at 1500."

"Where are we going?"

"I'll tell you later." We just need to make sure everybody's on board by 1700. And there's one more thing."

"And that would be . . . ?"

"You and I are taking a freight train, right behind the passenger train."

"That'll teach me for hanging around with the teacher's pet."

"Can you get Bud to help us round people up? We'd better scrap the flying for today. It'll be all we can do to get everyone ready to move out on time."

"Why don't *you* ask him? After all, he's your new best buddy." Melford grinned; he was always grinning. And Pete was right about Don and Bud Rollins. Don hadn't spoken with Bud much, but he sure remembered Bud's support that day in formation. The second impression had stuck. They'd all become friends.

"No time. I've got to go to town and sell my car. No place for it here, and I don't think we're coming back. I'll see you later, Pete. I've got to hustle."

Pete yelled after him. "You know, you ought to take Bud with you. I'll bet he'd get you get a 'G' for that car!"

"Probably so! I'll meet you back here at 1500."

35

The trains rolled out of the Morrison Field spur right on schedule. The nation's rail industry, despite huge losses of workers to the military service, was now at the beginning of a boom triggered by wartime demand. More powerful diesel locomotives came on line, replacing the old steamers. Throughout the industry, "luxury-type" club, lounge, and tavern cars disappeared to make more room for troops. Records for carrying passengers and hauling freight were broken and broken again. Before the war ended, annual figures would reach 740 billion ton miles of freight, ninety-six billion passenger miles, and gross revenues of $9.5 billion. The railroads were truly an integral part of the nation's war effort.

The two lieutenants joined Conductor Cal Dane and Brakeman Gene Talbot in the caboose of the eighty-three-car freight train, while the rest of the officers of the now-renamed 49th *Fighter* Group cruised in front of them aboard the converted luxury passenger train. The caboose was fire-engine red and thirty-nine feet long, with a small tower, called a cupola, in the middle. The brakeman kept his watch there, most often keying on the forward cars' wheel journal boxes, commonly called "hotboxes." It was not uncommon for the packing material in these journal boxes to overheat, then smoke and ignite. If the train wasn't stopped, the axel would overheat and fail, causing wheels to lock up and a possible derailment. Last thing they needed.

The cupola split the caboose in half. Dane and Talbot had a woodstove and two bunks in the forward cabin, while Don and Pete shared the aft cabin with the caboose's office, consisting of a desk and file cabinet. They slept on blankets on the floor. Throughout the day there was little to do, so with each stop for water, Don and Pete began walking the length of the train, checking the tie-downs on the flat cars. After a few stops, they'd checked them all, so they just kept repeating the process. Without the inventive task, they'd have died of boredom, but Don took the job Wurtsmith had given him seriously. He paid little attention to the obvious differences between his trip accommodations and those of the rest of the group.

By day three of the journey, the officers were getting a little tired of the caboose, let alone the hard floor. Dane and Talbot made sure there was food at each stop, but there was little talk between the four. As West Texas went by at 28 mph, Don decided they'd been burden enough for Dane and Talbot and told Pete they'd look for a better place to bunk. At the next stop they found bedding and blankets, which they piled into a canvas-topped half-ton about halfway toward the engine. It would be a bit noisy, but they'd get used to the racket and wind and cold after a while. It was just after dark when they finally settled in. Don started to lie down and then thought better of it.

"I'm heading back to the caboose to tell Talbot where we are. Besides, I need to rustle up some food. Want a sandwich if I can find one?"

"Sure. All this homemaking would make anybody hungry. You know, I'm sure glad Wurtsmith gave us this plum assignment. The last thing I'd want is a six-day trip to San Francisco on a luxury passenger train, complete with dining cars, bars, picture shows, dancing girls, and sleeping cabins."

"Well, I suppose I oughta tell you that Wurtsmith didn't pick you. He dropped this one on me and told me to pick an officer quartermaster."

"What?"

"Well, I'd rather do this with a good guy than have to deal with a lousy attitude. Sorry. I had no idea we'd be eating and sleeping like a couple of hobos."

"Lucky me to have such a good friend. Well, Yank, this hobo's hungry."

"Okay, be back in about twenty minutes. If you can help me find a lamp or flashlight somewhere, I'll try not to fall off the train while I get the food."

"It'd serve you right for stickin' it to your buddy."

Don laughed, sort of. They found a flashlight packed in a crate on the floor of the truck's passenger side, and Don headed out. Pete had to admire the guy's determination to do his job: all those tie-down checks and getting food for his "command," and it was no easy trip back to the caboose in the cold, windy dark. Don was a good troop. If Pete had been in Wurtsmith's shoes, he'd probably have chosen Don for this detail, too. But jeez, the guy sure made you shake your head sometimes.

Don returned with peanut butter and jelly and enough bread for four sandwiches, two for now, two for breakfast. But Pete went through his first one and kept right on eating.

"Aren't you going to save one for breakfast?"

"Nope. Tomorrow morning, I'm going to eat half of yours, Yank. I'm bigger than you, so I need more food. Second, it's the least you can do after getting me into this."

"Quit your bellyaching."

"No chance. You owe me." Both took a couple of bites, surprised at how hungry they were. "By the way, did Wurtsmith ever tell you where we're going?"

"Besides San Francisco, no. At least nowhere specific. But he said we're going to sea and we're going where the Japs are, so I don't think it's Hawaii."

"Too bad. I could use some rest time on the beach with some grass-skirt dancers and a couple of drinks."

Don went on like he hadn't heard a word Pete said. "You know, we haven't had any training at all, so it can't be to a combat unit, at least not yet. Then the way the Japanese are attacking everything, there may not be too many places left to go. Maybe we're going someplace on the West Coast for P-40s first and then we'll go to sea."

"I like the Hawaii plan better. We can train in the P-40 there and still log some beach time. See? Perfect!"

"I think you can rule out Hawaii."

"What do you know? You're just a lieutenant. I'm puttin' my money on Hawaii."

"Nope. Don't think so."

Pete shook his head. "Jeepers, I can't believe this. Two years ago I was chasing girls in Oxford."

"Oxford?"

"Mississippi. That's where the University of Mississippi is. Girls all over the place."

"You have a one-track mind, Melford."

"I met this sweetie named Karen about a week before I left. Boy, she woulda been worth some real attention. Guess I'll never know. And now look at me. I'm sitting here on this clackety train, in the dark, with a flashlight, a peanut butter and jelly, and a Yank for company. And I have no idea where I'm going."

"I wonder what it's like."

"What?"

"Combat. Nobody's ever shot at me before. I can't wait, though."

"For combat? You're nuts, McGanley. You know, I need to find you a girl before it's too late."

"Haven't you ever thought about it?"

"I hate to disappoint you, but not really. Why don't we take this thing one step at a time? I doubt there's anything fun about combat. And I don't have any desire to see anybody get killed, especially me. My uncle Herb got killed in France in World War I. I don't think you'd find the war as glorious as you think."

"It's not the glory."

"Then what is it about this war that makes you so anxious to see it close up?"

Don paused. "Oh, I don't know." There was another pause and then he perked up. "You're right. I'm nuts. Never mind. You know, it's too bad we didn't think of using this half-ton sooner. Talbot said we'd be in San Francisco day after tomorrow."

"So we wasted four nights of decent sleep in that caboose when we coulda been livin' it up in this motel room, right? Well, Yank, at least you got us away from two shower-needy guys who didn't even want us there."

"Not their fault, though. And they kept us from starving. I'll bet they're pretty good fellows once you get to know them."

"Good like you, Yank." Pete was grinning in the dark.

Don couldn't tell if Pete was mad or not. "Well, I'm going to get some sleep."

"I'll try not to steal your sandwich overnight."

The yakking finally over with, Don lay back with several blankets on top of him, glad for the dark and the clattering of the rails. But the idea of combat remained a loud, constant voice in his head. He knew he'd wanted to fly, but the flying alone was just an escape tunnel. He was on his way somewhere else, to combat. That's where he could stop running from his home, his lack of ability, his failures, and his personal pain, and all those feelings and memories he couldn't share with anyone. He hated them; he hated himself for them, and he couldn't make them go away. But in an odd way, he knew that what he was running so hard from was the same thing that drove him on.

36

January 8, 1942

The train pulled into San Francisco's main depot at Townsend and Fourth Street in the late afternoon. Don and Pete had long since found the truck containing the group's records. They grabbed a couple of clipboards to look important and started ordering yard workers to unload the flat cars, beginning with the records truck. They checked it for gas. By golly, it had some in it. Pete got directions from the yard workers and they jumped in and headed south on Highway 101.

The Cow Palace was easy to find, a huge arena with its own turn off the highway. The drive took less than twenty minutes. The place was almost empty; they'd beaten just about everybody here, including Wurtsmith. As buses arrived from the train station, it became obvious that the Cow Palace was going to be home for the night, not just for the 49th, but for other units as well. Don and Pete left the records in the ticket office, told the guard who they were and what the boxes were, and set off to find Wurtsmith and some food. They found neither. Beyond that, there was nothing else to do but find a place to sack out, so that's what they did.

✧　✧　✧

Next morning, there was no mistaking the aroma in the main auditorium. Some smart fellow had set up tables of hot coffee and breakfast rolls. They attracted a crowd in a hurry. Don and Pete ran into Bud Rollins as they headed for the goods.

"Hey, McGanley, for once there's a good reason to follow you around so early in the morning. Hope you guys enjoyed the trip out here."

Pete moved closer to Bud, looked around quickly, and whispered, "Does the major know?"

"Know what?"

"About the girls in New Orleans. You know, they hitched with us all the way out here. I thought for sure we'd get caught."

Rollins wasn't convinced. "What a bunch of bullshit! Nice try, though."

Don grabbed a couple of rolls and coffee from the table and spotted Major Wurtsmith standing alone all the way across the auditorium, by the exit doors. For a change, the Major wasn't issuing orders to somebody or reading papers. Don turned to his buddies.

"There's the major. I don't know about you guys, but I think I'll go find out where we're going."

"He probably doesn't know, either," said Bud. "But I'll be happy to guard the hot rolls while the major reports to you on the group's progress. You let us know what you find out. Dismissed."

Don ignored Bud's laugh. "Don't you want to know?"

"I already know," said Bud. "It has something to do with the war we're in. And since we're in it against the Japs, and since we've just traveled three thousand miles in their direction, my guess is that we're headed where they are. Nobody's given me a rifle and steel pot yet, so I don't think we've been assigned to some infantry division. And now that I know how to fly, that leaves an air base. Any questions?"

"I'll be right back."

Pete shook his head. "Gee, Bud, that was good."

"For Christ sakes, that guy's so churned up about all this. He's been like a little skitter bug since the first day I met him."

"You shoulda been on the freight train. He's all whipped up about being shot at. Combat. But I'll tell ya, he's okay . . . for a Yank."

"Yeah, I know. Just kinda makes me shake my head sometimes, ya know?"

"Me, too."

Pete watched Don walk away and knew exactly what was on his mind. It was the same eagerness he'd seen at Primary Training. Don carried it all the way through pilot training, down to Morrison Field, and across the country. He seemed to think he needed this war for some crazy reason. And he needed approval, though Pete wasn't sure from whom. He guessed that Don wouldn't answer if he asked. The guy didn't have too many friends, probably only a few his whole life. Pete felt glad that he and Bud were among them.

✧ ✧ ✧

"Major Wurtsmith, sir?"

Wurtsmith had just taken a seat behind a table piled high with folders. "Morning, McGanley. Get something to eat?"

"Yes, sir."

"I didn't get a chance to tell you yesterday. You and Melford did a fine job getting the freight train here. I hope the caboose wasn't too uncomfortable."

"Well, sir, we found some bedding and moved into one of the half-tons after a couple of days. Worked out okay. The caboose was getting a little crowded, and I just thought it would be better for the crew if we gave them some extra space."

"Good idea."

"Yes, well, sir, I was just wondering. Do you know where we're headed? The group, I mean?"

"Yes."

A long pause. Wurtsmith gave the lieutenant his undivided attention, but did not speak. This was a good young officer. He deserved to know more, but two things prevented it. First, Major Wurtsmith had probably said too much already; second, he didn't know much more detail himself. Over the next several weeks, orders would change almost daily as the war in the Southwest Pacific intensified. But he liked the kid.

"You're headed to the Hotel Whitcomb on Market Street where you'll bunk with three other officers until the twelfth at 0700, at which time you'll report to Pier 38. In the meantime, you have no duties. Grab a couple of buddies and enjoy San Francisco."

Don got the message and smiled back. So much for the West Coast idea. A pier meant a ship; they were going overseas right away. He started to ask how he was supposed to get to the Whitcomb, but decided against it. Major Wurtsmith was busy enough. But the man was a straight shooter and at least he recognized Don and Pete for having ridden that damned freight train all the way from Florida. Don appreciated that, and after spending too many years at the bottom of the household totem pole, it felt good for a change that someone seemed to like and have confidence in him.

"Anything else, Lieutenant?"

"No, sir." As badly as he wanted to know where they were going, he wasn't about to stand around and kiss the man's can over it. Plenty of guys did that sort of thing; he refused to be one of them.

37

The next three days in San Francisco were good ones for the 49th Fighter Group, unless you were in command. The officers in charge tried to get manifests right, requisition unit supplies, and organize personnel records. They were futile efforts: all three of these changed daily, almost hourly.

However, the rank and file did not suffer such problems. Devoid of direction and supervision, they were scattered all over the city, bound only by orders to show up with their gear at the correct pier, on the correct date, at the correct time. Newly paid with extra travel money, they contributed handsomely to San Francisco's economy and made darned sure that the bartenders didn't feel lonely. Boys chased girls, and the girls chased back. There were plenty of whirlwind romances to be had, few of which stuck. During the day, Don, Pete, and Bud roamed around together. By night, Melford and Rollins went on the town while their younger buddy broke off early for the Whitcomb. Don was far more anxious to get going, arrive somewhere, and start flying airplanes than to pay attention to a fantastic, energetic, bountiful city like San Francisco. Bud and Pete thought he was nuts and told him so.

The Whitcomb was a grand hotel. It had a huge, elegant lobby that featured bands almost every night. Built after the 1906 San Francisco earthquake, it was used originally as the temporary City Hall. It even had jail cells in the basement, still there in 1941. But it was a hotel after 1912, famous for attracting big shots from the political, entertainment, and business worlds. Don spent most of his evenings listening to the bands, or "orchestras" as they were billed by the hotel, and watching people who seemed desperate to cram a lifetime's worth of living into a few short days and nights.

✧   ✧   ✧

Don was up early on January 12, 0200 to be exact. He was already checked out of the Whitcomb, gear in hand, sitting and waiting, when Bud and Pete came downstairs. It was mostly downhill to Pier 38; three-quarters of a mile down Market Street, a right on Third, then a left on King Street to the piers. They carried everything they had in their forty-pound canvas B-4 bag: underwear, a dress uniform, one flying suit, a flying jacket, flying goggles and cap, boots, heavy socks, and a spare khaki uniform. Don had no civilian clothes at all; had worn none since leaving Staten Island over eight months ago. A footlocker containing extra items from his previous time in the army had been loaded on the train with the bulk cargo at Morrison Field, supposedly to be delivered back to him at their final destination, wherever that was.

It was cool and overcast in San Francisco. At least that made the trek from the hotel easier. But at the pier the "easiness" ended. Stragglers arrived on foot, by bus, taxi, and private auto, at all hours of the morning. So much for 0700. For the next eleven hours, the growing horde of uniformed officers and enlisted men milled around Pier 38, either waiting for orders or starting rumors, and looking up at the huge *U.S.S. Mariposa.*

Built in 1931 by Bethlehem Shipbuilding, the vessel was originally christened the *S.S. Mariposa*, one of the four sister ships of the "White Fleet," operated by Matson Lines. The "U.S.S." designation came courtesy of the War Department after December 7, officially making it a proud member of the nation's fleet of warships. With a 632-foot length, a 79-foot beam, and a 32-foot draft, the *Mariposa* was right up there with the great liners of its day.

Normally, a crew of 359 would be serving about 700 luxury-minded passengers on the upcoming voyage, but like the train ride from Florida, the trip at hand had nothing to do with luxury. The crew's complement was stripped to the bare minimum to make way for two thousand-odd troops on this initial wartime manifest. (Before the war ended, the number of troops per manifest would double, then double again.) The ship's top speed of twenty-three knots was its only defense, except for zigzag courses and intentional avoidance of great circle routes and standard shipping lanes. Such routing would lengthen the trip a few days, perhaps a setback to the urgent need for men and supplies in the forward area, but better than ending up at the bottom of the Pacific Ocean.

Don had never seen a vessel like the *Mariposa* before. The *Hunter Liggett* couldn't hold a candle to this thing. He couldn't wait to explore it; that is, if they ever got on board. The gangways were in place, and crewmembers were visible at the deck railings and at the windows of what must be the bridge, but nothing was happening. Frustration grew on Pier 38 as the day wore on, with no word of when to board. There was no food, no drink, and no place to sit.

The chaos reflected a country unprepared for war. Practically everywhere Don had gone since pilot training, there'd been little information and lots of confusion. If he hadn't worked directly for Wurtsmith, he wouldn't have known anything. They were at the start of a war where needs far exceeded the planning to meet them. Precious few knew what was going on, and no one knew who or where those precious few were. It was a condition that would continue for months.

Don, Pete, and Bud stood around doing absolutely nothing, all . . . day . . . long. They were starving, but several forays around the piers had turned up nothing but other uniforms looking for the same thing. Finally, just before 1800, an army captain with a bullhorn appeared at the forward gangway. In the dark, he looked like a silhouette against the pier's floodlights.

"Attention! Attention!"

"About damn time," muttered Bud. And then he added, loud enough for more than a few people to hear, "Whoever's running this screwed-up show oughta be hung!" Heads turned. For the first time in his life, Don was glad he was so short.

Don shared Bud's impatience, but he kept quiet. Besides, Bud would say enough for all of them. Captain Bullhorn continued, "We'll be boarding in a few minutes. You'll be assigned your cabin as you board. Go immediately there and stow your gear. There will be no personal gear allowed on deck when we sail. Anything found untended will be tossed back onto the dock. Ladies and gentlemen, we are headed into a war zone."

"Brilliant announcement." Bud was muttering again.

Pete took a fast look around. "He said ladies? I don't see any ladies."

And the army captain continued, "There will be no cameras allowed on board, no lights on at night, and no portholes open at night. Do not keep diaries or write any record of the trip. There will be no mail, coming in or going out. For the next several weeks, tend to your cabins and your personal gear. When it's time to board, we will call you by the first letter of your last name. Stay clear of the boarding ramps until it's your turn, and we'll get this process finished that much faster."

"Several weeks. Did you hear that, Bud? Long trip comin'." Pete was trying to slow Bud down before his mouth got them all in trouble.

"Hear what? My stomach? Sure, Pete, I heard it. I've been hearing it for the last five hours." And with steadily increasing volume, he said, "Jesus, this is bullshit!" Then Bud just yelled, "Hey, Captain! How about feeding the troops?" The hungry troops nodded and grumbled their agreement. Some applauded. But Captain Bullhorn had already turned away from the rail. Bud muttered to himself again, "Asshole."

"No, listen!" Pete kept trying to get Bud's attention. "I mean the guy said we'd be sailing several weeks. We're going a long way, and I'm going to find out about these so-called ladies."

"Yeah, guess that rules out Hawaii. Maybe we're going to Japan, get this thing over with quick." Bud was still steamed up. "Or maybe they're going to have us rot on this dock until the war ends. I hope these clowns don't run the war like this. We'll be dead in minutes."

A "few minutes" until boarding turned out to be over two hours. Bud was working himself into a near frenzy as he tried to stir up a riot on the pier. It was a miracle he hadn't been carted away by now.

"M through R, clear to board now!"

"You sure, Captain? We can wait a couple more days, no problem!"

Don spoke up, "Look, Bud, slow down. We can get our gear put away and meet at the forward rail . . ."

"The *bow*." Pete was grinning. Amazing, the guy never lost his sense of fun.

"Great, Pete, thanks. Okay, Bud? We'll meet at the *bow*, and go find some food. We'll be eating before you know it."

"Yeah, yeah. But only if I don't run into that idiot with the bullhorn first."

✧ ✧ ✧

The three lieutenants found the *Mariposa*'s main galley just after 2200 hours. It was nearly empty, the stainless steel countertops wiped clean. The cold lockers where the food was undoubtedly kept were locked up.

"What are you men doing here?" An accusatory tone behind Pete, Bud, and Don startled them a little. He was a big fellow, apparently one of the chefs, still in his tall hat and whites. "Dinner's over. You have no business here."

Bud wasn't in much of a mood to take crap from some cook. "Is that so? Look, pal—"

Don cut him off. "Sir, we were just looking for something to eat. Been a long day."

"Like I said, dinner's over."

Bud's cup of patience ran over. "What dinner? While you were feeding filets mignons to the big-boy kiss asses, we were standing on the docks, thirteen hours worth!"

Once again, Don stepped in, physically this time, between Bud and the chef. "Haven't had a bite in quite a while, sir. Think you might be able to scare us up some food?"

"What's the matter? Doesn't the army feed you guys?"

"Yes . . . when they get around to it," Don replied quickly and smiled. "I guess they just haven't gotten around to it yet, and since its past ten, I think we might be out of luck for the day."

Amazing what a decent approach will get you. Don and Bud were a study in contrasts: One wearing a conciliatory grin, the other with balled fists, furrowed brow, and a contorted, snarling face.

The chef seemed to soften some, looking the three officers over. After a minute or so he said, "Come with me." He led them through the galley to the refrigerated locker, then held his hand up and went in alone.

Pete was trying not to laugh. "Gee, Bud, I thought you were going to kiss the guy."

"Very fuckin' funny."

"Well," Don said, "I think we'll be okay."

The chef returned with three roasted ducks. "Do me a favor and eat up in here. Don't want anyone to come snooping by while we're raiding the ship's stores, do we? We'd all be on Captain Bligh's rack in no time." He grinned. "*Bon appetit*, boys." And he left. And they ate.

38

The eighteen thousand-ton *U.S.S. Mariposa* sailed just before midnight on Monday, January 12, 1942, to a destination unknown. Rumors flew and would continue to fly until either the destination was finally revealed or they docked and had a chance to ask some local where they were. War news and batches of rumors circled about the ship, all bad. What were they getting into?

It was the intent of the Japanese Imperial Staff to establish a "Co-Prosperity Sphere" from Manchuria and China south to Formosa, continuing along the outer chain of islands through Java, New Guinea, and the Solomon Islands. Original plans had called for a "New Order" rather than "Co-Prosperity Sphere," but it was decided that "New Order" sounded too much like the Nazi Third Reich. Call it what you like. The Co-Prosperity Sphere was nothing more than an ironic name. Conquered people, except for some collaborators, did not prosper under Japanese rule.

The allies, the Australians in particular, were truly shocked at the speed and ease of the Japanese advance down the island chains. During the 1930s, warnings of the "Yellow Peril" were met with skepticism, borne out of nothing more than simple prejudice. During the 1930s, Great Britain, the United States, and Australia responded to Japanese aggression by cutting off oil and scrap metal exports. The need to accumulate those raw materials forced Japan to go elsewhere to secure them, but it also led to the need for hard currencies.

They collected those currencies by manufacturing and selling cheap products in the depression-ravaged countries they would soon fight. Toys and household display items gave the impression that the Japanese entrepreneur thought small, built small, and earned small, befitting the physical size of the average Japanese, and hardly threatening to much larger Anglo-Saxons.

Behind this curtain of blind prejudice, the Imperial Navy rose virtually undetected, easily outsizing the U.S. Pacific Fleet by late 1941. It also led to a gross underestimation of the conquerors' planning ability, and the equipping, training, and sheer ferocity of the Imperial Japanese fighting man. As the allies got their education throughout 1941 and early 1942, the question, especially for the Australians, now became Japan's intentions regarding their own continent.

Japanese strategists, in particular Admiral Isoroku Yamamoto, had no intention of conquering the Australian continent. Army planners had long since researched the idea of invading not only Australia, but also India. Their estimates included the need for at least twelve full divisions and a resupply system so extensive and complex that the double invasion was quickly dismissed as "reckless."

Instead, the Imperial Staff sought merely to isolate the Aussies from the British and Americans, secure a self-sustaining resource pipeline through their island conquests, and remove the three hundred thousand or so westerners from the Co-Prosperity Sphere. If attacks on the Australian continent became desirable in the future, the Japanese would have a powerful network of forward operating bases from which to strike. Next step: Sue for peace.

Late in 1941, the Japanese plan was working nicely . . . almost. Churchill was facing a possible Nazi invasion after months of bombardment, and had long since pulled troops from Southeast Asia back to England for homeland defense, and rightfully so. The United States was hanging onto their isolationism. But, China was a problem. With the Americans' financial help and the growth of volunteer fighter groups, the Chinese were hanging on and draining Japan's resources. Nearly one-fourth of the entire Imperial Army was engaged there. So the Japanese adjusted the grand strategy to include eliminating the U.S. Pacific Fleet, hoping to simultaneously cut the U.S. umbilical cord to China and prevent the Americans from helping the Australians.

As tactically successful as Pearl Harbor was, Yamamoto's failure to corral and destroy the Americans' aircraft carriers left the U.S. Pacific Fleet with military muscle they could bring to bear much faster than the Japanese expected. A December 11 declaration of war on the U.S. by Adolph Hitler turned eyes toward Europe, but it wasn't enough to completely keep the U.S. out of Southwest Asia. Maybe the British couldn't add much against the Japanese after losing Singapore and Hong Kong, but the Americans could. As part of an initial commitment of 40,000 troops, the 49th Fighter Group under Major Paul Wurtsmith sailed southwest on the *Mariposa* toward a fire-hot cauldron of desperate, furious fighting.

39

L ife on the high seas went pretty much as Captain Bullhorn had briefed from the dock before boarding. The ship was dark at night; nobody wrote letters and few left their cabins. The food was great, though. Three times a day the officers gathered in the dining room, an elegant setting with huge chandeliers that hung gracefully over circular tables of eight, formally adorned with white tablecloths, china-like plates, silver service, and centerpieces. They were treated to full course meals served by professional waiters. Not bad at all, except there were no seconds. Still, the three first-class meals were the highlight of the day for Don. He could only imagine rich people cruising in such luxury, wondering if they ever really appreciated their good fortune for being able to afford something like this.

Beyond meals, there wasn't much to do. The ship's lounges turned into day rooms thick with cigarette smoke and poker games that went on and on, day after day, night after night. Don played a few times in the first few days, breaking about even, but the games got more and more feisty, the pots grew bigger, and the betting got heavier. He decided that he had better things to do, even though he didn't know what they were.

Officers were quartered in two- and four-person staterooms that now held six men. Some had nice views, others just portholes. The best suites undoubtedly belonged to the captain, the ship's officers, and Major Wurtsmith. Who knows how many enlisted folks were crammed together in their cabins. With space so tight, little time was spent in quarters outside of sleeping, unless one was lucky enough to be the only one there. It seemed like every nook and cranny on the ship was stuffed with matériel or troops.

Instead, Don spent most of his days on the main deck, looking out over rails, fascinated by the sea. He'd gotten a taste of it aboard the *Hunter Liggett*, but not like this. This ship was incredibly huge, yet dwarfed by the massive Pacific. He stood there quietly, glad for his military experience: in the CMTC, two enlistments, and pilot training. And now, in a strange way, he was glad for the war. Where would he be without any of it? Probably repairing carpet sweepers, or working as a lithographer, or delivering groceries. Yeah, he was happy to be here, staring out at the relentless swells, with a fight against a deadly enemy lurking beyond them. It was kind of funny that he had no idea where he was headed, but at the same time, he was damned glad to be headed there.

"What's the matter, buddy, don't you like poker?" Bud's bass voice startled Don out of this daydreaming.

"Not really. I lose too much."

They both leaned over the rails and stared at the ocean. Off in the distance, a singular thundercloud boomed away but didn't scare anybody. As they stood there together, Bud tried to think of something to say while Don hoped he wouldn't say a thing. It was just the look of them.

"You're a strange guy, McGanley."

"Who? Me?"

"Yeah, you."

"Why? Because I look at the ocean and keep my money in my pocket?"

"No. Because there's something eatin' at you. I may be a big ol' Kentucky-born coal-mine boy, but I ain't stupid."

"I thought you came from Knoxville."

"I do. Pop worked for Black Mountain Mining Company. Coal. We lived in Harlan County, Kentucky then. But Pop got crippled in a mining accident when I was eleven. He got a big insurance payment after the accident and we moved to Knoxville. He took a job with KUB and bought a house on Broadway Street for five hundred bucks. That was 1933."

"What's KUB?"

"Knoxville Utility Board. You know, utilities. Electrics and stuff. They light up your house after dark."

"Very funny, Bud."

"Had to walk three or four miles to school every day, unless I happened to have seven cents for the trolley, or somebody picked up my thumb and gave me a lift."

Don made a mental note, though there was no reason to. Seven cents; the streetcar down Victory Boulevard was only a nickel, same as the Staten Island Ferry to Manhattan.

Bud kept on. "Stayed a lot with my grandparents, though. They had a pig farm outside of town. During the school year, I got a job at Standard Knitting in town. Don't tell anybody, but I used to push a sewing cart around the floor. Delivered thread and fabric to the ladies at the machines. One time I got caught . . . I mean somebody said I was looking up a lady's dress. Can you believe that?"

"Well, were you?"

"Almost cost me my job. At twelve bucks a week, Pop woulda killed me. And later on the union boys came in and tried to stir things up with the machine ladies. Things got pretty tense then. Even my aunt joined the picket line."

"What did you do?"

"Stayed home. I needed the job for sure, but I needed my health even more. I'd rather hit the Central line than that picket line."

"What's the central line?"

"Central High School. I went to Knoxville High. Central was our big football rival. I was on the offensive line. Got my head bopped most of the time, but like I said, I'd rather beat heads with Central than fool around with that picket line."

Memories flashed in Don's head about that football coach who'd told him to go home until he could wear long pants. "What happened?"

"Nothin'. The union never got in, and the whole thing blew over. Had to quit the job anyway when I got into ROTC."

"ROTC?"

"Yeah, Reserve Officer Training Corps, at UT, the University of Tennessee. They had a rifle range on the top floor of one of the buildings. Shot .22s to our heart's content. I got into the flying cadets from ROTC."

Don would have told Bud about the CMTC, the journey through civilian employment to the infantry to his selection to the Flying Cadets, but he never got the chance. Someone else might have resented Bud going on and on about himself, but Don decided he didn't, at least not too much. He listened, sort of. The Tennessean was now among the small, select group of people he really trusted; people like Pete, his sister Elizabeth, Old Man Beattie, Sgt. Malone. Bud was big and brawny, a little foulmouthed at times, but confident and jovial, and there when you needed him.

And still talking. "Went to Maxwell for Primary, Macon for Basic. Ground-looped a PT-17 on my first solo. Well, it wasn't a ground loop, exactly." Bud laughed, but he'd caught Don's attention.

"What happened?"

"I only had five hours of flight time when I soloed."

"That's quick. My instructor didn't let me solo until I had almost ten hours."

"That's 'cause your instructor didn't have a contest going to see who could solo their student first. The guys at Maxwell put a keg of beer on it. Al Marsini, he was my instructor. He was bound and determined to drink first. Don't get me wrong; Al was topnotch, a real pro. I called him 'Mussolini' once. He didn't like that too much. Anyway, we were flying late one afternoon, he just climbed out and asked me if I could solo this thing, the Stearman. What're you going to say? 'No?' So I said, 'Sure, sir.' I tried to smile and just about choked on it, but I guess he didn't notice. He told me to taxi out, take off, climb to two thousand feet, do a 360 turn and have a look around, and then come back downwind and land."

"That's about what we did on our first solo, too."

"Well, I gunned the engine for takeoff and just broke ground when I got hit by some wind, from the cross runway, I guess. I hadn't had much practice with that, and before I knew it, the left wingtip dug into the ground, and I cartwheeled a couple of times, bounced around some, and headed into the trees. Ended up upside down about twenty-five feet up in the trees." Bud laughed again. "Soloed, though. Flew about as far as the Wright Brothers!"

"Upside down, *off* the ground, *in* the trees?" Don couldn't begin to figure out how the heck that happened.

"Yeah. Wrecked the airplane. I was hanging upside down, and the gas from the overhead tank was dripping down on me. Marsini came running up right away, yelling at me to unstrap and get outta there. He must've been runnin' alongside me down the runway. I'd give anything to have seen his face when I started cartwheeling. Anyway, when he got to me I was crying like a baby 'cause I thought they'd wash me out. But I unstrapped like he told me. Forgot how high I was and fell about fifteen feet to the ground. Could've broken my damn neck."

"They didn't wash you out, though."

"No, but I didn't know it then. Marsini helped me up and asked me if I was okay. He hardly said anything else all the way to Operations. Then they took me to the dispensary. The doc looked me over for about thirty seconds and said there was nothin' broken. Guy barely checked anything even though I was pretty scratched up. I'll bet he was just some damned orderly anyway. I went back to my room and started packing."

"For what?"

"I was damned sure I was gone. My roommate, Danny Romano, he was an okay fella, but our only relationship was last names starting with "R." Hardly ever saw him. Anyway, he kept telling me to stop packing, that they wouldn't throw me out. Well, nobody told me to leave so I showed up next day in the same flight suit. The thing still smelled sort of like gas, but I realized that somewhere along the way that I'd shit my pants, too. Hell of a mix!" Bud belly laughed at it all. "Wanna hear the real kicker?"

"Sure."

"Next day I soloed!" Bud was still laughing. "Marsini walked me out to another Stearman and asked if I thought I could fly it without embarrassing him." Bud hung over the rail, still laughing. Don laughed with him. "I don't remember what I said, but I soloed, and guess what?"

"I give up."

"Marsini got the keg!" Bud laughed at the memory. After that, it took him a couple of minutes to calm down. "I did Advanced in Orlando. Marianna. Best thirteen weeks of my life." He winked. "Know what I mean? So where'd you go?"

"Craig Field, Selma."

"Any good?"

"Sure. During our advanced flying we got some gunnery in the P-36 down at Eglin."

"Yeah. Well, never mind."

Bud was asking about girls, but he let the whole thing slide. He liked Don, even if the New Yorker was kind of different. But he'd done Bud a good turn with that roast duck. And the kid was polite, a good listener, and happy as a clam in the army, even with a war on. Funny, but it seemed that the war made life *easier* for him when everybody else was scared to death. Don was eager, more like *overeager*. For what, Bud had no idea. But he took the crappy details and never complained, and always got the job done. If the shooting started, Bud knew he would fly with him any day, and that was no small thing.

"Well, gotta get back to the game. These Midwest boys ain't as smart as they think. All I have to do is play dumb and the good old army might as well write their paychecks direct to me. I'll see you later."

"Okay."

Alone now at the ship's railing, Don was astounded how Bud could just laugh off the whole Stearman accident. He made up his mind that he'd never make a mistake like that. And if he did, he hoped he'd die in the crash. But he'd truly enjoyed Bud's company, even though he was just as glad to be alone again. In a way, he found himself wishing that he could be like Bud: happy-go-lucky, satisfied in his own skin, that sort of thing. There was no way he'd ever tell someone else about a screw-up like Bud's, no way in hell. But he was glad that Bud liked to talk so much about himself, because he didn't have to talk back. He had enough trouble keeping his own history right where it was.

Now Don relaxed some and turned his attention over the rails of the *Mariposa*'s main deck, and thoughts of Bud's accident gave way to the stunning view of the Pacific. It was January but not all that cold, mostly overcast and calm on deck, the prevailing winds almost matching the speed of the ship. It was a serene setting out to sea, where the gray colors were just right. The thunderstorm still crackled in the distance. Lightning flashed intermittently against the sky, but not too much, bothering no one, and the roll of the waves against the ship were almost intoxicating in their relentlessness. This was awesome, just watching it all. In a passing thought, he decided that if he hadn't become a pilot, he hoped he'd have been smart enough to join the navy. Same thought he'd had aboard the *Hunter Liggett*. Now he let his mind wander, trying to imagine where he was headed and what it would be like. The ocean was like that, too: full of mystery. He folded his arms over the rails and looked all the way to horizon, wondering how many miles it was out there, and what lay beyond.

40

Day three at sea: Don ate breakfast quickly and then headed for the lower decks. Though no one had given direct orders, word was out that the troops were expected to stay in their assigned areas, which meant staterooms or dayrooms. Passing over the poker once again, Don took an extended stroll along the main deck, found the stairs, descended another deck, and explored that. Not much else to do, so why not take in the whole ship? Even though the *Mariposa* was a pleasure cruise ocean liner, he didn't think of it as such. Stuffed with troops and equipment in just about every corner, it was anything but. He'd just keep snooping.

Several of the passageways and stairwells were either blocked off or locked up. But every chance he got, he descended. Despite all that dead reckoning he'd learned in pilot training, the endless passages and stairs soon had him turned around so much that he no longer knew which end was up or what direction he was headed. So what? He was curious to find out what lay ahead or below. Besides, it wasn't as though he had somewhere else to go, and no one had stopped him. As a matter of fact, he suddenly realized that he hadn't seen anyone in quite a while.

He reached what he guessed was the lower deck, or whatever it was that the maritime people called it. Before him was a double-sized door, with a sign fixed on it that read, "Authorized Personnel Only." A lock and chain hung unsecured beside one of the handles. He pulled the door open and entered.

This had to be the cargo hold. Alongside a fleet of jeeps and half-tons parked bumper-to-bumper were some huge crates, at least ten feet high by twenty wide, maybe thirty long, unidentified except for "U.S. Army Air Corps" stenciled in black. As he wandered among them, an armed private, obviously a sentry, came up behind him.

"Excuse me, sir, this is a restricted area. You shouldn't be here."

"Are you the only guard here?"

"Well, sir, I'm sorry, but..."

"Relax, Private. Do you know what's in these crates?"

"Sir, I really don't think..."

"Look, Private, I think you can see that I'm not Japanese. I was just curious to know what's down here, that's all. You've done your job. I'm leaving."

"Thank you, sir." As Don headed for a large door along the hold's bulkhead, the private called out and walked toward him. "Uh, sir, I heard some officers talking, and I think they're planes."

Don perked up. "Did you hear what kind?"

"T-40, I think, sir."

"No such animal, Private. Was it P-40s?"

"I guess so, sir. Are you a pilot, sir?"

"Yeah." *Jeez! P-40s. They must be ours!* He turned to the youngster, that is, the youngster who was barely younger than Don was. "Tell you what, Private... uh..."

"Carlson, sir."

"Private Carlson, you've done a good job. Sorry if I caused you any trouble. I'll leave the way I came in." Don headed out and then stopped short. "Private, there's a lock and chain on the door here. Isn't it supposed to be locked?"

"It's not, sir?"

"That's how I got in here, Carlson. Well?"

The kid's eyes were like saucers. "Oh, God! Yes, sir. I guess Bobby forgot to lock it when he left. I was supposed to check it. Oh, no!"

"No harm done. I'll get it when I leave." Don smiled and Carlson relaxed a bit. He started to leave again. "Hey, Private, had breakfast yet?"

"No, sir."

"I'll fix that. Stand outside the door, and I'll get you some chow. It may take a while because I don't know my way around the ship very well, but I'll scare something up and bring it back."

"Thank you, sir!" The boy saluted enthusiastically.

Don headed up to the main galley, where he found the cooks busy preparing the noon meal. He grabbed an egg sandwich, no, *two* egg sandwiches, and went quickly back to the cargo hold. He smiled to himself as he left the hold and secured the chain and padlock. Not long ago he'd been a private, just like Carlson.

✧　✧　✧

Don took the stairs two at a time, made a few wrong turns, and ran toward Pete's stateroom. He couldn't wait to tell Pete and Bud about the P-40s. But the stateroom was empty, Bud's, too. He checked his watch, and realizing he was late for the noon meal, hustled to the dining room. They were supposed to be in place by 1130. Seating was open, but the tables soon took on a character of their own, with the same group of guys sitting together meal after meal. Bud, Pete, and Don ended up at the same table, a small miracle but a welcome one. That day, his two best buddies had saved his spot between them. A waiter was serving soup when Don got to his seat, still panting from running up stairwells.

"Jesus," said Pete, "you look like you've just seen a ghost. You all right, Don?"

"Where you been, Captain, on the bridge checking the course?" Bud was such a smart ass.

"No. Guess what I found below."

"Below where?" asked Pete.

"In the cargo hold." Don lowered his voice to a whisper. "Boys, we have P-40s on board."

"And that's not all," Bud interrupted as he looked to his left, where a file of female officers, nurses he guessed, strolled into the dining room and took their places at the table next to them. The table had

had a "Reserved" sign on it for a couple of days but had remained empty. The men figured it was for the brass, so the tables closest to it were the last ones filled. No one in his right mind wanted their eating habits scrutinized by the big shots.

But this wasn't the brass. It was a table full of nurses, instant attention magnets that worked perfectly. The rumble of noise in the room ground to a halt, then slowly increased again.

Bud said, "I wonder where they've been the last few days."

"Can you believe this? The brass had 'em down below to protect 'em from us!" Pete was almost laughing as he spoke.

Bud gave the nurses a big wave and a smile. "Well, they can't protect 'em now! Ladies, how are y'all?" One or two waved back, the others ignored him.

The rest of the meal, Don tried to tell his buddies about the P-40s, but no one was interested. The chitchat was all about girls and changing prospects for the "cruise."

Don noticed that one of the nurses was different from the rest. She sat taller and straighter. She talked less. And she was pretty. No, she was *really* pretty, kind of beautiful. He began to pay more attention: not staring, but quick looks, long enough to take her in but short enough not to get caught. If she even hinted that she might look toward him, his eyes darted away.

41

The next meal was more of the same. Women remained the number one subject. Between peeks at the nurse, Don kept trying to tell the boys about the P-40s, but couldn't get anyone to listen to him. What the hell was wrong with these guys? Here they were, probably headed to a combat zone. The very planes they might fly were sitting below in the cargo hold, and no one cared? He couldn't understand it . . . and peeked at the nurse again. And with all this spare time on board, wouldn't it be a good idea to have a briefing or pass out P-40 manuals? Peek.

Bud Rollins was telling one of his off-color jokes about a loose farmer's daughter. Don shook his head. *They can hear us. And we're supposed to be officers.* Benny Andrews from Miami, Florida, strolled up and took his place as the table broke into laughter. Peek. He couldn't stop himself.

"Hi, fellas. Got stuck in the head."

"Head?"

"That's navy for the john. Hey, Don, what's the big joke?"

"I don't know. I wasn't listening." He nodded toward Bud. "Ask him yourself." Peek.

The crass talk around the ladies disgusted Don. He sat quietly the rest of the meal, peeked, then got up and left before the waiter brought dessert. Being January, it was already dark. Good. Knowing that most guys would head for the poker games, he went straight to his stateroom, hoping for some quiet time to himself. He climbed to the top bunk and lay on his back, hands clasped behind his head. Everything was perfect: lights out and nobody here to bother him.

He just stared at the ceiling. His mind relaxed enough to allow some thoughts in, but they weren't about the P-40s. They were about the nurse—the *beautiful* nurse. Anything that might distract him was shoved to the back burner so he could concentrate on this gal he didn't even know.

Up until now his "love life" had consisted of one incident years back, when he'd walked into Vic's room looking for another chance to earn a nickel by shining his older brother's shoes. Vic was on top of some girl whose dress was hiked up above her shoulders. She was naked below, and Donald could see legs spread wide and firm boobs bouncing gently as Vic arched his back and pumped feverishly. Both of them were grunting. Good thing Edna and Johnny weren't home.

"What are you doing?" Donald asked.

Vic rolled off the girl, who grabbed clumsily at her dress. The big brother with all the answers caught his breath. His eyes were halfway out of his head and he made no effort to cover himself. He whispered to his little brother.

"Donny. Shut the door, will ya?"

Donald was amazed how cool his big brother was. It was almost impossible to surprise Vic. He was so quick to turn anything to his advantage. In seconds, Vic had totally collected himself.

"Wanna try it?"

"Try what?"

"This. It's fun, Donny. Don't you worry. She won't mind."

Donald looked at the girl, who looked back, giving no indication whether she minded or not. She had pulled her dress back down, but Vic pulled it back up again as Don walked over to the bed.

"What do I do?"

"Just climb on. Come on, Bess, help him out."

And she did, even though Donald was a bit young yet. His body didn't work quite right, and he was clumsy. He got off almost as fast as he got on. And so his "love life" began. He never saw the girl again, hadn't felt anything special, and couldn't remember her name even though Vic had said it. Right now it wasn't worth the worry; just another thing his big brother taught him. He'd played Vic's game, and that was it. Now, lying in his bunk, Don knew that the brief encounter years ago had nothing to do with love.

But this nurse was different. He could feel it. And he wondered what she was really like. Would she ever be interested in him? She probably came from a rich family, insulated from the economic trauma of the 30s, and perched at the top of her class, with friends. In the dining room, she said little, but seemed comfortable and popular within the group, something he'd never been. He hoped she was as kind and gentle as she looked.

Ah, yes, "as she looked." There was a kind of growing tightness in his chest as he visualized her. Her image was crystal clear as he started a slow, full-body exploration in his mind. She had dark brunette hair, shoulder length with a slight, stylish curl. Her face was delicate, with creamy skin, a sharp but dainty nose and ears, a small mouth with perfect, white teeth, and lips that were just the right fullness, lightly accented with red lipstick. Her eyes were soft. Delicate shoulders led down to rounded breasts that looked smooth under her uniform, and the curves of her waist and hips gave way to slender, toned legs and ankles. He kept looking at the ceiling even though it was pitch black in his stateroom, wondering if he'd ever get to touch her, then imagining that they were alone and he was allowed, hoping that no one else had ever been there before him.

Good thing he was alone! He could feel his own heartbeat and blood rush. "Jesus, you dumbass. Calm down." Still, he kept her image right where it was. He had no idea how long he lay there, but it was a while, eventually long enough for him to slow himself down. In the quiet dark, he faded toward sleep a couple times, then forced himself to return. This was a feeling he'd never had about anyone. He wanted to hold on to it. But he was nervous and scared. Was this love? Geez, he'd never even spoken to her and wasn't sure if he had the guts. He'd been around girls before, and it was no big deal. Why was this so different? He wished he was taller, and better looking. Had she noticed him?

Well, he had no answers now. At least he knew he'd see her the next day.

42

Now there was a new reason that meals were Don's favorite time of day. He spent the next several sneaking more peeks at the nurse. One time he thought she caught him at it, but he wasn't sure. But if she caught him looking at her, wasn't she sneaking peeks, too? It was like some silly cat-and-mouse kid's game, made even more silly because it was being played by two adults. Good thing no one noticed; anyone paying attention would figure out pretty fast that there was something going on between them.

Fortunately, the officers' dining room returned to better decorum once the newness of the nurses' presence wore off. Bud Rollins told his dirty jokes elsewhere. Don preferred it that way. In the McGanley household, even Vic knew better than to use any type of vulgar language around the table.

The poker room was another thing, though. The pilots chattered on about conquests back home, the nurses' measurements, and opportunities to come. Maybe the nurses did their version of the same thing, though probably in more civilized language. It was part of the age-old axiom about putting boys and girls together. Sooner or later . . .

For the next several days, the dining room game went on. Don quit mentioning the P-40s. No one seemed to care, and since the pilots hadn't been told about them, he decided that it was meant to be that way. Instead, he found himself increasingly nervous playing his game with the nurse. She came to every meal, sat in the same place, and dined as gracefully each time. And Don peeked. If she noticed, she didn't let on. On day twelve at sea, he was just outside the dining room door when someone bumped into him. He turned, and there she was.

"Do you want to say something to me?"

"Uh, well, I . . ."

"Well, you've been staring at me for the last week. I was just wondering why."

He tried to gather himself. "Uh, because you're . . . um . . ."

"I'm what?"

"Pretty. You're very pretty." Her face softened, the beginning of a smile, and he asked, "What's your name?"

Now the nurse was taken aback a bit. "Mary-Louise. What's yours?"

"Don McGanley."

"And where are you from, Don McGanley?"

"Staten Island, New York. How about you?"

"Glens Falls. Ever heard of it?"

"Yes, I have. It's upstate. We used to go there on weekends when I was little. I have an aunt and uncle living up there, on a farm. Lots of places to play." He felt like a dummy, babbling on like that. He was pretty churned up. "What was your name again?"

"If I tell you, will you remember it this time?"

Geez, he felt like an idiot. He wanted to say something right, but nothing came. His face turned red; he looked down so she wouldn't see it. "Golly, I'm sorry." Then his memory kicked in and saved him. His head popped up. "Mary, right?"

"Mary-Louise, after my great-aunt. I was told the family name goes way back."

"I'll never forget it. Pleased to meet you, Mary-Louise . . ."

"Anderson."

"Okay. Pleased to meet you, Mary-Louise Anderson."

She liked that. He messed up but made it right, and she liked the way he did it.

Mary-Louise had grown up among well-to-do folks in upstate New York, classy but not snobby. Several of the pilots had come around asking her friends about her, but they all had some sort of chip on their shoulder; they seemed to think they had it made. It made her feel like some sort of prize in whatever game they were playing. She didn't like it. But this fellow was different, barely taller than she was, nice looking but not some hulky Buster Crabbe. He seemed a bit vulnerable, maybe unsure of himself, but willing to try. Donald didn't know it, but he'd done things just about right as far as Mary-Louise Anderson was concerned. She liked him.

43

Week three at sea: The cruise was getting long for everyone. No announcements or briefings, just guessing and rumors. With all the boredom and the cramped quarters, there were surprisingly few incidents, and even those didn't amount to much. Most of the time guys slept, played poker, or just lounged on deck. Don spent a lot of the day at the railing, just thinking about nothing, except when his mind was on Mary-Louise Anderson. He imagined her in a nice dress; wondered what she looked like when she was just lounging around.

"You spend a lot of time here, don't you?"

She'd startled him. He was so deep in thought, about her, that just about anyone could have walked up without him knowing it.

"Me?"

"Who else?" She laughed. His bashfulness was kind of nice. "I've seen you standing out here almost every day. We see each other at every meal, but you don't come up and talk to me."

He didn't answer that. She started to say she was interested and that she knew he was, too, then thought better of it. "What do you think about out here?"

He was still recovering. No way would he answer her honestly now. He wasn't ready. "Oh, nothing much." He turned his gaze back over the railing. His cheeks burned, though. He was nervous.

"Do you like the sea?"

"Yeah."

"Do you like being out here by yourself?"

"Yeah."

"Should I leave?"

He stood up abruptly. "No!" He said it too loudly, stiffened even more and turned to look at her. *Beautiful!* He took a deep breath. "I just wonder where we're headed, don't you? They haven't said a thing about it, and we're supposed to do the fighting."

"We were told at commissioning that they'd send us to combat areas, so I guess that's where we're headed. Jungles and snakes—I hate them!"

"More than they told us." He turned back to the railing.

"I guess there's a reason for that. You're a pilot, aren't you?"

"Yeah."

"What took you from Staten Island to being a pilot?" She'd surprised him for a second time, referring to his hometown. She remembered. He was nervous as hell just looking at her, couldn't imagine in a million years why she'd be interested in him.

"I joined the army and got into pilot training from there."

"Is your father a pilot?"

"No. He works in a grocery on Staten Island, called Roulstons. It's a local chain. He used to be the manager, but they demoted him to cashier when the Depression hit. I don't think he even knows I left home." That one said a lot. She caught it right away.

"What about your mother? Did she know you wanted to be a pilot?"

"Oh, she knew what I wanted, but she never wanted me to go into the service. We kind of fought over that before I left home. But she gave up, I guess. She even gave me her car when I left for flying school. My elder brother Vic had bought it for her for 422 bucks back in 1936. There was this Chevrolet garage on Bay Street and the salesman was Vic's pal, so he got the car cheap. But Mom never got a license and never drove it. She always took the streetcar or bus. It was a nice car, though: gray two-door. It ran okay but the brakes were pretty loose. I was going to use it for my license test when I was eighteen, but my brother-in-law convinced me to use his new '38 Pontiac. The steering was real tight on it and I flunked the test twice, so I ended up going back to Mom's car and finally passed. I had that Chevrolet all through pilot training and at Morrison Field. When we left for San Francisco, I had to sell it quick. Only got 136 bucks for it." *Damn! What a drawn-out babble that was! She must think I'm an idiot!*

A long pause. "Do you miss Staten Island, Don McGanley?"

"No." Again he answered too fast, too emphatically. But Mary-Louise had already filtered through the small talk about the dumb car and driver's test. She liked him and could see he was nervous, but didn't mention it. Even if he had a past that left him unhappy, he was polite. She couldn't help but think he must be a good man; a trustworthy one, but also determined, driven, and guarded. With so many guys out there looking for cheap thrills these days, it was good to meet someone different. It might take time, but she would find out about him. Oh, and he was good looking, too. She liked the way he combed his thick dark hair.

"I'll bet your parents miss you."

He didn't answer.

"Don't worry. They do."

He turned his head partway to her and raised his eyebrow. "How do you know?" Don was uneasy, but he liked this girl, even though it was obvious that she wasn't going to let this go. But at the same time, he didn't stop it, at least not yet, because it was *she* doing the prying, not some busybody he didn't care about.

Mary-Louise spoke softly, "Because parents, for all their personal faults and for all their mistakes, still love their children. It's just that they can't always show it or don't know how to show it, but they still love them. Sometimes their own troubles get in the way."

"You think so, eh?" Don needed to stop this. She was perceptive, too much so. If he'd had his head on straight, he would have asked about *her* family and perhaps where this keen insight came from. But he was off guard now. She'd managed to maneuver him into a secret place where he didn't like to go. He was unnerved that she'd gotten there so easily. Time to shift gears, and quickly. "You know what? I like you, Mary-Louise Anderson."

She looked right at him. "Why?"

That unnerved him even more, but he managed an answer without stammering. "Oh, I don't know. Because you're shorter than I am." He smiled and tried to look relaxed. "How's that?"

"Not very convincing." She laughed lightly, but knew she was inside his defenses. "You're hurt, aren't you? Tell me why."

"What do you mean?"

"What happened to hurt you so much?"

He felt dark. It took some long seconds for him to answer. "Nothing."

"It's okay now, you know." She was looking right at him. He couldn't hide anywhere. She saw that, saw how uneasy he was. And wisely stopped. "Know what I'd like to do?" And before he could answer, "Let's get up early and watch the sun rise. I've read about ocean sunrises in books and poems, but I've never seen one. Want to?"

Don realized he'd been looking down. He gathered himself and looked up. "Sure."

"Okay, then. I'll set my alarm for 4:30 a.m. and see you on the portside main deck."

He'd recovered now. "Portside? What are you, some sort of pirate?"

"No." She turned her nose up, but smiled. "I'm educated. Portside is the left, where the sun will come up. We're headed mostly south. So actually, the sun will come up toward the stern, but on the portside."

"You are a pirate."

"No, actually, one of the ship's officers told me."

"He didn't say 'portside' though. It's not even a word."

"It is now."

"You planned all this, didn't you?"

She smiled.

"Okay, I'll meet you at the portside stern. And by the way, set the alarm for 0430."

"I thought I said that."

"You said 4:30 a.m. Incorrect military time. If you're not careful, you could miss me and the sunrise by twelve hours." She laughed; he loved it. "Tell you what," he said. "We've been through so many time zones that I don't really know what time it is anymore. So let's just meet a half hour before sunrise. First light. How's that?"

She smiled softly at him and let her eyes rest on the young fighter pilot for a few moments. "Okay, Don. Until a half hour before sunrise then." She leaned over, kissed him on the cheek, and walked slowly away.

He just about melted. Don looked around quickly. Normally there were lots of guys roaming around on deck, but not now. How did she know that they were alone? Or maybe she just didn't care. Don turned back toward the ocean and leaned on the rails. He churned inside. He was a loner, had been one throughout his past, and remained one by choice. Yet this lady had challenged his barriers and won easily. Then just as easily, she let him off the hook. He realized that he didn't mind any of it.

The ocean view was there for the taking. He stood there for another half hour, looking out to sea, but didn't see anything. Except her.

44

Don couldn't think of a place he'd rather be: on deck, alone, at the stern, portside. It was forty minutes or more before sunrise, but a full moon was still up. He fought to focus his mind on the ocean. He could see the gentle whitecaps of the Pacific in the distance and the wake flowing away from the side of the ship. And then he looked aft, where the bluish-green churn from the two steam turbines marked the *Mariposa*'s path as far back as a mile. As the ship rocked slightly from side to side, he stared out over the rails at the vast, unending water, as impressed now as he was the first time he'd seen the sight. He tried to think about flying and airplanes and combat, but his reason for being here was none of those things. The reason was Mary-Louise Anderson. His heart was beating against his skin, for crying out loud. It wasn't supposed to do that first thing in the morning.

He tried to concentrate on the reason for this voyage, but two voices were talking to him at once. What will happen now? *I wonder if she's coming.* Where are we going? *I hope she does.* What will combat be like? *Maybe she won't.* I want to get to it—bad. *I want to see her—bad.*

He gave up and let his mind settle on Mary-Louise. She was beautiful in many ways, not just the way she looked, but also in the softness of her voice and the caring in her manner. She unnerved him. Even if he saw her coming a mile away, she'd still catch him off guard. She was amazing.

"Good morning, flyboy," Mary-Louise broke the silence.

He jumped, startled, and looked back over his shoulder at her, noticing the first rays of light on the horizon. He composed himself and faced her. "Good morning, Miss Anderson."

"Am I late?"

"Nope. Sun comes up in about fifteen minutes, maybe sooner."

She took a place beside him and they both leaned on the rails. For a few minutes, neither spoke. Then she said quietly, "You look so alone out here."

"That's the way I am, I guess."

"Why?"

"Oh, I don't know." His head dropped. "It's always been that way." Damn! He talked too much.

"Do you have brothers and sisters?"

"Yeah. Three brothers and one sister. I'm number four."

"So how can you be alone with such a big family?"

"Easy," he said with just a hint of bitterness in his voice, but she picked it up. Things were slowly coming together. He seemed to be so hurt. She wanted to help.

"Was it difficult at home?"

No answer.

"My mother and father and both of my sisters came to my nursing graduation. My parents cried, but so did I."

"I graduated from high school in January of 1938. Nobody came."

She noted the faint but pained look on his face. "But I'm sure they were proud of you. Your brothers and sisters, too."

No answer.

"And now you're a pilot. That's pretty hard to do, isn't it?"

"I guess."

"You're being modest. You know, I've never met a pilot before I met you. Are you any good?" She said it with a smile, expecting him to laugh, but he didn't.

Don turned and looked intently at her. "I have to be or I'm dead."

She looked right back. "Don McGanley, I came here because I want to watch the sunrise with you. You don't have to be or do anything else. Just be here with me, so you won't be alone and I won't be, either." They both turned back to the rails. Then she said softly, "I love it here."

It was getting lighter. They had five, maybe ten minutes before sunrise. Mary-Louise shuddered just a little and whispered something about being cold. Don had no coat or jacket with him and started to put his arm around her. Then he stopped, his arm awkwardly hanging in the air before he drew it back. She saw it, and saw him glance sideways at her, trying to be sly about it. He was struggling like some kid on a first date. It was endearing to her.

Over the past days she'd wondered whether she had a future with Don. She'd sensed it more each time she caught him looking at her. She'd let herself hope as they'd stood at the ship's rails on the lido deck. And now she knew. It would just take time, and that was the only question she had left. Would they have enough?

"Donald. I like that name."

"Mine?" By now Don's brain was bombarding him with signals. He could barely hear her over the rising noise. *Hey, stupid, why don't you kiss her?*

She smiled. "Yes, yours. Donald McGanley. Do you have a middle name?"

"Thomas. Only used when I'm in a lot of trouble."

She laughed, but softly. Oh, geez, he liked the way she did that. He inched just a little closer to her. Oh hell, he knew what to do, all right. God, she was beautiful! So why was he just standing there? His heart was beating faster and his mind was screaming at him, *Kiss her, ya dumbass!* But he didn't move. Mary-Louise turned toward him.

"Well, you'll be in a lot of trouble if you don't kiss me, Donald *Thomas* McGanley. I stayed awake all night, just like you did, and I don't want to be disappointed."

"How do you know how I slept?" *Go ahead and grab her!*

"You're stalling, Donald Thomas McGanley. Are you going to kiss me good morning, or do I have to embarrass both of us and make the first move?"

Don turned toward Mary-Louise just as the sun peeked over the horizon. He smiled at her; at least he thought he smiled. Jesus, he didn't know what he did! *Come on! Do it now! What the hell are you waiting for, dummy?* "Oh, I don't know."

"Yes, you do."

Go ahead and say "I love you," dummy! The sun rose and let loose a blinding streak of orange. *Kiss her, you idiot!*

The sun was brilliant on the water. Rays shot over the swells and arced into the sky, a spectacular shot that would last only seconds. Don reached up for her cheek, almost made it there, and then pulled his hand back. He put both hands back on the rails, looked out to sea. *I can't!*

"You know what? I wouldn't have missed this for the world, Mary-Louise Anderson. I'm glad you were here." His hands dropped off the rails, fell to his sides. And then he turned and left.

EASTERN AUSTRALIA

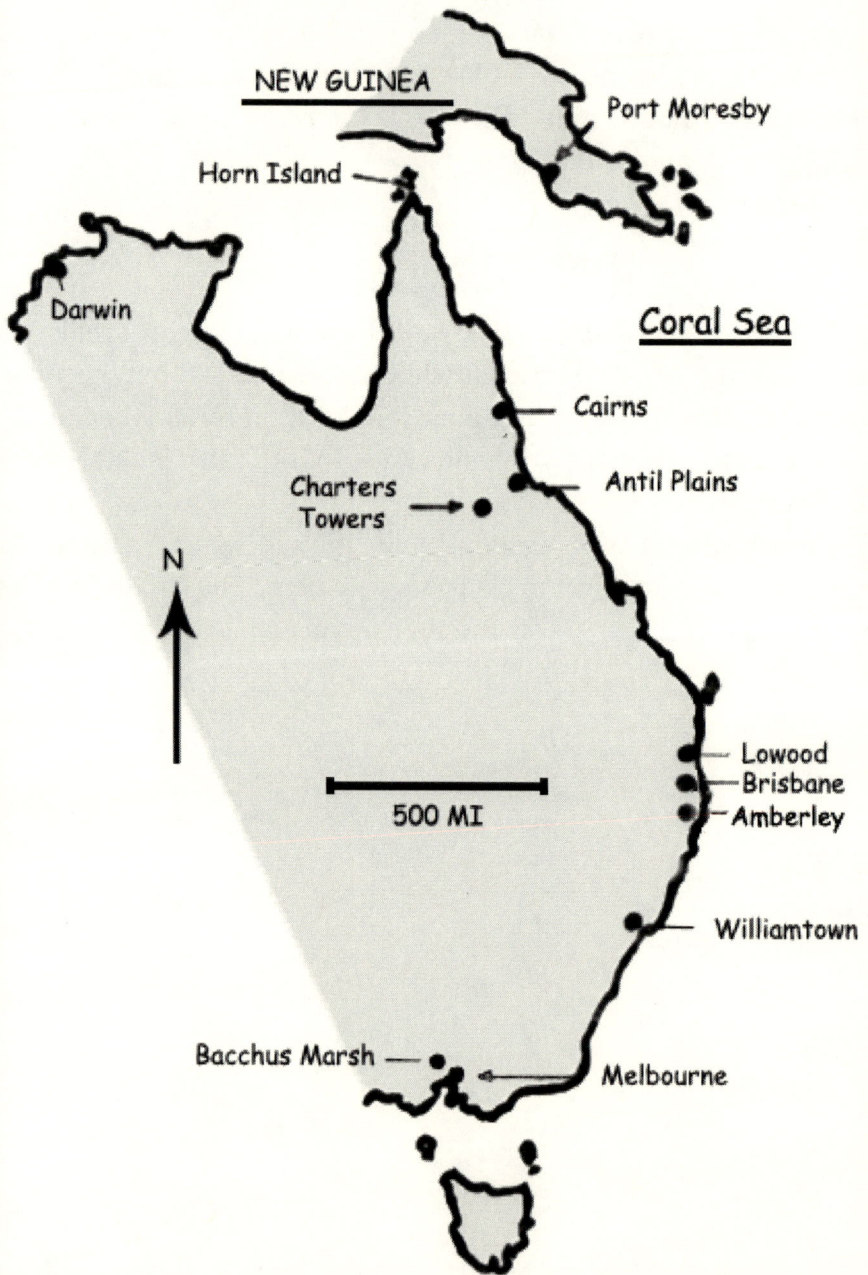

NEW GUINEA

Port Moresby

Horn Island —

Darwin

Coral Sea

Cairns

Charters
Towers →   • Antil Plains

N

500 MI

— Lowood
— Brisbane
• Amberley

• Williamtown

Bacchus Marsh —   Melbourne

Part 4

45

January 31, 1942

The *Mariposa* docked in Port Phillip Bay, Melbourne, Australia, just after noon. Unfortunately, the troops were told they wouldn't debark until 0900 the next day. Why? No one knew. Just another delay brought on by some big shot in charge who had no idea what he was doing. Irritating for most.

But for Don the delay left him a chance to see Mary-Louise again, even though he couldn't make up his mind what he would say to her. But she wasn't at the evening meal. Maybe breakfast. He got up early, packed his B-4 bag, and headed for the dining room, where he picked at his breakfast while he waited for her. She never came. In fact, none of the nurses did. Apparently, they'd already left. He'd blown it.

✧   ✧   ✧

The officers and men of the 49th Fighter Group dropped off footlockers and B-4s and assembled on deck at 0900, right on schedule for a change. The officers moved toward the ramp first, carrying only what they wore: khaki pants, shirts, ties, and flight caps. As they debarked, the same army captain who'd hollered from the rails three weeks ago in San Francisco told them to form up into two columns, just clear of the dock. Once again, there was a lot of wondering: *Where are we going, how far is it, and when will we start flying?* But no one complained because they were off the ship and moving. They were told to follow the man in front of them, and follow they did.

Don marched along head down for about an hour before Pete broke the silence. "Why so glum, Yank?"

Don didn't want to tell Pete or anyone else what was on his mind, but he hadn't fooled anybody. "Nothin'. It's just hot here. I can't believe I'm wishing for regular army utilities. They'd be a lot more comfortable than these shirts and ties."

"Pretty girl, wasn't she?"

"Who?" He was caught off guard. That seemed to happen a lot.

Pete laughed. "Who? How about that nurse you've been ogling at for the last two weeks. What's her name, anyway?"

There wasn't much use in trying to fool anyone, much less Pete or Bud. "Mary-Louise Anderson. But she didn't like me much anyway, so let's forget it."

"You know, we need to find a good party somewhere and get you hooked up with someone."

"Look around you, Pete. I don't think we're going to a party. Let's just forget it."

"You need a nice gal, Yank. Leave it to me. Once we get to the base, they'll probably turn us loose for a day or two while the brass figures things out. We'll head into town, and I'll take it from there. What do you say?"

"I say which base and what town? For cryin' out loud, Pete, we don't even know where we're going. I tried to get it out of Major Wurtsmith more times that I can count, but he wouldn't tell me."

"Don't change the subject. Boy, do you ever need to loosen up!"

"Pete, I thank you for being my social watchdog, but all I want to do right now is get busy with what we're here for, okay?"

"Don, look, we've been friends a long time now."

"Almost a year."

"So why don't you tell me what's going on with you, besides that pretty gal on the ship. You're always wrapped as tight as a rope. Gotta come from somewhere."

There was a slightly longer than normal pause and then Don laughed. "Okay, okay, you're right. When we get to this Australian paradise of yours, we can go find your long lost love, and you can find mine."

But Don hoped that wasn't so. There were other things to do now. They were getting closer and closer to the fighting with every step. So far the Japs were just a mixture of dangers, rumors, and fears about a horde of Mongols bent on taking over the entire world. It was long past time to get on with stopping them. The no-news, no-flying, no-training, no-briefing stuff was frustrating. They were marching like grunts, dressed like clerks, and sweating like pigs in the muggy 85-degree heat. Perhaps at the end of this hike things would start to happen. By his account, they couldn't start to happen fast enough.

As Don got lost into his own thoughts, Pete could only shake his head as he walked alongside. He and Don were good friends. No doubt the Yank would be a good man to have along in a pinch. The guy was serious, focused, and hardworking. Pete had never seen him get angry at anyone but himself, even when the raw deals came his way. It was almost as though Don expected them, the way he took things in stride. And he was a loner. Come to think of it, Pete couldn't remember Don approaching him or anyone else to ask for anything. It was always the other way around. He never told a joke and never talked about himself or his family or his years growing up on Staten Island, except for a few superficial statistics. Although Pete had tried several times, he couldn't get near Don personally. He wondered if anyone ever had. But he knew this: something was eating at the yank. Perhaps someday he'd find out what it was. For now, march on.

Shortly before dusk, those in the front of the two columns could see buildings up ahead, enclosed in an old gated fence with a sign that read "Bacchus Marsh." The place was deserted, obviously a base of some sort, but no longer used. After walking all day, the group was just happy to be anywhere they could get off their feet and sack out.

No one in authority said anything about food, and no one asked. The officers were directed to some old barracks and "quartered" there, with no beds or bedding. Without complaints, they picked out their own spots on the floor, lay down, and went to sleep.

✧   ✧   ✧

"Hey, there's food!" Don was startled out of a deep sleep, disoriented and sore from yesterday's trek. He looked at his watch, but couldn't read it in the pitch dark. Who cared what time it was? He was hungry; everyone else was hungry. Somebody yelled "food," and people were scrambling. Outside the barracks, a tent had been set up with a single floodlight overhead, and it looked like a line was forming. Sure enough, each man got a two-inch diameter potato and a piece of mutton, not much for the first meal since leaving the *Mariposa.* Don was sitting against the barracks with an empty mess plate when Pete walked up.

"You going to get something to eat, or do you expect the buffet to come to you?"

"Already ate."

"Oh . . . yeah. Well, I forgot to think. You were probably first in line."

"If I'd moved as slow as you do when I was growing up, I'd have starved to death. Number four out of five kids. Not a good place in the lineup, especially when there's only three potatoes."

"Yeah? What about kid number five?"

"Baby brother. I split my potato with him, assuming I didn't have to give my portion up."

"This is a joke, isn't it?"

"No, absolutely true."

Pete didn't know what to say about that. He looked down at his mess plate. "Never had this kind of meat before. Know what it is?"

"Mutton, I think. Lamb or goat or something like that."

"Not the best I've ever had, but it'll do, I guess. Nice of the brass to bring along a chuck wagon. You know, I just saw Wurtsmith. He said we're staying here the rest of the day and getting on a train tomorrow."

"Did he say where to?"

"Nope. Maybe he doesn't know yet."

"He knows, all right." There was frustration in Don's voice, caused by that itch to start flying that he couldn't scratch. It had been almost six weeks since he'd even seen an airplane. Pete was smart enough to see that Don was better off without company right now. He tossed the New Yorker a casual wave, said something about finding Bud Rollins or a poker game somewhere, and headed off to put some distance between them. Smart guy, that Pete.

Don looked around, trying to decide how to spend the rest of the day in a place where there was nothing to do. Not much to see, really, so he headed out the gate and wandered away into the wooded area that surrounded the "base." He took up a spot next to a tree he couldn't identify and made himself comfortable in the still, humid air, if that was possible. At least he was in the shade. He allowed the mystery of their destination and the P-40s he'd seen to fade. A slow gaze around his spot uncovered a snake not more than fifteen feet away. He'd heard that Australia was full of poisonous snakes. So what? After the march the day before and no shower today, he was getting a little ripe. No, he was actually *very* ripe. If that appealed to this guy, then let him have it at it.

He thought about Mary-Louise. He hadn't spoken to her since that morning at the rail, only saw her a time or two after that and only for a few seconds. He looked for the snake again. It was still there, flicking out its tongue. He shut his eyes and started to smile as he remembered a time when she'd told him how scared she was of reptiles and jungles and such. He wondered where she was now and if he'd ever see her again. He wished to hell he'd kissed her that morning on the ship, but she'd pushed him before he was ready. He said out loud to himself, "I think I love this gal," without worrying whether or not anyone had heard him, because no one had. And he made up his mind that he wouldn't blow it a second time if that second chance ever came.

46

Melbourne, Australia, February 20, 1942

Mary-Louise Anderson was beat. She claimed a corner on the third floor of a new hospital, only a skeleton of a building, but at least a quiet place for now. She tried to close her eyes for a few minutes.

Since the *Mariposa* had docked in Melbourne three weeks ago, the advance team of eight nurses had been working up to twenty-hour days setting up a tent hospital in Royal Park. In hot, humid conditions, they received and stored medical supplies, set up wards, and equipped makeshift operating rooms. The operation was to be up and running by the time their unit arrived, maybe a week from now. Under destroyer escort, they'd sailed from New York on the *U.S.S. Thomas H. Barry* on January 23.

Established early in 1940 as the 56th General Hospital, the unit was originally stationed at Fort Jackson in Columbia, South Carolina. After Pearl Harbor it was re-designated the 4th General Hospital. Staff numbers grew rapidly, including more than 120 nurses by the time it sailed from New York. When Mary-Louise volunteered for army duty while working at Lakeside Hospital in Cleveland, she was immediately assigned to the 4th and sent to San Francisco with seven others. They were among the first American nurses in Australia.

The nurses had been officially quartered at hotels downtown, but it wasn't worth losing sleep by going back and forth to the work site. Instead, they slept in the tent wards. Hotels served only as a place to take an overdue bath or keep footlockers and personal gear.

The War Department's Medical Corps was growing fast at that time, reorganizing as it went. When the war started, only 1000 nurses existed in the entire army. Six months later, there were 12000. Hospitals were categorized as Field, Evacuation, General, Station, and Surgical as they receded from the front lines and graduated in levels of care. Later on, portable surgical hospitals, called "Backpackers," were established in the forward areas, but not until the last months of 1942. "General" hospitals were the first level with electricity and running water, providing long-term recuperation and therapy, after which troops could return to the front. (Those who couldn't were shipped to Station Hospitals or Surgical Hospitals, which usually meant that for them, the war was over.)

Construction of the ten-story, one-thousand-bed hospital next to Royal Park was to be complete sometime in May. Once open, the Australians would turn it over to the Americans at no cost, a reciprocal part of the lend-lease agreement between the two governments. As construction progressed, the nurses transferred the medical operation from the tents to the building, floor-by-floor. There was no extra time to waste: sick and wounded were already arriving.

Mary-Louise was glad she was here. There was purpose in this chaotic, frenzied life. She'd made good friends, especially Kate Maine, who kept her moving long after her body had given up. Kate was a special breed: tough but straight, funny and fun, and dead serious when she needed to be. She was a natural leader, a role she took on even though she was not officially named as such. The nurses responded to her. Everyone seemed to understand the serious nature of the war they'd been drawn into, and the race against time to get this place fully operational. Despite long hours and endless tasks, no one complained and no one slacked off. A lot of that was due to Kate Maine's leadership.

"Tired?" Kate Maine looked down and smiled at Mary-Louise, who looked right back up and smiled through a couple of dark-circled eyes.

"Of course not."

"You're hard to find sometimes."

"Intentionally."

Kate sat down next to her best friend. Friendships seemed to be made quickly and easily, especially now. The growing war made everything more intense: by fear, unknown, adventure and danger, and the notion that no one knew how much time they really had left. "Well, what do you think of this little adventure we've gotten ourselves into?"

Mary-Louise said, "I'm glad we're here. It's not exactly what I expected, though."

"That's for sure. Four months ago, we were civilian nurses at Lakeside. Remember that place on East Ninth where you all took me for my birthday?"

"Yes, I do. We were all going to marry rich Cleveland doctors and settle down on huge, sprawling estates on the south shore."

"So much for that. And I'm a long way from Nashville."

"You don't sound like a Tennessean."

"Nashville, *Illinois*, Mary-L. Population 3,210. Fifty miles east of St. Louis."

"Do you miss home?"

"Not really. Nashville was just a small farming town. If I'd stayed, my mother and dad would've probably hitched me to some local guy by now. I'd be knee-deep in diapers and growing corn or soybeans or wheat or something. Remember 'Blue Moon'? Red Jankowski used to have a bar down by the railroad station. Half the town would go to Red's on Saturday night, drink Falstaff, and listen to 'Blue Moon.' Only a few people had electricity at home, so Red's was the only place we could listen to the radio." Kate sort of sighed as she reminisced. "Oh well, I saw a cute fella on the ship."

"Which one was that?"

"He waved at us, remember?"

"You mean the loud one?" Mary-Louise added, "He was obnoxious!"

"But he was really cute." Kate had a sly look on her face.

"If you think so. Did you talk to him?"

"We were supposed to stay away from the boys, remember? I guess they didn't want us to get pregnant." Kate laughed. "Well, once I talked to him, maybe a couple times. His name is Bud Rollins. He wouldn't tell me his real first name." She winked. "I didn't listen to that silly order any more than you did."

"It's probably awful."

"What is?"

"His first name."

Kate looked away, kind of gazing at nothing. "I wonder where he went."

"I have no idea, except that it's where the fighting is."

"I'll bet you're wondering where your guy went, too."

"Which guy?"

Kate laughed again. "Mary-L, you're a sweetie, but you don't fool anybody." She paused, waiting for some sort of response, but didn't get one. "I saw you two at the railing one day. Come on, what's his name?"

Mary-Louise debated with herself. Maybe Kate was her new best friend, but she was a talker, too. She'd been thinking a lot about Don McGanley lately, but she kind of wanted to keep it to herself. She'd liked the way he was . . . gentlemanly and not loud like so many of the other flyers had been. And he was private, and vulnerable, and distant, which only made her want to learn more about him. He didn't curse, either, or at least she hadn't heard him.

She knew she was attracted to him and wanted to find him again. And she'd been willing to kiss him. No, it was more than willing: She'd *wanted* to. She hadn't felt like that about anyone before. She'd kissed boys a couple of times, but never for real. Her mind went to that sunrise on the *Mariposa*. Why had Don walked away like that? She wasn't angry over it, not hurt, not even sure if disappointed was the right word. He needed her or somebody. He just didn't know how to ask. Maybe that's what it was. Oh well, she was here in Australia now, and he was God-knows-where, at least until this war was over. Most likely, she'd never see Don again, anyway.

"Hey, you!" Kate caught Mary-Louise daydreaming.

"Don McGanley. His name was Donald McGanley. He was from New York City."

"Well, what was he like?"

"I don't know. He was quiet, and very polite, you know, kind of different."

"You're not saying much."

"Neither did he." She paused. "I just know I liked him."

"And he liked you."

"And what makes you say that?"

"He looked at you all the time. Actually, it was kind of cute the way he'd take these quick peeks at you in the dining room. I counted them one day, eight times in one minute. Are you going to sit there and tell me you didn't notice?"

"Well, okay, maybe I did. He was real shy. I had to go talk to him. I don't know if he ever would have talked to me on his own."

"Cute."

"I wish I could have seen more of him. He was so private. He'd start to tell me something and then he'd stop. I think he wanted to talk to me, but he was afraid."

"Of what? Us?"

"I don't know." Mary-Louise looked away from Kate. "I wish I could have seen him more. I really liked him."

"You said that. Maybe you love him, but you're too scared to think it or say it."

"I'm not scared, and it's none of your business, Kate."

"Ha! I'm right!" Kate let that sink in. "Well, I can understand why you two didn't talk much. You know, you don't exactly come across as the down-home type, Mary-L. You can be a little stiff with all this upstanding, debutante stuff. I'll bet that scared him off."

Kate sure was blunt, but accurate. Mary-Louise's family was pretty well off. She'd grown up in the best part of Glens Falls, the eldest of three girls, learned proper manners, and wore dresses all her life. One of her younger sisters had been somewhat of a tomboy, complete with ball, bats, and shorts. Mary-Louise had tried to put a stop to it, taking her shopping for "proper attire." Her father, dutiful and wealthy, owned some successful horses in Saratoga and frequently traveled back and forth to New York City on business. Her mother was a chapter president of something called the PEO, apparently some super-secret organization of the well-to-do which did not include men. She wouldn't even tell Mary-Louise what it was. Maybe the Andersons weren't filthy rich, but they were plenty influential around the community, with a lot more money than most. The way they raised their three girls reflected it.

"I'm not stiff."

"Sure you are. You're the prim and proper queen of the prom. Maybe he thought you were a snob."

"What?"

"We all did before we got to know you. So maybe he thought so, too, and didn't want to take a chance. Men can't handle it if we brush them off, you know. I suppose you two didn't do anything more than talk." Kate had a sneaky look on her face.

"*That's* none of your business."

"That means no."

"Busybody."

"That's what friends are for. So I'll tell you what. We'll keep an eye out and watch for both of them. Bud and Don sat at the same table all the time, so they must know each other. I bet they're friends, and if we remember them, you can bet they remember us. Trust me, I know men."

"I'd like to see him again."

"That, Ms. Mary-L, is obvious."

47

The train carrying the 49th Fighter Group left Bacchus Marsh for Newcastle in New South Wales. From there they went by truck to Royal Australian Air Force (RAAF) Williamtown, arriving on February 10. It would be home for the next three weeks. The group was now officially made up of the 7th, 8th, and 9th Fighter Squadrons, with Don, Pete, and Bud assigned to the Ninth.

Williamtown was a real military airfield with real barracks, and best of all, three Wirraways (Australian T-6s) lent to the Americans by their Aussie hosts. Don was the first man up the next morning, the first to volunteer, and the first to fly. He went up seven times over the next seven days, short around-the-flagpole sorties, but priceless half hours after going so long without flying. He wore out the Wirraway with plenty of high-G aerobatics, and even scared the crap out of his copilot by doing a full-rudder snap roll, a maneuver forbidden during pilot training. Even so, an instructor at Craig had showed him one; might come in handy in combat.

While taxiing in from his seventh sortie, Don slowed and gazed at two brand-new P-40s that had flown in while he was airborne. And they had U.S. markings!

✦　✦　✦

February 26, 1942

"Who's ready to go?"
The Operations Officer stood before a dozen lieutenants and pointed toward the two P-40 E-models. He talked as though they'd

all been joyriding through the war, and now it was time for the "Junior Birdmen" or "Yardbirds" (from the *Snuffy Smith* comic) to grow up.

Don resented it. This guy had a lot of gall to look down his nose at them. Whose fault was it that they hadn't flown? Theirs? Three weeks on the ocean and no briefings, no manuals, nothing to prepare them for what lay ahead. Don's six rides at Morrison Field and seven here at Williamtown, a total of nine hours, were the most in the group, but that hardly qualified as P-40 training. No one standing there had done any regular flying in almost 80 days. He'd heard about enough from this guy: *Ah, the hell with it.*

"I am."

"Okay." The Operations Officer looked down and started to write on his clipboard.

Bud Rollins jabbed him in the ribs and whispered, "Are you nuts? When you going to learn, McGanley? Never volunteer!"

"Better than standing around listening to this."

"What do you know about a P-40?"

"I worked on them back at Mitchel. An airplane's an airplane."

"And a rowboat's a ship, just like that *Mariposa*, right?"

"Well, we got to start sometime. I'm tired of doing nothing."

The Operations Officer finished his scribble, motioned toward one of the P-40s. "Good. Take that first one. Fly around for a while, get the feel of it, and land. Make a long downwind and give yourself a good five- or ten-mile final approach. Don't rush."

"Yes, sir." Don headed toward the P-40, but stopped short and looked back. "Don't I need to get a parachute, first?"

"In the airplane!" The yell came from a crew chief in the cockpit. "C'mon, Lieutenant, I'll give you a quick course on this baby."

The crew chief extended his hand and pulled Don up on the wing. He climbed in the cockpit and looked around. *Jeez, big airplane!* At least the starting procedure was the same.

"Okay, Lieutenant, when you're ready to take off, feed the throttle in slowly. There's plenty of power. Once you're rolling, hold the stick in neutral and it'll just fly off the ground. Piece of cake!"

"Okay."

"Once you get the gear and flaps up, put the throttle at 2,300 (RPM) and 30 (inches of mercury). That oughta give you about 230 mph. Flies like a dream."

"Thanks for the info, Sarge. How long have you been around these airplanes, anyway?"

"About twenty minutes. Just got the scoop from the guy who ferried it over here. No sweat, though."

Not exactly. There was plenty to sweat about. The P-40 produced up to 1200 horsepower, twice what a T-6 did. That meant lots of rudder was needed to counter the engine torque. The main wheels were less than ten feet apart, short by most standards, which made it less stable. And it was a "taildragger," with the nose so high in the air it was hard to see over the cowling, especially for Don. And finally, the blue skies above belied difficult weather conditions. It was windy, almost twenty miles per hour, all crosswind. Those winds would push against the flat side of the vertical tail, causing the airplane to nose back into the wind, "weathervaning" in pilot-speak.

He hadn't thought about all that; his hands were full now. This was his first test in a *real* fighter. He was awed by it: its size, its power, its immediate response to *his* commands as he pushed the throttle forward. Practically standing to see over the nose, Don went straight about forty yards, then stepped on the left brake, and turned onto the runway. Just as the untrained, unskilled, but well-intentioned crew chief advised, he added power slowly.

Immediately, the P-40 began to drag to the left from the engine torque. Don added right rudder to straighten out, then wind gusts from the same direction slapped against the tail, and the airplane weathervaned back to the right. Hard left rudder to stay on the runway, hard right, then left, and right again. *Shit!* That simple takeoff, "hold it neutral until it flies off the ground," had now turned into a wild, swerving, seesaw-type battle between Don and the P-40, which had somehow forgotten who was supposed to be in charge. The fighter went off the left side of the runway, bucked and heaved over sand and grassy clumps, still accelerating. Screaming at himself, Don said the hell with it all and yanked back on the stick. Four thudding but ever-lengthening skips later, he was in the air.

✧   ✧   ✧

The P-40 flew like a dream; at least the chief was right about that. Don was settling down now. As he returned for landing he started to enjoy the view below, the feel of the P-40, and the powerful hum of the Allison engine. He knew the rest of his squadron mates had probably laughed themselves silly at his takeoff, and he knew that now they'd be watching him return for landing. The Operations Officer had told him to fly around the airfield and then set up a long, easy straight-in—nothing fancy. Don thought about that. A tight, circular "overhead" pattern might seem more risky, but it would also allow him to see his landing point all the way through his final turn. On a straight-in, the runway would disappear over the nose as he got closer and slower.

He decided to keep his speed up on final; the lower nose attitude would help him keep sight of the runway longer. He also noticed that the crosswinds were increasing, probably well over 20 mph by now. Just above the ground he'd have to dip the wing into the wind and add a lot of left rudder to straighten the nose for landing. He'd had almost no practice doing it; at pilot training they cancelled flying for crosswinds like this.

With two miles to go, he reminded himself out loud, "Okay don't get cute. Just put it on the ground and walk away. Screw 'em. Let 'em laugh."

The airplane that had been so smooth at altitude fought him all the way down the final approach. The nose drifted back and forth with the changing wind gusts. For a second it would try to level off or even climb, the next second it felt like it would fall out of the sky. Just above the runway, he moved the stick right and added left rudder. The plane sank immediately. He added power and pulled back on the stick to avoid landing hard. The plane "ballooned," a slight climb, though it felt like more than that. *Christ!* Another seesaw ride. Finally, the right wheel touched about halfway down the runway, but it seemed like he was going farther right, off the runway. He stomped the left rudder but the left wheel still hung in the air. Back left with the stick, just enough to start it down.

But it was too much correction. The left wheel hit and the P-40 swerved to the left, off the runway and into the sand and weeds. Don was no longer a pilot, just a rider bucking over the small dunes. He fought for control, but one at a time, the wheels dug into the sand. He was thrown forward and down as the tail came up and the left wing caught the sand. He braced himself with one hand on the dash, the other in front of his face, and ducked. Finally, mercifully, the P-40 thumped to a stop, standing on its nose, about twenty degrees past vertical. He felt the blood rushing to his head and then he smelled gasoline. *Get out!* He tugged at his lap belt and shoulder harness, both of them held even more secure by his weight. At least he'd gotten his canopy open. He'd fall right out if he could get this fucking harness off.

He couldn't see the gas, but it was leaking for sure. Strong smell! Still struggling with his belt and harness, he heard shouting. An Aussie. The guy had come running from an adjacent field, just a local farmer, but Don's eyes bulged wide when he saw a lighted cigarette flopping from the Aussie's lips.

"You okay, mate? Thought you'd be a goner for sure! That was the . . ."

Don's eyes bulged. "Get the fuck outta here! Now!" The Aussie looked stunned but backed away as Don yelled again. Jesus, he'd be blown to bits if the idiot dropped the cigarette. Hell, the airplane was about to blow anyway. *Forget the fall, just get out!* Don finally managed to twist the harness buckle and fell straight down, bouncing over the windscreen, and through the prop. He hit the ground with a thud, rolled to his feet, and ran.

Amazingly, the fighter never blew. Far enough away, Don stopped and bent over at the waist with his hands on his knees, trying to catch his breath. He turned around, slowly stood up, and watched it. His instinct for survival slowly but surely gave way to the realization that he'd screwed up. He found himself wishing the P-40 had blown, with him still strapped in it.

Within minutes, a jeep sped up to him, a driver and the Operations Officer. The captain leapt out and grabbed Don by both shoulders.

"Lieutenant, are you okay? Lieutenant? Lieutenant!"

Don didn't answer. He just stood in a daze, staring blankly at the banged-up P-40.

48

The best way for a boss to react after one of his pilots wrecks an airplane is to get that pilot back in the air again. Bud Rollins' primary instructor knew that after his first solo attempt, and the 9th Fighter Squadron's Operations Officer knew it now. Two more P-40s flew in from Melbourne the same afternoon Don crash-landed, with more due in. The next morning, he dropped the dumb wisecracks about "Yardbirds" and "Junior Birdmen" and pulled Don aside.

"Lieutenant, I'd like you to fly today. Feel up to it?"

"Yes, sir!" He really did. Don hadn't slept a lick, hadn't even tried. He kicked himself all night long over the accident and wondered if he'd ever get another chance. And here it was.

"Good. I'm sending you up with Rollins. You guys stay together in formation, get comfortable flying the thing, and then come back for one landing. Fly a long straight-in to the runway."

"Yes, sir."

The Operations Officer looked directly at Don. "McGanley, I'm not going to stand here and tell you not to worry about yesterday. If you fly long enough, stuff like that will happen. How many hours do you have in the P-40?"

"None."

"Not correct. Twenty-five minutes, remember? Here's the point. If you let yesterday affect you now, then you won't have learned much. I want you to put that sortie to work for you. Go up there and make yourself better." He paused, then grinned at Don. "After all, you're the most experienced P-40 pilot we have." Don grinned back and went to round up Bud Rollins.

✧   ✧   ✧

There was no wind that day; not a cloud in the sky, either. Don and Bud took off uneventfully and headed east. They rat-raced over the vast, open Pacific, taking turns as the leader. The Warhawk performed beautifully: loud, powerful, responsive, and smooth. Supposedly it could reach thirty-one thousand feet, but there was no need to go that high today. And it was fast, topping 350 miles per hour several times during dives. It was as much fun as Don had ever had in an airplane; they could have stayed out there until the gas ran out. With Bud leading, they headed back, splitting up for separate straight-ins about 10 miles from Williamtown.

As he'd done the day before, Don flew the long straight-in. He'd meant to ask about flying a simple overhead pattern and landing, but after yesterday, he didn't think it was a good idea to question the captain. He'd ask after he got down. Now, having slowed to landing speed three miles from the runway, Don pushed the throttle slightly forward to maintain 105 mph. The engine didn't respond. He looked down as he pushed the throttle forward even more. Still no response.

"Aw, shit!" Don's heartbeat accelerated as fast as his speed decayed. His eyes darted to the engine instruments. Manifold pressure was fine, but engine RPM was rolling back no matter what he did with the throttle. He looked at the runway; he'd never make it. The ground was rocky below and patchy trees gave him no place to set the airplane down. "Come on, baby, don't do this to me."

But the airplane wouldn't listen. Don felt the first nibbles of aerodynamic stall, a buffeting which would continue until the P-40 simply refused to fly. Then it would roll over and slam into the ground. He was a dead man. *"Goddammit!"* he yelled as he unstrapped and pulled the canopy back. He ran the trim wheel back to keep the nose up, then held the stick level and slightly back as he stepped out onto the wing. It was all he could do to maintain his balance in the wind as the plane shook with rapidly increasing intensity. There was no time left. Don reached for the D-ring on his parachute harness and pulled as he dove off the trailing edge of the wing. The parachute opened immediately. After two short swings, he landed hard. The P-40 crashed in seconds, only fifty yards away.

49

Don sat head down against the side of the barracks. He was thinking about that dumb flight doc. "Take the day off," he'd said, right after his second post-crash examination in as many days. What the hell kind of advice was that? Didn't he realize what had just happened? Didn't he know he was talking to the same guy as the day before? The jackass acted like being in an accident was like eating a sandwich. Even the fellow who'd picked him up in an ox cart seemed to see his plane crash as a non-event. And one smartass who Don didn't even know had passed through the medical tent and made some crack about being "on your way to becoming an ace."

He felt sick. He remembered the pit in his stomach when he'd pushed the throttle forward, saw the relentless decay in speed, and knew he wasn't going to make it. How could this happen? He leaned his head back against the building and clamped his eyes shut, as if that would make it all go away.

"There you are." It was Bud Rollins. "I just heard what happened, Don. Jesus, that was close! You okay?"

"No!" Don practically shouted it without looking up.

Bud was quiet for a minute. "Don't be too hard on yourself, fella. If the damned airplane don't work and you can't land, you jump. That's what you did. I'd say you did the right thing."

"Well, I don't. I should've rode it in. And that damned thing yesterday should've blown up."

Rollins sat down. "Look." He started to tell Don about his own landing, an unceremonious splat, but he changed his mind.

"Bud, I'm over here by myself for a reason. If I wanted company, I wouldn't be sitting here. Now give me some room, okay?"

"Don, you did the right thing. I just came from Ops. Even Wurtsmith was talking about it. In fact, he's looking for you now."

"Two friggin' airplanes! I can't believe I did—"

"Did what? You worried about yesterday, too? Look, those two days had nothing to do with each other. Nothing! The Ops O blew that yesterday, plain and simple. Too damned windy, especially since nobody's flown these birds before. If it was so easy, then why the hell didn't he fly? And today? The airplane quit working, and that's it." He paused. "Hey! You know, all we can do is what we're told, and with all the wonderful flying we've been given, hope like hell we don't kill ourselves before the Japs get their chance. Personally, I'm kinda glad you're still around to do all the volunteering."

Bud grinned as he said it and looked for a reaction, but got none. Don still sat with his forearms resting on his knees, head down. Bud's grin changed to a frown. "What the hell's the matter with you, Don?"

Don still didn't answer. Bud said, "You know, I'm kinda slow sometimes, but I think I've got this figured out. For some reason, you think you've got to prove something to yourself, don't you? All this eager beaver stuff isn't to show off or impress us, it's to impress *you*."

"Look, Bud—"

"No! *You* look! I don't know what happened in your life to make you feel like you have to be first all the time, but I'm tellin' ya that it's about *fuckin'* time it stopped! Christ, if they took volunteers to stand up in front of a firing squad, I swear you'd be at the head of the line! You think you're the only one around who's had it tough or fucked up a few times? Well, join the club, McGanley!"

"I just wrecked two goddamned airplanes! What do you think I should feel?"

"Scared! Relieved! Or how about just glad to be alive? Glad you had enough skill and moxie to get through the first one and walk away. And glad that you had the sense to jump out of the second one when most of us wouldn't have got out in time. You know, I don't know what the captain was thinking with that 'Who's ready to go?' crap. I felt like flattening his face after the 'Yardbird' stuff, and then he tries to push us into something we're not trained for. But you were the only one with the guts to speak up and try. Maybe that was dumb. I sure as hell had no intention of saying anything. But the way things turned out these last two days, I'd say you're pretty damned lucky. With all the cards stacked against you, you're still alive and kickin'. Now, lighten up, McGanley, before you force me to get your attention, right in the fuckin' chops!"

Pete Melford came around the corner. "Thought I heard you guys. So has everybody else. Hey, Don, Wurtsmith's looking for you."

Don said, "Pete, leave us alone, will you?"

Bud held up his hand. "No, Pete, stay here! We can take turns knocking some sense into McGanley's head." And he turned to Don. "Look, McGanley, nobody expects you to be happy about this, but you have to quit frettin' about everything. You act like this war is something we should *want* to get into. What are you, nuts? You're carrying around some crap that you should have dumped a long time ago, and it ain't doin' you one damned bit of good. Anybody with a lick of sense would rather be someplace else, like home."

"You don't know what you're talking about, Bud."

"Yeah? Well, I'll tell you this. I don't want to get killed because you've got your head up your ass trying to prove something to yourself! We don't fly solo around here. We fly in groups, flights, you know? We're going to need each other to stay alive."

Then Pete took his turn. "This war—some of us are going to get killed, Don. Planes are going to crash. We're probably going to get bombed. The only way we're going to get through this is to look out for each other and keep our heads screwed on. And maybe we can get home in one piece."

Don didn't answer. *What home?*

Bud's turn again. "He's right, Don, and you know it, don't you?"

Finally, Don looked up, and Pete said, "Why don't you come into town with me and Bud? I spoke to some Aussies and they told us where the ladies like to go. Look, it's just what you need. I'll even let you have the pretty one."

"Not tonight, Pete."

There was dead silence. Pete and Bud looked at each other. Their friend was down with no way to pick him up. The guy seemed unreachable. Both of them had known guys who came into the service for all kinds of reasons: some for the adventure, some because of pedigree, and some for the pure ego of being a pilot. Don was different, driven by other reasons. Bud shook his head, but ever the conniver, Pete winked at him, like he had an idea, a way to appeal to what mattered to Don most.

Pete said, "I know where we're going."

Don stood up in a hurry. "Where?"

Pete looked over at Bud, then back at Don. Pete thought to himself, *Look at this guy. Two seconds ago he was ready to shoot himself. Now he's an eager beaver again.* "Lowood Station," he said. "I think it's near Brisbane. We leave day after tomorrow. I saw our names on a roster at Operations. You know, I heard MacArthur's in Brisbane. He'll probably come out and meet us. That means your execution is postponed, Don." Pete waited for Don to react. He didn't. "We're in the 36th Fighter Squadron, Eighth Group."

"What? What about our group, the 49th, with Wurtsmith?"

"They're off to Darwin, wherever that is. All three squadrons. The scuttlebutt is that more P-40s are coming in tomorrow morning. They'll gas and go. Anybody who doesn't fly one out goes to Darwin by train in the afternoon. We weren't on either one of those lists, so I snooped around. Then I saw the list for Lowood, P-39s. We're all on it."

Don couldn't believe it. "P-39s? Since when? We've been flying these P-40s . . ."

"Aw, come off it, Don. You and Bud are the only guys that have flown the 40s. Look, they're changing people around left and right. No one's had any idea what's going on since we got off the ship anyway. I guess if we're gonna get into combat, it's going to be in

P-39s. You should be happy; you're the one who's so all-fired ready to get into this war. What difference does it make if it's in a P-40 or a P-39?"

"Wurtsmith, that's what." Don didn't know what to think. He'd worked hard for Wurtsmith and wanted to stay in his group. If he were ever going to have the chance to prove himself, it would be because of Wurtsmith. Now he'd screwed up and Wurtsmith was going to dump him.

Pete said, "They're talking about the Japs invading Australia."

"Where'd you hear that?"

"Aussies. Amazing what you can find out when you ask around. But they can't do that until they take New Guinea."

"New Guinea?"

"Big island north of us. That's where the Japs are advancing. The Aussies are trying to hold New Guinea, but they don't think they will. Someone said they might send Americans up there. Maybe that's us."

Don was shaking his head. Bud turned to Pete. "New Guinea, eh? Well, Pete, sounds like paradise. Let's go get packed. And as for you, McGanley, I suggest you go find Wurtsmith before he finds you."

50

February 27, 1942

The *U.S.S. Thomas H. Barry* docked in Melbourne. Unfortunately, a nasty storm rocked the ship as she passed through the Bass Straits, leaving most of the passengers hopelessly seasick. A good percentage of the 4th General Hospital's personnel had to be carried off the ship.

But that was yesterday. The ship's arrival boosted morale in Melbourne. Now there were 120 nurses on station, not just eight. Duty shifts became more reasonable. Twelve hours was still common, but that was a lot better than those marathons Mary-Louise and Kate had been working. And now there were men around to unload cargo. Even better, word came through the rumor mill that a bill in Congress was proposing full officer pay for nurses. For years, they'd been given officer-like rank, but not the title, and only a fraction of the pay and benefits of regular officers. It was a small piece of good news at a time when little good news was available.

The reprieve was short, though. Wounded were pouring in from all over the Southwest Pacific Area (SWPA) in the face of the relentless Japanese advance. Since the Pearl Harbor attack, Wake Island, Guam, Burma, Hong Kong, Rabaul and Kavieng, Singapore, Timor, Java, and Bali, just to name some, had all fallen. In early March, Lae, Salamaua, and Finschhaven on the northern coast of New Guinea were attacked and secured, all within three days. And the news from the last American stronghold in the Philippines was worsening. How long the remaining garrisons could hold out was anybody's guess, but the situation didn't look good.

Even Australia's northern coast came under attack. On February 19, the Japanese raided Darwin to cover their landing at Timor, destroying nine P-40s and a slew of transport and merchant ships, probably why Wurtsmith was headed that way. Almost four hundred casualties were evacuated by American aircraft, trains, or hospital ships, either to Sydney or Melbourne. The *Thomas H. Barry* barely arrived before the staff was overloaded again. And there was more. Nurses were told that before long, they would begin rotating temporary duty assignments on hospital ships.

Ship duty could be perilous, though it wasn't supposed to be. Besides the white paint with red crosses on both sides, the Second Geneva Convention in 1906 mandated additional markings. A thick green stripe was painted all the way around, well above the water line. At night, white floodlights lit up the entire vessel, and additional green and red lights accentuated the markings. There was no way to mistake a hospital ship for anything else. It was an internationally recognized war crime to fire on them.

But the Japanese still attacked and strafed them on occasion. One ship was actually sunk. Hospital ships were less safe in port, where they could easily be moored next to combat vessels. That happened at Darwin, where one was strafed and bombed. And at night, hospital ships lost their Geneva protection when the identifying lights were turned off to prevent giving away the harbor location. Because of the danger, wounded were usually boarded in the early mornings. Ships sailed as soon as possible after that.

Fortunately, such duty was still months away. Completing the new hospital in Melbourne topped the Medical Corps' priority list, with the most optimistic projection being sometime in early May. Between caring for sick and wounded, moving equipment to new floors, or long hours in the operating room, there was no one to spare.

✧   ✧   ✧

Days off were welcome, and rare, but today was one of those days. One of the nurses got hold of a car, and five of them, including Kate and Mary-Louise, drove across town to Albert Park Beach, a splendid and popular spot named for Queen Victoria's husband. March is normally a transitional weather month in Australia as summer moved toward autumn. But today was going to be a hot one, almost thirty-five degrees Celsius. Two of the nurses brought Aussie men-friends along, who seemed more than happy with the five-to-two odds. The men bounced easily from one gal to the other, obviously intending to try all of them on for size before deciding on the winner, if they ever got that far.

This was a rare chance for Aussies to turn the tables. Yanks were invading the continent now. Newspapers were full of caricatures of American GIs: socially aggressive, better paid, always on the prowl. So far there'd been surprisingly little trouble between the American and Aussie competitors, but the war was still young.

Kate and Mary-Louise moved off by themselves and had barely stretched out towels before they had company. One of the Aussies sat down next to Kate, no doubt attracted by the way she generously filled out her bathing suit.

"So what's your name, girl?"

"Kate Engaged."

"Oh, well, how about your friend, then?"

Kate motioned toward Mary-Louise. "She's Mary-Louise Engaged. What's the matter? Aren't our friends good enough for you?"

"Uh, no, I mean, sure they are. I just wanted to meet ya, that's all. Don't get all bothered about it."

Kate nodded toward the three other nurses, grouped on the sand about 30 yards away. "I thought you came with Cathy."

"I did. We're good friends."

"Well, if you want to stay that way, you might stop staring at my chest and go pay some attention to her."

That took care of that. He got up and left. Mary-Louise held her laugh as long as she could, then couldn't hold it anymore. "Scared him off, didn't you?"

"Just protecting you, Mary-L. Bathing suits seem to have some strange effects on men."

"Well, yours does. He never looked at me once. You didn't have to tell him I was engaged, did you?"

"I'll call him back . . ."

"No! That's okay. I just thought it was funny. And you're not engaged, either."

"I will be."

"To who? That big guy on the boat?"

Kate gave her a sly look. "I know what I want, Mary-L. Do you?"

"And how do you know?"

"I know. You watch. We'll see our boys again."

"I *don't* have a boy, Kate."

Kate laughed. "Whatever you say."

"He went his way, I went mine."

"Whatever you say."

"Will you stop saying that? Let's just get a tan, okay? And don't let me burn."

"Whatever you say, Mary-L."

51

The 36th Fighter Squadron left Newcastle by train, traveling over four hundred miles up the east coast to Lowood. There they began checking out in the P-39 "Airacobra."

Built by Bell Corporation, the P-39 was supposed to be the new "wonder fighter," a revolution in technology and design. The canopy opened on both sides like a car door. The engine was mounted in the fuselage *behind* the pilot, employing a large crankshaft to turn the propeller. A nose wheel made steering for takeoffs and landings much easier. A 37mm cannon fired straight from the bullet nose, and two .50 caliber machine guns fired synchronously through the prop. Thirty caliber guns were added to each wing, starting with the D-Model. Six fuel tanks in the wings were protected by additional armor plating.

The P-39 was a big guy, tough and heavy. Though its engine horsepower matched the P-40, armament and extra plating cost it speed, altitude, and maneuverability. Such liabilities put the "wonder fighter" well short of expectations, and the War Department nearly shut down the pipeline. A lot of them ended up in Russia. Then came December 7, and suddenly production increased and accelerated. Before the war ended, Bell would build more than 9000 P-39s.

Don flew the Airacobra twenty-six times from March 21 through April 26. Pete flew twenty-four, Bud Rollins twenty-three, the rapid-fire sorties doing all of them a world of good. Amazingly, they proceeded without incident. Proficiency grew and confidence with it. Pete and Bud noticed that Don seemed to have put the P-40 incidents behind him. Even though his silly eager beaver thing was still alive and well, at least the kid was doing better. And they noticed something else: McGanley was a damn good pilot.

For a change, things were happening fast. The 36th deployed its way up the east coast of Australia, from Lowood to Rockhampton, and then to Antil Plains for twenty days. On April 26, the squadron flew on to Cairns and then continued to Horn Island, the last jump-off point between Australia and New Guinea. Final orders came two days later. The squadron was to be in place at Jackson Field, near Port Moresby, on April 29.

The dangers of flying in and around New Guinea were well known. The Aussies at Horn Island told plenty of stories about the coastal fog, Japanese raids, and rustic conditions at the allied airfields. And there was a story about six B-26s that had tried to find Port Moresby in bad weather, without ADF to navigate by. The leader attempted to descend with three wingmen flying tight. Though unsure of their position and threatened by mountains, the risk paid off. All four made it through the clouds and landed safely. The others stayed above the cloud deck, hoping it would eventually break up enough to get down. It didn't. One B-26 descended alone and was never heard from again. The other circled until the gas ran out. The crew bailed out, including a war correspondent who wandered in the jungle for twelve weeks until he lucked out and made his way back to civilization, barely alive. No one else was ever found.

But those were stories. Now, for the first time, rumors and wild guesses gave way to a real forward-area briefing for the first nineteen American fighter pilots set to deploy to New Guinea. This was it. Combat! They gathered in front of their fighters just before 1100 hours, joined by their new squadron commander. Don could hardly stand still as he spoke.

"We'll take off in three flights of five and one flight of four, starting at 1130. Look your airplane over good. We'll be landing at Seven-Mile Drome, seven miles northwest of Port Moresby. Keep radio silence throughout. If the weather is good at Port Moresby, we'll find the strip visually. If there's cloud cover, the airfield will turn on a mobile ADF. The gas tanks are being filled to the top and you'll be fully armed in case we run into Japs. They've been raiding the area every day. If we happen to see them, follow your flight leader. Don't engage unless your leader does. If you get separated, head for the south coast of the island, find Port Moresby, and then head northwest to the airfield.

"Remember the mountains. They're almost twelve thousand feet high not too far north of the field, so don't guess if you're in the clouds. The runway runs northwest-southeast. Land to the northwest. Everyone flies a straight-in approach to the runway, starting ten miles out. When you land, go to the end of the runway and turn right. There's a drainage ditch all along the strip, so don't try to turn off until you get to the end. Remember that there's someone right behind you, so don't dawdle. Get off the runway as quick as you can. Park next to the first aircraft you come to, just off the parallel taxiway, then report to me in the Operations Tent at the far end of the taxiway. Questions?"

Someone spoke up. "Captain, why the late start today? If the Japs are raiding, wouldn't we want to be there sooner so we can gas up and get after them?"

"Not today. The Aussies say they have enough airplanes to handle the Japs, and they don't want us overloading the airfield during their morning patrols." (Hardly. In fact, the Aussies were down to a handful of serviceable airplanes, but the Americans didn't know that.)

"We want to do this smoothly. If all goes right, any raids will be over by the time we arrive, if they come at all. We fly in after the patrols land, then the Aussies fly out. If we show up in the middle of a fight between Zeroes and returning patrols, there'll be more airplanes out there than horse sense. The Aussies don't want that; neither do we. All I want is from you guys is to be ready, just in case. Just follow your flight leader. Now, anybody else?" The group of pilots stood silent. "Okay, see you at Seven-Mile."

Don's heart was pounding as he finished up his preflight. Number 6942 was streaked with oil, either a little bit of a leak or a sloppy spillover from servicing. Not unusual, and nothing was dripping now. Probably okay. As he finished he patted the aircraft nose, the way a cowboy would pat his horse just before he climbed aboard, and sat down under the left wing. They'd be taking off soon, right into the teeth of the war.

This was what he'd wanted so badly. For a second, he wished his mother and father were watching him now. And his brothers, and all those other people who'd tried to stop him from becoming a pilot. Even Mrs. Blanchet, the old librarian at Curtis. What would they all think as they watched him climb into his cockpit and start the engine? How would they feel if he never came back? He wondered. Well, they probably wouldn't think much about it. Hell, why would they? They didn't even know he was here.

But *he* knew. He *wanted* to be here. He had to be here, going into combat. He needed to know he wasn't too dumb, too small, too this, or too that. He thought about the two P-40s he'd crashed, and that time when he'd forgotten to strap into his Stearman. *Idiot!* He couldn't believe he'd done such stupid things, but he had, right in front of everybody. Never again.

Someone blew a whistle. "Okay, let's get moving!"

Don jumped up too fast and bumped his head on the underside of the wing. He put his hand on his head and brought it around to his face. Good, no blood. He shook his head at himself, then climbed up on the wing, into the cockpit, and strapped in. He looked to his left and right at the pilots climbing into their P-39s. He took a deep breath. "God, don't let me screw up." Then he pressed the starter.

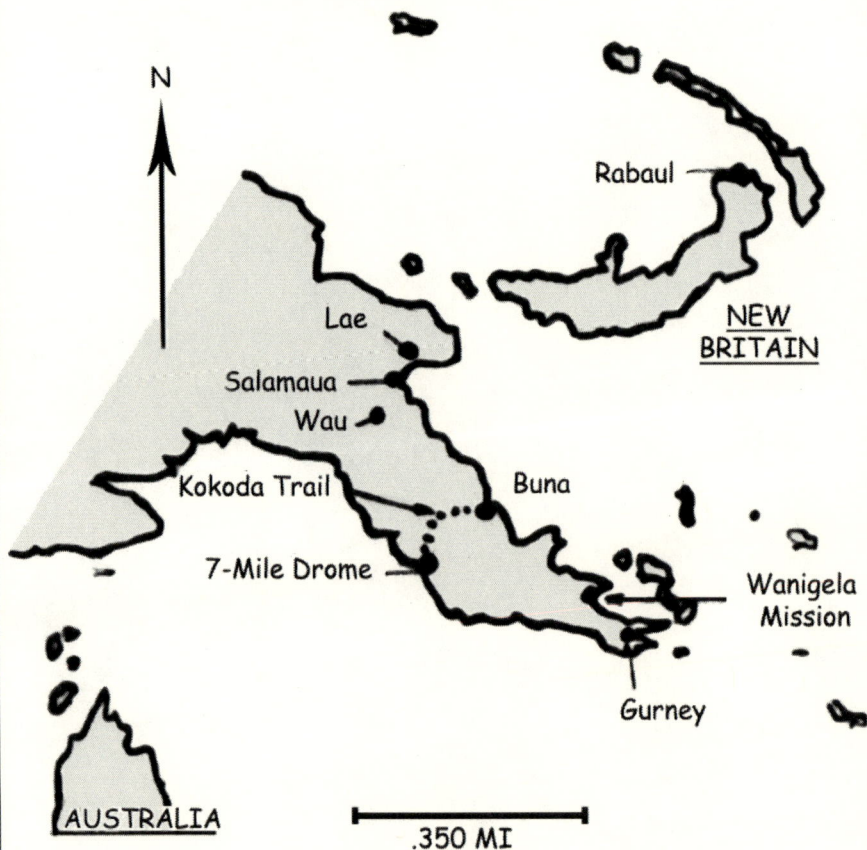

NEW GUINEA

N

Rabaul

NEW
BRITAIN

Lae

Salamaua

Wau

Kokoda Trail

Buna

7-Mile Drome

Wanigela
Mission

Gurney

AUSTRALIA

.350 MI

Part 5

52

New Guinea appeared in the distance just under two hours later. A couple of scattered clouds did little to obscure the southern coastline and the Owen Stanley Range beyond. They were big mountains all right, and he could tell it was windy; it looked like there was a layer of dust in the air. As the commander had said, the ADF beacon was off.

The weather was fine, but Don had other problems to worry about. An oil leak started from the propeller shaft about 150 miles short of Port Moresby. By the time he descended for his approach to Seven-Mile, the mixture of oil, salty sea air, and dirt from increasing winds had turned his windscreen almost opaque. Two miles from the runway he couldn't see straight ahead to save his life. The twenty-seven-hundred-foot runway, built from crushed coral and a light gray in color, seemed to disappear before him. He unstrapped and raised himself up, almost standing, until he could see the ditch and parallel taxiway off to the right, with some palm trees beyond. He picked up five P-39s already parked on the parallel to the right. All he had to do now was watch for the beginning of the ditch, then look for sand and grass on each side of his canopy. If he could see ground on both sides, then the runway must under him. Hell of a plan!

But he made it, touching down smoothly, dead center in the runway. Happy to be down but still unable to see forward, Don rolled out toward the end, keeping an eye on the ditch to the right. Then without warning, he caught a huge dark blur just left and forward. A rough bump made him tumble to the left, and his P-39 veered off in the same direction. He hit the right rudder hard while pushing forward on the top of both rudder pedals, the brakes. He managed to get the airplane stopped, pointed sixty degrees to the left, but still on the runway, barely.

"What the hell was that?" He'd hit another airplane, going the other way. "What? What's he doing? Damn it! Who is that jackass?" The combination of shock and anger swallowed him up. First the P-40s in Australia, now this! Jesus, when was this crap going to stop? He suddenly realized he was still on the runway, and other guys in his flight would be landing behind him. Dealing with this clown who couldn't follow simple orders would have to come later. Now he needed to get off the damned runway. He cobbed the power to get moving again and nearly overshot the turn at the end. He did a hasty, sloppy job of parking the P-39, climbed out the door, leapt to the ground, and looked at the left wing. Bashed in. At least he didn't smell gas. He sprinted all the way to the Operations Tent at the far end of the taxiway. Whoever this idiot was, he was going to kill him! He barged into the tent.

"Goddammit, where's the CO?" Luckily, the closest person to him was a huge, obviously seasoned sergeant who blocked the view beyond.

"Whoa, there! Easy, Lieutenant. What's the problem?"

"I'll tell you wha . . ."

Sergeant James Casey put a firm grip on his arm and steered him outside and back a few steps. Casey talked quickly, before Don could get a word in. "How'd you doin', Lieutenant? Heard there was a little problem out there with a couple wingtips. Don't sweat it. We'll get your airplane patched up, and you'll be back in the air tomorrow morning."

"Goddammit!" Don was still steamed, but at least he wasn't hollering anymore. "Some idiot can't follow a simple direction, and now I'm going to get my head handed to me."

"I don't think so," Casey continued. "First of all, it was the Ops O who clipped your wingtip. I heard him explain the whole thing to the CO right before you came in. Relax, Lieutenant."

It started to dawn on McGanley that this smart sergeant had saved him from himself. Don took a slow breath.

"Okay, okay. You can let go of my arm, Sarge."

"Casey, Sir. Pleased to meet you. I think you'll find that in a couple of minutes, the CO will want to see you. Judging from what I've heard so far, I say you're in the clear."

"Okay, okay. Thanks." Now Don was embarrassed for losing his cool. Not a small thing that Sergeant Casey had done for him.

"Don't mention it, Lieutenant. Just walk in there nice and calm, and things'll be fine. I've got some things to do, sir. I'll see you around." He took a last look at Don. "You okay, Lieutenant?"

"Yeah, okay. Thanks, Sarge." Don turned and walked slowly into the Ops Tent. The Ops Officer and CO were standing behind a table writing on a portable blackboard, assigning airplanes to pilots, pilots to flights, and flights to missions. Two guys finished talking to the Ops O, then turned and passed him on their way out. Now Don stood before his Ops O.

"McGanley, you all right?"

"Yes, sir. Sir, I . . ."

"That was you and I who bumped on the runway. We're out of the mission."

"What mission, sir?"

"Strafing raid against Lae and Salamaua, up on the north coast. Raids on Port Moresby have been coming from there. We're going to give them one back, for a change." He couldn't miss the look of anger and disappointment brewing on Don's face and motioned him aside. "Look, Lieutenant, the runway incident was my screw-up, not yours. Don't worry about it. We'll get the bird fixed, and you'll be on the first patrol tomorrow morning. I guarantee it. Go grab something to eat, then head out to your airplane and make sure nothing else is bent. After that, see if Sergeant Casey needs any help getting us settled in." Then he turned back to his blackboard and the first operational mission for the 36th Fighter Squadron.

Well, that was just *fucking* perfect! This was what he'd worked and wished for, and now he was screwed right out of the first mission! He walked along the row of P-39s until he came to 6942 and plopped down under the damaged wing. His eyes welled up. Good thing he was alone He felt like a loser. He looked up now and then to make sure no one was watching him. He was still sitting there when the rest of the pilots returned to their gassed-up airplanes, cranked up, taxied out, took off, and headed north to attack the Japanese.

53

0435 hours, May 1, 1942

For Don McGanley, it was day one of the Second World War. He was ready. For the moment, though, he'd have to wait because he was stuck in the middle of eight cots. Dawn was still two hours away, and besides, each officer had his .45 at hand. Snooping around in the dark just might just get you shot as an invading snake, an encroaching Japanese soldier, or just for waking somebody up.

✧   ✧   ✧

The Operations Tent was still set up at the southeast end of the runway. When Don arrived a small crowd was gathering near the entrance. He could hear an enthusiastic voice among the group but couldn't see who was talking. Something about a gun. Army Second Lieutenant Danny Edwards was bragging about Seven-Mile's newest defense, a four-barrel, .50 caliber machine gun.

"All you guys have to do is bring the Nips to me and my crew'll peel 'em off for you. We'll put so much lead in the air they'll think it's raining bullets. The gun'll be over there." He motioned toward the palm trees behind the parked P-39s. "The Aussies told us that the Nips seem to be concentrating more on airplane revetments we're building along the runway. They'd be done by now, but guys spend half the time diving into ditches and the other half rebuilding what the Nips shoot up. You fellas just bring them to us, and they'll never know what hit 'em!"

Somebody from the other side of the circle spoke up. "Sonny, you ever fired one of those things before?" Ah, the unmistakable voice of Bud Rollins.

"Nope, but we're planning some gunnery practice this morning after the first takeoffs. Don't worry, we'll handle the gun."

"I'm not worried about that. I'm worried about whether you can tell the difference between a P-39 and a Zero. Here's a tip for you: if the gear's down, it's probably one of us." Laughter.

"Don't worry, sir. We'll be ready."

"I feel better already."

More laughter, quickly broken up by the Operations Officer. "All right, listen up! Tail numbers and names are posted. Once you've got your airplane and flight assignment, get away from the Ops Tent. Go check out your airplane and make sure it's ready to go."

True to his word, the Ops Officer assigned Don the No. 2 position of the first patrol. He was in tail number 6942, the same bird he'd flown the day before. He hustled over to his P-39 and checked it over carefully. Casey's boys were good. It was fixed, armed, and gassed. And they'd found the oil leak; fixed that, too. Don smiled. He'd remember these guys.

The four-ship took off one at a time, the leader circling the field while wingmen joined to the right side, called *echelon* formation. They climbed and headed to a point twenty-five miles north of Seven-Mile, where they set up a holding pattern over the Owen Stanley peaks, fifty miles back and forth. The objective was to place themselves between the enemy bases and Port Moresby. Yesterday's mission against Lae and Salamaua hadn't done much militarily, except to serve notice that the Americans were on the island. No doubt the Japanese would come.

According to the just-departed Aussies, the first raid of the day usually came before dawn. It was more of a nuisance than a military strike, using slow, four-engine flying boats. They would have been easy targets for the Americans, but at high altitude, in the dark, with lights off, they were hard to hear and impossible to see, even with spotters looking and listening. Fortunately, though, the Japanese rarely hit anything, except people's nerves. But after sunrise it was a different story. The enemy attacked at irregular intervals, using two-engine "Betty" bombers or Zeroes, sometimes both. These were the raiders the patrols needed to intercept.

The holding pattern was the best way to conserve gas and lengthen the mission. The Americans flew a loose formation so they could concentrate on scanning the skies. There was no chatter on the radio. The flight leader's only instructions before takeoff were to "follow me, form up in loose right echelon, and shut up!" until the enemy was spotted.

✧　✧　✧

This was Don's first combat mission: he looked around the cockpit and then out at his fellow flight members. He loved what he saw, looking closely at his flight leader, awed by the way he appeared at the controls of his fighter, and realizing that *he* looked exactly like that.

He wondered what it would be like when they met the Japs. What would they do? What would the Japs do? No tactics or dogfighting tips had been discussed or briefed. They should have paid more attention to that back at Antil Plains. In fact, all the flying he'd done since Advanced Training was little more than "Go get some hours." or "Don't bust the airplane." *"Don't bust the airplane." What a joke that was!*

He guessed he'd just light out after the nearest Jap, then made a note to himself not to fire until he was close enough to hit something. He noticed the shadow of his P-39 glancing off the clouds. In all of his flying so far, he'd never noticed that before. It occurred to him that he might get a perception of sudden movement in his peripheral vision and, thinking it was an enemy fighter, react to it by mistake. His index finger seemed to fit so naturally on the stick's trigger. Jeez, he could easily squeeze off every round he had, shooting at nothing.

And then when he really needed it, he wouldn't have any ammo left. Better not do that.

As their flight, call sign "Philly," circled, his mind circled too, engaging and reengaging the desire to fight without really knowing how to do it. And what would it be like to see another airplane catch fire and explode. He thought out loud to himself, just as he had when they left Horn Island, because it was damned important. "God, don't let me screw this up." Not once did he consider that he might be killed, or that he'd be trying to kill another man.

The time went by as fast as Don's thoughts buzzed through his head. The flight leader finally broke radio silence. "Philly, we're heading back." It had been two hours. They'd burned almost all of their 105 gallons and had seen nothing. Don felt let down. What would he have done in combat? He wanted to know—*needed* to know. Now it would have to wait another day.

As the four P-39s approached Seven-Mile, the pilots saw that fog from Port Moresby Bay had blown over the field. It was not an unusual condition; the Aussies had warned them about it. Sometimes the fog lifted as fast as it blew in. Other times it sat over the field for an hour or more. There was almost no way to tell what would happen, and they were running out of gas. From above, they could easily see the runway through the fog, but landing through it would be different. The flight leader led them through a downwind leg, dropped his gear, and broke off in a left-hand descending turn to final approach. Don waited three or four seconds and then followed. As he descended, the visibility got worse. At 150 feet, he was in the soup.

"Philly 2, go around!" It was the leader's voice, loud and frantic. Don cobbed the power and pulled up out of the fog. At 250 feet, he was in the clear again as he flew right over a P-39 on the runway. His leader had crash-landed. Looking straight down, Don could see that the P-39 was mostly intact, but cocked about thirty degrees to the left of the runway heading. Part of the landing gear trailed about five hundred feet behind it. It would take a while to get the runway clear again.

He started a left hand climbing turn over the field, barely passing three thousand feet before he noticed that the fog was already starting to lift. It figured. Had they waited another five minutes, the whole flight of four could have landed in the clear. Instead, three airplanes were stranded in the air, low on gas and ideas.

The allied fields around Port Moresby were nick-named for their distance from Port Moresby: Three-Mile Drome, Seven-Mile Drome, Thirteen-Mile Drome. The trouble with going to another field now was that he didn't know their exact location or what condition they might be in. He made a call in the clear on "Golden Voice," the squadron radio frequency:

"This is Philly 2. I'm climbing to seven thousand feet. How long to clear the runway?"

There was no answer: the boys in Operations, including the radio operator, had probably joined the cleanup effort. More calls to Operations would be useless, so he kept silent. Wouldn't it be great if the Japs attacked now? Since Don's first flight departed on patrol, two other four-ships had taken off at staggered intervals and headed toward the same area they'd patrolled, hopefully to maintain coverage. But without the ground radio manned, there was no way for patrols to alert Seven-Mile of incoming Japanese, and no way for any ground signal to be relayed to the fighters now circling over the field.

Don checked his gas. Ten gallons, maybe fifteen minutes of flying time. He scouted the area for an alternate landing site and noticed the coral reef out over Bootless Inlet. It looked lush green, with long reed-like grass growing up through the coral, called Kunai grass. Just yesterday he'd heard someone call it Fisherman's Reef. He figured he could "dead-stick" in there if he had to. All he had to do now was position his orbit so he could get there unpowered and hope he'd never have to test his theory.

Luckily, both the fog and the runway cleared quickly. Don pulled his throttle to idle and entered a descending spiral for landing. This was going to work out: gear down, flaps down, runway in front of him, and gas left to burn. Those previous musings about combat were long gone. All he wanted to do now was land.

54

" Japs over the field!"

Whoever had left the radio station in the Operations Tent was back, screaming into the mike on Golden Voice. Don was less than fifty feet in the air, but shoved his throttle full forward in a second go-around. There were two small hills that made a "Mae West" just to the left of the runway, and he broke hard to go between them, scanning back to his right for Japs.

As he cleared the hills, he saw Zeroes about a mile off the runway's northwest end, headed inbound. There were three of them, flying in trail, staggered. It was a typical strafing formation, flown that way to keep from accidentally shooting the aircraft in front. If there were more than three, Don didn't see them. He took one last look at his gas: six gallons, perhaps five minutes of flying time left. He set the throttle at about three-quarters power, enough to accelerate downhill and keep positive pressure on the carburetor. The last thing he needed now was to demand too much of the engine and lose it to a vapor lock or fuel starvation. He broke back to the right, directly at the formation as the lead Zero opened up against revetments along the runway. Ground personnel, many still out there after pulling the disabled P-39 clear, were scattering as bullets smacked into the ground around them.

Don bore in on the second Zero from its right front quarter and squeezed the trigger. Nothing. "Shit!" He'd disarmed his cannons before landing! Instantly, he flipped the three toggles up and pulled hard to the right to keep his nose ahead of the target. The Jap hadn't seen him yet. Don fired. Immediately, chunks flew off the Zero as it started trailing smoke. Don flew right through the formation and yanked hard to the right as the third Zero pulled straight up to avoid a collision. Tracers shot across his canopy.

He kept going right, turning a full one hundred eighty degrees, bisecting the runway. He snapped his head right. *Jesus! More Zeroes!* There were at least five of them, still bearing down on the revetments! He reversed his turn to the left, and almost immediately felt a "Thunk! Thunk!" right behind his cockpit. Looking behind him he could see he was trailing smoke, and two Zeroes that had broken off their attack were now after him. He headed out over the treetops toward the bay as more bullets zipped by.

The P-39 engine was liquid cooled, unlike the Zero's radial, air-cooled engine. Apparently, he'd been hit in the coolant. The engine was quickly overheating and losing power. He was running out of options and gas with Zeroes on his tail. Only seconds to live. He dove toward the water.

But he remembered some advice from a pilot training instructor who'd joined the cadets at breakfast one day. The instructor had been grounded for flying under the Pettis Bridge in South Carolina, turned in when some local who'd been fishing instead of working was miffed because he couldn't catch anything. The instructor said, "Somebody gets on your tail, you get low and then lower. Here you are trained to fly smoothly, but (in combat) forget it. Fly as sloppy as you can."

Don jerked the stick: first left, then up, then down as he alternately stomped on the rudder pedals. The throttle was fully forward, but he pushed on it anyway as the engine belched and choked. He was no more than twenty-five feet above the water, eyes straight ahead and locked forward as his P-39 wobbled back and forth, almost out of control. But he kept at it. He tensed, ready for the burning pain that came with being shot.

After what seemed like minutes, though it was only a few seconds, he noticed that the tracers had stopped. He climbed slightly and looked back, trying to see through his own smoke. *No Zeroes?* He couldn't believe it! *Where are they?* Maybe they'd given up or scared themselves flying so low. Maybe someone else chased them away. Whatever it was, he didn't care. In a well-timed miracle, Fisherman's Reef appeared dead ahead, tall Kunai grass making it look smooth as silk, effectively hiding the sharp, rocky coral beneath it.

He waited until he knew he could make it, then lowered the landing gear. The wheels touched softly, but chunks of rubber flew up and past the canopy as the tires and gear assembly disintegrated. The fuselage screeched against the coral, and the prop snapped off and flew over the top of his canopy. He stomped the rudders right and left, trying to keep straight, but control was impossible. The P-39 rolled half right, started to flip, and then flopped back down, crunching to a halt. Sometime during the crash landing, the engine quit. He looked at the gas gage: empty, probably why he hadn't blown up.

Finally stopped, Don clenched his eyes shut and hunched over, expecting the Zeroes to reappear behind him and finish him off. But it was eerily quiet. Why the Jap pilots had broken off their pursuit, he still couldn't guess. He just sat there in his chewed-up, smoldering P-39, then slowly rose out of his hunched position. He realized he was breathing hard, almost hyperventilating. He told himself, *Slow down, slow down . . . slow . . . down!*

And then he thought out loud, "I can't believe I'm not dead."

55

The area around the Operations Tent was a crowded, chaotic place in the aftermath of the first attack since the Americans arrived. Incredibly, no one on the ground had been hurt, though the airplane revetments along the runway were shot up pretty good. Ground crews and engineers were busy redigging them. Pilots "rubbernecked" from just outside the tent, trying to stick their heads in and catch a glimpse of the portable chalkboard to see what would happen next. It would be a typical scene in the weeks to come. Every damn day someone in authority had to throw the pilots out.

The Japs were long gone now, well before anyone had a chance to refuel and get after them. One Zero had gone down as well as one P-39. The Operations Officer shouted over the noisy chatter of excited pilots who'd barely made it on the ground before running out of gas. "Who are we missing?"

"McGanley, sir!" It was Pete. He and Bud had spent the last half hour looking for Don up and down the airstrip. Nothing. "McGanley's missing."

"Anybody know what happened?"

Lt. John Caldwell spoke up, "Yeah, Captain, I saw him get jumped by two Zekes and head out for the bay. They must have gotten him."

"Who got the downed Zero?"

"I did, sir!" said Caldwell. "I finished him off."

"No, you didn't!" Danny Edwards had turned the .50 caliber gun over to his crew and just arrived, panting like a rabid dog after running all the way in from the gun position. "McGanley got him. I . . . I saw him dive on the Japs . . . just as they reached the strip.

He . . . he blew right threw their formation and got one. I saw . . . saw it all!"

Caldwell had a real stupid look on his face. "Well, I . . ."

Bud Rollins walked over to Caldwell and looked directly into his face—a cold, menacing glare. He inched ever closer to Caldwell, nose to nose, and spoke slowly in a low, steely voice, "Maybe you oughta shut up."

The chatter abruptly stopped. Caldwell started to open his mouth to speak, but Pete stopped him. "Pretty fuckin' good idea, Caldwell, don't you think?" Pete *never* used that kind of language. Even Bud turned and looked at him.

"Anybody else see it?" asked the Ops O. Caldwell said nothing, and no one else spoke up. "Okay, then, get out there and check out your airplanes." He rattled off ten names and told those pilots that they were now on a two-hour alert in case a second wave of Japs showed up. The area started to clear out in a hurry. "Caldwell!"

Caldwell turned back toward the tent. "Yes, sir?"

"Make sure you know what you're claiming, Lieutenant. If you still think the Zero is yours, then write up a report. In the meantime, you're the SCO."

"SCO, sir?"

"Summary court officer. Someone has to gather McGanley's effects for shipment home. You've got the job. Go get his gear and pack it up. The clerk will add a letter from the CO and give you the address. When everything's ready to go he'll send it off on the next courier plane to Australia."

✧   ✧   ✧

Bud and Pete walked silently together toward their P-39s. Pete could tell that Bud was really steaming. He started to speak first, but Bud beat him to it. "I oughta kick his ass."

"Don't waste your time. The Ops O took care of it. Besides, I need you around to cover me, you know? You can't do that after they court-martial you." Even Pete thought his attempt at levity was pretty poor. Don was a good man. They were both hurting.

"At least he got our first kill," said Bud. His teeth were clenched. "I'm going to make damned sure his family knows that. I've got a feeling they should know."

"So do I. I'll help you." They walked on.

"Hey! Hey! Lieutenant Melford!" It was the kid from the gun battery, Edwards, running toward them.

Pete answered, "Lieutenant, uh, Danny, isn't it?"

"Yeah, I . . ."

"Hey, thanks for what you did back in the Ops Tent. McGanley was a good friend of ours."

"I don't know, but . . ." It looked like Edwards was starting to cry.

"Kid, don't worry about it," said Bud. "If you blubber every time a guy gets killed, you're gonna be crying all day long. It's dangerous around here, ya know?"

"But I think I might have gotten him."

"The Jap? Then why didn't you say so?"

"No . . . Jesus!" The kid was fully crying now. "I think *I* got him. McGanley. Oh, shit!"

"What do you mean?"

"He flew through those Nips right in front of me. I . . . I saw the Zeros first and just opened up. I was scared shitless. God, I'm sorry!"

Bud and Pete looked at each other, then back at the kid. He was coming apart. Pete said to him, "Danny, it was combat. We all know it. Don knew it, too."

"Oh, no! No! God, *no!*" The boy's face was in his hands and his fingers pushed against his eyes, as though that would stop the tears.

There was no way anyone could get mad at the kid. What for? It wouldn't do any good now. Bud thought back to that morning before takeoff when Edwards had been so proud of his new gun, promising to take care of the Japs for them. He'd been the one to tell the kid not to shoot the good guys down, and now that's exactly what had happened. If Bud was going to get mad at anybody, he might as well be mad at himself. He truly felt for the kid, took a step toward Edwards and put a hand on his shoulder. "Kid, we've got our airplanes to check out. Why don't you come along and help? Take your mind off things for a while." Bud paused. "And stop blubbering. Christ, if you make me blubber, I'll have to kick your ass, too."

Edwards gave Bud a questioning look. The kid's face was sopping wet, but at least he was trying to compose himself. He and the two pilots headed again toward the P-39s.

Pete said, "Not bad, Bud, even for you." Bud nodded. As bad as they felt, the kid gave them something to focus on besides Don. It hadn't taken very long for this war to get real lousy; they'd have to stick together to get through it.

Danny Edwards hung around long enough to get hold of himself. He actually learned a few things about the P-39, and then he left, muttering something about his gun crew. Pete and Bud teamed up and took longer than most to check over their airplanes, just to keep busy. They headed slowly back to the Ops Tent about a half hour later.

Pete turned to Bud. "You know, you're a real softie at heart."

"Go jump in a lake."

Pete laughed. "See? Just like that. See how nice you can be?"

"Maybe I'll just kick *your* ass." Bud actually felt a little bit better.

Pete laughed again and slapped his buddy on the back. Then there was yelling behind them, and Danny Edwards was running right at them, hollering as he went. They turned. "Hey, he's back! McGanley's back!"

56

Conditions were tough at Seven-Mile. Even though the Aussie 75th Squadron had occupied the field for a while, there wasn't much to the place besides the airstrip. "Barracks" consisted of canvas tents set up on the edge of the jungle, a mile or so away from Operations. A single ton-and-a-half shuttled the pilots from the tents to the strip each morning and then back again at the end of the day. The tents were A-frame design, one pole across the top and a pole at each end, with the canvas staked down tight. Each of the eight cots had a pillow and wool blanket, more like an itchy mattress. With almost no space between cots, the protocol as guys arrived was to take the middle cots first, so that the later arrivals wouldn't have to crawl over bodies to get to an empty one. A canvas *lister* bag hung from one of the end poles and contained about thirty gallons of water, the only safe source besides Operations and a waterfall located about a half mile into the jungle.

Tents were open at each end, supposedly to allow the thick, humid air to pass through and keep the place reasonably cool. Nice idea, but still air was still air. Rains came frequently, and so did the mosquitoes. The pilots had been warned about malaria and dengue fever in Australia, but the danger there was nothing compared to this place. It was hard to imagine how anyone could exist in New Guinea *without* getting one or the other, even though the docs provided Atabrine and Quinine pills to prevent it. Damned mosquitoes! There were no lights, and here in the dark, packed in, there was no way to see or get away from the little buggers.

Food, or lack of it, presented another problem. Rumor had it that the first supply ship from Australia had been sunk by the

Japanese. For the time being, everyone ate bread or hardtack "biscuits" topped with a mixture of melon rind and sugar, which the pilots generously named "jam." Their predecessors had left behind a few tins of corned beef, but it was mostly lard, really. The Aussies proudly claimed that the corned beef had made the journey from "hoof to can in less than ten hours!" Assuming that one day some decent food would show up, Sergeant Casey promised the boss that his engineers would build a chow hall. Another nice idea, but months away.

Fortunately, the engineers took the time to dig a latrine ditch about hundred yards from the tents, and constructed toilets by placing wood planks across the span. One-foot-diameter holes were cut into the planks for obvious reasons. Someone even thought to build three-foot walls around the planks, an accommodation which did not go unnoticed. Dysentery set in almost from the first day: at least a guy could suffer in relative privacy. On the other side of the tents, Casey's men dug slit trenches for air raid defense.

Both ditches got plenty of use. One morning, in the pitch dark, a flying boat bombardier got closer than usual with his bombs. Everyone scattered. No one got hurt, but two new arrivals took a left instead of a right and dove headfirst into the wrong ditch. Despite a valiant attempt to clean themselves up, the two were banished from the tents and the ton-and-a-half. They ended up walking the mile or so to the Ops Tent that day. The Ops O asked where the hell they'd been, but took one whiff and didn't wait around for an answer. In tough places and tough times, there was finally something to laugh at.

✧　✧　✧

After the strafing mission against Lae and Salamaua on April 29, raids against Japanese bases there stopped in favor of scramble missions and patrols. The pilots showed up at the Ops Tent just before dawn each morning, grabbed a biscuit and "jam," and then rubbernecked into the tent, trying to find out their assigned tail number as well as its "110," or in-commission, status. After that, they headed for their airplane and sat alert underneath the wings. Three pistol shots would signal an inbound raid, after which all alert birds were to be airborne within two minutes.

It wasn't good enough. Most of the time, the enemy was already on top of Seven-Mile when the warning came. And sometimes Seven-Mile wasn't even the target. The 36th mission was defense of Port Moresby and the surrounding airstrips. Some were barely occupied; all were vulnerable. In the chaotic days of May 1942, the pilots scrambled without knowing which airfield was being attacked. Frequently outnumbered, they simply tried to find, engage, and destroy as many of the attackers as possible. It was a tough order: losses in planes, men, and equipment started to mount up.

✧　✧　✧

Pete, Bud, and Don sat alert under the wing of Pete's P-39, each of them nursing their way through a hardtack biscuit and jam.

Bud spoke up first, "Long way from home, boys."

"Yeah. I wish the home folks could see us now. Hotshot pilots winning the war against those wimpy yellow buggers," Pete mused. "Not so wimpy, are they?"

Bud said, "Nope. Not by a long shot. Last raid I was just sitting there in line for takeoff. They strafed two of us on the taxiway and got Benny right after he broke ground. Never even got his gear up. Fuckers! I was scared shitless."

Don added, "I still don't know why they didn't finish me off that first day."

"You were lucky," said Pete.

"Yeah, I guess so."

"Tell me, you still glad you're here?"

Don spoke slowly, "Yeah, I suppose."

Now Bud leaned forward and looked at both of them with a lot of interest. Pete held him off with his eyes and turned again to Don. "Still feel the same way about combat?"

That first combat mission flashed back to Don. He'd nailed that Zero. Then he was fighting for his life with two more on the tail. There were bullets everywhere. That was a bit hairy, but everything he'd done seemed natural to him. Johnny came to mind: what would his father think about that? Then he blocked out the thought. "Oh, I don't know."

Yes he did. He just couldn't make himself explain it all to them. He wanted to be here until the job was done. War over. Then he'd consider what to do next. Pete's eyes met Bud's. Maybe this wasn't such a good time to go into this. Somehow, Bud kept his mouth shut. Not a small feat.

Pete said, "I know. You're saving yourself for that nurse."

"Aw, come on, Pete." Out of the frying pan and into the fire. Don didn't know which subject to avoid first.

"No, really. I'll bet Mary-Louise is just dying to see you again."

"Mary-Louise?"

"See? I knew you were in love, soldier-boy."

"Knock it off, Pete."

"Have you written to her?"

"No."

"Why not? The mail plane goes to Brisbane and Melbourne."

"I don't know what her unit is."

"C'mon, you don't have to know. Just put 'Cute nurse from the *Mariposa*' on the front, and it'll go right to her."

"Very funny."

Pete turned serious for a moment. "But if you wanted to, you could get a letter to her." Don looked at Pete. Pete said, "You know it, too." Then there was quiet for a minute.

Bud said, "I remember a nurse I'd like to meet again. I just don't know her name. First chance we get to go to Australia, I think I'll go look her up. Since she was on that ship with Don's girl, they're probably in the same unit."

"She's not my girl."

"Good idea," said Pete. "You ought to go with him, McGanley. Get your brain out of combat and into softer pursuits. If Bud's company is too unsophisticated for you, I'd be glad to offer my services."

Don laughed. He knew damned well what these guys were doing. Ever since Bud chewed him out after the P-40 crash, those two had been working on him. And maybe at the proper time and proper place, they'd be right. Maybe, but not now. "We'll see. Well, I'm heading for my cockpit."

"What for? We're parked in the middle of the pack. You'll save yourself about . . . oh . . . zero seconds. Besides, it's hotter than hell up there."

But Don was already on his feet. "Better'n getting strafed sitting here. If I'm going to die in this war, I'll be damned if I'm going to die on the ground."

57

Mary-Louise Anderson and Kate Maine worked together on the fifth floor of the brand-new 4th General Hospital. It had opened the second week in May, right on schedule, and none too soon. Casualties poured in as before. Two troop trains arrived earlier that day with wounded sailors and airmen from Darwin. Ever since the first Japanese attack on February 19, the vital northern seaport seemed to be under one long raid. The rumor mill promised that an invasion of Australia was inevitable. It just forgot to say when, where, and how many Japanese ships, divisions, and planes were coming.

As usual, the nurses were whipped from a long-day's work, though morale was high among them. The business of saving lives and restoring health brought equal shares of pain and purpose and return. And word was out again that the nurses' roles would soon expand. Some would be temporarily assigned to troop trains, others to the hospital ships which would soon be making regular runs to Darwin, New Guinea, Guadalcanal, and other forward areas.

With all the unpredictability, wartime romances went full circle as young soldiers met nurses, nurses met doctors, doctors met locals, and locals met soldiers. No one knew how much time they had, just that it was precious and not to be wasted. In this one-day-slow, one-day-hellacious environment, Mary-Louise and Kate worked the last hour of an unusually long shift: no bedpans or baths for now, just a few more pulses and blood pressures in the officer's ward. Mary-Louise bent over what she thought was a sleeping patient. He opened one eye and grinned at her.

"Looks like I got the pretty one."

She took his right wrist and gently forced a thermometer through his lips and under the tongue. "Where you from, Lieutenant?"

"Hiahi Heach."

"You're funny. Any pain?"

"Li'l."

Mary-Louise checked her watch and gently withdrew the thermometer from his mouth. Pulse eighty-four, temperature one hundred: not too bad for someone recovering from shrapnel wounds. "What do you do?"

"Pilot."

"I have a friend who's a pilot."

"Yeah? What's he fly?"

"I don't know. I just met him on the way over here. On board ship. You know, he never told me what airplane he flew."

"What ship was it?"

"The *Mariposa*."

"No kiddin'. I was on the *Mariposa*."

"You were? When was that?" she asked.

"January. We docked on the thirty-first."

"So did we."

"You must have been in that group of nurses."

"I was."

"They discouraged us from mingling with you lovelies." He was waking up fast.

"We were told the same thing."

"We figured that. I guess the big brass isn't as dumb as I thought. But they didn't exactly *order* us. I heard there were a few connections here and there."

Mary-Louise smiled. "Maybe you know my friend. His name is Donald McGanley."

"Your *connection,* I suppose?" He was fishing, but she didn't bite. At least he got the message, and answered her. "Don't know the name. But I know the guys in my outfit. He must have been in the squadron that split off before we went to Darwin."

"Where did they go?"

"I don't know that, either. We were all at Cairns. Then they started separating people. Maybe the P-39s went to Port Moresby, up in New Guinea. There was some scuttlebutt among the Aussies about all the action up there." He shook his head. "Thank God I never had to fly one of those crates!"

"Why do you say that?"

"Oh, I don't know. It's different, weird airplane. The canopy opens like a car door. But I guess I shouldn't be saying all this."

"Why? Do I look Japanese?"

"No. You look like somebody I'd like to get to know."

The young pilot seemed like a nice guy. She'd heard plenty of pledges of love and received a few proposals, too. She understood. But he'd been given something to help him sleep through the pain, and she noticed his eyes getting heavy again. Come to think of it, she was surprised he'd woken up at all. Mary-Louise said softly, "Well, now you know me. But I'll bet there's someone waiting for you back in the states. Why don't you get some sleep now. You'll be leaving for San Francisco in a few days."

He was almost asleep anyway. Mary-Louise checked the young pilot's chart. 49th Fighter Group. Come to think of it, that number sounded familiar. She thought to herself, *Hmm, so they split up.* What was the name of that place, again? Port-something. She'd have to find out.

58

Seven-Mile Drome, May 6

It was raining like hell. There'd be no flying that day, at least for a while. Even the Japanese were smart enough not to attempt a raid in this crap. Don, Pete, and Bud sat in one of the makeshift shelters the engineers had hastily built, just palm fronds over a frame.

The engineers amazed Don. They worked hard and fast in between Japanese raids, repairing revetments, patching the runway, setting up tents or covered shelters. There were few leaks despite the relentless rain that fell in sheets. The rainy season was supposed to be heaviest from January to the end of April. Well, this was May, so why all the rain? He'd rather be flying.

Pete and Bud were chatting away, Bud's voice the loudest, as usual. They were talking about girls again, and Bud kept mentioning that "doll" he'd met one time on the *Mariposa*. "Maybe I'll write her a letter."

"Really? Okay, what's her name?"

"How should I know? But she looked great to me."

"You mean she had big . . . you know."

Bud belly-laughed. "Tits. Yup!"

"You know, Don's girlfriend ought to know her."

"You're right! McGanley, why don't you write to that little babe of yours and find out this girl's name for me?"

Here we go again. "I don't have a babe."

"So you keep trying to tell us," said Pete. "Won't work, fella. Look, this is your big chance to do a buddy a favor. All we're doing here is sitting in the rain. Why not use the time wisely?"

"I don't even know her unit."

"I think we solved this. Sure you do. She's a nurse, got off the ship with us, and probably stayed right there in Melbourne. Just send a general delivery to the army hospital there. Stop being such a shy boy and help your buddy in need. Besides, we're getting tired of badgering you about this stuff." Pete grinned his usual.

"So am I."

"Well, then?"

"Maybe."

Bud sighed. "Well, that's a start." Then he changed the subject and turned back to Pete. "Did you hear? They're putting bomb racks on the bellies."

Don perked up. "Really?"

"Yes, really," said Bud. "I heard some guys talking to the boss about it, attacking ship convoys with five-hundred-pounders. I guess the swabbies need our help."

Pete asked, "Five-hundred-pound bombs? Where are we going with five-hundred-pound bombs?"

"Wherever the convoys are."

Don was glad they were talking about something else, about flying, even though he wondered exactly how he was supposed to aim a bomb.

Bud continued, "I'll bet it's a piece of cake."

"Pete and I did gunnery practice, but that was strafing a little raft in the Gulf of Mexico. We never dropped any bombs."

"We strafed once, but only a few of us. The fourth guy in my flight drove it right into the ground, so they stopped the training right there. Before we could start up again, we were in the war and they graduated us."

"Yeah," said Pete. "Same thing happened to us. After the attack, they didn't care how many sorties the guys had left. Don and I were already finished flying, though, the Friday before. As soon as we were done, we skedaddled out of there and went to my house in

Meridian. That's where we were on the seventh. You guys realize how many days went by before we flew again?"

"Seventy-seven," replied Don.

Bud looked at McGanley and rolled his eyes. "That many? Maybe somebody ought to tell the CO that. Remember that little speech? 'Yardbirds' he called us. We all just stood there and took it."

Don added, "Somebody should have spoken up."

"Why didn't you?" Pete asked.

"Maybe I should've. And now they want us to go drop bombs on ships, for Pete's sake!"

"Hey!"

Don shook his head. "Don't get me wrong. Dropping bombs is fine with me, but this is the umpteenth time they've asked us to do something without a peep about how to do it. I don't know how they expect us to hit anything, but you can bet they won't like it if we miss."

"Well, this is a switch, McGanley. I'm surprised you're not first in line to help them load, in a driving rain, no less. You frustrated or somethin'?"

"Yeah, I am, I guess."

"Well," said Bud, "when in doubt, T.L.A.R."

"What's that?" Don asked.

"That Looks About Right."

Pete laughed. "I like it."

Don shook his head. "And how in the hell are you supposed to hit a moving target that's shooting back, for Pete's sake?"

"I said I resent that."

"Simple. Bomb the ships that don't have guns, McGanley." Bud and Pete laughed.

Don didn't. Ever since they got to Australia, just about everything had been screwed up—marches, changes in airplanes, units, and commanding officers. There were even rumors that the current air commander, General Brett, was on his way out. And now that they'd finally gotten to New Guinea, things were still screwed up. There were raids every day, and there seemed to be no rhyme or reason to the response, except to scramble like a bunch of ants and hope the Japs didn't shoot them up before they got off the ground. And now, with the Japs coming from one direction, they were headed in another, to bomb ships no less.

Ah, the hell with it! Despite himself, Don joined in the laughter with his two friends. If the three of them really knew what was going on, they wouldn't have laughed at all.

✧   ✧   ✧

The Japanese plan to create a Co-Prosperity Sphere, originally set for fifty days, was now in its sixth month. They'd completely missed the American carriers at Pearl Harbor, and allied supply lines to Australia remained open. The only way to cut them and isolate Australia was to extend their conquests another three thousand miles southeastward to include the Solomon Islands, New Caledonia, and all of New Guinea. At the same time, the Japanese hoped to force a final confrontation and finish off the American fleet.

On April 29, the Imperial Staff ordered the execution of Operation Mo—the invasion of Port Moresby. The invasion force and a cover group of six warships left Rabaul on May 3, cut through the St. George Channel, and steamed south around Woodlark Island, aiming for an amphibious landing near Port Moresby on the tenth. At the same time, a larger strike force of two carriers, two heavy cruisers, and six destroyers covered landings in the Solomon Islands. After supporting their respective landings, the two Japanese fleets would converge in a pincer movement against the Americans, thought to be operating somewhere in the Coral Sea.

But the Americans had broken Japanese codes and knew of the plan. U.S. Task Force 17 rendezvoused with two other task forces by May 6 and faced the enemy with two carriers, eight cruisers, and ten destroyers. The P-39s from Seven-Mile Drome were among several Army Air Corps units ordered to prepare to bomb Japanese convoys, just in case the navy asked for extra air support.

But no attack orders ever came. Instead, Don, Pete, and Bud flew three straight days of scramble missions over the Owen Stanley Range, all with empty bomb racks. While the pilots wondered what the hell was going on, two fleets operating a thousand miles to the east hammered away at each other with wave after wave of carrier-based fighters. They fought to a tactical draw with heavy losses on both sides, but in the end, the Japanese invasion fleet turned back. By May 9, bomb racks were downloaded from the P-39s. It would be weeks before the pilots would find out how close they'd come to being invaded, and perhaps overrun.

59

May 15

D on had flown eighteen missions in May so far, the most in the
squadron. There were patrols over the Owen Stanley Range,
and he'd flown several missions to protect Wau, an Australian
holding south of Lae and Salamaua.

There were gold mines near Wau and the village of Bulolo. No
doubt the Japanese would try to take them, so escort missions
protected C-46s and B-26s sent in to resupply or reinforce the
Aussie garrison there. Fighters remained overhead while transports
landed on a short, ridiculously sloped uphill runway. (Only an idiot
would try to land there, but if the allies could use it, so could the
enemy.)

It was not uncommon for engagements between Zeroes and
P-39s to take place while supplies were unloaded below. In a quick
but furious fight three miles north of Wau, Bud got his first kill when
four Zeroes attacked two C-46s approaching the strip. In three days
near Wau, Don and Bud added two "probables"—unconfirmed
kills—apiece. Both of them kidded Pete, who shot down three
clouds, all confirmed.

But most missions were scrambles to defend Port Moresby and
its surrounding airstrips. Warnings continued to come late or not
at all. American losses were high, in pilots, planes, and spare parts.
Close to two dozen P-39s from the 36th and the newly arrived 35th
Fighter Squadron were lost in May alone, including eight shot up on
the ground.

The Japanese airmen were not the small, inferior men they'd been made out to be, just as Pete had said. Most of the attacks had come from their crack naval unit out of Lae, all seasoned combat veterans. Their decade of experience in China and East Indies' campaigns allowed them to match up quite favorably against the young, green Americans.

And Japanese tactics were sound. Instead of coming strictly from the north, as they had earlier in the month, they attacked from all directions and varied the size and make-up of their attack groups. One day there were forty bombers and fifteen fighter escorts; the next only a few Zeros. The randomness kept everyone on edge.

Still, the Americans were learning fast. A new commander took over at Seven-Mile and made two smart decisions. He increased the number of alert planes from ten to twelve and moved the alert birds to the end of the runway. Response time was reduced from two minutes to thirty seconds. It all seemed so simple, though no one had thought to do it.

✧ ✧ ✧

It was early afternoon. Don sat alert in his cockpit, broiling in the afternoon heat and humidity. He was careful not to touch hot metal of the canopy rail; good way to get burned. But he loved being in the airplane. It was the perfect place to be if you didn't want to be bothered. Pilots had to stand ready, but more often than not, afternoon alert was more quiet than the morning. It was a nice break.

He was alone with his own thoughts. As much as he liked Pete and Bud, the constant badgering . . . Well, it was okay: he just didn't want to talk about girls or himself all the time.

But his friends had been right about one thing. He'd wanted to write to Mary-Louise. Don pulled out a paper and pen, silently proud of himself for not grabbing a pencil from the Ops Tent. The paper was damp from the humidity; no way he could write anything legible with that. He looked up and around; no one was watching. Good. His thoughts drifted toward the nurse, and he began writing.

Dear Mary-Louise,

I am hoping you remember me from the Mariposa. I was the fellow you spent a few minutes with at the railing, and we saw the sun rise together one morning.

Our unit made it safely to New Guinea two weeks ago, and it's been pretty hectic here ever since. There aren't too many comforts around here, but so far I've kept my health and have luckily steered clear of lead poisoning, at the same time dealing a case of the same to one of Tojo's little yellow lads. I have several probables as well, but since they are not confirmed, the army doesn't count them.

I hope you will spare some time to write a letter to the guy who got such a kick out of spending time with you.

Sincerely, Don McGanley

Later that afternoon, Don's letter went out on the courier plane headed for Brisbane and Melbourne.

60

May 29

D awn broke with brilliant colors and a slight southeasterly
breeze. Out to the east, thunderheads were sharply silhouetted
against the sky. No doubt there'd be rain later. It was hot, humid, and
dead quiet.

Of the twelve pilots on alert, eleven sat underneath the wings
of their P-39s, thankful that the breeze was just strong enough
to blow away the mosquitoes and provide some relief from the
sopping-wet air. Don was the only pilot sitting in his cockpit. The
way the planes were situated, his canopy blocked the breeze. His
stomach felt lousy, and he was sweating like a pig from the heat
and a slight fever brought on by several days of diarrhea. But he
couldn't worry about that now: Everybody had been dealing with
dysentery since they got here. All he wanted was to be ready if the
signal came.

Don was daydreaming in the quiet. He'd only slept a couple of
hours, and though the missions had been piling up, twenty-six now,
he figured he wasn't any more run down than anyone else. Actually,
he *loved* it. He knew damned well that Bud had been right: he was
fighting two wars from his P-39, the one against the Japanese and
the one against himself. But he was happy right here, in a cockpit in
New Guinea.

His daydreaming drifted to Mary-Louise. Had she gotten his
letter? What did she think of it? Did she even remember him? He had
a clear image of her, right next to him as they leaned against the rails
on the *Mariposa.* He tried to keep his vision of her and remember

things she'd said to him, but for some reason, it wasn't working very well. He was shaking a little, didn't feel right. *Damn stomach!*

✧   ✧   ✧

Pop! Pop! Pop! Sudden shots from the Ops Tent shattered the quiet. Don instinctively reached forward, selected his rotary switch to the left tank, and primed the fuel manifold. He set the throttle about an inch forward to keep from over-speeding the engine on start-up, and mashed his foot on the energizer. The Allison engine sprang to life. He pushed the throttle forward, turned onto the runway, saw someone running toward him. It was the aerodrome officer, whose job was to clear the airplanes for takeoff with a hand signal. Don would be long gone by the time he got in place. Eighteen seconds after the shots were fired, he was off the ground.

Golden Voice came up on frequency. "Head east-southeast!" The visibility was perfect: distant clouds blocked the sharp rays of the sun, and the sky straight ahead was clear. Don scanned 360 degrees for Japs but saw none. He pulled his throttle back into a "cruise climb" to save gas. One by one, the other alert birds caught up. No one formed up and there was no radio chatter. The P-39s passed over Port Moresby in a staggered stream, several hundred yards apart, climbing as they went. They would continue as high as the P-39 would go, literally "hanging on the prop," and hope to catch the Japanese below them.

There was no way to know the size or makeup of the enemy. Hell, the direction of attack was only a guess, too. Japanese "Betty" bombers flew in large, flat arrowhead formations of six to nine aircraft. Attacking from the rear meant facing concentrated 20mm cannon fire. It was better to dive on them from the front. If Zeroes were escorting, then the battle would turn exclusively toward them.

The Americans had to remember to avoid turning fights in their heavier, less maneuverable P-39s. Once engaged, the Zeroes would enter a zoom-and-roll maneuver, climbing almost vertically until their heavier pursuers ran out of airspeed and literally fell out of the sky. From there, it was a simple maneuver for the Zeroes to roll in behind the Americans. This simple zoom-and-roll had cost the 36th several airplanes and pilots already.

Don had been at twenty-four thousand for several minutes without any sightings. He was above most of the other airplanes, lucky to be in one of the newer F-Models with an electrical fuel pump. Most of the other alert birds were D-Models that had to level off around twenty thousand or even a little lower. He began to wonder if the air-raid alarm had been false, or if they were heading in the wrong direction, or if the enemy had somehow slipped by. Getting farther and farther away from the field seemed a dumb thing to do so he slowed as much as he could without stalling. If he didn't see something soon, he'd have to come up on the radio or turn back toward Seven-Mile.

Then the radio came alive. Someone hollered, "Hey, there's a fight down there!" Another squadron had been alerted from one of the other airfields, probably Thirteen-Mile. There they were, some ten thousand feet below and to the left, tangled up with at least half a dozen Zeros. Someone was trailing smoke, but Don couldn't tell who.

It didn't matter. He shoved the throttle forward as he pushed over into a steep dive and picked up two Zeroes in a left turn, directly in front of him. They weren't engaging anyone and apparently hadn't seen him yet. He glanced down at his speed: just under four hundred miles per hour. He continued the dive, got below the two Zeroes, then pulled straight up into them, straining as hard as he could against the Gs. As he reached thirty degrees nose high, the Zeroes rolled out of their left-hand turns. Perfect shot at their bellies, totally unseen. At two hundred yards, Don opened up on the left Zero with his 30mm cannon. He saw a flash of fire immediately, then it blew up.

Don yanked hard right to avoid burning debris and suddenly had a face full of the second Zero, only fifty to seventy yards ahead, also turning hard right. No zoom maneuver: fatal mistake. *Shit, I'm going to hit him!* He fired again as both airplanes sliced through the horizon, then yanked left and back on the stick, eyes and teeth clenched tight, bracing for impact. The concussion from the explosion threw Don against the top of his canopy as he flew past the debris that used to be the second Zero.

He opened his eyes wide, heart pounding, almost hyperventilating, but it was over. He'd destroyed two Zeroes in less than six seconds. He spun his head around looking for other airplanes, but saw none, not even his own guys. He flew back to level flight, pulled the throttle back, and took a deep breath. He looked around again: nobody. He turned back to a westerly heading and started climbing again, just in case.

"Oh!" A gut cramp made him lurch forward. "Damn!" His body was burning up. He forced himself to ignore it. Thankfully, it slowly abated.

Passing twenty thousand feet, Don had a clear view of the mountains to the right and New Guinea's southern coast to the left. Clouds were broken, but the visibility was perfect between them, the sun behind him. He thought for a moment how strange it was that he was up here alone. Five minutes ago there'd been planes everywhere. He scanned the sky. Where the hell was everybody? He considered coming up on the squadron frequency but what would he say? *Hello out there, this is McGanley. Where are you guys?*

He looked at his fuel. Plenty. In ten minutes he'd be back over Seven-Mile and check there for Japs. If there were none around, he'd land and gas up and wait for the next alert warning. At least it would give him some time to hit the latrine ditch. He was soaked in sweat and his guts ached even worse than before. More cramps. He squeezed his eyes shut against them. *Just let me get home!* Again the cramps let up. He opened his eyes, picked up some movement: a black spot on his canopy, to his left.

Two airplanes were heading in the opposite direction: one big, one small. A B-17! He'd seen plenty of them in flight during the coastal flying in Australia so he was sure of it. The smaller one was a Zero, trailing the bomber but still out of firing range. They were maybe three miles south of him and about three thousand feet below.

He yanked the stick left, shoved the throttle full forward, and headed straight for the "Flying Fortress" to cut the Zero off. Thick cumulous buildups blocked his view for several seconds and then he regained sight of the Zero, one o'clock, still behind the B-17. He rolled in behind the Zero with lots of overtake. All three airplanes were close now, but he didn't fire; didn't want to hit the B-17. The Zero must have seen him, though. He pulled up suddenly into a zoom-and-roll. Don lost him among the clouds and turned left again, looking back high over his right shoulder to see if the Zero came down after him.

It did. The Jap was damned good. Don headed straight north, away from the B-17 and toward the mountains, and dove straight into the most concentrated group of clouds he could find. Safe there.

Or so he thought. Updrafts and downdrafts rocked the P-39, tossing Don around the cockpit. He lost his grip on the stick and throttle, G-forces pinning him forward. He couldn't sit up or read any instruments, had no idea what his airplane was doing. It felt like it was coming apart. He thought, *I'm dead!* Suddenly, he was out of the clouds and back in smooth air, going right at the Owen Stanley Mountains, way too fast, way too nose low, out of control. His eyes bugged. He yelled out loud and pulled, but the stick wouldn't move. His vision went black, but he kept pulling. Then he felt the stick gradually become lighter in his hand, realized his eyes were shut, opened them, and saw nothing but deep blue sky.

He pushed full forward on the throttle, surprised that it wasn't already there. It had been pulled all the way back. *When the hell did I do that?* Now he rolled the P-39, got the nose down, leveled off. He spun his head around, looked behind him, then left, then right. The Zero was gone. So was the B-17. He realized he was hyperventilating, and sweating. He started to throw up, fought it back, and forced himself to take slow breaths.

Damn! You stupid ass!

The gut cramps came back. He had to get back to Seven-Mile before he threw up all over the place or crapped his pants. He checked his gas. Still plenty. Good. He shoved the throttle forward and headed home.

61

"God, McGanley, you're a maniac up there!" Bud Rollins was hollering from beyond his right wingtip as Don pulled the mixture all the way back. The engine cut off.

"What?" Don started climbing out of his parachute. He remembered now that it was several sizes too big. Good thing he hadn't had to use it. If he'd had to bail out, the opening shock would have raised his voice about three octaves, assuming he didn't fall out of the damned thing. At least his gut felt somewhat better now; he was in between cramps. Bud was still hollering.

"I said nice shooting, buddy!"

"What are you talking about?"

"You got two of them! I saw the whole thing! They both blew up, no chutes. Nice going, kid!"

Don climbed down off the leading edge of the wing. "I was lucky to get back." He hadn't given the two kills a minute's thought. That crazy dive into the clouds had almost gotten *him* killed. And he felt lousy, drenched in sweat.

"Yeah, but everybody made it today. Makes a big damned difference when we see them first, don't it? I'll tell you what. We owe a round to whatever general decided to send us those F-Models. I don't think they ever thought to look up for us."

"Yeah." Don hadn't realized how dead tired he was, and he'd taken off only forty-one minutes ago. And the cramps were coming back; he was still dizzy and sweating. He wanted to double over, but not with Bud there. And Bud was still talking.

"Hey, I just came from Ops. I told the boss everything I saw. He wants you to write down all the details right away. We've got some big shots coming in, and he said something about putting you in for a medal!"

Don never heard him. The cramps were back now. He had to get to a trench. He looked at Bud, mumbled. "Give me a second." He stumbled toward the trees behind the parked airplanes, but didn't make it. Nausea and gut cramps racked his body. He fell forward, face first. That's the last thing he remembered.

✧   ✧   ✧

It was dusk outside, almost pitch black in the tent, and hotter than hell. Don's face was soaked, his mouth parched. He shook. He could hear people talking, but it all ran together, and he couldn't make much out of it. He remembered that Bud had taken him to the doc's tent after he collapsed, and he vaguely remembered the doc saying something about dysentery, right before he shoved a spoonful of God-knows-what into his mouth. The doc said it would help with the cramps, but it burned like the dickens. Something told him not to swallow; he spat it out. The doc had stepped out, but Bud stayed with him and eventually brought him back here.

Now Don tried to focus his eyes and listen to the talk around him. No use. He was boiling hot. A voice was talking about girls and cold beer. Then there was laughter and somebody mentioned Seattle, the Miami mob, and an uncle who'd tutored Al Capone. More laughter.

Now lights were flooding the tent, the ton-and-a-half driving up. His eyes ached as he squinted against the bright beams. Then it was dark again. More voices. Now a wave of chills. He shook. His body ached everywhere. He tried to pull his blanket on top of him, but it was underneath him and wouldn't budge. He rolled onto his side, took a deep breath, and tried to make himself fall sleep. Hopeless. Chills.

Pete sat down on the cot next to Don. Bud stood beside him. Don was turning his head turned back and forth, eyes closed, shaking and sweating. They couldn't see much in the dark, but they didn't have to. Pete looked at Bud. "Malaria."

62

Fourth General Hospital, Melbourne Australia: June 6, 1942

Mary-Louise Anderson stood over the same fellow who'd been on the *Mariposa*, the same guy from the railing at sunrise, the same guy who'd left her there. He looked so vulnerable, lying there in bed. Obviously he'd lost weight, and there hadn't been much extra to lose to begin with. Over the past day and a half, she'd spent a lot of time in this room, wondering what she'd say to him when he woke up, and wondering what he'd say back. The letter had arrived only a few days ago. It was quite short, but she'd read it over and over. The guy was so different from anyone she'd known before.

In Glens Falls, she'd been something of a society girl, only meeting the right young men: eligible, proper young men picked out by her mother. Even so, the boys had been self-acclaimed big shots, usually headed for law school, medical school, or Wall Street, but no less the breast-grabbing bores that all her friends complained about.

But Don was different. He'd been shy, unassuming, and polite. She thought of his letter: "I *hope* you remember me." She smiled. And on the ship she'd remembered how tortured he looked as they stood before the sunrise. She'd mentioned the idea of kissing, and he looked like he'd faint. Another smile. Now Mary-Louise stared again at Don: a long, slow stare that she didn't care to stop anytime soon. Oh, yeah, he was the one.

"You're here early, Miss Anderson." The doctor had entered quietly. "You're not on duty until 0700, are you?"

"Uh, well, no, Doctor, but the ward's full. I thought I'd help out some."

"How's he doing?" The doctor wasn't blind. He'd been in theater for three months and seen this plenty of times before—the malaria *and* the nurse's reaction to a patient.

"No change. Fever's down, and his vitals are good. Seems to be sleeping well."

"Normal for this stage. Any blood or unusual darkness in the urine?"

"No, Doctor."

"Good. Watch for it. I've seen two cases of it since midnight. Both are men out of New Guinea, so be on the lookout and get somebody in here if you see it. Check every pan before they throw it out. If the kidneys shut down, we'll be on a short leash."

"Yes, Doctor."

"The next several hours will tell us a lot." He started to leave and then turned. "Good-looking young fellow, isn't he?"

"Yes, he is. And ... aren't they all?" She paused. "I'll do the bedpans right now."

"I'll check back in a couple hours, Miss Anderson." The doctor smiled and left. He knew what was going on, but he also knew a good nurse when he saw one.

For the first time in weeks, Mary-Louise didn't feel tired. She was excited, almost shaking. Kate Maine came in right at 0700, and they started on the rest of the bedpans and vitals, the usual start to their morning shift. They worked quickly, without a word, finishing just as the sun replaced the red sky, instantly brightening the room—the start of a good day. There were no new inbounds, and several of the patients, like Don, were going into the recovery phase. They'd found no cases that the doctor had warned about. Kate stepped out of the ward to grab a coffee, and Mary-Louise found herself at Don's bedside again. *Wake up, Don McGanley.* On cue, he stirred. Now *she* was shaking; she made herself take a deep breath and leaned over him just slightly. He started to open his eyes.

"Hello there, flyboy." She placed her hand gently on his forehead. "How do you feel?"

His eyes felt like lead, closed almost as fast as they'd opened. He was drained and disoriented, his mouth dry and pasty. "L-lousy. I . . . I don't . . . but . . ."

"You're safe. Go back to sleep." A woman's voice? At Seven-Mile? Don tried to open his eyes again. No use. "Where's . . . the . . ."

"Go to sleep."

He could have sworn he felt a kiss on his forehead. Then he drifted off.

✧   ✧   ✧

"That's him, isn't it?" Kate was right in front of Mary-Louise's face. "Mary-L, that's Don, isn't it?"

"Maybe."

"Stupid answer. I know he is. I checked the chart, and you've been buzzing around him like a bee ever since he got here."

"Lots to do."

"Trying to figure out what you're going to say to him?"

Mary-Louise looked a little flustered. She said, just above a whisper, "Kate. Just keep it down, will you please?"

"What are you being so coy about? I know you got that letter from him." She caught the look from Mary-Louise, the kind you get when you've been a little too nosy. "Okay, okay, but I'm going to ask him about my man as soon as he wakes up. You stop playing dumb, Mary-L, and I'll stop talking so loud that EVERYBODY CAN HEAR US!"

"Kate, for God's sake!"

Kate laughed. The war was fast paced. Guys came and went, so did romances. She knew that the nurses there were dedicated, to be sure, but she also knew that everybody was on the lookout for the right guy. This war brought endings just as fast as it brought beginnings. There wasn't much time to waste if you saw something you liked. Kate was after Bud, if she could ever find him, and she knew that Mary-Louise was after Don, coy or not. Well, then, the guy was right here. She couldn't ask for a better chance than that. "He's not going to be here much longer, you know."

"There's almost no fever, and it doesn't look like anything's affected his kidneys or liver."

Again Kate laughed at her friend. "Mary-L, I'm going to start hollering again."

"Okay. Yeah, I know. Why don't you let me worry about that."

"Because you move about as fast as a snail, and because I'm your friend, and because I don't want you to miss your big chance." Mary-Louise started to interrupt; Kate stopped her with a raised hand. "And because I don't want to miss mine."

63

June 9, 4th General Hospital, Melbourne, 1600 hours

"How you doin', sonny?" Bud Rollins stood over Don's bed, the smile as wide as ever.

"Bud." Don smiled back, but this was getting old. People were sneaking up on him left and right.

"Correct. You've had a nasty bout of malaria, fella. But don't worry about it. You're not alone. Half this place is full of guys with malaria."

From the hallway they heard a loud "Shhhh!" Bud turned and got a stern look from a nurse who'd just stuck her head in the door. He waved at her and turned back to Don. "That's only the third time they told me to shut up!" He laughed.

"What're you doing here?"

"Oh, I hopped a ride on a B-26 out of Antil Plains. Got here this morning. You should get out and see Melbourne. Nice town."

Don looked confused. "Antil Plains?"

"Yup. We're out of Seven-Mile. I guess the brass is reorganizing everything. Figured we'd had enough for a while. Most of the squadron left Seven-Mile a few days ago. Replaced us with some guys from the other fields around Port Moresby." Bud could see the confused, almost pained look on Don's face; he knew exactly what it was. "Don't worry, you didn't miss anything. Everything's all screwed up, but the war's still on."

"You're a pain in the neck, Rollins."

"So are you, McGanley. What of it? We're at Antil Plains to 'reconstitute.' I guess that's fancy talk for getting back on our feet after we've had our asses shot off."

"Then what? Where do we go then?"

"Who knows? The squadron's standing down until further notice. No flying at all. So the skipper gave everybody a fourteen-day pass. I bugged the Ops O for a while, and he finally told me that we'll start flying Aussie P-400s when everyone gets back, but he wouldn't tell me what we're doing after that. All I know is that we can't do much about the Japanese from Antil Plains, and maybe they won't come that far south . . . I hope. Fine by me. We need the break."

Don didn't answer. He was still drained from the malaria. Between that and the dysentery, he was down to 112 pounds. At least both were coming under control now, but it took more than a small effort just to raise his head and arms. He looked over toward the window. "They won't let me out of here until I gain back some weight."

"Well, don't get too anxious. It was pretty rough up at Seven-Mile the last few days. We lost four guys and five airplanes the last day we were there. Kyle, Jarman, Walsh, and 'Bigs'. And three more guys came down with malaria right after you. The Japs even gave us a send-off, about two dozen Bettys' worth, right before we took off. They ferried us out in B-26s."

"Where's Pete?"

"Across the hall. I think he found a nurse he likes. If you're lucky, he'll maybe break away and come see you for a few seconds."

"Lucky me."

"And how about your little nurse? She around here?"

"How should I know? Maybe, I guess."

"You *guess*?" Bud walked past three beds to the door, opened it, and said back over his shoulder, "Well, I'll see you later, buddy. Get on your feet, and we'll have a beer or two before we head back to

Antil. Now I've got a nurse of my own to find!" He pulled the door open and came face-to-face with a very angry shift supervisor, Nurse Lt. Kate Maine.

"Shhhh!" She looked square into Bud's eyes as he turned toward her. She gave it to Bud in a shouting whisper. "This is a hospital, mister, not a train station! You raise your voice again and I'll have you thrown out!" Then her angry look changed to a stare of recognition. Then her eyes softened. From the *Mariposa*. He was just like she remembered him.

"Well, I know you!" Bud's grin was a mile wide; his voice just as loud as before. "I'm Bud. Remember me?"

"Nurse . . . Kate . . . Katherine. Katherine Maine." Now she smiled. "You bet I do, flyboy."

✧ ✧ ✧

Since Mary-Louise volunteered to work a double shift, she'd been given three hours off to catch some sleep. She'd gotten none, though. She walked through the double doors of the seventh-floor malaria ward, passed the first three sleeping patients, and stopped at Don's bed. His eyes were closed, but he must have sensed something; they slowly opened.

"Hi there, Don McGanley."

"You sneaked up on me."

"It's the shoes. They don't want us clopping around here like a bunch of horses or making a racket like your friend Mr. Rollins."

"Where is Bud? Is he still here?"

"Left with my friend Kate. I don't think we'll see them for a while." Don and Mary-Louise looked at each other, for just a few quiet seconds, though it seemed longer.

"It's good to see you again, Miss Mary-Louise Anderson."

"Nurse Lieutenant." She smiled, then there was another quiet moment. "I got your letter." He said nothing; she added, "What took you so long to write?"

Don laughed out loud, then quieted when she put a finger up to her lips to shush him. Amazing, these women. Get right to the point, don't they? Didn't she realize he almost didn't write at all? Still, he couldn't take his eyes off her. She was so beautiful, exactly the way he'd pictured her just about every day these past months. It seemed like time had stopped since they were last together, that they'd stood at that railing only this morning. He wanted her to be his. Then she said, "You owe me an explanation."

"For what?"

"What do you mean, 'For what?' You know what I'm talking about."

"I'm sick. You should be taking care of me." *I should have kissed you.*

"Stalling, your standard maneuver." *I could love this man, if he'd just let me.* She walked over to the other side of the room, returning with a folding chair, and sat down. "I don't have to start my next rounds for a while, Don McGanley. So I'm just going to sit here until you talk to me."

I love you. "Maybe I'll just lie right here and look."

"That's a start at least. And what are you going to look at?"

"You. All I've been looking at the past six months is bugs, snakes, Japs, and people like Pete and Bud."

"So why me? There're plenty of other nurses around here."

"You're the first one I've seen. I've been sick, remember?"

Goodness, afraid of your own shadow! Okay, we'll play the game. "Shall I call another nurse, then?"

"I don't see any more around. Guess I'm stuck with you."

That's right, mister. You are!

"How long am I going to be here?"

"If you gain enough weight and the malaria symptoms stay away, the doctors might release you in about ten days."

"Good, we're supposed to start flying about then."

"That leaves you some time in Melbourne before you have to go back."

"I doubt it. I have to get back. I'm not on a pass."

"Yes, you are. Your squadron notified the hospital since several members of your unit are here. You started a two-week pass a couple of days ago. If you have pass days left after your discharge, you'll be free to stay here in Melbourne. But the doctor wants you back for a check each afternoon until you leave." Don frowned. "It's either that or go back to your unit."

"Well, I heard it's a nice town here. Maybe I can go out and get a decent meal."

"There're a couple of nice parks, too. If the weather's okay and you feel up to it, we can spend some time walking through them. How's that?"

"Sure." A long, quiet moment followed as they looked at each other, looked away, and then back at each other again. There was a lot going on; they both felt it.

"I loved your letter." She said it quietly; he smiled but didn't answer. She could see that he was running out of gas: the eyes were tired, almost half-closed. She reached for his wrist to take a pulse, just to do something or look busy. Instead, her two hands ended up wrapped around his.

Mary-Louise wondered if she'd rather have it this way, playing mental games with Don, or the way it was with Kate and Bud. They were off somewhere, unwilling to waste time or opportunity. Mary-Louise had seen them together for only a few minutes, but they seemed so sure about each other. And they let each other know it, as well as anyone else within earshot.

She wanted Don to tell her how he felt, even though she already knew. She just wasn't sure how hard to push him. One thing was certain, though: there wasn't much time. He'd be gone in a couple of weeks; maybe her opportunity would be gone as well. She couldn't just leave it at that. Life was too short, and this was too important to her. Shy or not, she knew she'd have to find out where they stood before he left for Antil Plains.

Mary-Louise realized that she was still holding his hand, and looked down. He'd already drifted off to sleep.

64

Finally they were letting him out of the hospital. He hadn't had a bit of fever in days, and he'd dutifully crammed down everything they put in front of him, whether it resembled food or not. He only had that day to get out and see some of Melbourne; the squadron wanted everyone back the next day. No B-26s this time; they had to go by train.

As for his guide around town, Mary-Louise had been whisked away to Brisbane early in the week after a large group of malaria victims arrived from New Caledonia. He asked when she was due back, but no one could tell him. He probably wouldn't see her before he had to leave. So much for not letting a second chance slip away, but there wasn't a darned thing he could do about it now. He'd blown it.

He'd heard about a little café that served the best lamb chops in town, so he planned to walk around some, go get his lamb chops, and then return to the hospital for his day check. After that, he'd just leave early, taking the night train instead of waiting until the next morning.

It was chilly outside. June was a winter month in southern Australia, with fog, frost, cold rain, and sometimes even snow. It was supposed to rain later that day. The temperature was a big change from the hot, humid air in New Guinea, but it felt good to him. It was a lot better than being cooped up in the hospital. Don had walked less than a full block when someone called out to him.

"Don McGanley!" He turned. It was a nurse running toward him. "Whew! I barely caught you. I'm Kate Maine. Mary-Louise wants you to meet her at Bennie's at nine o'clock."

"Bennie's? What's that? I thought she was in Brisbane."

"She was. Came back late last night. Do you know where Bennie's is?"

"No."

Kate pointed down the sidewalk. "Just go straight on toward Royal Park. Nice little diner a couple blocks up on the left. Don't worry, you'll like it after all the hospital food. And by the way, your friend says he'll meet you at the train tomorrow morning."

"What friend?"

Kate laughed. "Bud Rollins." Don was just like Bud had described him.

"Oh. Well, where is he? I thought we were going to get a bite or something."

"No way. Mr. Lieutenant Rollins and I have plans. So do you. Well, it was nice to meet you, Don McGanley. Have a good time." Kate pulled a light sweater around her shoulders, backed up a few steps, turned, and ran back toward the hospital as fast as she'd come.

"Thanks!" *What plans?*

✧   ✧   ✧

Bennie's seemed like a nice place, but he decided to wait outside for Mary-Louise. He shivered a little, but knew it was from the cold and not the malaria. He turned up the collar on the loaner coat they'd given him at the hospital and checked his watch, minute by minute. He felt himself getting nervous, the same way he'd felt nervous on the *Mariposa*. He shook his head. He'd known a few pretty girls before, but never one like Mary-Louise. He couldn't figure out what she saw in him.

But he'd savored every single minute with her, enjoyed just thinking about her. The sunrise at the railing had been quiet and private, just the perfect setting he needed. And for the past ten days he'd waited, more like anticipated, her arrival at his bedside each morning. She never pulled up the chair and sat with anyone else.

He never saw her holding another's hand. He was thinking about seeing her now, and—

"Hello, there." She'd sneaked up on him again. He looked at his watch: 9:00 a.m. He looked at her. *Beautiful!* She said, "I thought you might want some breakfast. You didn't eat at the hospital, did you?"

"Nope, I was waiting for you." He made that up.

But it sounded good to her. She said, "Well, let's go. It's freezing out here, and I'm starved. They didn't feed us yesterday. I got back late."

They found a table near the door and sat. The coffee was splendid. He could see her shaking. "Cold?"

"Yes. Takes me a while to warm up in the morning. I walk to the hospital every day from the barracks in Royal Park, but I haven't gotten used to the cold weather yet. It changes fast around here. Only a couple months ago I was at the beach." He just looked across at her. They were quiet for a minute, then she added, "I thought we'd go over there after we eat."

"The beach?"

She laughed. "No, Royal Park. That okay?"

"Sure. This is my first day out of the asylum."

She laughed again. "Good. I knew you had a sense of humor in there somewhere, and a walk is the perfect thing for you. Maybe this fog will burn off and it'll warm up some by the time we finish. Do you have any other plans for today?"

Just you. "Nope, just a day check later this afternoon."

The eggs, sausage, and toast were perfect. *She* was perfect. Right now there was no malaria, no war, no hospital, no nothin'. Just her.

Then he stopped in mid-bite. "Oh, no!"

"What? Do you feel sick?"

"No. Oh, damn!" His face turned red, swearing in front of her. "I'm s . . . sorry."

"Don, what's the matter?" She reached out, alarmed, and put her hand over his forearm, looking for signs of sickness.

"I . . . I don't have any money. They just shipped me down here when I got sick."

Mary-Louise looked down and smiled to herself, trying like crazy not to laugh out loud. He looked helpless, like he'd committed some unforgivable sin. She looked up again and saw real pain in his face and realized that this was really important to him. She liked the way he cared, the way he wanted to do everything right for her. She understood. She put her hand into her bag, pulled out a five-dollar bill, handed it under the table to him, and whispered, "Give the waitress an extra ten percent. Locals rarely tip with the war on, but the Yanks have their regular paychecks. They love you guys here."

He looked across at her. Suddenly she looked even more beautiful, and the food tasted even better.

65

Royal Park was only a couple more blocks. They entered at Gateside Street and walked around the Australian Native Gardens. It was an ornamental setting, lush with color and exotic birds: cuckoos, parrots, falcons, and several types of wrens. They headed into the park, stopping at the Burke and Wills Cairn, a stone and mason monument to the nineteenth century explorers who attempted to traverse the entire continent, south to north and back again. They'd died on the return trip. The cairn marked their starting point. Mary-Louise wanted to show him the zoo, only a little farther, but she could see that Don was still a bit weak from the malaria. So they headed back toward Gateside Street, passing a line of strange-looking gum trees and an orchard of eucalyptus and casuarina trees.

They said nothing, enjoying the cool morning air as they walked in the park's distinctive quiet. They reached the large oval of native grassland at the park's southern end, surrounded and protected by a railing to prevent intrusion. A path of sand and light gravel crushed gently under their feet. They stopped at the railing, leaned on it, and took in the grassland before them. *We've been here before.* It was time to talk, but neither seemed to know how to begin. Don reached for her hand, took it, and squeezed it softly. She moved closer to him, until she was leaning against him, just slightly. They both felt the contact.

Don began, "I feel like I'm in Central Park. There's this big city all around us, but you'd never know it."

She loved the touch. "With a war on. That's even more amazing." Then she looked at him; she could see how tired he was even though they'd only been walking thirty minutes or so. "Are you okay?"

"Yeah, just a little tired, I guess."

They leaned over the railing, and he was on the *Mariposa* again. He knew damn well it was time, tired or not. He peeked left and right to make sure they were alone; he could feel himself stirring. His heart was racing. *For Christ's sake, settle down!* He knew if he looked at her, she'd look back. Then he'd be committed. He started to put his arm around her; maybe that would slow things down a bit. But when he turned slightly to do it, so did she. Without thinking, both his hands came up to her face and cradled it gently. *It's so soft!* And he leaned forward and lightly touched her lips. He slowly pressed closer. She was smooth and warm and giving. He heard a soft murmur and let one arm slide around her shoulders while the other fell to the small of her back. Her head lay naturally on his arm, and he could feel her body as she gently pressed herself into him. They kissed like they'd both been dreaming about ever since the *Mariposa:* full, slow, and sensuous—completely honest. God, what a moment. Then he relaxed, started to let her go, looked at her, and touched her lips again. He heard her murmur again, felt her again, and thought how wonderful this was. For those few moments, they were the only two people on earth. Finally, he leaned back, still holding her.

"I've never done anything like that." He took a deep breath and realized he was panting. He hadn't breathed at all when he kissed her.

She laughed at first. "Did you peek?"

He wasn't sure how to answer that. "Well, yeah, but only for a second."

She was happy. Then she paused, became more serious, and looked up at him. "When do you want to tell our parents?"

"Are you sure?"

"Yes."

"Whenever you want."

"Yours, too."

He didn't answer at first. Then he said, "I'm not sure they'd care."

"I am."

"How do you know?"

She looked straight at him. "You're good, you're their son, and you're off to war. And there's a lot at stake. You mean more to them than you give them and yourself credit for."

"How do you know?"

"I know."

"You know what my mother used to say when I'd leave the house for a job or an interview or anything?"

"No, what?"

"She'd say, 'Don't embarrass me.'"

"Don."

"I told her when I left home that I wouldn't be coming back. My father, he never even said good-bye the day I left for good. Just went to work like it was any other day. So why would he care about me now? Or us, for that matter?"

"That hurt you, didn't it?"

"Maybe, but not anymore. I've got other things to worry about now." He turned and leaned on the railing again. He could feel his teeth clenched tight. All that perfect, quiet calm he'd felt just seconds before was gone.

"It hurt you, Donald. That's something you have to face and forgive." Don didn't answer. "They'll always be your parents. You shouldn't forget that. It's a tough job, especially the way things are these days. And, honey, I want to meet them."

Honey. She might as well have shouted the word. "I don't know."

"Well, I do. I also know you want their love and approval. You need it. We all do. So let's go meet them together. And you'll see that what you thought was missing at home was really there all along. Maybe they just didn't know how to show you then, but I'm sure they do now."

He looked at her and decided there was no point in saying any more about it. Whatever his parents felt about him, or what he felt about them, was not important now. All he cared about was her. He couldn't have loved her more. "Okay, okay, you want to meet my parents, we'll meet them."

She smiled. "Good. Now, there's a church I go to here in town. It's not too far from the hospital. The reverend is a wonderful man. Let's go talk to him."

He leaned away from the rail. "Lead the way."

"One thing first." She turned to him and looked straight at him. "I let you kiss me, and we decided to get married. Don't you think you ought to tell me you love me?" She smiled; he smiled back.

"I'm the one who made the first move. Look at the risk I took. I didn't even know you'd kiss me back."

"Liar."

"So maybe you should tell me first."

"After I had to wait *six months* for you to make the first move? Look, Buster, do you love me or not?"

"Sure do."

"Goodness, you men are scared of your own shadow. I love *you*, Don McGanley, and I'm not afraid to say it or feel it or show it."

"Good for you. Now, shall we go see this preacher? My train leaves in exactly eighteen hours."

66

They stood before the Reverend Davis just after four o'clock that afternoon. Don repeated everything perfectly, but his mind was running off in different directions. He couldn't believe this beautiful woman loved someone like him. Why was that? He really had no idea. There were no doubts at all about loving her. He'd been certain about that from the very beginning. He wondered why he hadn't just said so right out loud, the way people were supposed to. He'd even flubbed a simple "I love you." He'd told himself he damned well better say it to her before he went back to New Guinea.

New Guinea. As he held her hand, and Reverend Davis talked, his mind drifted away to Seven-Mile Drome, the fight going on there right now, without him. He was ready to get back; he *needed* to get back. Why did he still feel that way, standing in a church? He couldn't answer that, but he knew that he had to win his war here, *right now.* This was the time. New Guinea was the place. He thought of sitting in a scorching-hot P-39 cockpit, the three-shot alert, the rush to the runway, and the pure joy of air-to-air combat. *That* would always be the best time of his life. Would Mary-Louise ever understand?

". . . now pronounce you man and wife. Mr. McGanley, you may kiss your bride."

Don turned toward Mary-Louise, who was already looking at him. She knew he'd been far away. They kissed, barely touching, then she embraced him tightly and held on for what seemed like a long time. She knew he'd never felt this from anyone else, and she wanted him to know that she could give him what he'd never had in his life. Slowly she felt him start to hold on to her, his grip gradually tightening. Her eyes misted, closed tight, then opened, and she let the tears fall. They continued to stand there in each others' arms, trying to protect each other, holding on. Reverend Davis' grin slowly faded as he watched them. This was not a newlywed embrace, charged with sexual tension and anticipation of what would surely come next. No, this was different. It was about help. One of them needed a lot of it, maybe both of them did. He couldn't tell which and decided not to ask.

$$\diamond \quad \diamond \quad \diamond$$

She lay on her side, watching him as he slept. They only had a few more hours before he had to be at the train station. She wanted to wake him but was trying to figure out how she'd go about it. *Ah, secret weapon.* She snuggled close, rubbing her breasts against him and kissing his face. It worked.

"Hello, there, Mrs. McGanley."

"Were you asleep?"

Don's eyes were still closed, but he smiled. "'Course not."

"We don't have much time. I don't want to waste it."

"What time is it?"

"Three."

Don stopped smiling, eyes still closed. "I've got to go back. I *want* to go back."

"Why?"

"It's what I do."

"I know that. But it's one thing to go back because you *have* to go. Why do you *want* to go?"

He was quiet for a minute. "To fly."

"That's not it. You didn't say it was for anyone else, or for me, or because others would have to go if you didn't. There's more to this, Donald." She reached across him, her arm cradling his head and shoulder, and let her breasts lie gently on his chest, her leg falling in between his. She wanted him to feel her. "Tell me what it is." He didn't answer, and it was quiet again. "You have to prove something to yourself, don't you? What do you have to prove?" She didn't expect him to answer, and he didn't. One night together wasn't going to get through this wall; it would take time.

But she was afraid for him. Whatever he chose to do about his hurt would affect both of them now. She said, "I want you to know something."

"What?"

"I want you to know that you don't have to live your life alone. Share it with me. I *want* you to share it with me."

He opened his eyes and rolled toward her. They were on their sides facing each other. He started to wrap his arm around her, but she stopped him. "I won't let you have me again until you tell me you love me."

"I already did."

"No, you didn't. You have to say it right."

"For Pete's sake . . ."

"Say it!"

"Okay, okay. I . . . love . . . you."

"Like you mean it."

He rolled his eyes. Then they narrowed some, kind of devilish. He said slowly, "I hope we made quadruplets. That'll teach you." He was becoming aroused again.

"No, it won't. Look, Mr. Stubborn, are you going all the way back to New Guinea without telling your *wife* you love her?"

"Nobody knows you're my wife."

"Oh, for heaven's sake! What are you afraid of? You think I'll tell everybody you said you love me? Maybe you think I'll send a wire to your hotshot pilot buddies and embarrass you." They both laughed at this ludicrous exchange. "Hmmm, maybe I will."

Tension was building in both of them, and they weren't going to stop it. Their eyes were locked. She pulled him toward her and rolled onto her back. He clasped her hands, flat against the bed, extended them out, and kissed her long and hard. They were panting for breath. He arched his back and looked down at her, then lowered himself again, kissing her as they began to move together. He whispered to her, "I love you." She murmured in response. He said it again, "Mary-Louise *McGanley,* I love you."

67

Flying, what little there was, started out of Antil Plains on June 20. At least half of the pilots were still laid up with dysentery or malaria. The airplanes weren't faring much better, only some beat-up P-39Ds and a few old Aussie P-400s. Parts were nonexistent. The squadron was lucky to get six airborne in one day. Pilots began recovering, but flying conditions droned on at a snail's pace for the better part of three weeks. This was "reconstituting?" Everyone was getting antsy. All the rumors about New Guinea were bad, and here they were, doing nothing. What in hell was going on, and who was running this show, anyway?

Good questions. Command and control of the Army Air Corps in the SWPA was nothing short of a convoluted mess. The air war was being run by General MacArthur's chief of staff, whose air-combat experience totaled a big, fat zero. The staff itself was a mishmash of Australian and American officers, many who gave out orders simply because they had rank to do it. Out in the field, paperwork requirements made the pipeline for supplies and spare parts longer than the war had lasted so far. And while the Allies were mired in this mess, the Japanese were moving.

Early in July, enemy troops landed at Gona on New Guinea's north coast. Virtually unopposed, they moved swiftly east toward Buna, brutally eliminating civilian resistance along the way. The total population of one village, suspected of housing collaborators and coast watchers, was summarily beheaded one by one. The Japanese held a sixteen-year-old girl to the last, who watched in horror until her captors turned their blades on her. An old coast watcher escaped to tell the story.

At Buna, the hopelessly outnumbered Australian garrison held out for less than a day, then escaped into the jungle. Within two weeks, more Japanese troops landed at Buna, and over ten thousand invaders began driving south on what was known as the Kokoda Trail, toward the Owen Stanley Range and their prime target, Port Moresby.

Fortunately, even the Japanese, with all their experience in fighting in Indonesia's jungles, became bogged down in New Guinea's repressive natural defenses. Huge rocky peaks and deep swampy gorges, sometimes less than a day's march apart, made moving heavy equipment almost impossible. Critters with no names attacked relentlessly. The Japanese struggled against malaria, dengue fever, and jungle rot, none of which cared which side you were on.

Meanwhile, the Australians poured all the reinforcements they could find into defense along the Kokoda Trail. American fighters out of Port Moresby attacked the Japanese columns with anything they could still put in the air.

But the Japanese were still winning. Word around MacArthur's headquarters in Brisbane centered on *when* the island would fall, not if.

✧　✧　✧

Enter General George Kenney, a short, stocky, tough-looking man chosen by Hap Arnold to run the air war in the SWPA. Although he wasn't due to take command until the first week in August, Keeney showed up in theater several weeks early and met with MacArthur in Brisbane. As the story goes, he practically bulldozed his way past MacArthur's chief of staff to get to the boss, who unceremoniously asked Kenney what the hell he planned to do to get the Air Corps in gear and win the godammed air war.

Kenney wasn't intimidated. First, he asked MacArthur who would run the Air Corps in theater, Kenney or the boss's chief of staff. If it was the latter, he was ready to accept transfer back to the states. If not, then the gentleman needed to butt out, now. Second, he asked for time to look around the forward areas himself, after which he'd return with an informed answer to the general's question. MacArthur apparently liked what he heard.

Kenney went up and down Australia's east coast, assessing flying, maintenance, and resupply operations that were either on their heels or not there at all. When he passed through Darwin he took note of an exceptional commander there, Paul Wurtsmith. Late in July, on his last stop, he visited Seven-Mile Drome and got a first-hand look at what the Americans had been going through the past few months . . . from a slit trench. Right on cue, the Japanese attacked just before noon, destroying several aircraft on the ground and torching two hundred gallons of gas. The P-39s got off too late to intercept anyone. This was a far cry from the staging and refueling base Seven-Mile was supposed to be. These guys were barely surviving.

Kenney had seen all he needed to see. He took command on August 3 and established the Fifth Air Force, which effectively separated Australian and American staffs. (The Aussies would have their own separate air force and staff, but under Kenney's overall command.) Then he set up a full-time parts depot at Charters Towers on Australia's northeast coast and sent out a directive authorizing field commanders to promote and decorate deserving pilots and crews. Changes came in a hurry, and none too soon.

68

Antil Plains, August 8, 1942

"Hey!" Pete Melford was just about out of breath after running all the way out from the Operations shack. Don was sitting under the wing of an Aussie P-400. Bud Rollins was leaning on the wing reading a letter. "I got some good news!"

"Christ, Pete, can't you see I'm reading?"

"Boys, we're first lieutenants!"

"What?" Don got up.

"I just came from Ops. There's a signed order by a General Kenney, two-star. He's the new big cheese around here. Word is that he's really stirring up the pot."

"Good. Somebody needs to light a fire around here."

"Well, he's doing it. Couple of mechanics told me we're getting a shipment of parts later today."

"So how do you know we got promoted?" Don asked.

"I saw the list."

Bud had a big smile on his face, his eyes still on the letter. "Good. I'll need the money."

"What's so funny, Rollins?"

"Looky here! Kate says we're getting married as soon as I can get down there."

"Kate who?"

"Nurse Lt. Katherine Maine, fellas. You can eat your hearts out."

"You asked her to marry you?"

"Nope. She just said we're going to do it as soon as I get some time off. Ha! Gotta love that gal!"

Pete said, "You're nuts. I met three nurses in Melbourne. Had a great time. C'mon, you can't just marry one you just met."

"Why not? She's ready, so am I. Besides, we didn't just meet. I ran into her on the *Mariposa*, way back in January. And she took good care of me down in Melbourne. Just 'cause you two guys got dumped doesn't mean I did."

Pete shot back, "Dumped? I didn't get dumped. I just think it's unfair to the female race to not make myself freely available. Got to give 'em all a fair shot, don't you think?"

"You're the one who got passed around. You got dumped. Admit it, Melford."

Don hadn't been listening. He stared intently ahead and mused out loud, "We need to get back in this thing."

Pete turned away from Bud and looked at Don. "Don't worry, fella, you're about to get your chance. We're leaving for Charters Towers."

"Charters Towers? Where's that?"

"North of here somewhere. They're setting up a depot. I told you. Kenney's got everything moving. I heard he went up there and cleaned house. Some colonel was running a paper empire, clogging up the parts pipeline. Kenney got rid of him on the spot. Now they're building their own spare parts, even taking parts off downed airplanes. Word is they're churning out airplanes quick."

"What are we supposed to do there?" Don asked. "The fighting's in New Guinea."

"Gee, Don, they didn't tell me. Ops O finally threw me out when he caught me snooping around. But I heard somebody say they launched a big B-17 raid from there just yesterday, the biggest one so far. So don't you worry, we'll be back in the fight soon enough. And why're you so all-fired anxious to get back to New Guinea, anyway?"

Bud shook his head and muttered at Pete, "Stupid question."

Pete continued, "Maybe we'll fly airplanes out as they fix 'em up, I don't know. Besides, I'll bet there's women at this place. It'll be my pleasure to fix you right up, unless you prefer those grass skirts and shirtless natives on New Guinea."

"For God's sake, Pete, don't you think of anything else?" Don was only half irritated. Pete was Pete. He thought of Mary-Louise, his wife, and kept it to himself.

Bud jumped in, "When do we leave? I hate to say it, but Don's right. We're not doin' much sittin' around here. I'd just as soon get on with this thing and be done with it."

"Day after tomorrow, I think. I told you. They threw me outta the Ops shack."

"You should've been a spy, Melford."

"Nah. I'm just happy to be a snoop."

Don said, "Well, I hope you're right. I'm with Bud. We need to get back into this thing."

✧　✧　✧

They arrived at Charters Towers in a flight of six on August 10. The depot that had been dead as a doornail since the war began was now growing into a massive maintenance operation. People were busy . . . and happy as hell about it. In one week, the number of in-commission B-17s on the field tripled, all repaired or rebuilt. P-39s were being repaired just as fast and were ferried out to forward areas at a rate of about one per day. Meanwhile, the pilots did some practice strafing at a gunnery range near Ross River. When orders to New Guinea finally came, they were more than ready.

Don flew out in a group of twelve, divided into two flights of six. They stopped for gas in Rockhampton and Townsville, overnighted at Coen, and took off for Seven-Mile Drome on August 30. Over the water he let himself daydream, even though he should have had his eyes open for Japs. He thought of Mary-Louise and how quickly everything had happened. They hadn't told anyone, not even the army. He shook his head at himself. He'd gone to Melbourne because of malaria, not to get married.

But he realized he hadn't thought of his new wife enough in the past five weeks, had only written to her once. Not exactly like a newlywed. She'd responded with three letters in three days, one with a picture of her holding a stray pup she'd found. He wrote back, promising to carry the picture with him into combat. And he'd talked about the weather, of all things. He shook his head again, though, *Jeez, shouldn't married people talk about kids or about the house they were going to buy, or something like that? The weather! She must think I'm an idiot.* Now he wondered for the first time if he'd see her again and thought it would be too bad if he didn't. *Just too bad?* He was sure he loved her; remembered how she got him to say so, but he wondered why his desire to get back to New Guinea was so important. Jeez, was it more important to him than his own wife?

69

September 4, 1942

Back in the air over Seven-Mile. Don hadn't shot at anyone since his two victories on May 29, over three months ago. Most of his flying since then had been waste of gas, but now he started to notice changes—good ones. Supply and parts runs came more regularly from the mainland. The P-39s were now protecting Seven-Mile's refueling station and attacking the enemy, rather than just fighting a Custer-like defense for their own survival.

Today's mission was a big one: first to strafe Japanese ground forces along the Kokoda Trail, second to draw their fighters out of Lae and Salamaua, and third to strafe whatever targets they could find at Buna. The P-39s headed north over the Owen Stanley Range. Don was No. 2 in a flight of six. Pete flew No. 5, all staggered in right echelon.

It was hard not to be awed by the huge peaks and valleys along the Kokoda Trail. Don wondered how anyone could move in the thick jungles below, but the Japanese had managed to push well over halfway across the island. No doubt about it: Port Moresby was the objective.

The P-39s had barely been airborne five minutes when they spotted the invading column. *Jeez, they're getting close!* One by one the Americans peeled off and took their turns opening up with .30 caliber guns. They made three runs each with hardly any return fire, but it was impossible to tell how effective they were. The Japanese scattered off the trail, and the terrain forced the pilots to pay more attention to their pullouts than the results of their strafing runs.

They could hardly see anything through the thick jungle. The flight had just reformed and begun to climb northward when the leader spotted a large formation of Zeroes.

"Japs twelve o'clock high!"

Don saw them right away, three large flights at least ten thousand feet above them, probably headed for Port Moresby. It looked like they hadn't seen the P-39s yet; most likely the olive green P-39s blended in perfectly with the jungle below. It was a good bit of luck: any fight now would be no fight at all. The Americans were low, slow, and heavy against the fast, maneuverable Zeroes.

The leader came up on the radio. "Nobody breaks formation. We'll let them pass, then climb and move in behind them." Don noticed that they'd slowed their climb to gain airspeed. Good idea. The formation loosened a little as the Americans divided their attention between their own position in formation and the approaching enemy. Thirty seconds later the Zeroes dived en masse toward them. They'd been seen.

The fighters came at each other head-on, an impromptu game of chicken, but the Zeroes hurt themselves by staying in a tight formation and attacking as a group. With a downdraft carburetor preventing pushovers and wingmen left and right, the only way to maneuver was up. The Americans opened up first with their superior wing guns, and several of the Zeroes pulled up. The extra speed the Americans gained in the minute before the fight allowed them a quick belly shot. Three Zeroes exploded as the flights passed each other.

But there the advantage ended. The Americans could easily have dived and accelerated away, but no one thought of that. Don's way to the left was clear; he yanked hard, felt his vision narrow, relaxed on the stick to clear his eyes. He looked left again and saw a Zero attacking a P-39 from the rear. He pulled his nose on the Jap and opened up, even though he was well out of range. But he made an impression. The Zero pulled up off the P-39's tail.

The sky was like a beehive now, planes going in all directions. Don saw black smoke to his right, real close, another P-39 with two Zeroes following and firing. He snap-rolled right, turned fifty degrees, and opened up again. Nothing hit home, but both Zeroes broke off the attack. They'd already hit the P-39, though. Thick black smoke trailed from it. Don saw the American roll over. He saw the pilot fall out and watched as a parachute opened. He looked behind him. Clear. He started a slow climb, keeping his speed up, and decided to stick around until the parachute made it to the ground. He flew one full circle to his left, keeping the parachute in sight while checking the sky around him. Funny how there were airplanes everywhere one minute and nothing there the next.

He kept a watch out and then saw two Zeroes, right one o'clock, slightly low. They were going after the parachute. He'd heard guys talk about this but hadn't seen it before: Japs shooting at parachuting pilots. Don pushed the throttle to the stop and headed for the lead Zero. The Jap wingman, on the right, must have seen Don coming and pulled up and away. Don ignored him, started to open up on the leader, and stopped himself. *Too far away, don't waste ammo.* He pressed in until he reached three hundred yards. The lead Zero must have glued his eyes to the parachute, and for some reason his wingman never warned him. Don sprayed his cockpit with bullets. There was no smoke and no explosion, but the Zero rolled slowly and the nose dropped. No time to watch it hit; Don turned sharply right and looked up for the second Zero. Nothing. He looked behind him, again nothing.

He looked back to his left, found the parachute again, and started another left-hand orbit to shield the descending American pilot. After one full turn, he picked up the second Zero again, left and low, just above the trees, heading for the parachute. Don rolled left and dived almost straight down, spraying tracers across the nose of the Jap. The Zero pulled up and left while Don pulled to a blackout to avoid crashing into the trees himself. He lightened up on the stick, eyes cleared, and saw the second Zero flying away.

By the time Don looked back, the parachute was just above the trees, about a quarter mile from a plume of fire and smoke, probably the first Zero that tried to gun the descending pilot. Don watched the parachute descend into the jungle and looked around for landmarks, a way to pinpoint the pilot's position. But the whole area was nondescript, a sea of rolling green in all directions.

The air battle lasted less than two minutes. By the time he looked up again, there were no Zeroes to be seen. Several plumes of smoke rose from the jungle below; no way of knowing how many were American and how many were the enemy. Don came up on the radio, "Anybody see who went down?"

"We lost one on the first pass, maybe one more. I don't know who that was." That sounded like Ben Gray, No. 6. It was becoming obvious that the leader was no longer with them. He'd have spoken up by now.

Don said, "I have the lead. Count off by position."

There was a pause, then, "Three," "Four," another pause and then, "Six."

Shit, it was Pete who bailed out. "Okay, okay. Gray, get above the peaks and radio a warning to Golden Voice, then head for home and give them Melford's location. Don't land until you're sure no more Japs are headed for the field. Go!"

Now Don looked at his gas: well over half. Without an external tank, they'd left Seven-Mile with just over a hundred gallons. "Everybody check your gas. Anyone got less than seventy gallons?" Quiet. "Okay, we're headed for Buna."

70

McGanley lay on his cot and looked up into the dark. The day's flying was over with no news about Pete. It was not unusual for guys who went down to remain missing for a month, even longer. The lucky ones were found by natives, the *right* natives, who fed them well, carried them everywhere, and saw them safely home. But now the Japanese were all over the Kokoda Trail; sometimes their presence was enough to discourage the natives from helping the Allies, in this case, a downed flyer.

Was Pete dead? Who knew? There just wasn't much use in dwelling on it now. Don felt strangely detached from it all and wasn't sure why. Was he screwed up since he didn't seem to feel some sort of heavy, dark sense of loss? He thought about Paulie Nelson for a minute. He'd been responsible for that. And he'd decided that he didn't want to feel that way again, ever.

But Pete had been a good friend from the first day of pilot training. He was the guy who kept trying to run his social life. They'd gone back to the Melford home in Mississippi together, gone to Morrison together, taken that train to San Francisco together, and on and on. He should feel more now, shouldn't he?

He forced himself to take a deep breath. Pete was a pilot "missing in action," like so many had been before him and like *he* could be any day. Heck, there had been lots of times where no one knew who'd been shot down until somebody simply wasn't around for dinner. Come to think of it, he hadn't seen a pilot jerk a tear since he'd gotten to New Guinea last April.

Maybe there was a good reason for that. War was different for fighter pilots, almost impersonal in a way. Pilots flew alone, packed into a heavy metal cocoon defended by an awesome array of guns and bullets. From inside they blasted away at a faceless enemy. There was no blood and guts to it and no holding a buddy in your arms while he died. Pilots counted victories by shooting down *airplanes*, not killing the men inside.

In the pitch dark, Bud Rollins crashed down on the cot next to Don. Wood cracked, but the cot held.

"Hey!" Don grabbed his pistol by instinct, then slowly set it back down below his cot.

"Sorry."

"For heaven's sake, Bud!"

There was no sound for a moment, then Bud said, "I was looking for you. We lost Pete."

"I know."

"Did you see it?"

"I saw him jump out. Parachute went into the trees."

"Was he near the Japs?"

"Don't really know. We were in a fight, off the Trail, maybe two or three miles from where we strafed them."

"Shit."

"All we can do is hope the friendlies find him first."

"I know. Jesus, this is lousy."

"Nothing we can do about it."

"I heard you did though. Heard you got a couple of Japs who went after Pete in his parachute. Good goin'."

"Got one. The other took off."

"Still, everybody's talking about it. You did good, buddy."

"I just react, Bud. You see those guys, you go after them."

"But you react so fast. Faster than me, for sure. Seems like you have ten eyes up there or somethin'" There was silence for a minute. "You don't give yourself enough credit, Don. You're the best damn pilot in the outfit, in my book. Pete's too, I'll bet."

Whatever you say, Bud. "He'll turn up. Don't worry."

"Hope you're right."

"Let's get some sleep. We'll probably be up early again tomorrow." Don stared into the black, thoughts swirling around him. He remembered Leslie Melford, Pete's little sister. She'd be crushed when she heard the news. The whole family would be, and he wouldn't be there to tell them what happened. Pete was a friend, a *real* friend. That didn't happen very often. Dammit, Pete mattered; so did his whole family. The next day he'd go see the commander, volunteer to be summary court officer, and write to the Melfords himself.

And what if it'd been him? *The best damn pilot, eh? That didn't amount to much.* Maybe Edna would cry, Elizabeth too. He had no idea what his brothers would think. And Johnny? Hell. Nope, he was on his own. He felt a tear roll out of his eye as he looked up into the dark. It trickled down to the edge of his ear, stopped for a second or two, and fell in. He needed to sniff to clear his nose, but didn't dare, not with Bud right next to him.

One cot over, Bud started to say something more, thought better of it, and closed his eyes. McGanley was a tough one to figure. Good guy, though. And he hadn't been kidding about the flying. It was amazing how fast McGanley saw things in the air. There was no hesitation in the guy. While everybody else was trying to figure out what to do, he was already doing it, like it was instinctive to him. And if you were a Jap, the instinct was deadly. He was, without a doubt, the best damned pilot they had. (A mosquito buzzed around Bud's head. He swatted at it and missed. The little shit would get him for sure after he'd fallen asleep. Bud only hoped it wasn't carrying malaria.) Well, not much he could do about McGanley tonight. It was obvious that the guy didn't want to talk, as usual. Maybe tomorrow.

71

B y the end of the first week in September, Japanese raids against
Port Moresby were coming twice a day. Large formations of
bombers and fighters pushed the Americans to the limit. Raids
on Buna took a back seat as the Americans threw everything that
would fly into the air just to protect Seven-Mile. It was like those
first hectic days in May all over again.

Don flew twelve missions in eight days. When he wasn't flying,
he was in a slit trench up to his waist in mud while mechanics
worked furiously to refuel or repair his airplane. The squadron
racked up kills as the Japs kept coming. Don and Bud Rollins had
three *probables* between them, but there was no time to fill out the
silly paperwork required to claim a victory. The enemy was close to
coming right over the mountains at them. Pilots slept with their .45s
in hand. The mission was survival.

And there was more to the onslaught than the overland drive
to take Port Moresby, though nobody at Seven-Mile knew it. The
Japanese planned yet another landing for September 9, this time
against the Australians near Milne Bay, down on the southeast tip
of the island. Things were getting tight. If the Japanese could take
Milne Bay, they could attack Port Moresby from two sides. If they
took Port Moresby, they'd have New Guinea at last. The next stop
would be Australia.

The Japanese landed on schedule and drove toward Milne Bay's
Field Three. But the Australians fought back, supported by mainland
B-17s that bombed their troop and supply ships. The B-17s didn't hit
much because of bad weather, sinking one troop ship and damaging
one minesweeper. But they disrupted the operation enough to

prevent the enemy from putting fresh supplies and reinforcements ashore. The Japanese fleet withdrew, stranding their own landing force. Within days, the poorly supplied invaders were completely defeated. Those who weren't killed or captured simply scattered into the hills. It would be the final Japanese attempt to land on New Guinea's south coast.

As for Port Moresby, the Japanese ground offensive was running out of gas, rations, and time. They reached as far as Imita Ridge, on the south side of the Owen Stanley Range. Then the Australian defenders, reinforced by the first American ground troops to land on the island, teamed with strafing fighters and the daunting jungle hazards to begin pushing the Japanese backwards along the Kokoda Trail. But this last drive on Port Moresby had come damned close to a victory. When the tide finally turned, the Japanese were less than ten miles from Seven-Mile Drome.

✧   ✧   ✧

September 15, 1942

"Hey, did you hear? We're moving again!" Bud came from the direction of the Ops Tent. Don was sitting in his customary place, under a wing of his P-39, chewing a piece of hardtack. They hadn't seen a Jap airplane over the strip in three days. Finally some quiet.

"What?"

"Yeah, they're moving us to Milne Bay, a place called Strip-One, or something like that." Don noted that it was Pete who usually did the snooping around the Ops Tent. Bud usually just took what came and got at it. Now, for some reason, Bud had picked up the rubbernecking.

"Never heard of it."

"Me, neither, but I heard we just beat back a Jap landing on the tip of the island. They're moving the Aussies out, and we're moving in."

"What about this place? I mean, what about the Buna raids and the runs against the Japs. They're still on this side of the mountains."

"Not our problem, I guess. Too bad the brass doesn't tell us much. Maybe you ought to write them a letter and tell them they need to fill us in." What a wiseass Bud was! But it was a standard song. Those good changes after Kenney assumed command worked fine until the last, desperate Japanese attempts to take Port Moresby and Milne Bay threw things back into a chaotic scramble. Nobody seemed to know who was doing what to whom. And if they did know, they never seemed to tell the guys who did the fighting. It drove Don nuts.

"Well, what're we supposed to do flying out of Milne Bay?"

"How should I know? I guess we'll find out when we get there. But I heard it's a pretty bare strip, less than what we've got here, all tents again."

"Nothing new about that."

"No, but I heard something else, too. The boss is going to assign permanent airplanes when we get there. You can name it, put your kills on it, sing to it, whatever you want."

"Hey, I like that."

"Me, too."

"Maybe things are looking up after all."

It was a result of General Kenney's initiative to recognize and motivate the frontline pilots and mechanics. Commanders were to be on the lookout for the go-getters, write them up for citations, medals, even promote them on the spot, and Kenney would support it. They'd shuffled all over the place in the past three months, seen their leadership change repeatedly, and flown a lot of patchwork airplanes. They'd fought dysentery, malaria, and the Jap advance over the Owen Stanleys. Now, giving the pilots their own airplane and their own mechanic seemed a great way to build some badly needed morale. Good move!

"So what're you going to call your fighting machine?"

"Nip's Nemesis."

Bud laughed heartily. "Not bad. You've been thinking about that for a while?"

"Yep."

Bud winked. "Well, don't forget to put those four Jap flags on it."

✧   ✧   ✧

The squadron spent four days moving to Number One Strip. Milne Bay was just over two hundred miles away, well under an hour's flying time, but the boss decided to keep sufficient force at Seven-Mile during the transition. The Japanese were still close, and B-26s and B-17s from Australia teamed with fighters stationed around Port Moresby to bomb and strafe retreating troops. Even though Jap air raids had slacked off, there was no reason to be careless. The Americans moved out as relief moved in.

Bud had heard right. Number One Strip was pretty bare. Mechanics and engineers got to work as fast as they arrived, setting up tents, digging ditches, and building airplane revetments. Any equipment left behind by the Aussies was pretty beat up, including one two-engine bomber they hadn't bothered to repair. It looked like they just grabbed anything worth having and took off with it, leaving the incoming Americans with nothing. No matter, though. Those Australians had fought heroically on this side of the Japanese pincer. The incoming Americans got the full word as they arrived. It didn't take much imagination to realize how close they'd come to losing the island.

Meanwhile, there was a landing strip to build. Engineers worked furiously to lay down Marsden matting before the next rains arrived. Marsden matting consisted of ten-foot-long-by-six-inch-wide steel planks with two-inch diameter holes down the middle. Soft earth or caked mud came through the holes, creating a friction that effectively held the matting in place. It took almost thirty thousand planks to build the strip, but someone was on the ball getting the equipment on site. The runway was finished before the last P-39 arrived from Seven-Mile.

However, the strip could be a godsend or an adventure. If the sun was right, the glinting beams made it easy to find. If the steel was wet, the surface could be slicker than hell. Pilots had to take more care landing on it than on a bituminous or crushed coral strip.

The commander called the pilots together once the full squadron was in place. They gathered around the Ops Tent after grabbing a quick breakfast.

"Welcome to Number One Strip. I just want to let you guys know about some changes coming and why we're here."

Finally! Don looked at Bud, this time with a nod and a wink and a huge grin. When was the last time *this* happened?

"First, most of our missions are going to go up the north coast or off toward the Solomons. The Japs have our marines trapped on Guadalcanal. We'll patrol the sea lanes and try to keep the Jap Navy off their backs. I've got Sergeant Casey and his boys loading extra gas tanks for the overwater missions."

Casey. Don remembered him well, though they hadn't crossed paths in a while. Casey was the guy who'd saved Don's skin that first day at Seven-Mile after Don and the Ops O had bumped on the runway. He was one of those go-getters, wounded more times than anyone could count because he wouldn't take cover when the Japs attacked. Too busy protecting his airplanes . . . or shooting back.

The boss went on, "You see enemy ships, report them. Any of the Jap ships get careless and stray away from the group, or if you see one dumb enough to be out there alone, let 'em have it.

"Now, the other guys will be headed up toward Buna. Our job is to get rid of fighter resistance so our bombers can attack the base without interference. Buna's the key. If we can get rid of Buna, the Japs will have no place to go after we run their asses back up the Kokoda Trail." The boss paused for a minute to let it all sink in. "Okay, we'll post the missions every morning. Anybody got any questions so far?" He answered, "Good!" before anyone had the chance to speak up. The boys got the message and chuckled together.

"Now, we've found out that the Jap fighters are using our frequency. Okay, we're going to let them." The pilots exchanged glances. "They haven't figured out that they can't speak English very well, so they'll be easy to identify. If you can hear them, they're within fifty miles. And you'll know they're fighters because the bombers don't chatter. As for us, keep the chatter down. Any questions about that?

"Okay, we're standing down the rest of the day. You are all getting your own airplane. Stop by the Ops Tent when we're through here and find out which one's yours. Take good care of the airplanes, fellas. They don't grow on trees. You can spend the rest of the day helping to get yours ready. That includes the name and painting whatever design you want on the nose . . . within reason." He paused for emphasis. "I don't want to have to explain to some visiting general what 'fuck' means." The pilots roared with laughter. "Now, I've got a boxful of Jap flag decals you can paste on for kills. They'll be at the Ops Tent, too. And from now on, I want all confirmed kills written up. I don't want to hear the word 'probable' any more than necessary. Write up the claim and sign it, and include the confirmation if you can. Everybody got that?" He scanned the group of pilots; they nodded. "Okay, that's all I have." He turned and walked away.

Don and Bud stood together. Bud nodded at the boss as he walked away. "I like that guy."

"You bet."

"Didn't give us any of that 'Hup, two, three, four, dismissed' crap, either."

"No, he didn't."

"That's because he's a first lieutenant, too, just like most of us. Smart guy."

"And we know what the score is for a change. A couple Aussies told me about the fight around here the last few weeks. Must've been pretty hairy. Think about it: we were sweating out Port Moresby at the same time. Jeez, Bud, you realize how close this was?"

"Well, things are looking pretty good now, at least it seems that way. C'mon, I've got three stickers to pick up, you've got four. Let's grab us a paintbrush and have some fun."

72

The Dutch hospital ship *Sumaritaan* docked in Melbourne, loaded down with the sick and the wounded from the forward areas. Stories about the fighting were horrific, the damage done by the war extending well beyond bullet wounds and missing limbs. Kids barely old enough to be away from home had seen things no one should ever have to see. Even the hospital ship hadn't been safe. Japanese fighters dived on them, coming out of nowhere, without opening fire most of the time. "Buzzing" the ship was apparently some kind of fun and games, but hardly funny to the ship's captain, who had to treat all threats as real and get everyone off the deck while he "zigzagged" the ship. The entire crew's exhaustion from long work hours was obvious, as well as their relief of finally being safely in port.

Now it was the 4th Army Hospital's turn to put in the overtime. Mary-Louise and Kate had been called in during off-duty hours to work sixteen hours straight, with lots more to do. They were grabbing a quick break. The coffee seemed to taste especially good even though it really wasn't, and it felt good to sit down after the last umpteen hours on their feet. Mary-Louise wiped her forehead.

"Whew! I've never given so much morphine and penicillin. The whole floor's one big infection."

"At least it's quiet now. Most of them will make it, I think. They've gotten this far."

"Plenty of them didn't, I heard. We're lucky. I can't even imagine what it's like out there. So many of them have legs or arms or hands missing. I really don't know how they cope with that. I don't think I could."

"But our job, Mary-L, is to help them do just that."

"Yes, yes, it is." She sighed, a long slow exhale as she tried to imagine how it must be out there. Mary-Louise watched her friend pull out a blank sheet of paper. "Another letter to Bud?"

"Yeah. I'm going to stay after that man until he catches me."

"I could never do that."

"What? Chase a man? Mary-L, don't give me that. You just did it differently, that's all. Caught him, too." She winked. "An inspiring hook and catch."

"It wasn't like that."

"Modesty, one of your best traits."

It was quiet for a minute. Mary-Louise leaned slightly forward, the small cafeteria table supporting her elbow, which in turn supported her hand, which held up her chin. She closed her eyes, realized how easy it would be to fall sleep, and opened them again. She mused, "I wonder when I'll see Don again."

"Has he written?"

"Once. I wrote him back. But it's been a while."

"I wrote Bud at Antil Plains. He wrote back, about ten lines. That's Bud, all right. But I don't know if he's even there anymore. They might be back up in New Guinea by now."

"I've heard the fighting up there is bad. I'm worried. Don and I have so much to talk about, and we don't know when we'll get the chance. It's hard enough just to get him started."

"Same with Bud."

She sat up. "Bud? You're kidding. You could be hundred yards away on the other side of an auditorium and you'd still know he was in the room."

"You know what I mean. We have a lot to talk about, too. But you can't let yourself worry about the war and what might happen to him. You'll drive yourself crazy. All we can do now is concentrate on our job here. That's the smart thing to do."

"I don't believe you. You need to talk to him as much as I need to talk to Don."

Kate looked at her for a long minute. "No, well yeah, I guess so. We haven't had time to talk much, really." Mary-Louise looked up at her as Kate said, "We've been too busy playing with each other." Kate's slow smile turned into a wicked, mischievous grin. "Ooh, gives me the chills to think about him. That guy can really do it."

"Kate!"

"What? Don't be such a square, Mary-L. Besides, I already told him we'd be getting married the next time I saw him. I told him I won't let him touch me until he says 'I do.' Hope I can hold out."

"You *told* him you were going to get married?"

"Yeah. I'm not going to wait around for him to think about running off."

"Did he answer you?"

"Not directly about that, but he'll show up here. You watch. That's an answer."

"I don't know how you can be so sure about someone you don't even know."

"You mean like you and Don? C'mon, Mary-L, how do you know *you're* sure?"

"Well, I've spent a lot more time with Don than you've spent with Bud."

"Mary-L, it's about quality, not quantity." Kate was still smiling.

Mary-Louise smiled back. Some people thought Kate was too brazen, too crass, and too loud. But Kate was Kate. Mary-Louise found her easy to talk to. "Maybe my idea of quality is different from yours."

"That's for sure. But I'll tell you this: Bud's my man. I've had a few fellas in my time, but he's different. I can *feel* it between us and not just between the sheets. I've never felt it before, but I know what it is. It's chemistry, Mary-L, and we've got it." Kate looked directly at her friend. "So, how do *you* know?"

"Same way you do. I knew it the first time I talked to Don. And I knew *he* knew it, too. I just wish he'd open up with me. He hurts, you know? I keep getting bits and pieces about his parents. He's never talked about his brothers or having friends when he was growing up, except to say that no one paid any attention to him. He's been alone, and now he seems so intent on being a part of this war. All he talks about is getting back to combat, like he's trying to prove something."

"Prove what? To who?"

"To himself. I know he loves me, but he doesn't like himself. I want to know why. What is it that makes him feel that way? And I want to help him get past it all, make him understand that there's nothing to prove to anybody." She paused. "You know, I worry about him not coming back. He worries about not *going*."

"Well, he seemed like a nice guy, I guess, but doesn't this sound like some sort of maternal instinct thing? Which need are you meeting, the one he missed at home or the one you have now?"

"But this is what I want. I don't want it to slip away."

"Maybe, but your life with him is in the *future*, not the past. I talked about kids with Bud, and he talked right back. Maybe neither one of us said the marriage word, but it was there, all right. We never mentioned the war once. He never talked about airplanes or combat or Japanese or anything like that. The only urgency that man ever showed me was for *me* and me alone, lust and all. Ooh, now I'm getting chills again . . ."

Mary-Louise shot a glance around to make sure they weren't being overheard. Kate kept right on, "So when this war's over, will Don have *you* or will he always be looking for something else? Not some*one* else, mind you, but some*thing* else. Mary-L, he can be in your bed, right next to you, and still not be there."

It didn't bother Mary-Louise that Kate pried into her life like this. Kate was a good friend, her best friend, right when she needed one. And these weren't normal times. The war complicated things because it kept her and Don apart, but it had also brought them together. Without a doubt, her new husband had problems to deal with, but didn't everybody? She didn't just love the guy; she wanted to help him. And she knew that he'd be totally devoted to her; he was just that type. They had plenty of foundation to build their life on. "We'll make it. I'll see him soon. You'll see."

"Honey, I don't have to see. You do."

73

Number One Strip was officially renamed in the last half of September, after an Australian squadron leader named C. R. Gurney. Guys asked around, but all they could find out was that Gurney had bought it in a plane crash.

The place was busy, though. The Japs weren't raiding as much anymore. Since their unsuccessful campaigns against Milne Bay and Port Moresby, the Japanese effort now seemed concentrated on getting their troops back to Buna safely. Meanwhile, the Americans went to work building up their base at Milne Bay. Supplies poured in, including concrete to construct cement floors. At Gurney they started with the mess hall, mainly to try and control those damned mosquitoes. The pilots proudly posted a sign over the door: "Through these portals pass the hottest pilots in the world!"

Indeed. *Nip's Nemesis* flew twenty-eight missions over the next six weeks: lots of patrol, some strafing, and very little air-to-air action. Don flew No. 2 in the flights most of the time, but led several other missions. A couple of guys had told him he was being considered for promotion to flight commander, a spot that usually went to guys more senior. He tried not to pay attention to rumors like that; there'd been a dozen a day ever since he first arrived in theater. This was a good one, though. He wanted the job.

The routine settled in at Milne Bay. The building continued. For a change, there was no practical use for the slit trenches. Some guys even found time to try and learn some *Motu*, one of the native tongues. Spare parts came in from Australia. Word from Guadalcanal was improving at least for now; so was the news from the Kokoda Trail. For sure the food could still use improvement, and the mosquitoes remained relentless attackers, but life as the hunter sure beat the hell out of life as the hunted. There was even time to write.

Dear Mary-Louise,

We're all writing letters now, so here's mine. We moved to Milne Bay back in September. The Australians have left the place to us, so we're building it from scratch. It looks like they took everything but the kitchen sink when they left.

So tell me, wife. How would you like your Jap? Do you want him on white or rye, with or without mustard? Or do you prefer chili sauce? Whatever you like, you shall have.

I got hold of a ukulele, too. I'll be happy to play you a tune when we see each other again. I miss you.

Love, Don

✧ ✧ ✧

October 29

Don jumped down from the wing of his P-39. It had been a dull mission, a patrol up New Guinea's north coast overflying Wanigela Mission, a new airfield the Allies were building east of Buna. Almost two hours of flight and he hadn't seen or heard a single Jap.

"Hey, Don!" Bud Rollins was yelling over the sound of several other airplanes taxing in to shut down. "Boss wants to see you."

"What about?"

"Who knows? He just told me to come get you." Don was trying to figure out what he'd done wrong and couldn't think of a thing. There'd been very little shooting in the past couple of weeks. Bud was still talking. "Actually, he wants to see both of us."

"Where is he?"

"Ops Tent."

The two lieutenants walked in. Good: no one else around. The commander was talking to the Ops O, motioning to the list of aircraft on the board.

"Boss, you wanted to see us?"

"Yeah." He led the two lieutenants out of the Ops Tent. "Come with me." They walked the short distance to the boss's shack. He motioned to a bench. "Sit down."

Don's mind started racing. *What the hell is this about? Promotion?* He really wanted this.

"Rollins, McGanley, I'm sending you down to Amberley. You're going to check out in P-38s. You leave tomorrow. As far as I know, it's permanent, so get your stuff together."

"Australia, sir?" Don's jaw dropped. "Wha . . . what's this about? Why us?" He was trying not to raise his voice. This was totally out of the blue.

"All I know is that I was told to send two good guys down to Amberley for P-38s. That's you two."

Transferred? "Uh, sir, I . . . I was hoping to . . . I'd like to stay with the squadron. Did I do something?"

"No, McGanley. I just need to assign two good guys. I thought you might like to get to another airplane. The 38's faster, goes farther and higher. I thought you'd enjoy this."

Don was trying to figure out how to say what was on his mind. "Sir, I was hoping to become a flight commander here."

"Yes, you've been considered. I'll pass the word down to Amberley about that. I know a few people down there and in Brisbane. I think you've earned a shot at it."

Bud hadn't said a thing during all this. It didn't really matter to him where he was or what he flew. A war was a war; he just wanted to get through it in one piece. And now that he was going back to Australia, he might get a chance to go see Kate in Melbourne.

But Don was different. They walked quietly away from the tent. When Don was sure they were far enough away, he stopped. "Goddammit! What the hell is this all about?"

"Maybe it's just what the man said. He needs two good guys and picked us."

"Goddammit!"

"Whoa, there! Relax, kid, I said two *good* guys." Bud could see how steamed up Don was. "I don't know about you, but I'm kinda flattered. Maybe those guys need a couple seasoned hotshots, you know? Just the thing to get a new squadron started. And he's right. P-38s will be a lot of fun. Look, once we get down there we can go see those nurses. Maybe that cute one who dumped you will give you another chance. Kate told me she really likes you."

"I'm not in this thing to have fun, Bud."

Bud took Don's shoulder and turned him so they stood face-to-face. "Okay, then tell me. What are you in this thing for?"

Don didn't say anything. He was mad at everything right now, especially himself for blowing up in front of Bud. If he'd had any sense, he'd have found a slit trench by himself and cooled off. He took a deep breath. "Ah, sorry. Don't listen to me."

"Well, I am listening. So talk."

"Ah, I just got caught by surprise, that's all. Sorry."

Bud didn't believe him. "Someday, McGanley, you're going to figure things out, put stuff in its proper place, and just learn to do the best you can, like the rest of us. And if you're smart, you'll learn to be satisfied with that. Quit taking everything so damned hard."

"You're right."

"I sure as hell am. You know, this isn't as bad as it seems." Then Bud smiled that big optimistic smile of his. "Think of it as an opportunity. Same with that nurse friend of yours. This whole thing could turn out to be the best thing that ever happened. Personally, I can't wait to get down there. And don't worry, the Japs aren't going anywhere."

Don looked up at him. They started walking again. Don didn't know why, but he said, "I didn't get dumped, Bud."

"Yeah, yeah. Well, you can go out for a nice dinner, then."

"We're married."

Now it was Bud's turn to drop a jaw. "What?!"

"I said we're married. Day before we left Melbourne. Last summer."

Bud was truly stunned. "Holy shit! Really? You little devil! Ha! Why didn't you tell me? Well congratulations, fella. Now we've both got a *real* reason to go to Australia." He slapped Don on the back, shook his head. "I can't believe it!" Bud put his arm around Don's shoulders, a huge smile on his face. He thought, *Finally, the kid did something decent for himself.*

But the two lieutenants were a study in contrast as they walked. Head down, Don's shoulders sagged as they headed for their tent to pack up their gear.

74

The P-38 was a whole new world. With two sixteen hundred horsepower engines, it could outmaneuver the P-39 even though it was twice as heavy. It could climb like a bat out of hell and reach the 30s easily. And it was armed to the teeth, with a 20 mm cannon and four machine guns in the nose. Then there were mounts that could carry two tons of bombs and rockets. No wonder guys were so anxious to get into the newly formed squadron at Amberley.

Don and Bud were paired for the checkout, which for them turned out to be one sortie. Most of the pilots were brand new in theater with no combat time, and needed more flights than that. So the two "grizzled veterans" were left alone to fly daily patrols over the empty ocean. No one saw a Jap. Even though they flew fifteen times in two weeks, it seemed like they were out of the war.

"Hey, we just got a three-day pass." Bud sat across from Don while they ate. The food was better than anything at Seven-Mile or Gurney, but it did little to help Don's mood. He hadn't said anything since they sat down, like he was somewhere else.

"What?"

"I said we got a pass. Let's get out of here and go see the girls."

"What the hell did we get sent down here for? We haven't done a thing since we got here."

"Good question."

"I was supposed to be a flight commander down here. These clowns here have no intention of doing that. We've been flying in circles and burning up gas for two weeks. What the hell is this?"

"I don't know. Why don't you ask the boss yourself?"

"Because I'm sure I don't want to hear the answer."

"Well, you'll love this."

"What?"

"We're supposed to go up to Moresby."

"Back to 39s?"

"I don't know. I don't think so."

"Then what for?"

"It's just for a few days, I heard. But that's not the best part."

Don looked down at his plate of food. His head fell into his hands. "I can't wait."

"When we get back from Moresby we go to Charters Towers."

"Huh?"

"Yep. We're going to pick up a couple of 39s and fly them back to Gurney."

Don looked like he was ready to shoot himself. "Like a couple of yo-yos. You know what they're doing, Rollins? Stickin' it to us, that's what! We were making some headway in Milne Bay and they pulled the rug right out from under us. I was supposed to be a flight commander. Then I was told I'd be one down here. And nothing's happened. Now we get sent back, where we get to start over at the bottom of the heap. Don't you see how we've been jerked around? We got sent down here for nothing, fake promises and all. I can't believe you're so easygoing about it."

"What're you worried about? We'll be back at Gurney before the end of November."

"This is a bunch of crap, Bud, and . . ."

"You don't listen too good, do ya, McGanley? You know what your problem is? You forget that we're just lieutenants. I could care less who the flight commander is, or the squadron commander, or the nearest general. I just fly where they tell me to fly and fight when they tell me to fight. If the damned Japs get in my way, I shoot 'em. And if I'm lucky, I'll live through all this shit and then I'll get to go home. Home! That's my goal, Don, my *only* goal. I don't know about you, but when I get there, I'm gonna grab Kate and do all kinds of things to her for as long as she'll have me. We're gonna have a bunch of kids and keep practicing like we can make more until the day they plant us. Now, you tell me what the hell's wrong with that?"

"What are you talking about?"

"You, for Christ's sake! Why are you so all fired up about fighting this war and being some fancy-titled asshole? This war seems like it's your own personal proving ground. Well, I've got news for you. Those are real bullets they shoot at us, McGanley, every damned day! You can be a big shot or try to prove to yourself or anybody else whatever you want, but if these bastards get you, then all you are is *dead!* So what's more important to you, *living,* or being some kind of *fuckin'* flight commander hero? And if the answer is flight commander, then why the hell'd you get married, anyway?"

"It's for . . . well . . . it's about . . ."

"What? Tell me, right now!"

Don looked long and hard at Bud. Ever since that first day at Morrison, back when Major Wurtsmith had ordered Don to get the new pilots up in the air, Bud had been there to stand up for him. They'd only been friends for eleven months, but it seemed like much longer. They'd marched halfway up the coast of Australia, bounced around Wirraways, P-40s, P-39s, and now P-38s, been bombed by Japs, shot at by Japs, and returned fire at Japs, with fourteen confirmed and unconfirmed kills between them. They'd lost Pete, their best friend, and saw plenty of others fail to return from missions. He'd found Mary-Louise, lost her, and then found her again, with the help of malaria, no less. So . . . maybe Bud was right. Did he really have to make rank or flight commander or prove something to his father or mother or anyone else back on Staten Island?

"Well, McGanley?"

"Sorry, Bud."

Bud's eyes rolled. "You know, Don, for some strange reason, you're my best friend. But sometimes, you need a good bop on the head, like right now."

"Okay, okay, Bud."

"Not good enough. I want to hear you say that your past is in the past. Whatever happened to you that put you on this screwed-up road to glory is going to get buried right now and stay that way. You're a good pilot, Don, the best I've seen around here or anywhere, and you've got plenty of guts. Remember those two P-40s back at Lowood? Nobody else had the balls to volunteer to fly them. We all shook our heads when you volunteered, but none of us had the guts. You did. So you don't need to be a flight commander or King Arthur or Jesus Christ to prove yourself to me or anyone else. Shit, how many times do I have to say this? Now, you understand, finally?"

Don laughed, but carefully. He paused for a minute and then answered, "Jeez, Bud, you gonna hit me?"

"I oughta."

"Okay. I get it. From now on, we fly and then we go home." *And I'll keep my thoughts to myself from now on.*

"I oughta clobber you anyway, just to make sure."

"Let's take that pass and go see the girls."

"Smartest damned thing you've said in months."

75

Husband and wife lay in bed together, his arm around her shoulder and her head resting gently on his chest. They hadn't moved in a while, eyes were closed, and breathing had finally calmed down to something much slower and more relaxed. They were thinking together, but no one spoke. *We're getting better at this. Slower, longer, exploring, dizzy, almost losing control. Wonderful!* They dozed, woke up, and dozed again.

Mary-Louise opened her eyes. It was still dark outside, but she had no idea what time it was. All she knew was that she wanted this to last; when the light came he would have to go. And then she wanted them both to be away from here, on their way home on the next outbound ship, she and her husband. *We've both done enough in this war,* she thought. It would probably go on for a long time, but so would their life together if they could just have the chance to live it. She took a long slow breath and let it out just as slow. He wouldn't want to leave the war, not until it was over and he'd conquered whatever it was he needed to conquer. And it wasn't the Japanese.

She spoke softly. "Are you awake?"

"Yeah."

"I thought you were asleep."

"I should be, the way you wore me out."

"I don't want it to stop."

"I know." He said nothing for a minute or two. "I can't believe this."

"What do you mean?"

"Married, here with you, everything. I never thought anything like this would ever happen to me."

"Why do you say that?" She wanted him to talk. There were so many times he'd started to say things to her, then stopped or changed the subject. Mary-Louise knew she couldn't have him completely until he let her inside his world. There was quiet for a while. She felt his arm tighten around her shoulder, and his fingers too, as if he was gathering strength.

"I don't know. I can't say."

"Yes, you do, and yes you can. Tell me, honey." More quiet. She looked again at the window. Still dark. Good, they had time. She whispered, "I want you to tell me why."

Don closed his eyes, tight. Here he was again, up against a past that wouldn't go away. For the umpteenth time he felt his father's hand around his neck, fist cocked, ready to hit. He tried to think of a better memory of his father, but he couldn't do it. And when he left home for good, no one bothered to see him off. Let the loser go. Did it mean anything to them that they might never see him again? Guess not. Don't embarrass me, his mother had said. It hurt.

But he couldn't say these things to Mary-Louise, not all of them anyway. "I just feel lucky, I guess."

What a bunch of baloney that was, she thought. She started to sit up and face him, then stopped herself. She hoped he was finally ready to let out some of those demons that had dogged him so long. One day she'd help him expose them all, and they'd be gone for good. Now she needed him to trust her, so she didn't push him.

"I heard you're more than lucky. Your friend Rollins says you're pretty good, as a pilot, I mean. How many planes have you shot down?"

"How do you know Bud said that?"

"Kate told me."

"Bud's been working on me pretty hard lately."

"Good!"

"Good? How do you know?"

"He talks a lot about you in his letters. He's writes a lot to her. That's a hint, Lieutenant McGanley."

"But I wrote again."

"You did?"

"Yeah. A few weeks ago, from Milne Bay. Didn't you get it?"

"No. What did you say?"

"Not too much. Uh, I can't remember right now."

She let him off the hook. "Don't tell me. I'll pick it up tomorrow." She sighed, a long, slow sigh. "So how many?"

"How many what?"

"Planes. How many have you shot down?"

"Forty or fifty."

"Really? That's the most I've ever heard of!"

"No, I'm kidding." Only four officially. The others don't count." His hand tightened gently around her shoulder, right after she slapped his chest.

She reached up and kissed him. At least it was a start, the first time he'd joked about the war or himself. He kissed her back. They felt good together.

She tried to imagine him in an airplane; she couldn't really do it, even though she'd seen snapshots of other pilots in their fighters. "Aren't you afraid when you fly?"

"No."

"But what about when they're shooting at you?"

"No time to be afraid. You just react. Sometimes I think about it later, I guess, but there's not much time for that, either."

"Do you think about me?"

He chuckled. "I knew you'd ask that."

"Well, do you?"

"Sure."

"You're lying." He laughed at that; she jumped right on him. "You laughed, that means I'm right." She kissed his chest and paused for a minute. "Don, you like it up in the air, don't you?"

"Yes, I do."

"Maybe someday you'll want to be with me more than you want to be in the air over New Guinea."

"That's not so."

"Yes, it is. And I can't do much about it with this stupid war on. We may both be in Australia, but we're zillions of miles apart."

"It's going to be more. I'm going to end up back at Gurney, Milne Bay. And that's if they don't change their minds again and send me somewhere else. First I'm shipped down here for P-38s and then I'm shipped back to P-39s. I feel like a yo-yo."

"Why? Did you do something wrong?"

"I don't know. I was told I'd be a flight commander in P-38s." He was quiet for a minute. "This kind of garbage has been going on since . . . forever. I'm sick of it."

"But that's combat, isn't it? Back to New Guinea?"

"Yeah."

"But I thought that's what you wanted. Now you're mad about it? Make up your mind, flyboy."

She had him there. He felt like an idiot. "Think you're pretty smart, don't you?"

"Yes, I am. And now that I know you're going back to New Guinea, Lieutenant McGanley, you just make darned sure you come back to me when this is all over."

"Agreed." He kissed her hair and then her forehead. She turned her face up to him; they kissed and wrapped their arms tightly around each other. Then their hands began to move and their bodies responded as they explored, rolling one way and then the other, trying to press harder and harder against each other. They held their kiss as they made love, frantically this time. They lost control again, dizzy and carefree, making sounds they couldn't stop, and finally fell against each other. Then they dozed off.

✧   ✧   ✧

She awoke again, having no idea how long she'd been asleep. But she knew time was running out; there was a hint of light out the window. Mary-Louise guessed he was still asleep but spoke anyway. "I'm going on the *Samaritaan*."

She was surprised, but glad when he answered, "What's that?"

"A Dutch hospital ship. The crew's Dutch, but they use Australian and American nurses. They've been telling us for months that nurses will start rotating out and back to the forward areas. Now they finally got around to it."

"When?"

"I don't know. They asked for volunteers at the hospital, and Kate and I signed up. The ships don't keep a regular schedule because *you guys* don't fight your war on one, either. They said they'd try to give us as much notice as they can."

He was taken aback there. His *wife* was possibly going into harm's way. He'd never thought about that before. A sudden shot of worry hit him; he'd never felt that before, either. Now he didn't know what to do about any of it and tried not to react to it. "Whatsamatta? Didn't you get enough cruising on the *Mariposa*?"

She couldn't tell if he liked the idea or not. In a way she wanted him to protest. Another side of her wanted him to support her. She decided to be matter of fact about it. "They said we'd all go sooner or later. I suppose it's our turn in the barrel, as they say. And I want to help, Don. All these sick and injured guys I see; they need us."

He realized how much he liked it when she used his first name. And he realized he was proud of her. He kissed her. "How long will you be out?"

"I don't know. But they always rotate the nurses when the ships come into port. At least they do in Melbourne. So I guess it won't be too long, a month or so." She paused. "I heard a rumor the other day. We're going to put up a general hospital on New Guinea as soon as you heroes make it safe. Maybe I'll volunteer again and get on the ship. If we stop in Milne Bay, think you'll be able to find room on your cot for me?"

"No way."

"What?" She looked hurt.

"You think I'd want you on my cot, in an eight-man tent, with a bunch of smelly, nosy pilots watching us? I mean, I'd be embarrassed. You know what I mean."

She snuggled up and made up her mind that she wasn't done with him yet. "It's only embarrassing if you're doing something naughty." She saw him smile. *Bashful,* she thought, *he doesn't know what to say.* She thought it was cute, but was smart enough not to say anything. What fighter pilot wanted to be thought of as "cute"? Instead, she put her hand on his chest and slowly stroked down, past his stomach, lower still, until she found him. "Like this."

76

December 3, 1942

The formation of officers stood at attention for the boss of Fighter Command, Paul B. Wurtsmith. Wurtsmith had met General Kenney at Darwin during Kenney's theater tour last July and made a heck of an impression, as he had on Don back at Morrison Field. Kenney told him he'd move up if he performed, and Wurtsmith did. The 49th Group fought off raid after raid at a time when the Australian people and just about everyone at headquarters thought an invasion of the mainland was inevitable. Perhaps the success Wurtsmith's group had in the summer and early fall of 1942 helped convince the Japanese to forget it. When Wurtsmith flew his P-40 into Milne Bay for this medal ceremony, he wore stars on his shoulders.

Good thing it was overcast. Without a wisp of wind, it was sweltering enough in the ranks without the sun beating on the men. But this was important, part of General Kenney's determination to make sure that those who fought the good fight got recognized for it. Don stood out in front of the formation with two others, facing Wurtsmith while the adjutant read aloud.

Award of the Silver Star, Donald T. McGanley, First Lieutenant, Thirty-sixth Fighter Squadron, Eighth Fighter Group, Air Corps, U.S. Army. For gallantry in action over Port Morseby, New Guinea, on May 28, 1942. This officer was pilot of a pursuit plane which participated in an attempt to intercept the enemy. Twenty-five Zeroes attacked, sending elements to the front and rear of our formation. In spite of their

numerical superiority and heavy fire from all directions,
Lieutenant McGanley turned and made a head-on attack
on the main flight and succeeded in damaging at least one
Zero. Instead of diving and attempting to escape, Lieutenant
McGanley, noticing an enemy fighter attacking a P-39 from
the rear, quickly went to the attack and succeeded in causing
the Zero to withdraw.

That was the *first* Silver Star awarded to Don, from the mission when they lost Pete. A second Silver Star was for the two victories on May 29. And next there was a Distinguished Flying Cross for seventy-five combat missions. He was the first in the unit to get the DFC.

Wurtsmith stepped forward after each reading, pinning the medals just above the left shirt pocket. "Long overdue, Mac. I'll make sure you don't have to wait so long next time."

"Thank you, sir."

"Sorry I didn't bring you along to Darwin with me. You've proven yourself here. Tough conditions, too. Damn fine job."

"Thank you, sir." Don didn't know what else to say. The ceremony ended abruptly; Don turned around, and Bud was already right in front of him, extending his hand.

"Congrats, Don. I never knew what a hero you were."

Don shook his head. He was embarrassed. It was bad enough having all the citations read, one for the other two officers and three for him, especially when half the stuff in the citations was pure junk. They sounded like somebody had typed them up for some soupy movie. Don said, "None of that stuff was even close to what happened."

"So what? You've been gung ho from the first day here. 'Bout damned time somebody noticed."

"They didn't even have the dates right."

"And they forgot the part where you had the shits and had to pucker yourself all the way back to Seven-Mile!" Bud was laughing now, even harder when Don threw his arms up. "Don't worry, though, buddy. We enjoyed hearing every word of it." Then Bud stopped laughing. "And you know, it looked like Wurtsmith remembered you."

"Yeah, yeah. He's a good man, Bud. I wish we could have gone to Darwin with him."

"But we'd have missed Seven-Mile, and you wouldn't have all those fancy medals now. Shit, you'd probably still be a slug like the rest of us. Now I'm waiting with baited breath for your fifth kill. I heard Kenney said he'd pin a medal on anyone who made ace." Don didn't react. "C'mon, fella, look at the bright side. Somebody big noticed. I thought that's what you wanted." Bud put his arm around Don's shoulders. "The big cheese figured out what the rest of us have already known for a while now. Who cares if some paper-pusher can't write worth a shit?" Bud paused. "Know what I think?"

"What?"

"I think you should take a look at what's happened over the past year and see how far you've come, and how far we've all come."

"Here we go again."

"Well, you seem to need it, or you need that good bop on the head. Maybe both. Think about it, Don. In a way, those medals were for all of us. So what if they're boring and written up stupid. We've been so busy bein' shot at and so worried about the Japs coming over the next hill that nobody's taken the time to tell us that we're doing our jobs pretty damned good around here. And it's not over. We're going to be here for a while yet, that's for sure. I don't know about you, but I'm *glad* you got to stand up there and take a bow. You oughta be proud, too."

"You think so, eh?"

"Damn right I do. I'm just sorry Pete wasn't here. He'd be proud of you today." Bud saw that Don was looking down. He'd embarrassed him. "Too bad you're married. Pete woulda found you a woman."

Don looked up and saw Bud grinning. "You're not going to start up with *that*, are you?"

"Nah, Pete's property. Tell you what, though, let's get over to the Ops Tent and join the party. If we can't get drunk, at least we can act like we are!"

"For Pete's sake!"

There was no flying that day. With little else to do, the boys dug into some extra C-rations, the newer canned stuff that actually had some taste. After a while, they broke into a chorus or two of "Don't Sit Under the Apple Tree," and someone actually got hold of some "coconut juice," New Guinea moonshine. Before long a pair of scissors appeared and the pilots started an impromptu hair-clipping party. There was no one to impress, so what the hell. It was a good party, right when the boys needed one.

✧　✧　✧

It was dark in the sleeping tent, had been for quite a while, but Don couldn't sleep. He wondered where all the mosquitoes were, and then realized a decent breeze was blowing through the place. That didn't happen very often. Nice change. There were some snores, but Don couldn't tell who the noisemakers were. No matter. It was a fine, quiet night. He thought about things Bud had said, two or three times now. Pete, too, and Mary-Louise. He couldn't hide anything from her, as hard as he tried.

He felt alone, like he was not good enough. Geez, he'd always felt that way. Why couldn't he shake that feeling? Pete had stuck with him, Bud stood up for him, Mary-Louise loved him, and Wurtsmith rewarded him. Two Silver Stars! Not one, but *two*. He thought about that sergeant at the CMTC, Malone it was. He hadn't remembered him in a long time. What the hell did all these people see in him, and why wouldn't he let himself see it? Wasn't it about time he did?

And what did he really want out of the cockpit of a fighter? A place where he could push aside the pain of Johnny's anger and indifference, forget what happened to Paulie and those two busted

P-40s? Wasn't it ironic that he felt safe in the very place he was in the most danger? Heck of a war he was fighting, and how would he know he'd won it? He realized, maybe for the first time, that he owed someone besides himself to do just that.

77

December 8, 1942

The *Samaritaan* sailed from Melbourne for Darwin, just under four thousand miles away. It would take a week to get there. The ship was three days behind her planned departure, having lost almost one-sixth of her crew in port, deserters now caught and jailed. Most of the deserters were Javanese who'd have been a lot smarter to wait until the ship docked closer to home before they took off. Now they'd probably have to sit in Aussie jails until either the war was over or a manpower shortage forced their release.

Kate and Mary-Louise roomed together in their own cabin, unusual but welcome. Duty was light on the way north, a leisurely life that wouldn't last long. As soon as they took on wounded, scheduled shifts would run twelve hours, but more like sixteen in reality. The weather was perfect, the seas calm. Clear nights followed spectacular sunsets, like the one right now, where high stratus clouds edged by sharp orange colors and streaky rays made the western sky look like some Monet painting. You just had to see the sight for yourself because the right words didn't exist to describe it. Mary-Louise and Kate leaned against the port railing of the *Samaritaan*'s top deck and took it all in, both thinking about the same thing: their fighter pilots.

"You thinking about Don?" Kate asked.

"Yes."

"I was wrong about him."

"What do you mean?"

"I mean that when I saw you two together this last time, I knew I was wrong. You looked . . . I don't know . . . you two just looked right, you know?"

"He's a good man, Kate. He wants to be here, flying I mean, and I know he's troubled sometimes. He won't tell me much now, but some day he will. I'll help him do that, and then we'll go home."

"Where's that going to be?"

"I don't know, probably New York somewhere. We'll meet his parents in the city and then go up to Glens Falls to see mine. Who knows after that? I'll just go wherever he wants." She paused. Kate looked at her.

"What?"

"I'm afraid."

"Of what?"

"This war. I . . . I don't know."

"Mary-L, you can't let yourself run scared like that. We both have a lot to lose. Everybody does. We just have to do our job. We pay attention to that and we'll be fine."

They were quiet for a moment. "Yeah, I know. But, God, I miss the *hell* out of him."

"Mary-L!" Kate feigned shock and laughed as she spoke, "Where'd you come up with talk like that?"

It was Mary-Louise's turn to laugh. "From listening to you talk too much about Bud. So why didn't you two get married when he came down with Don?"

"We decided to wait until after the war. We're going to be apart so much, so we figured we'd be man and wife when we could live like man and wife. I got him, though. He promised me his last night here. After that, we—"

"Wait a minute! *Promised* you? I thought you weren't going to let him touch you until you got married."

"I lied. You'd lie too if somebody did those things to you. Mary-L, when he . . ."

"Never mind, Kate. I get the idea."

"For Christ's sake, Mary-L, you're married. You ought to be the expert here. What's all the shock about?"

"I'm not shocked."

"So tell me what Don does."

"I will not!"

"Must be good. I'll tell you, Bud's all over me, his hands and his fingers, and he knows what to do with his . . ."

"Will you stop?" Mary-Louise turned back toward the fading light on the horizon and let her mind drift back to their night in bed, too: how careful and gentle he was and how they'd lost control. They'd made love three times, or was it four?

She looked up. The colors were almost gone from the sky now, and she could see more and more stars as the pale light disappeared from the horizon. She forced herself to think of the wounded they'd board the next day and the help they'd need. The medical staff had already been told that the *Samaritaan* would spend minimum time in the harbor since the Japanese were so fond of attacking Darwin.

Kate looked at Mary-Louise, who seemed like she was somewhere else all of a sudden. Kate supposed she had a right to be. She was the married one. What kind of wife would she be if she wasn't afraid? Enough for now, though. She stood silently next to Mary-Louise, half wondering how long she should wait before she brought the girl out of it. A half hour passed, it seemed, though it was only a few minutes.

"Mary-L, anybody home?"

"Oh, sorry, Kate, I was thinking about the wounded. We'll be busy tomorrow."

"Yeah, I suppose so. I guess our boys will have to wait, won't they?"

"And so will we. Let's leave it at that, okay?"

"Okay." Kate knew when to back off. The girl talk was just a little fun. Kate hoped it didn't offend her. In fact, she knew it didn't. They'd be fine. Kate made up her mind to personally see that Mary-L got safely through this brutal war so she and Don could make those rounds in New York, and have that life together.

78

Darwin was a mess. The *Samaritaan* arrived at 2300 hours, the smell of oily smoke guiding the ship into port. The place had been hit the day before. One destroyer was severely damaged and two munitions buildings totally flattened: a couple of stray rounds had apparently started a chain reaction, then secondary explosions did the rest. Over twenty men were badly injured around those buildings alone. The runway had taken two or three direct hits, but those had been patched already. Finally, two doctors and a nurse had died in a direct hit on the station's clinic, leaving the wounded and sick with only makeshift care until help arrived.

While the *Samaritaan*'s medical staff spent the night identifying and assigning casualties to wards on the ship, the head doctor met with the Australian station commander. They scheduled the ship's departure for 0500, or as soon as possible once casualties were aboard. One doctor and one nurse from the ship's staff would stay behind, at least until Brisbane could assign permanent replacements for those killed in action. Kate was picked.

Medical staff response to the emergency was cool, fast, and efficient. At 0600, after only seven hours in port, the *Samaritaan* was back at sea. Normally, hospital ships made two or three stops to pick up the wounded and the sick, but the Darwin casualties plus malaria victims and wounded from New Caledonia and New Guinea filled up enough beds for the head doctor to direct the ship back to Melbourne.

✧　✧　✧

It had been a long, hectic day, or was it two? Mary-Louise had been on her feet since the *Samaritaan* made port, working nonstop through the night and then starting her shift without a break, with nothing but a couple of pieces of fruit to keep her going. She hadn't even realized that Kate was left at Darwin until a doctor told her, three hours after they'd left port. Now finally off duty, Mary-Louise was too tired to eat a full meal, so she'd come up on deck to eat a last piece of fruit before heading off to bed.

The breeze on deck was heavenly; warm and not too strong. She felt herself starting to relax as she closed her eyes and faced the wind. They'd done well today. Moving so many critically wounded GIs was a huge medical risk, but well worth it. The men were bedded down now. Those needing morphine had received it, wounds had been dressed, and sponge baths finished. Now the wards were finally quiet, at least for a while. As shifts got back to normal, nurses who'd worked straight through could finally relax.

At times like this, Mary-Louise could clearly see the impact of her role in this war. Thoughts about going home were replaced by an intense desire to save the lives of these men. She was proud of her service, of theirs. She thought of her husband, wondering where he was and if he was safe. She was proud of him.

And when would she see him? She hoped there'd be a letter from him when she got back to Melbourne. She thought back, back to the *Mariposa*, when she'd caught the cute second lieutenant sneaking peeks at her in the dining room, then when she'd met Don for the first time. And then the sunrise on deck, when he was too shy to kiss her even though they both knew it was the perfect time. She saw his face as he woke up from his bout with malaria, too weak and disoriented to know where he was. She thought about breakfast at the café, how he'd looked when he realized he couldn't pay the check. Royal Park, where he finally summoned the nerve to kiss her for the first time, and they both knew they wanted to get married. And then they were together in the dark, locked as close as their bodies could get, but not close enough. She loved Don more than anything. What was he doing now, she wondered.

And the breeze still blew, lightly and peacefully. Mary-Louise drew a long, deep breath, took one last look across the rail, and decided she ought to head for her cabin. No doubt the next day would be another long one. As she turned away from the railing she heard a buzz back to her right, toward the sun. She looked in that direction but couldn't see anything through the glare, though the sound was getting louder. Clangs from the ship's bells suddenly echoed across the deck.

"Get below, all hands get below!" The voice was deafening, as was the continuous clang, clang, clang of warning. Mary-Louise ran for the stairs, only twenty-five feet away, which would lead down to the next deck, to the door into the ship's interior, and safety. She reached for the railing as the first bullets ricocheted against the ship's siding, pinged off the railing of the stairs, and thudded into the teak floors of the deck.

It was just a playful run of fun for a couple of Jap pilots on the way home. The planes were gone as fast as they came, the single pass leaving damage so slight it almost wasn't worth reporting, though the captain surely would. But as the Zeroes climbed away from the *Samaritaan*, Mary-Louise lay unconscious and bleeding, less than three feet from the stairs which led to the door below.

✧ ✧ ✧

Strafing attacks against hospital ships didn't happen often, especially at sea, but they happened often enough to keep the crews and medical personnel on edge. As soon as the immediate danger was over, crewmembers did a sweep of the decks to check for damage. No one was allowed on deck until the sweeps were finished and the captain gave an "all clear." That usually took more than an hour. Sometimes the "all clear" never came.

Two crewmembers found the American nurse almost immediately. Help arrived less than two minutes later, two doctors and another nurse, breathing hard after running up three or four sets of stairs.

"It's Anderson! Head wound! Get some pressure on the side of her head, right there!" She was still bleeding; at least there was a pulse. One of the doctors yelled at the nurse. "Bad! We'll get her below. Run ahead and get the OR ready for us. Move it!"

79

December 16, 1942

The sun was just starting to rise. Four P-39s cruised smoothly at 21,000 feet, headed east-northeast, about ten miles off the New Guinea's northern coast. Don was in the lead. Bud led another flight of six about five minutes behind them.

Patrols up the coast had been largely uneventful of late. The Japanese were mostly on the defensive now. Fifth Air Force had control of the air over the island. There was an unmistakable, growing feeling among the allies that the war was beginning to go their way. No one had heard talk about invasion fleets or the likely loss of New Guinea or the possible invasion of Australia since last September, three months ago. In fact, the Japanese had been rolled all the way back along the Kokoda Trail to Buna. It looked like a matter of time before they'd be pushed off the island entirely.

But the battle for New Guinea was far from over. The enemy, though depleted and far outnumbered, dug in at Buna, surrounded there by Aussies and Americans since November 21. P-39s out of Milne Bay and Port Moresby had been strafing their positions every day since, weather permitting.

This was the first time the Allies had seen the enemy in such a defensive crouch, and they would soon find out what that really meant. The Japanese would not give in to surrender, regardless how hopeless their situation might be. They fought intensely to the death. The costs in time, resources, and casualties necessary to root them out to the last man would drag out the siege at Buna until long after the outcome was known. The pattern would repeat itself for three and a half more years as the Americans inched closer to Japan, island by island.

The nature of the air battle was no different. Maybe there were fewer enemy airplanes in the air and fewer raids against American airfields, but the Japanese were far from stopped. Dead ahead, Don picked up a large group of enemy bombers about two thousand feet above them, headed south, probably for Port Moresby. He maneuvered to put the sun directly behind the P-39s. They'd be practically invisible. Perfect. He looked to his right at Art Anderson and pointed to the bombers ahead. Anderson nodded and passed the signal along. Flight leaders had made it clear before they left Milne Bay: no radios unless engaged, in case the enemy was listening.

Don scanned above and behind the bombers looking for Zeroes, which usually lagged there, then pounced as the Americans attacked. No Zeroes, though. As the Americans approached, they noticed that these bombers were different from the Bettys they were accustomed to seeing. These were "Sallys," older, smaller, maybe a little faster. They'd heard about them, but hadn't seen many so far, perhaps another indicator that the Japanese were being stretched.

Most of the Sally's guns were 7.7mm machine guns, instead of the Betty's notorious and lethal array of 20mm cannons. There was one 12.7 mm gun in the dorsal turret that the attackers needed to avoid; coming out of the sun at high speed would help a lot with that. Still, lighter armament overall meant less range capability for the bombers' guns and less potential damage if the Americans got hit.

Don gave the skies behind and above the Sallys one last look and saw clear air. The Americans split and attacked, diving and firing on the outermost bombers first. The Sallys were in a single group in a wide arrowhead formation, total of nine. Unusual. Normally, there would be two or three groups of bombers, staggered horizontally and vertically for mutual support.

Don opened up on the leader from the formation's nine o'clock position, in a dive, *Nip's Nemesis* burbling slightly as it approached maximum speed. He aimed for the cockpit, spraying a three-second burst down the left side of the bomber. The left engine blew up almost immediately as the Sally nosed violently over and to the left. Probably got the pilot, too. Then the whole bomber exploded. He pulled up, overflew the formation, and then yanked hard left to circle around for another pass. He lined up in the bombers' front quarter, no longer out of the sun and slower now, the sharp turn costing him airspeed. One more pass oughta do it; three of the Sallys were down already. He scanned the skies to the north one more time. *Shit!* Zeroes, at least two formations of them, a dozen at least.

He yelled into his mike, "Zeroes trailing the bombers, one thousand feet high, two groups!" The light colors of the Japs airplanes had served them well. They were close. "Get the bombers! Stay in tight and get the bombers!" Don hoped his three wingmen would stay engaged, maybe nail a few more and stay close enough to the bombers so the Zeroes couldn't fire without the risk of hitting their own airplanes.

Don broke off his attack on the bombers and aimed straight for the Zeroes. He needed more speed and altitude but had neither. Some of the Zeroes were already firing even though the P-39s were way out of range. For their part, the Sallys were cutting loose with their 7.7mm guns, following the P-39s as they passed. The air was full of bullets, and the sun's bright, low angle, which was such an advantage only seconds before, was now a problem, disorienting to say the least. Worse yet, it turned Don's instrument panel into a black hole: he couldn't afford to take his eyes off the Jap fighters long enough to check his airspeed. Head on, he picked out a target right in the middle of the Zeroes. They were flying nice and tight, no lateral maneuverability. *Stupid*, he thought. He put his finger on the trigger and fired.

Twenty miles back, Bud Rollins picked up the fight when Don's Sally exploded in midair. He cobbed the power and climbed; 20 seconds later he heard Don's call about the Zeroes but stayed silent. Little bastards were probably using the same frequency and listening.

He saw a huge fireball dead ahead, then another to his right. Damn! Still too far away! He headed for the smaller fireball, the Zeroes, gradually picking up more and more airplanes. Rollins' flight had the sun at their backs, the same advantage Don's flight had had. Even though the Zeroes had a light paint job, they looked like black dots when they turned. Jesus, there was a bunch of them! At least they didn't seem to know that the second flight of P-39s was there.

Don's first pass into the Zeroes scattered the whole flight, with a nice dividend. One blew up in front of him, a lucky shot perhaps, but he'd take it. Meanwhile, the Sallys had had enough. One of them banked hard and right to escape and ran into a wingman, causing a huge fireball, the large one Bud had seen seconds ago. Another Sally started smoking, probably hit by shrapnel. After two passes by the P-39s, several bombers were down, the remainder scattered. Rather than chase them all down, Art Anderson, now east of the bombers, broke off, called his flight to follow, and headed for the Zeroes. He picked up the fight to the north, McGanley against six Zeroes, maybe a minute away.

The odds among the fighters were evening up now. Bud's flight closed fast from the east, Anderson and four more from the south. Good thing! Don was low on airspeed, helpless against the highly maneuverable Zeroes. He pushed down toward the water to gain airspeed and separate from the fight. All he'd wanted to do was break up the escort so they couldn't help the bombers. Then, with enough speed, he'd turn east into the sun and get his flight out of there.

Bud's flight arrived, almost invisible until the last, a total surprise. The Zeroes closest to him seemed to be pulling down and away. It would take too much time to chase them down. The second group, the one Don had attacked, was scattered like flies. Easy pickings. Bud's flight blew through the disorganized Zeroes. Two went down right away, without any defensive reaction. The three that remained evidently saw the six P-39s bearing down on them and shot skyward to get away and out of the fight. Bud chose not to follow them, and the fight was over.

✧   ✧   ✧

Don's eyes were now on the water and his rising speed, with no idea that six Zeroes from the second group had followed him down. Two of them opened fire on his P-39. Now it was the Japs who came out of the sun. Don never saw them, only felt several loud, sudden thumps, like the ones he felt that first day over Seven-Mile. His body jerked, a reflex, bending over to the right. His head hit the canopy and he felt a sharp burning in his right side and hip. He instinctively rolled right and pulled, into the attacking Zeroes, forcing them to pull up. They flew right over him.

I'm hit! He looked up and right and saw another Zero firing, tracers coming right at him. Then there was another loud thump, then more pain, same spot. He screamed out loud and shoved on the throttle, already full forward, turned harder right into the Zero, which also shot past, directly overhead.

They'd never catch him now. He checked his cockpit: 8,400 feet, 320 mph. By the time the Zeroes turned around to follow, he'd be way too far ahead, out of range. He looked back to make sure. The Zeroes must realized the same thing Don did; they didn't bother to try and chase him down. Don started a slow left turn to parallel the coast and headed southeast toward Milne Bay. He scanned his engine instruments; they all looked okay. He pulled the throttle back and set his manifold pressure at 2300.

Nip's Nemesis had taken some hits, but it was a good airplane, flying smoothly. Don took one more look behind him, high and to the left, and then the right; he couldn't stop a yelp as he twisted around. He looked down and saw blood all over the upper right thigh of his flight suit. He was breathing heavily; he forced himself to take a long, slow breath, yelped again as he straightened up, and took another breath. He spoke out loud to himself, "That's enough for one day."

80

Two doctors and three nurses worked into their third hour of surgery. They'd stopped the bleeding but were carefully picking bone fragments from the frontal lobes of the patient's brain. Most of the damage was on the left, likely to affect language, motor skills, and intellectual abilities. The blood-brain barrier, which screened toxic substances from the brain's blood supply, was almost nonexistent in spots. If Mary-Louise survived at all, doctors were in for a full-time fight to prevent infection and further bleeding. Coma was all but certain. There was no way to determine the extent of damage until she woke up. They could only hope to get the fragments out, stabilize her condition, and get her home alive.

✧　✧　✧

"Ah, damn!" Don kept pushing on his side and hip. Every second it got worse as the adrenaline wore off. His left hand was on the stick while he used his right to try and stop the bleeding. It wasn't working very well; he was soaked in red, with more blood seeping through his fingers. His right hand sank into the wound; he'd been hit in the same area at least twice. And he couldn't move his right leg. He bent forward a little, and tightened down hard. No good. He forced himself to take slow, deep breaths, started feeling a little dizzy. *Jeez, this hurts like hell!* Behind him, two flights of P-39s moved up on his right.

✧　✧　✧

The nurse took a pulse and tucked the bed sheets good and snug around Mary-Louise while the doctor flashed a light in her eyes.

"Well, doctor?"

"Pupilary response in both eyes, so that's good. Mid-brain looks okay, as far as I can tell." He placed his stethoscope on her chest, listened.

The nurse asked, "Will she make it?"

"I don't know. X-rays showed we got all the fragments out. But there was considerable damage, and lots of blood loss. Not much more we can do now. We'll see what kind of impairment she has if and when she comes out of the coma. There's bound to be some. And it'll be a long road back for her after that. They'll have to get her to a neurologist when she gets back to the states."

"Lucky to be alive."

"That she is. If this happened out in the field somewhere, she wouldn't have had a chance. At least the sulfas were effective. We seem to have stopped any infection, at least for now."

"Do we continue them?"

"No, let's go with penicillin, one injection every six hours for a few days. I don't think we should worry about any reaction it might have with brain tissues. There's been some concern about that. Let's just make sure we hold off infection for now. I don't want to have to go in again."

"Yes, doctor." The nurse shook her head slightly. "I don't know her very well. She came on board just before we left Melbourne. But she worked like a mule at Darwin. I wish I had twenty more like her."

"Yep, she seems like a good kid." They stood there together for a moment. "C'mon, kid, don't give up." He touched her forehead gently, and left.

✧ ✧ ✧

"McGanley, you okay?" No answer. "Don, this is Bud. Are you okay?" Still no answer. "McGanley, *goddammit*, answer up! You're going down! Level off!"

Now he heard. Bud was screaming at him, but he sounded a long way off. He tried to check his altimeter but couldn't read it. His head spun. But instinctively he pulled back on the stick, reached level flight, and then started climbing. Then he relaxed without knowing it and started to nose over again. He no longer knew where he was, how low he was, or how fast he was going. He felt sleepy. It was getting darker outside.

"Don, *shit*, stay with me!" It was Bud again. There was no smoke trailing Don's airplane. Bud saw the bullet holes all along the right fuselage, on the cockpit door, right behind the neatly painted *Nip's Nemesis*. It was a miracle they missed the engine and drive train. The airplane was pretty shot up. And he could see that Don was partially slumped over. "Talk to me, Don. Where are you hit?"

He was thinking about how good it felt in this cockpit, on a combat mission, in the best place in the world. New Guinea—just an island in the middle of God-knows-where, but he was a fighter pilot here.

"Don! C'mon, kid, stay with me, now. Pull up a little bit. C'mon, pull up a little bit. Don! Dammit, answer me!" *Nip's Nemesis* was rolling slightly to the right, passing twenty-five hundred feet. "We're puttin' in at Wanigela Mission. Five minutes and you'll be on the ground. Say somethin', McGanley! Mary-Louise, remember her? Hang on, dammit!"

Someone was calling him, but he couldn't hear it very well. Johnny, finally? Or Vic? Pete? Bud? Paulie? He couldn't tell. It was almost dark. Sleepy, dizzy. No pain at all; he was fine now. In fact, everything was okay, finally. He could see blurry instruments in front of him, tried to focus on them and the canopy rails on either side, but couldn't. He saw the stick in his hand, but couldn't feel it. Then he mumbled, slowly, barely audible, "I don't need to do any more."

Steadily, darkness started closing in from all sides. He couldn't stop it, no strength left. He exhaled slowly, and let the darkness come.

✧ ✧ ✧

Nine hundred miles to the southeast, a hospital shipped steamed along at twenty-one knots, headed for Melbourne. She would make good time getting there by riding the East Australia Current. Among the patients was a young nurse locked in a coma with severe head wounds. Within two days they'd transfer her to the first ship bound for the United States. She would still be asleep when she arrived at the Presidio Hospital in San Francisco three weeks later.

✧ ✧ ✧

On December 16, 1942, just north of Buna, twelve American P-39s destroyed three Sally bombers, got credit for two more that collided, and downed three Zeroes. Two pilots became aces: Donald Thomas McGanley from Staten Island, New York, with six confirmed kills, and Wilford T. Rollins from Knoxville, Tennessee, with five. They lost one man.

Epilogue

September 12, 1962, U.S. Air Force Academy, Colorado Springs

The freshman had his chin tucked firmly down and in, the way freshmen, or "doolies," were supposed to as they sat in Mitchell Hall, where the cadets took their meals. Since they'd arrived at the Air Force Academy in June, doolies "caged" their eyes straight down at the academy emblem at the bottom of their plates. If called upon by an upperclassmen, they could look up, but only to answer the question asked.

Two tables away, Cadet Third Class Chuck Coles stared across the Mitchell Hall floor at the doolie. Coles had the feeling he was staring at himself. Christ, the doolie looked just like him! As the meal period ended, seniors and juniors began to get up and leave, until there were only the doolies and a few third classmen (sophomores) left. Coles got up, walked over to the doolie's table, and spoke to the highest ranking cadet he could find.

"Howdy! Chuck Coles. You guys Tenth Squadron?"

"Yeah."

"Who's that smack over there?" Smack: another endearing name for doolies, along with "squat."

"Andrews."

"Where's he from?"

"Don't know. Ask him if you want."

"No, that's okay. I'll drop by Ten after the meal. Any problem if I go see him?"

"No, I don't think so, but the AOC (Air Officer Commanding) has a problem with guys being bothered during Call to Quarters, just so you know. Hard-ass! He wants people to be studying so we can lead First Group in GPA. No screwing around or noise in the halls. He usually patrols around for the first hour, but if you come after 2100, you should be okay."

"Thanks."

"You know, you guys look a lot alike." He paused, looking back and forth at Coles and the doolie. "In fact, it's kinda *scary* how much you look alike."

"Yeah. Hey, thanks a lot."

Call to Quarters was the evening study period, running from 1945 to 2230 each night. It seemed long, but with six classes to prepare for, the time was valuable, usually all that the cadets could get in one day. Afternoons after class were wiped out by marching, rifle drill, or intramural sports, and the evening meal was mandatory. If cadets were lucky enough to have periods off during the daytime, they frequently spent them getting some extra "rack," or sleep.

Chuck rapped lightly on the door of Cadet Fourth Class John D. Andrews and Cadet Fourth Class Morton A. Jenkins, Class of '66. He opened the door without an answer, the normal custom, and walked into the dorm room. Both beds were made up neatly with red blankets, the class color. The room was spotless, except for the desks, which were strewn with textbooks. Both freshmen snapped to attention.

"You guys busy?"

Jenkins answered, "Uh, sir, we were just studying."

Chuck stared at Andrews, who stared back, and then looked straight ahead. There was a long silence. Then Chuck turned to Jenkins. "Mr. Jenkins, I need a minute or two with Mr. Andrews here. Think you can hide next door for a bit?"

Jenkins jaw dropped. "Uh, sir . . . yes, sir."

"Thanks. I'll come and get you when I'm finished."

"Yes, sir." He gawked one more time at his roommate, then at the upperclassman, and left.

Chuck turned to the doolie. "Have a seat and relax, Andrews."

"Yes, sir."

"I mean it. Have a seat and relax." Andrews sat. There was a long minute of silence. Chuck took a couple of deep breaths. "Mr. Andrews, have you noticed how much alike we look?"

"Yes, sir."

"Where are you from?"

"Stevens Point, Wisconsin, sir."

"Mansfield, Ohio." Chuck could see that Andrews was stiff and uncomfortable. "You like the Academy, Andrews?"

"It's okay, sir. It's going to be hard."

"Well don't worry. You kind of get used to it. Some guys yell more than others, but now that the academic year's started, that stuff backs off a lot. Getting through basic summer is the tough part."

"It's the academics, sir."

"A lot of guys have more trouble with the military transition."

"Sir, that was easy. It's the academics that are hard. I had to go to college for a year to get boned up on math and science."

"I know what you mean. After I was accepted, the academy sent me two math books to complete before I showed up. Well, don't worry. There're lots of smart guys around who can help you out. If you have trouble, don't be afraid to ask."

"Yes, sir."

"So you went to college for a year. How old are you, then? Nineteen?"

"Yes, sir. Turned nineteen on July 10."

"What year were you born?"

"1943."

Chuck stared long and hard. "Any brothers or sisters?" His heart was pounding so hard that he could hear it through his chest. *What the hell was going on?*

Jack sensed it. His answer came slow, deliberate, and calculated. "Two sisters, sir, but not really. Half sisters. I was adopted."

Chuck's eyes got wide. "So was I."

There was a pause. "Really?"

"Yeah. And my birthdate is July tenth . . . 1943."

They were stunned. Jack could barely speak. "Jesus!"

"Yeah. What's your first name, Andrews?"

"John, sir."

"Is that what you go by?"

"No, sir. It's Jack."

Chuck stood up. "Well, Jack, why don't we do a little research."

"Yes, sir."

"I think we're related somehow. We gotta be. Look in the mirror. Same height, same looks, exact same age, and both adopted. Anyone ever told you about your real parents?"

"Not much. They were killed in the war."

"Like mine. Tell you what, Jack, let's you and I find out. We can use the phones in the library. And drop the 'sir' shit, okay?"

✧ ✧ ✧

Both boys had known of their adoption for several years. Birth certificates reported the Presidio Hospital in San Francisco as their place of birth and the Harrell Adoption Agency as their guardian. Harrell policy prohibited disclosures about natural parents, so there'd been no secrets for adopting families to keep over the years. When Harrell went out of business in late 1946, whatever records they had identifying natural parents and next of kin disappeared as well. There were a million Andersons in the United States, and no way to figure out which one they needed to find. Dead end.

But researching Presidio Hospital records was a different matter. A series of phone calls to San Francisco put the cadets in contact with a helpful nurse, who went through basement records and found out that a Nurse Lt. Mary-Louise Anderson, wounded in the Southwest Pacific Area and permanently impaired, had delivered twin sons there on July 10, 1943. All the record said was that the boys were given up for adoption and released to the Harrell Adoption Agency on August 30.

And then came an incredible stroke of luck. As part of academy training, cadets learned the biographies of the academy's big shots, among them the newly-assigned Vice-commandant of cadets, Col. Wilford T. (Bud) Rollins. The colonel had been among the first Army Air Corps pilots in the Southwest Pacific Area during World War II. Jack remembered his bio from Basic Training. Southwest Pacific Area, just like Mary-Louise Anderson: maybe, just maybe. Wouldn't hurt to ask, anyway.

✧   ✧   ✧

The phone rang at Colonel Rollins' quarters. Mrs. Rollins was just finishing up the dishes after having a friend over. The colonel was out of town, and she just never wanted to sit and eat by herself, being the social butterfly that she was.

"Mrs. Rollins."

"Good evening, ma'am. My name is Cadet Third Class Coles. I was told that the colonel is TDY this week."

"Yes, he is. I expect him back Saturday. How can I help you, Cadet Coles?"

"I was wondering if you could please leave him a message for me."

"Certainly. What is it?"

"Well, I know he served in the Pacific Theater during World War II."

"Yes, he did."

"Well, ma'am, I just wondered if he ever heard of a nurse named Mary-Louise Anderson."

Dead silence.

"Hello? Mrs. Rollins?"

"Ye . . . yes, I'm here."

"Can you pass the message to him, please? I can call back when he gets home, or I'm in 18th Squadron, Cadet Coles, if he wants to get hold of me." Again there was silence. Chuck looked at the phone like there was something wrong with it. "Hello?"

"Yes, uh, yes, I'll get hold of him and pass him your message."

"Thank you, ma'am, and I'm sorry to bother you in the evening."

"It's no trouble at all, Mr. Coles. Good night."

Twenty minutes later, there was a knock at Coles' door. "Hey, Chuck, phone call at the CQ desk for you. It's Colonel Rollins."

"Thanks."

"What the hell did you do?"

"Nothing. I'll be right there." CQ duty was the academy's equivalent of hall monitor, a crappy one-day assignment answering phones and making sure the halls stayed quiet during Call to Quarters. Chuck picked up the phone. "Cadet Coles."

"Colonel Rollins, Mr. Coles. I heard you called my home this evening."

"Yes, sir, I'm sorry for the inconvenience, but . . ."

"Not at all. Are you available for dinner tomorrow night?"

"I guess so, sir, but I heard you were out of town until Saturday."

"Not anymore. I'll see you tomorrow about 1700."

"Uh, sir?"

"Yes, Mr. Coles."

"I don't want to be rude, but may I bring another cadet with me? It's amazing, but we almost look identical, like twins."

Bud paused only for a second. *Holy shit!* "Absolutely."

A senior, called a "firstie" at the academy, loaned Coles his car for the evening; Chuck and Jack arrived at the Rollins' home in Douglas Valley right at 1700. Because he was a doolie, Jack had to wear his uniform, so Chuck did the same. Now the twins stood together in front of the door, which opened before either of them had a chance to knock. "Good evening, gentlemen." The woman, perhaps in her mid-forties, was not what you'd call beautiful, but she had a classiness and toughness about her that made her unmistakably attractive. "I'm Kate Rollins. Come in."

✧　✧　✧

Kate and Bud sat on the sofa across from the cadets. Chuck and Jack looked like their parents, all right: same facial features as Mary-Louise, same slight build as Don. And if these two weren't twins, then Mendel needed to redo his genetic theory.

Kate knew that Mary-Louise had given birth to twins, but hadn't been able to find them. Harrell kept their placement strictly confidential. It was as though Don, Mary-Louise, and their twins had fallen off the end of the earth. Clearly, someone cut procedural corners, skipped the effort to find families, and made it all stick. And the army had no record of the McGanley marriage. By the time Kate and Bud got a private investigator involved, Harrell was long gone. But now, neither of them doubted that they were looking at their best friends' twin sons.

Kate was trying not to cry. Bud's eyes went from one cadet to the other and said, "Amazing."

Chuck didn't waste a second. "Sir, Mary-Louise Anderson was our mother, wasn't she?"

Bud exchanged a glance with his wife. Kate took her time. She took in a deep breath and nodded as she answered, "Yes, she was. And my best friend. I went back through my things today. Here's a picture." Kate and Mary-Louise stood in their uniforms, arm in arm in front of the hospital in Melbourne. The cadets stared at the photo, transfixed.

Jack asked, "Ma'am, what happened to her?" He looked down at the photo one more time.

"She was on a Dutch hospital ship, returning from Darwin to Melbourne. A Japanese fighter strafed them. She was the only one hurt, but the wounds were bad; head wounds. They barely saved her on the operating table, but there was a lot of damage to her brain. At the time, no one knew she was pregnant. They didn't find out until after she got to the Presidio. My guess is that they didn't even know there were two of you until the day she delivered."

Kate looked at the two cadets. Their eyes were intense, completely fixed on her.

"After you were born, she was transferred to an institution in Glens Falls, New York. She passed away in 1948 after a brain hemorrhage. There's more to tell, certainly, but we'll get to that. Here's another picture of her, taken at a place called Prince Albert Beach, shortly before she married your father."

The cadets continued staring at both pictures. Bud and Kate left them with their own thoughts for a few minutes. Bud couldn't imagine how he'd have reacted if he were in their shoes right now.

"She was a pretty one," he said, finally.

"And a wonderful nurse," added Kate. "She married your father in June of 1942."

The two cadets looked up, at the exact same time.

Bud said, "I didn't even find out about it until he told me a few months later. That's how private he was. And neither of them got around to telling the army. There were other things to do."

Chuck asked, "You knew him, sir?"

"Yep. His full name was Donald Thomas McGanley. Smart pilot. Fast thinker in the air, the best we had. Got the Air Corps' first kill in New Guinea. He became an ace the same day he was killed in action. I was there. His picture's up in the aces' gallery in Arnold Hall. Did you guys know that?"

"No, sir." they said it together.

Bud laughed at that. The boys were exactly alike. And then he thought what a dumb question he'd asked. Of course they didn't know his picture was up. How could they? But Bud was glad they knew now. "Interesting time back then. We were very, very good friends."

"Sir, what kind of a guy was he?" Chuck asked, but it might as well have been either of them.

Bud rubbed his hands together and looked up at the ceiling, as if he was trying to decide what to say and how to say it. "Let me tell you guys. He was a hero, but he never figured out what that meant. He succeeded, but he never realized that, either, I don't think. He was hell-bent on overcoming something he just couldn't put his finger on."

Now Bud's eyes were watering; Kate's, too.

The cadets exchanged a glance. "We don't know what you mean, sir," said Jack. "Overcome what?"

Bud sighed. "I figured we might get to this. But before we do, you guys need to understand how important it is that you're here, with all of your lives before you. You're going to have opportunities your parents deserved but never had. Their opportunties were lost; that happens in wartime, as I'm sure you realize. But your parents gave you fellas a good start, both of them did. And now they'll live on through you two. You would have been very proud of them. I'm damned sure they'd be very, very proud of you." He fought back tears. "This makes their lives worthwhile. I wish they were here to see you two."

"So do we." They said that together, too.

"Tell you guys what. I ordered some pizzas. They should be here any minute. Let me go grab a couple of beers and we'll eat right here, and Kate and I will tell you guys a story."

Acknowledgments

Years ago I read a historical novel called *The Gates of the Alamo* by Stephen Harrigan. I've always been interested in the battle, and was impressed by the depth of his research. But what struck me most about his book was his main character: a flawed, conflicted, but decent man caught in a big event, and how important his legacy was. An important theme in life, I think; one of personal significance for me, and the reason I wrote this book.

A Cockpit in New Guinea is a historical novel based largely on my dad, a World War II fighter ace now living in Tennessee. Much, but not all, of what happens to Don McGanley actually happened to my dad (with the obvious exception of the last air battle), though I reserve the right, with Dad's permission, to keep fact versus fiction to myself. I maintained this approach with most of my characters because I wanted to use true personal events and real places as much as I could and protect privacy at the same time. I gathered personal stories through countless interviews, and wish to extend my warmest thanks to those of the World War II generation who graciously and patiently told their stories and answered my questions, some of which I needed to make quite personal. Those interviews are reflected in my attempt to make my characters and their lives authentic.

I must document, however, that some characters are absolutely real, like Generals Kenney and Wurtsmith. Kenney's published memoirs offered a valuable personal take on the chaotic days of 1942. General Wurtsmith really was my dad's first operational commander, at Morrison Field in West Palm Beach. His role in my book appears totally from my dad's point of view.

Without exception, librarians in New York, San Francisco, Fort Myers, Seattle, Portland, San Diego, and Knoxville were patient and supportive. I did all the research for this book by myself, on purpose, because I simply didn't want to miss any of the fun. The more I read, the more engrossed I became, and the deeper I dug. I spent hour upon hour just reading *Time* magazines from 1937 through 1941. And the sorting process was fascinating. Personal diaries tell you one thing, biographies another, army records another. And then there's the Internet, textbooks, and folks who've written their own books, all with their own points of view. In dealing with historical events and perspectives of those events, the narratives in this book are my best effort to present corroborated facts and viewpoints from multiple sources. I did not intend to teach history, but to present information I thought was germane to the story as accurately as I could. My deepest thanks go out to all those who researched and recorded the wealth of historical and technical material for someone like me to find.

I had three readers before I went to press: Jerry, my neighbor and a retired teacher, my sister-in-law Kristin, also a former teacher, and my wife, Lynn. They waited patiently for over three years while I went back and forth with my writing, tweaking, adding, and changing, until I realized that I'd never stop. I handed them my "perfect" manuscript and sat as still as I could through their thorough, honest, and unabashed critiques. I owe them all a huge debt of thanks.

I'm not a doctor, but thank goodness my aunt is. Her fifty-plus years of experience in internal medicine helped me fill gaps in my medical research so I could present believable medical scenarios and jargon consistent with the times. Thanks, Auntie!

And finally, how could I forget my dad? I scoured his military records and personal letters. We went through dozens of interviews and hundreds of questions about his life experiences, attitudes, and personal feelings. Obviously, the last air battle is virtually all fictitious since he's still around today, but the lion's share of flying experiences in this book are exactly as he recounted them to me. We used models and waved our hands around like a couple of fighter pilots in the bar, just to make sure I got them right. I can't thank him enough.

The process of producing this book was an engrossing, satisfying experience for me. I hope you enjoyed the story as much as I did telling it.

Edwards Brothers,Inc!
Thorofare, NJ 08086
09 December, 2010
BA2010343